Love and famil[...]
precio[...]

Daddy's
Christmas
Miracle

Three all-new stories to warm your heart
this winter from favourite authors
Rebecca Winters, Marie Ferrarella
and Shirley Jump

Daddy's
Christmas
Miracle

REBECCA
WINTERS

MARIE
FERRARELLA

SHIRLEY
JUMP

MILLS &
BOON

Mills & Boon, an imprint of Harlequin (UK) Limited, Eton House, 18-24 Paradise Road, Richmond, Surrey TW9 1SR

DADDY'S CHRISTMAS MIRACLE
© Harlequin Enterprises II B.V./S.à.r.l. 2011

Santa in a Stetson © Rebecca Winters 2010
The Sheriff's Christmas Surprise © Marie Rydzynski-Ferrarella 2010
Family Christmas in Riverbend © Shirley Kawa-Jump, LLC 2011

ISBN: 978 0 263 89357 1

025-1111

Harlequin (UK) policy is to use papers that are natural, renewable and recyclable products and made from wood grown in sustainable forests. The logging and manufacturing processes conform to the legal environmental regulations of the country of origin.

Printed and bound in Spain
by Blackprint CPI, Barcelona

Santa in a Stetson

REBECCA WINTERS

Rebecca Winters, whose family of four children has now swelled to include five beautiful grandchildren, lives in Salt Lake City, Utah, in the land of the Rocky Mountains. With canyons and high alpine meadows full of wild flowers, she never runs out of places to explore. They, plus her favourite vacation spots in Europe, often end up as backgrounds for her romance novels, because writing is her passion, along with her family and church. Rebecca loves to hear from readers. If you wish to e-mail her, please visit her website at www.cleanromances.com.

Dedicated to the Smart family,
who never gave up or lost hope. You and your
courageous daughter are an exemplary model
in faith for the rest of us.

Chapter One

"The bus is coming. Bye, Dad. Don't forget I'm going to Jen's house after school for a sleepover. Her mom is driving us all home tomorrow so you won't have to worry about it." Allie leaned across the front seat of the truck and gave him a hug.

"I haven't forgotten anything, but I think your cold's worse," Colton Brenner said. Throughout the week, her congestion had become more noticeable. "Maybe you'd better give this party a miss and have an early night."

"I can't! It would ruin the whole weekend!" She sounded so upset he was sorry he'd said anything. "We've made too many plans, but I promise not to stay up late. The decongestant pills you gave me are in my purse."

"If you're not improved tomorrow, I'm taking you to the doctor."

"Everyone has a cold right now. It's not a big deal." Her warm brown eyes slid away from his. When they did that, it signaled she didn't want to get into a heavy discussion with him.

"But not everyone is *my* daughter." He kissed her cheek. "I love my children."

"We love you, too." She opened the door and got out.

"Later!" his son called from the backseat.

He turned. "Bye, Matt. I'll be at your wrestling match at three o'clock."

"Don't forget it's in Livingston."

"Would I do that?" They high-fived each other before he jumped down. "We'll go for pizza after."

"Cool!" Matt shut the door.

Colton—Colt to his friends—sat back in the seat, eyeing his fifteen-year-old twins as they waited for the school bus that would drive them into Bozeman eight miles away.

Every morning he brought them down to the entrance of the Circle B to make sure they got off safely. The family always ate breakfast together and talked over the day's plans. His housekeeper Noreen picked them up at the same spot after school. It was a ritual he'd started years earlier and had never deviated from.

When their mother had pulled her permanent disappearing act, he'd made it his mission to be there for them in every possible capacity. He loved them more than life.

This morning their breath curled in the invigorating air. Twenty degrees above zero wasn't bad for mid-November in the Bridger Mountains of Montana. He could remember other Novembers at twenty below. Unfortunately the weather couldn't be good for Allie's cold.

More snow wasn't forecast until tomorrow evening. With a lull between storms, this was the best time for him and his foreman to ride up to the north forty with some of the hands and finish repairs on the fencing. If he left with them now, he'd be able to get in a good six hours of work before he had to leave for Livingston, twenty-six miles away.

Now that football season was over and Matt's team had lost in the playoffs, Matt had joined the wrestling squad. His school's first preseason match was today. The boy was shooting up, but he wanted to get more buff. Colt smiled. He remembered wanting the same thing at Matt's age.

After his children boarded the bus, he waved to the driver before heading back to the ranch house three miles up the mountain. His eyes took in the blanket of snow covering evergreen forests and copses of aspens. He loved it all, from harshest winter to the glory of summer, when wildflowers filled the alpine meadows. Every season highlighted different aspects of the ranch's beauty and brought him renewal.

Thanks to his Scottish ancestors who'd emigrated here in the late 1800s, the setting of the Brenner cattle ranch was the most beautiful mountain spread this side of the Continental Divide. He counted his blessings.

The one thing missing from his life hadn't mattered to him in years. He'd long since put the pain of his travesty of a marriage behind him. Though everything else had failed during those nightmarish twelve months of supposed wedded bliss, he and his nineteen-year-old bride had made perfect babies together. Matthew and Allison...nonidentical brunettes who came with their own individual spirits.

Loving his children, working the ranch to leave them a legacy for the future, was his reason for living.

THIRTY-YEAR-OLD Kathryn McFarland had the distinction of having been kidnapped from her parents' mansion on South Temple in Salt Lake City, Utah, and lost to them for the first twenty-six years of her life. The people at Skwars Farm, Wisconsin, who'd taken her in had called her Anna Buric. Her origins were a mystery to everyone. Then one day a miracle happened.

She was found!

In an instant, she'd become Kathryn McFarland. And like the pauper who'd suddenly been thrust on the throne as the Prince of England, she inherited lands, titles, wealth and a loving, illustrious family eager to embrace her.

That was more than four years ago. Yet every time she let herself inside her penthouse condo at the McFarland Plaza in downtown Salt Lake, she experienced alternating waves of gratitude and guilt—gratitude because she'd been united with the most wonderful, generous parents imaginable and guilt because she needed her own space.

She knew it seemed unfair to her family that after waiting twenty-six years to get their little baby back, Kathryn had returned a grown woman who needed her family desperately, but secretly needed her independence, too.

They'd lost all that time with each other. So had she, with them. It was only natural for her to live with them and bask in their love, but it couldn't go on forever.

Kit Talbot McFarland, Kathryn's sister-in-law, knew exactly how Kathryn felt. She, too, had been kidnapped as a baby in the same bizarre case twenty-six years earlier, and had been found a few months before Kathryn.

But in the process she'd met Cord, one of Kathryn's two older brothers. It wasn't long before they were married and now had a little girl and another baby on the way.

From the beginning Kathryn shared a unique bond with Kit. She, too, suffered untold guilt for not spending more time with her birth parents and family, who lived in California. Kit and Kathryn were painfully aware that both sets of parents, the McFarlands and the Talbots, had suffered "empty arms syndrome" for more than two decades.

To some degree, Kit's two-year-old daughter helped satisfy that ache in the Talbots' lives, but Kathryn had no husband or children. She wasn't even close to starting her own family. Which was why Kathryn's parents couldn't understand why she wouldn't continue to live with them in their home in Federal Heights, only a few miles from the plaza.

They didn't outwardly pressure her. It was more the pleading in their eyes, the unspoken message, hinting they wanted her with them. All those silent hopes played havoc with Kathryn's guilt.

Thank heaven for Maggie!

There weren't enough words to describe Kathryn's love for her older sister Maggie McFarland, the mother of a one-year-old boy. She, along with her husband, Jake Halsey, had been the ones to find Kathryn in Wisconsin and bring her home.

Soon after their family reunion had made headlines in every newspaper in the nation, Maggie and Jake married and built a house in upper Federal Heights. When they were settled, Maggie insisted Kathryn move into the penthouse where Maggie had been living in order to have some breathing room.

Their mother's fear of another kidnapping had made her so overprotective, she'd almost suffocated Maggie at times growing up. Now that Kathryn was finally home, Maggie could see the same thing happening to her sister and told her she needed to get out of the house and on her own.

"There needs to be spaces in your togetherness," she'd whispered to Kathryn at her wedding.

"Listen to Maggie," their oldest married brother Ben concurred in a low voice. "She knows what she's talking about."

Cord nodded. "We've all lived with horrific guilt for twenty-six years because no one heard the kidnapper come into the house and steal you away. Now that you've been found alive and are home again, everyone needs to get on with their lives. No more guilt. No more looking back."

With those words, Kathryn understood her siblings were her best friends and allies. Between them, they took care of the move and got her settled on top of the McFarland Tower. Every window looked out on a superb view of the Salt Lake Valley and the mountains encircling it.

From the kitchen, she had an eastern exposure and could see Mount Olympus, covered in snow. This morning while she'd been working with Cord, he'd told her there was fresh powder up Little Cottonwood Canyon in Alta, where he and Kit lived.

They'd made plans to ski tomorrow. Their first outing of the season. She couldn't wait. Cord was a fabulous skier and had given her lessons every winter. Kathryn was getting pretty good at it, if she said so herself.

Cord was the true mountain man of the family. In that regard, they were soul mates—like the first McFarland who'd claimed a lot of land in the Albion Basin for his own before the turn of the last century.

She'd seen it for the first time in summer, when the meadows were a riot of wildflowers. A euphoric Kathryn had thought she loved that season best until fall arrived and the trees turned to gold and flame everywhere she hiked.

Then came the majesty of winter, so white and gorgeous. She hated to see it go, but when spring followed and the primroses poked their pink heads out of the melting snow, the signs of new life filled her with indescribable yearnings for the changes yet to come. After living in a flat part of the country so many years, she couldn't get enough of the Rockies and was a constant visitor to Cord's mountain home.

When she heard her iPhone ring, she'd just taken a bite of peach yogurt. It was probably her brother making final arrangements for tomorrow. She clicked on and said hello.

"Hi, Kathryn. It's Bonnie Frank." The woman worked at North Avenues Hospital in the patient advocacy department funded by the McFarland Foundation.

"Hey, Bonnie. How are you?"

"Ask me tomorrow morning when I haven't been on my feet all day."

Kathryn chuckled. "I hear you." She took some more bites. "What's going on?"

"The E.R. just contacted me. A teenage runaway was

admitted a few minutes ago after collapsing on a downtown street. Nancy Isom was the head nurse on duty and she couldn't get any information from the girl, so she called my office asking for you. I know it's dinnertime, but do you think you could drop by the hospital sometime this evening and interview this one? I've gotten absolutely nowhere with her."

"I'll come now." The sooner she dealt with the problem, the sooner she could get to bed. A day of skiing gave her a real workout and needed to be fortified with a good night's sleep.

"You're an angel. I'll let them know you're on your way."

Kathryn rang off before freshening up in the bathroom. After making sure she had a McFarland Foundation brochure in her purse, she put on her parka and left the condo.

The private elevator took her to the underground car park where the security guard waved to her. She got in her Jeep and took off for the hospital, located a mile away. She phoned her parents en route to see how their day had gone.

After all those years, when she'd wondered if she had a mother and father who were even alive, it seemed miraculous that Kathryn could call them up whenever she felt like it. She adored them.

THERE WAS ONE SLICE of pizza left in the pan. Colt glanced at Matt. "Do you want to wrestle for the last piece?"

He screwed up his face. "That's all right, Dad. I want to live to see another day. You can have it."

Colt laughed. "I liked that reversal you came up with before the ref blew the whistle. Good job."

"Thanks." Matt reached for the pizza, as Colt knew he would, and made short work of it.

The waitress came to refill their glasses, but Colt shook his head. After she walked away, he pulled out his wallet and left a couple of bills on the table. "Shall we?"

They both got to their feet at the same time and shrugged into their parkas before heading for the entrance to the pizza parlor. "Hey, Dad, want to see a movie?"

"Sure. With your sister gone, we'll make it an official guys' night out." They walked into the frigid air. "What's playing?"

"The latest vampire film."

"I thought that was a chick flick," he teased.

"It is, but Marcus was talking about it at the match. He said it was pretty good."

"I guess I can stand it if you can. Allie can't seem to get enough of the *Twilight* series."

Two hours later Colt said, "Believe it or not, I liked it."

"Me, too!" Matt blurted, eager to talk about it as they left the theater.

Halfway to the truck, parked around the corner, they heard, "Hi, Matt! Hi, Mr. Brenner! Where's Allie?"

He glanced around, surprised to see Carrie and Michelle, two of Allie's good friends. Colt would have thought they'd be at the sleepover, but evidently they hadn't been invited. Allie had given him the impression it would be a big group. It appeared somebody must have hurt somebody else's feelings. Diplomacy was called for.

"She made other plans. Did you two like the film?"

Michelle smiled. "We loved it."

"Did *you?*" Carrie asked Matt.

"It was okay," he answered in a quiet voice, hiding his enthusiasm.

Colt got a kick out of his son, who acted like a typical male around girls. At that age, shyness hadn't been one of Colt's problems. His ease around girls had probably facilitated his early marriage. Would that Matt took a little longer to grow up before he made a commitment that would change his life.

They reached the corner. "See you girls later. Don't let any vampires bite you tonight."

The girls broke into laughter. "Bye, Mr. Brenner."

"Bye, Matt." Carrie again.

His son said something indistinct before they parted company and headed for the truck.

On the way home he turned to Matt. "This morning on the bus, did your sister say anything about a quarrel with her friends?"

"No." He darted him a curious glance. "Why do you ask?"

"Because I thought all Allie's friends were going to be over at Jen's tonight."

Matt shrugged. "I don't know, but she was kind of quiet on the bus."

Her cold could account for that, but Colt still wasn't reassured. An uneasiness had crept over him he couldn't explain, but she'd hate it if he phoned her at Jen's. No teenager liked to be checked up on at a party.

He rubbed his jaw where he could feel the beginnings of a beard. "I guess we'll find out tomorrow after she gets home."

"Dad?"

Did Matt know something after all? "Yes?"

"I think something's wrong with Blackie's hind leg."

"He needs reshoeing," Colt murmured, his mind still on his daughter. "In the morning we'll get it taken care of before we load up more hay to take to the west pasture." He drove up to the side of the ranch house and turned off the motor.

"After that, is it okay if I go skiing with Rich? We'll buy a half-day pass."

"Sounds fun."

They both got out and walked around to the back. "You want to come with us?"

"I'd like to, but Noreen says the kitchen disposal is having problems. Since Ed's arm is still in a cast, I promised I'd take a look at it. If it needs to be replaced, that could take some time." For a variety of reasons, Colt wanted to be on hand when Allie got dropped off. "Let's go skiing next Saturday. Maybe Rich's dad will want to come, too."

"I'll ask him."

"Sounds like a plan." Colt followed him to the back porch. They stomped the snow off their cowboy boots before entering the house. Ten minutes later they both said good-night.

Colt checked with Noreen, who lived in the older

house on the property with her husband, Ed, Colt's ranch manager. Noreen hadn't heard from Allie. Not that he expected her to call, but when he entered his study, he knew he wouldn't sleep until he'd talked to his daughter.

Without hesitation, he called her cell phone. Her voice mail came on. He asked her to call him back when she could, then rang off.

Frustrated when another twenty minutes passed with no response, he looked up the Wagners' number in the phone directory. Even though it was ten-thirty, he called them, but their voice mail came on, too. He left the message that he'd like Allie to call her father, then he hung up.

Maybe the Wagners had taken the girls to a movie or ice skating. The thought that they were all out together should have relieved him. Colt was probably obsessing for nothing, and yet…

His thoughts flew back ten years to the time when he'd gotten a strange foreboding about his grandmother. It had been early morning. Though he'd just arrived in the upper pasture with some of the hands, he turned right around and galloped home to discover his grandfather weeping over her body. "Her heart stopped beating a half hour ago, Colton. She's gone."

Unnerved by the memory, he decided he couldn't sit around waiting for the phone to ring. He hurried down the hall and took the stairs two at a time to Matt's room. His son was listening to his iPod.

When he saw him, he sat up in bed with a jerk. "Dad?"

"Get dressed and come with me to Jen's house."

"What's wrong?"

"Maybe nothing. I just need to make sure Allie's all right."

"Okay." He slid out of bed to put on his clothes.

"I'll meet you at the truck."

ON HER WAY INTO THE E.R., Kathryn glanced around the lounge filled with friends and relatives of the patients. The place had never looked busier. She approached the desk and spotted Nancy, who was simultaneously talking on the phone while she entered information on the computer. The two women had become friends while Kathryn was getting her RN degree.

As soon as she saw Kathryn, she flashed a smile of relief and hung up. "Thanks for coming so fast. Our uncommunicative runaway is down the hall in the isolation area, Room Six. Her tests just came back. She's got the H1N1 virus."

"Is she coherent?"

"Oh, yes, but she won't tell us how long she's had symptoms. I think she's been sick for a while. When they wheeled her in, she was very upset about being brought to the hospital. She told us to let her go. If she's refusing to talk, it's because she's terrified about something. When the ambulance picked her up, she had no ID on her."

"Where was she found?"

"Down near the Rio Grande Café. A pedestrian saw her collapse and called 911."

One of the homeless shelters was near there. The airport, the Greyhound bus depot and the Amtrak station were all close by, and it seemed possible she'd come in from out of town.

"Did she speak with an accent? You know—Alabama, Boston, Texas, New *Joysey?*"

Nancy laughed at her imitation and thought for a minute. "Nothing stood out. I'd say she's from somewhere in the western states, but no central Utah drawl if you know what I mean." They both smiled.

Good. That narrowed the field a little. "You want me to tell her about her condition?"

"Yes. I'm hoping that when you do, she'll break down and open up to you. See what you can get out of her, will you?"

"Sure."

Kathryn went around to a back room where she shed her parka. After removing the brochure from her purse, she stowed everything in a locker, then washed her hands. Donning a surgical mask and lab coat, she then slipped a small notepad and pen in her pocket along with the brochure and found her way down several halls to Room Six.

They'd hooked up an IV to the pretty brunette lying there in a hospital gown with her eyes closed. Before she did anything else, Kathryn opened the girl's locker and took her bag of clothes out in the hall to examine.

She'd been wearing a North Face parka, navy jeans, a red, long-sleeved pullover sweater, Nike Air Morgans with hook-and-ladder fasteners, and tube socks. Everything higher end and clean. No smell of smoke. All items could have been purchased in a major department store anywhere across the nation.

After Kathryn returned the bag back to the locker,

she walked over to the computer and brought up the police report first.

> Jane Doe. Age 14–16. Caucasian. Picked up at 4:10 p.m., Friday, Nov 19. A pedestrian, Ronald Ewing, 50, Grantsville, Utah, saw her slump onto the sidewalk at 300 south, fifth west, Salt Lake, and called emergency on his cell phone. Approx height 5´5˝, weight 115 pounds, brown hair, brown eyes, teeth in excellent condition. No evidence of alcohol. No needle marks. No sign of drugs hidden on her body or in her clothes. No purse or wallet. No money. No injury marks, no sign of assault, rape or foul play.

There were a lot more things Kathryn could add simply by looking at her. Aside from the fact that she had the flu, she was the picture of health and excellent hygiene. Her nails were well cared for, her shoulder-length hair had a gloss to it.

The hospital stats indicated a fever of 101.4 when she was brought in. No vomiting or diarrhea. They were hydrating her and giving her medicine to bring down her temperature. Since the last check of vital signs, there'd been a drop of one degree. That was good news.

She was someone's darling.

Kathryn snagged a stool and sat down at the side of the hospital bed. "Hi, Anna. I'm Katy."

The girl opened her eyes. They were velvety brown. Lovely eyes. Anxious.

"Don't let the mask scare you. It's a protective mea-sure because you're fighting the H1N1 virus, but judging by the progress you're already making, it's not such a serious case. Unless I made a lucky guess, I know your name isn't Anna. I gave you *my* old name. The one I was given after I was kidnapped. It's as good as any."

Anna blinked. If Kathryn didn't miss her guess, she'd gained the girl's attention.

"I brought a brochure with me. My family had it printed when I was taken from them." She pulled it out of her purse. "Let me show you the picture of me at the top." Kathryn held it up so she could see it. With her other hand, she pulled down the mask so the girl could see they were one in the same person. Then she put it back in place.

"It was taken four years ago. You'll notice what it says beneath the picture. 'Kathryn McFarland, lost for twenty-six years, has been FOUND!' You're probably feeling too tired to read it, Anna, so I'll read it to you." Kathryn continued to read.

May 3 marks the twenty-sixth anniversary of the abduction of our fourth child, Kathryn Mc-Farland, from the McFarland home in Salt Lake City, Utah. Born April 2, she was only a month old at the time she was taken.

Soon after the kidnapping and community search, the Kathryn McFarland Foundation was founded and now honors Kathryn's memory by finding missing children, and preventing them from going missing in the first place.

When Kathryn was kidnapped, our community and many others joined together to help us find her because there was an immediate recognition that she was everyone's child and that we are all in this together.

Child abductions across our nation since its beginning have highlighted the need for legislation to enhance our ability to protect our children from predators of all types. When a child is kidnapped, time is of the essence.

All too often it is only a matter of hours before a kidnapper commits an act of violence against the child. That is why we're pleased that the U.S. Senate has acted to pass legislation creating a national AMBER Alert system, which galvanizes entire communities to assist law enforcement in the timely search and safe return of child victims.

Since its inception, the foundation has assisted approximately seventeen thousand families and law enforcement agencies in their searches. We have seen over eight-five percent of those children returned home safely. This is what continues to give us hope.

Kathryn put the brochure down on the bedside table. "Someone out there—*somewhere*—is dying inside because you're missing, Anna. I don't know how long you've been missing, or why. I don't know if you were kidnapped and let go, or if you left home of your own free will.

"What I *do* know is that a beautiful young woman like you is very lucky not to have been exposed to serious danger. I also know that anyone who loves you is in agony right now, fearing the worst."

The girl's eyelids fluttered closed, but they couldn't hold back the trickle of tears.

"My family went through so much agony, they would have died if they hadn't decided to do something positive with their pain. Did you hear those statistics? Seventeen thousand families assisted. That figure has changed since four years ago. It's now twenty-three thousand, with an eighty-five percent rate of success.

"I have parents, two brothers and a sister who've dedicated their lives to helping children unite with their loved ones. Now that I've been found, I've devoted my life to helping someone like you get the help you need.

"Consider me a friend who's going to make certain you get well and are safe. My brother runs Renaissance House, a shelter for homeless women to assist them in getting reestablished. It's only a mile from here. After you're released from the hospital, I'll take you there. You'll like it. The big, beautiful mansion was my home before I was kidnapped. After that, my family moved. They couldn't bear the pain of living in a place where I had been stolen right out of the nursery during the night. Since that time, my brother turned it into a halfway house. He did it because he hoped that one day *I* might walk in."

Suddenly the girl broke down crying. Kathryn stood up to lean over her and smooth the hair from her temples. "I didn't tell you all this to make you cry. I just wanted you to know that you're not alone. Sleep now, Anna. I'll stay right here and take care of you. I'm a nurse who did my training in this hospital. You're among friends here."

After a long silence, "My name's Allie."

Joy.

"I like that name much better." She handed her some tissues. "Go ahead and blow your nose, Allie. You must have been congested for a few days now."

The teen nodded and blew hard. Kathryn handed her a receptacle. "I'm going to get you a cold drink. Fruit punch, Sprite, root beer, Coke, you name it."

"Fruit punch, please."

She had manners, too. "Coming right up."

Kathryn hurried down the hall to the desk. She pulled her mask down again. "Her name's Allie. She wants some fruit punch."

A beaming Nancy lifted her head. "I knew it! You have the magic touch. Be back in a tick."

In another minute, she returned with two cans. Kathryn thanked her and joined Allie, who'd reached for the brochure on the side table and was reading it.

"I'll raise your head so you can drink without choking. Say when."

Before long Allie had drained her drink. Kathryn took the empty can from her. "Better?"

"Yes, thank you."

"Shall I lower your head now?"

"Not yet. Where did that kidnapper take you?"

Kathryn sat down on the stool once more. "New York, then Wisconsin."

Allie's red-rimmed eyes studied her in fascination. "How did you find your parents?"

"I didn't. My sister and the man she's married to now found *me*. When my family came into my hospital room to see me for the first time, we all looked so much alike there was no question I belonged to them."

She blew her nose again. "You were in a hospital, too?"

"Yes. I'd been in a car accident and had broken my leg. Because of my cast, everyone had to be very careful when they hugged me, especially my dad. To this day, I don't know which one of us squeezed harder."

"My dad can squeeze hard."

"That's one of the great things about having a father. It still makes me cry to think how many years I lived without my parents." Kathryn's throat swelled with emotion. "I love mine so much, you can't imagine. My dad's incredible."

"So's mine. That's why—" She suddenly stopped talking and tears gushed from her eyes.

Unable to stay seated after realizing how upset the teen was, Kathryn stood up and clasped Allie's free hand. "The longer I live, the more I realize that none of us is exempt from pain." She handed her more tissue. "How long have you been sick, Allie?"

"I've had a cold all week. After I left the bus station I started to look for a taxi, but then this man on a bike grabbed my purse and rode away. It had all my money in it. That's when I got dizzy and fell down. Then another man walked by. He saw me and called the police. I begged him not to because then Dad would find out."

She grabbed hold of Kathryn's arm, staring at her with imploring eyes. "Dad doesn't know I came here. He thought I was at a sleepover. I planned to be back home by tomorrow so he would never find out. He *can't* find out!"

"Why not?"

"If he knew the reason, it would hurt him too much."

Oh, darling girl...

Chapter Two

Not two seconds after Colt parked in front of the Wagners' house, their car pulled into the driveway. Reed was with his wife. No one else was in the car.

Colt got out and walked over to them. Wendie rushed toward him. "It's good to see you." She gave him a hug and said hello to Matt, who'd trailed him.

"Hey, Colt." Reed broke out in a broad smile. "To what do we owe this honor?"

"Matt and I just got out of a movie and thought we'd come by to see how the sleepover's going before we drive home. Allie had a bad cold when she left for school. I almost didn't let her go and wanted to see if it was worse."

Both of them looked surprised. "What sleepover?" Wendie asked.

The question was like a punch to the gut. "Obviously there wasn't one. I thought something was wrong when I saw Michelle and Carrie at the movie. Did Allie come home with Jen after school?"

"No. I picked her up and took her to the orthodontist. Tonight she's been tending Chelsey and David so we could go to a wedding."

An icy sensation crept through Colt's veins.

"You haven't seen her since she left for school this morning?" she asked.

"No."

Matt shot him a worried glance.

"Come into the house," Reed urged. "We'll find out from Jen where she is."

The four of them went inside. Reed called to his blonde daughter, who came into the living room dressed in army fatigue pajamas. The second she saw Colt, she froze.

"Hi, Mr. Brenner." She didn't look in the least happy to see him. It was very unlike her.

"Pumpkin?" her father inserted. "Do you know where Allie is? She didn't come home from school today."

Jen averted her eyes so fast that it reminded Colt of his daughter when she'd told him her cold wasn't a big deal and she didn't want to talk about it.

Wendie put an arm around her. "If you have an idea where she is, tell Colt so we won't have to phone everyone we know. It's late. We'd hate to have to disturb people who might be in bed by now."

Jen kept her head bowed. "She made me promise not to tell."

"Tell what?" Colt asked, trying to remain calm.

"Yesterday she told me she wouldn't be at school today. She said she'd be back the next day and asked me do her a favor, so I did."

"What favor?"

"When our homeroom teacher took roll this morning, I—I told her Allie was in the restroom and would come in with a late pass," she stammered. "That's why the school didn't call you."

"Jennifer Wagner!" Reed exploded.

"I know that was wrong, Dad. I'm sorry, Mr. Brenner. Allie said that in case you called here, I should get Chelsey to tell you all the girls had gone to a movie. But Allie was positive you wouldn't phone." Her voice wobbled, producing another moan from her parents.

Colt's body shuddered in reaction. "You have no idea where she went?"

"No. I'm really sorry. I shouldn't have agreed to help her." She started crying.

"It's not your fault, Jen. My daughter put you in an impossible position. For that *I'm* sorry."

Matt's stricken expression set off another alarm bell. "Maybe you should call the Greyhound bus depot and find out if she got on a bus this morning."

For his son to tell him that... "What do *you* know about this?"

His gaze didn't flinch. "Nothing, but last week when Rich and I went to the Bozeman Bowl after school, I thought I saw her going in the bus depot. Rich said I was just seeing things because a lot of girls wore North Face parkas. That night I asked her about it. She said she hadn't been downtown, but she got mad about it. I thought that was kind of weird for her to be upset about a simple question."

Colt whipped out his phone to call information. The minute he was connected to the depot, he told the person who answered to put him on with the manager. "This is an emergency."

"Just a moment, sir."

He felt as if someone had just sucked all the air out of his lungs.

"This is Mr. Padakis, the manager. How can I help you, Mr. Brenner?"

"My daughter's been missing since seven this morning. I thought she went to school, but I now believe she may have taken a bus today, probably this morning. Her name is Allison Brenner. She's fifteen. Before I call the police, can you find out if she purchased a ticket? Any information you can give me would be helpful."

"I'm sorry to hear this. Give me a moment. I'm looking in the system now. Yes, here she is. A. Brenner, Circle B Ranch. She bought a round-trip ticket to Salt Lake City."

Salt Lake? Allie didn't know anyone there. They had no family there.

"The bus left at 7:40 a.m. She's due back tomorrow at 5:00 p.m."

He gripped the phone tighter. "What time does that bus start back to Bozeman?"

"Let's see. 8:30 a.m."

That made it an eight-and-a-half hour trip. He checked his watch. She would have arrived in Salt Lake by four today. It gave her fifteen, sixteen hours to do whatever she planned to do in that amount of time. The stone in Colt's throat made it nearly impossible to talk.

"Thank you very much, Mr. Padakis."

"I hope everything's all right."

"So do I," he whispered in shock and hung up. In the next breath he reached blindly for Matt and hugged him hard. "You weren't wrong. She went to Salt Lake on a bus this morning."

Matt's head flew back. "You're kidding."

"I wish I were, but that gives the police something to go on."

A dozen questions filled Colt's mind.

The Wagners looked pained. "What can we do to help?" Wendie asked.

"Thanks for offering, but this is a matter for the police. I want them to find out how many other passengers on that bus were headed for Salt Lake. Maybe she has a boyfriend who talked her into going."

"No." Jen shook her head. "She would have told me."

"I thought she told me everything, too, Jen." Colt's features turned grim. "The fact that none of us, including her own twin, knew her agenda, let alone that she asked you to lie for her, tells me my daughter has some deep-seated problems. Come on, Matt. Let's go home. I'll phone the police on the way."

The Wagners walked them out to the truck. Colt gave Jen a hug before he drove off with Matt and made the call. He didn't hang up with the chief detective until they'd reached the ranch.

As he shut off the motor Matt turned to him. "Are they going to look for her?"

Colt nodded. "They'll make inquiries, but he told me not to be too worried since she bought a round-trip ticket. The Salt Lake police will be at the bus depot in the morning when she shows up, so he told me it would be a waste of my time to fly there."

"But we're going to go anyway, right?"

He'd never loved his son more than at this moment.

"Right." They walked around back and entered the house. "We'll have to leave for the airport at five. That's not very far away. I'll wake you in time."

"I don't think I'll be able to fall asleep."

"Try. We're going to need all our energy tomorrow."

Matt paused at the foot of the stairs. "Your birthday's a week after Thanksgiving. Maybe she went to Salt Lake to get you a special present."

He rubbed the knot in the back of his neck. "Don't I wish that were the reason."

Matt's expression closed up. "Why do you think she went?"

Since Mr. Padakis had first mentioned Salt Lake, Colt didn't want to admit—let alone put a voice to—an uncomfortable thought working its way through his psyche. "I don't know, Matt."

And because he didn't know, he wasn't about to speculate about something that could destroy the world he'd created for his children. He'd always believed he'd raised them in a happy emotional environment.

But if Allie's disappearance, even for a forty-eight-hour period, had anything to do with what he was thinking, then it meant he'd built his house on sand and it was too late to hold back the dreaded flood.

Matt started up the stairs. Colt watched him go. There'd be no sleep for either of them tonight.

He wandered into the living room, gravitating to a picture of his daughter on her first horse. The image blurred.

Did I fail you, Allie?

Was that what this was about?

"KATHRYN?"

"Hi, Cord. Sorry to phone you this late, but the hospital called me in on a teen runaway case. I'm going to have to cancel our ski plans for tomorrow."

"I won't pretend I'm not disappointed. I'd rather ski with you than anybody."

"I feel the same way about you. But since Kit's expecting again, she'll be thrilled to have you all to herself. Give her my love."

"I will. When you get a chance, I want to hear about your case."

"Of course, but not tonight. Get a good sleep."

Kathryn rang off, then made a call to Maggie. The moment she answered Kathryn said, "Forgive me for calling you so late. I'd like to ask a favor of you, but first I need to know your plans for tomorrow afternoon."

"Jake and I were going to stay home and play with Robbie. Kamila might come over with Jared. Why?"

"I need to take a missing teen back to her family. She's in the hospital getting over the flu and can probably go home tomorrow. But she lives in Bozeman, Montana, and—"

"You'd like me to fly you there?" she finished for Kathryn. "That's not a long flight. I'd love to do it. Meet me at the hangar at twelve-thirty. I'll have you there by two. Robbie will nap while I'm gone."

"You're the best, Maggie," Kathryn said. "I'll call you in the morning if the doctor decides she should stay in the hospital another day. Otherwise, plan on it."

"Sounds good. Do you know something?"

"What?"

"You've become a workaholic. That's how I used to be before I met Jake."

"Yeah, well, we all can't be as lucky as you."

"You could have married Steve."

"I could have, but he only proposed to me because he couldn't have you."

After a long silence, Maggie said, "What are you talking about?"

The time for honesty had come. How strange that this was the moment. "Kit's brother was already clerking for you when I arrived on the scene. It was *you* he loved. You were the reason he left California. When he asked me to marry him, I told him I was flattered, but I didn't want to be your substitute. He got all red in the face, but he didn't deny it."

"I had no idea." Her sister sounded shocked.

"Of course not. That's because you were so in love with Jake, you didn't know if you were coming or going. I can't say I blame you. Jake Halsey's the kind of man who is so attractive he gives every woman a heart attack. Unfortunately, there's only one of him. If I didn't love you so much, I'd scratch your eyes out."

Maggie laughed, then sobered. "Honestly, Kathryn, I love him so much, it scares me."

"Steve saw it, too. That's why I told him that until he went back to California to get away from you, he'd never be happy."

"So *that's* the reason he suddenly left."

"Now you know the whole truth. When I told the family I couldn't marry him because I loved him like a brother, I meant it."

She heard Maggie clear her throat. "Your turn's coming, Kathryn."

"No. I've had plenty of possible turns, but I've discovered I'm not the marrying kind. I crave my freedom too much. Maybe being a captive at Skwars Farm for twenty-six years made me claustrophobic over the whole institution. My psychiatrist says we need to explore it, but that's for another day. Talk to you tomorrow. Love you."

After she hung up, she left the empty isolation room and crossed the hall to check on Allie. The teen was asleep. Her long bus ride and the flu had left Allie on the verge of exhaustion when she'd left the depot.

Whatever had caused Allie to leave home had worn her out, physically and emotionally, but her vital signs looked good. She could be released tomorrow, but would have to stay in bed at home for another night at least till the flu had left her system.

Without wasting any more time, Kathryn slipped back across the hall to make the most important phone call of the night. It was quarter to twelve. If Allie's father suspected nothing and still thought his daughter was at her best friend's house enjoying a sleepover, then he was in for a huge shock.

But if he'd discovered she was missing and was frantically looking for her, then it was past time to end his anguish.

Allie had painted a picture of a loving family. Like Kathryn, Allie had put her father on a pedestal no other man could hold a candle to. She was an exceptional girl. It meant she had an exceptional father. There'd been no mention of a mother.

Kathryn reached for her note pad where she'd written down the phone number Allie had given her and punched in the digits.

WHILE COLT WAITED for the detective in Salt Lake to call him back, he went up to Allie's bedroom. He'd already given the police a description of what she was wearing when she'd left for school, including her backpack. Colt hoped that a thorough search of her room might reveal a clue to help him out. Anything…

She always stashed her money from odd jobs and babysitting in a drawstring purse hanging in the closet. None was there. Naturally she'd used it to buy her bus ticket. To his dismay, he found her cell phone in the bottom drawer of her dresser. She'd turned it off, killing that one glimmer of hope she might call him.

His daughter had been planning this for a long time. The pit in his stomach yawned wide.

Expecting to hear from the detective, he was ready to answer when his cell phone rang. He pulled it from his pocket and clicked on. "Detective Martinez?"

"No," sounded a female voice. "Are you Mr. Brenner?"

He blinked. "Who's this?" Colt knew he sounded terse, but couldn't help it.

"I'm Katy McFarland." Katy was the nickname she used with young people. "The first thing you need to know is that your daughter Allie is fine, but she's asleep right now. She gave me your phone number so I could call you."

Adrenaline gushed through his veins. "Where is she?" he cried out. "Who are you?"

"I'm a medical caseworker for North Avenues Hospital in Salt Lake City, Utah, and was called in when your daughter was brought here around four-thirty this afternoon. She became dizzy after getting off the Greyhound bus. A passerby saw her on the ground and called 911. There was no ID on her. An ambulance picked her up and brought her to the E.R. Your daughter has the H1N1 virus, but it's not a serious case."

Colt staggered to the bed and sank down.

"She's really all right?"

"I wouldn't lie to you, but I have to tell you her biggest fear is that you won't be able to forgive her for what she did. In case you didn't know it, she worships the ground you walk on, so that makes a girl nervous to disappoint the most wonderful father in the whole world."

She'd imitated Allie's way of speaking to perfection, charming Colt, who was close to speechless at this point. "I don't know how to thank you."

"You just did, so don't think about it anymore. We've got her on an IV to treat her flu symptoms. If she continues to improve, she can probably be released tomorrow provided she gets nursing care at home for another day."

Colt jumped to his feet. "My son was the one who figured out she'd taken the bus somewhere. The police are attempting to locate her in Salt Lake right now. Matt and I will fly to Salt Lake on the earliest flight out of Bozeman in the morning. We want to be with her until she's out of the woods."

"You don't need to do that. To be frank, your daughter didn't want to stay here tonight. She has begged me to let her go home tomorrow. In the event that she's well enough, I've made arrangements through the hospital to fly her to Bozeman by private charter in the afternoon. I'll accompany her and take care of her for another day until she's up and around."

"I can't let you do that."

"It's my job."

"No one has a job like that," he argued. "No wonder our hospitals are in financial trouble."

"The patient advocacy department is funded by a private donor, so it's not a concern. More importantly, your daughter made a deal with me. She would tell me your name and let me call you if I nursed her till she was better. We shook on it."

Good grief.

Allie, Allie. What was going on inside her? After a certain age, she'd only wanted Noreen around and Colt hadn't hired another nanny. Yet in her vulnerability today, she'd reached out to a stranger. Why?

Colt wanted to ask this woman if she knew what had driven Allie to do what she did, but now wasn't the time. It was enough to know his daughter was safe in a hospital, getting treated for the flu of all things.

He took a deep breath. "How soon can I talk to her?"

"As soon as she's awake. Housekeeping has brought me a cot so I can stay with her tonight. If she should wake up, I'll let her use my phone to call you. Otherwise, call my number in the morning and I'll put her on."

He pursed his lips. "I may phone you before that to find out if you're real or if I'm having an out-of-body experience."

She laughed quietly. A husky kind of laugh that resonated inside him. "There's nothing more terrifying than not knowing where your child is. Until you can hug her and kiss her, I know you won't quite believe you have her back."

Whoever this woman was, she could read minds. It gave him goose flesh. "Ms. McFarland?"

"Yes?"

"Thank you," he whispered.

"You're welcome, Mr. Brenner. We'll talk in the morning. Good night."

She hung up first, leaving him dazed.

When he gathered his wits, he left the room and walked down the hall past the guest bedroom to Matt's room. His son had fallen asleep, but after what they'd been through, he decided to wake him up.

"Matt?" he called softly to him.

He made a sound and turned toward him. "Is it time to go?"

Colt sat down on the side of the bed. "We don't have to go anywhere. Your sister's been found." In the next few minutes, he told him about the phone call.

Matt reached over and hugged him. "Do you think I'll catch it?"

He hadn't seen that question coming. "I don't know. Let's not worry about that now. Go back to sleep."

"They're really going to fly her home?"

"That's what the nurse said."

"Whoa. Well, good night, Dad." Matt laid back down and punched his pillow to get it in the right position.

Colt eyed his son for a moment. The biggest care on Matt's mind now was whether he would come down with the virus. Would that the flu was all that plagued Colt. Unfortunately for him, this new knowledge was only the tip of an enormous iceberg.

After leaving Matt's bedroom, he headed for his study again. He called both detectives and left messages that Allie had been found. Following that, he e-mailed the Wagners to tell them the good news. There was no one else to inform.

Wired and restless, he went to the kitchen to make himself some coffee. Caffeine was the last thing he needed, but it was the only drink he wanted.

His premonition that something was wrong with Allie had borne fruit. Two times he'd experienced this. Both times there'd been bad news. He dreaded the thought of it ever happening again. His heart might not be able to take it a third time.

Noreen was going to be surprised when another woman besides herself would be waiting on Allie. Colt had gotten the surprise of *his* life when a Ms. McFarland, rather than the detective, had phoned to let him know his daughter was in hospital. Sick, but safe.

The woman had sent an essence through the phone line he couldn't describe. He had to confess that his curiosity had been aroused. For several reasons, he knew it would be a long time before tomorrow afternoon rolled around.

Colt wasn't sure he could wait. If he talked to Allie in the morning and didn't hear improvement, then he'd fly to Salt Lake with Matt as planned.

KATHRYN HAD SET her watch alarm for six-thirty. After she got up from the cot, she checked her patient's vital signs. Everything looked good. Her temperature was down to ninety-nine. While Allie still slept, she stepped outside to use the restroom and freshen up. She ordered breakfast trays for both of them, then put on a new surgical mask.

As she reached the room, the E.R. doctor was just coming out. "She's doing fine. Keep her on the IV until you're ready to transport her."

"I've arranged it for this afternoon."

He nodded his approval before walking away.

Kathryn went back in the room. "Good morning."

Allie looked happy to see her. "Hi."

"The doctor said you're coming right along. Let's get you up to the bathroom, then you'll feel even better."

"I've never had to go so badly."

"That's what an IV does to you." She raised the head of her bed, then helped her get up and walk to the bathroom while she rolled the IV stand. "Do you feel dizzy?"

"Not really."

"Good, but I'm still going to stay right outside the door. If you start to feel funny, just tell me."

"Okay."

When Allie came out again, she said, "I feel ten pounds lighter."

Kathryn laughed. "You probably are. Need help getting back to bed?"

"I don't think so."

To her relief, Allie made it without support. "Do you feel any nausea this morning?"

"No. I'm hungry."

"I'm glad to hear that." She helped ease her back

on the bed. "Our breakfast should be here in a minute. While we wait, why don't you call your father. I promised him you would."

"I'm afraid to."

Kathryn made a face. "Afraid? Of the most wonderful father in the whole world?"

"By now I'm sure he knows I asked Jen to lie for me. I think Dad hates lies more than anything else."

"But he loves *you* more than anything else, Allie. Once you tell him the reason behind this incident and let him know you're sorry for not being honest with him, he'll understand and love you all the more." She pulled out the phone and pressed his number. "Here. It's ringing."

With reluctance Allie took the phone from her. Almost immediately she said, "Hi, Dad. It's me." Whatever he answered in response caused the tears to roll down her cheeks. "I miss you, too. I'm so sorry for what I did."

Kathryn slipped out in the hall to give them privacy. The trays eventually arrived. She took them in the room and put them on the table that slid over the bed. Propping herself on the stool, Kathryn reached for hers and devoured her toast and eggs. In a few minutes, she heard Allie saying goodbye.

"I love you, too. Here she is." She extended the phone to Kathryn. "Dad wants to talk to you."

She took it from her and put her empty tray on the side table. "Good morning, Mr. Brenner."

"It is now." His voice sounded deeper.

"Are you grounded yet?" she teased.

He chuckled. "Almost. Like you said, it will take hugging her to convince me completely."

"The doctor says she can go home. If all goes well, we should be in Bozeman by two."

"That's even earlier than I'd hoped."

The man couldn't wait to get his daughter back. "She can't get home fast enough either. We'll be coming in on a Cessna CJ2."

"All the comforts of home for my daughter. I'm very grateful."

"I'm thrilled she's doing this well. Before we hang up, there is one thing. Allie stowed her backpack in one of the lockers at the bus depot, but the receipt with the access code for the computer was stolen along with her purse. I'm afraid you're the only person who can authorize someone to open it."

"I'll take care of it right now and ask them to ship it back to us."

"Hopefully by the time she's ready to return to school, it will have arrived. See you in about six hours."

"I'm counting down the time."

The comment made her smile. She hung up.

"Katy?"

Bemused by his comment, she was slow to flick her gaze to Allie. "What is it?"

"I'm glad you're going to be taking care of me."

"You are?"

She nodded. "People die from the H1N1 virus."

The poor thing had been so frightened to tell her father what she'd done, she was only now realizing the state of her health.

"Well, it's not going to happen on my watch. While

you graze the TV channels, I'm going to go home and
pack a few things. Then I'll be back. I expect your
breakfast to be gone."

"I want to eat."

"Good. You know the button to press if you need a
nurse to help you to the bathroom again. Can I get you
anything else before I go?"

"No. Just hurry."

"I promise."

Nancy had gone off shift when Kathryn approached
the desk. Sue was on duty. Kathryn caught her up to
speed on the Brenner case, then she left the hospital for
home.

It was cold and cloudy, but no storm was pending yet.
For Allie's sake she hoped there'd be little turbulence
on the flight to Montana.

Once she'd reached her condo, she packed a suitcase, then took a shower and washed her hair. After
she'd blow-dried it, she slipped on fresh underwear and
walked over to the closet.

She gave a few outfits consideration, then made her
choice of a pair of camel-colored wool pants and matching cashmere sweater with a crew neck. She toned it
with a dark brown suede blazer she'd picked up with her
family in Rio. The suede boots in the same tone were
comfortable, yet dressy. Her topaz studs added the right
touch.

The clothes she'd worn at the farm had been nothing
like the outfits Maggie wore. Her sister, with her long
legs and slim figure, looked like a fashion model without even trying. With her sense of dress, she'd helped
put a wardrobe together that suited Kathryn. Their

family's local and national prominence dictated that they be ready for the camera whenever they went out in public.

Both sisters were blonde and five foot eight, but Kathryn's figure was a little fuller. Sometimes from farther off, people thought the two of them were twins. But once they got up close, the differences in their facial features became evident.

Kathryn had a wider smile and naturally dark-fringed eyes. Since becoming a mother, Maggie wore her hair shorter, the way Kathryn had done at the farm. Now they'd reversed things.

She rummaged through her accessories drawer and pulled out a chiffon scarf in a geometric design of leopard-skin colors. Once she'd caught her shoulder-length blond hair at the nape with it, she applied a pink frost lipstick, sprayed herself with her favorite wildflower scent and was ready.

Before she left the condo, she phoned her parents. Her mother answered. "I'm so glad you called, darling. Come on over and have lunch with us."

"I wish I could, but I'm on a case and won't be home for a few days." Her mom understood what that meant. Any lost child took top priority. Thanks to her psychiatrist's suggestion, Kathryn found that if she took the time to explain things to her mother, she didn't get so upset if Kathryn couldn't be with them.

"Where are you going?"

"I'm taking a teenager home to her family in Bozeman. Her name is Allie Brenner. She came down with the H1N1 virus, but it's a light case. Maggie's going to fly us there in a little while."

"Was she a kidnap victim?"

"No. She came to Salt Lake for a reason, but didn't tell her father where she was going. He thought she was at school."

"Oh, dear."

"When she got off the Greyhound bus she became dizzy. Someone called the police and she was taken to the hospital without any ID or money. She wouldn't tell anyone anything. That's why I was called in."

"The poor child."

"My feeling exactly. Something's going on with her, Mom. I have no idea why she came here, but she finally trusted me enough to let me contact her father."

"He must have been out of his mind with grief."

Kathryn would never forget the way he'd answered the phone. Talk about a terrified parent. "He was…and so grateful for the call."

"Of course. No one knows better than I what that phone call was like when Maggie told us she'd found *you!*" Her mother broke down weeping.

Afraid it would get her started, Kathryn said, "Allie's frightened, too, and for some reason is clinging to me. Since she needs watching, I decided to see her back safely."

"Well—" her mother sniffed "—you and Maggie take care. Call us when you get there."

"I promise. Love you, Mom."

Chapter Three

The gleaming white-and-blue Cessna with gold strip-ing stood out from the overcast sky as it descended and made seamless contact with the runway. Colt had been given permission to drive his Xterra as close as the rules allowed to pick up his daughter.

Matt whistled. "Sweet. How would it be to own one of those?"

Colt agreed, but right now he'd focused his gaze on the door, waiting for it to open. The second there was movement, he started forward.

"Allie!" he cried when he saw her in the aperture wearing her parka.

"Hi, Dad!"

He took the last steps to reach her and pulled her into his arms. She gave him a squeeze that almost knocked his hat off. "Do you have any idea how happy I am to see you?" Without letting her go, he carried her the small distance to the car. Matt opened the rear door so Colt could help her into the seat. He kissed her forehead. "Are you all right?"

"Yes, but I'm glad to be home."

"Amen to that." In a second he had her strapped in. "I'll be right back."

When he started for the plane again, his breath caught at the sight of the stunning blonde woman who'd just stepped out on the tarmac. Impressions of caramel swirls among vanilla cream flew at him like reflections off a glacier sparkling in the sun.

She was the epitome of feminine elegance, the kind of trait a few women were born with that had nothing to do with what they wore. Although what she was wearing was perfect down to the shape of her slim waist shown off in a suede jacket. It drew his attention to her womanly hips and long legs. A white parka lay over one arm. She held a small suitcase in her other hand.

"Whoa," his son murmured behind him. Matt was old enough to appreciate the sight of a truly gorgeous woman.

His comment said it all, jerking Colt back to his senses. He reached for her suitcase. "Welcome to Montana, Ms. McFarland. I'm Colton Brenner. This is Allie's brother, Matt."

Her startling blue eyes shifted to his son. "How are you, Matt?" She shook his hand. "Did anyone ever tell you that you and Allie look a lot alike? Except you're the handsome one."

While Colt chuckled, a warm blush spread over Matt's face. "Call me Katy."

For some reason she didn't look like a Katy to him. "Matt? If you'll help her in the front seat, I'll stow this in the back. Let me have your parka."

"Thank you." As she handed it to him, their arms brushed. He could smell her fragrance. All of it was unexpected, increasing an unbidden awareness of her. Colt didn't like it. He'd never experienced such a strong reaction to a woman before, not even when— A grimace marred his features. *Just don't think, Brenner.*

Out of the corner of his eye he saw her climb in the backseat next to Allie. She had a mind of her own. It was just as well. Now she wouldn't be seated next to him to provide a distraction he didn't need while he took them home.

He walked around and got in behind the wheel. As he drove away, he could see the Cessna taxiing out in preparation for takeoff. "You people have provided an amazing service for our family. You'll have to tell me where I can send a contribution."

"That's very generous of you, but the patient advocacy program is in place for that very purpose. The only thing of importance is that your daughter is back with you safe and sound."

And troubled.

He glanced over his shoulder at Allie. "I was worried about your cold, honey. We should have done something about it a few days ago."

"A lot of my friends have had one. Do you think they've had the H1N1, Katy?"

"Probably. We might not have known about you if you hadn't taken that long bus trip. It exhausted you and caused your temperature to spike."

Colt turned onto the highway headed toward the ranch. "Next time you're sick, I'm not waiting to get you in to see the doctor."

"I'm sorry about everything. Hey, Katy? Do you think Matt will catch it?"

Colt's eyes met their guest's amused gaze through the rearview mirror. It was only a moment, but he felt a connection. The same kind of feeling he'd experienced with her over the phone. He gripped the steering wheel tighter.

"Tell you what. If he gets a cold, your father can take him in to be tested."

"I'm not going to get it," Matt grumbled.

Time for a change of subject. "Noreen is fixing your favorite dinner. I hope you'll be able to eat a little of it."

"Breakfast tasted good, and I ate part of my lunch."

"Sounds like your appetite has picked up. I don't think you ate a solid meal all week."

"That's because my throat was sore. Do you like enchiladas, Katy?"

"I adore them. In fact, I could live on Mexican food."

Matt leaned forward. "That's what *you* always say, Dad."

Colt stepped on the gas. The sooner they reached the ranch where they weren't all trapped together, the better.

"Is it hard learning how to be a nurse?" Allie asked.

"Only if you have trouble with math and chemistry."

"I guess *you* didn't," Matt said.

"But I'm a klutz at logic. My last boyfriend showed me his LSAT books. I took some of the sample quizzes and failed them."

"What does LSAT mean?"

"It's a test to see if you can get in to law school."

"I didn't know that. Give us an example."

"It's hard to think of one."

"Try." To Colt's astonishment, Matt was being amazingly persistent.

"Okay. Let's say a person in a cold climate buys a stylish coat, even though it doesn't keep him warm. You assume this person will sacrifice comfort for appearance, right?"

They both said yes.

"So then you have to read five different situations to see which one the same assumption applies to. But it's hard and tricky. For example, an acrobat asks the circus to buy him an expensive outfit to impress the audience. Do you think that's the same thing?"

Silence reigned. Finally Allie said, "I don't get it."

"Neither do I. Did you, Dad?"

"Well, let's think about it. The guy in the cold climate needed some kind of a coat, warm or not. The acrobat didn't need an expensive outfit. Any kind of outfit would have worked."

"I still don't get it."

"Neither do I," Katy assured him. "My brain doesn't work like your father's or Steve's. As I said earlier, trying to do his homework was worse than figuring out a Chinese puzzle."

Both his children laughed and kept on chatting with her.

Steve. Her latest boyfriend out of how many? What was she? Mid-twenties? Her age was hard to tell.

She was a catalyst, stirring up conversations they'd

never had, prompting them to ask questions they wouldn't have thought of. *Disturbing the peace and tranquility of his well-ordered life.*

KATHRYN NOTICED her host let his children carry the conversation the rest of the way to the ranch. They traveled under a low ceiling of clouds. She was glad they'd beaten the latest storm front.

At the entrance to the Circle B, he turned off the main road and they began the climb through a mountain fairyland flocked with snow. It spoke to her heart of hearts.

She felt it happening again. That spurt of adrenaline racing through her body.

The first time she'd experienced it was at the plane when she'd seen the tall rancher striding toward her wearing well-worn cowboy boots and a black Stetson. Rugged, powerful. She'd immediately thought, *here* was a man to match his mountains.

Over the years at Skwars Farm, she'd roomed with many families in a rotation. The last family she'd been with had a daughter, Nelly, close to Kathryn's age. Nelly had a driver's license and could take the family car into town. She always stopped at the library to bring back more Louis L'Amour books for Kathryn, who'd gotten hooked on *High Lonesome* years earlier.

Ever since Kathryn had been old enough to fantasize, she'd pretended to be Considine's woman. Considine was the hard-hitting outlaw whose code of honor in the face of all odds helped him survive on the American frontier.

Talk about an out-of-body experience—just a little

while ago he'd come to life in the form of Colton Brenner.

Fantasizing was a tool Kathryn had used to survive during her twenty-six years in captivity. Her psychiatrist couldn't emphasize often enough that it played the key role in helping her cope during the years she was floundering.

But it had been four years since her family had found her and she still couldn't shut off the mechanism that caused her to dream beyond the boundaries of reality. Staring at Colton Brenner, imagining he was the hero of her young girl's dreams, wasn't healthy.

Already she sensed this twenty-first-century family man had staked out his own territory a long time ago. Only a special few had entrée into his inner circle. Kathryn got the distinct impression she was an unwanted guest here, existing on borrowed time because of an unexpected turn of events involving Allie. If nothing else, his set boundaries guaranteed an end to her flights of fantasy, breaking the dangerous quarter-of-a-century cycle.

The car wound around one more curve in the road lined with walls of dense evergreens covered in snow. Suddenly they came upon a vale nestled between the mountains containing a fabulous western-style ranch house. Smoke curled from the chimney.

She picked out the barn, the bunkhouses and bungalows, another house, outbuildings, pens and corrals. In the far distance, she saw the stream that crossed the property and beyond it a herd of cattle.

"We're home, Katy."

"I can see that." She squeezed the teen's arm. "I've

decided the name Circle B doesn't do this place justice. It should be called something evocative like Cloud Bottom Ranch."

Everyone in the car laughed, even the children's father. He said, "Our ancestors started what was then called the Ayrshire Ranch on just six hundred acres and a little bungalow. They hoped to raise Ayrshire dairy cows, but the experiment didn't last long.

"Each generation of Brenners that followed bought other small parcels of land and grew crops. It got renamed the Circle B after my great-grandfather brought in Angus cattle. No one could pronounce Ayrshire properly anyway. He wanted something simple and straightforward."

She smiled, remembering the problems people had with names like her kidnapper Antonin Buric and the Skwars families. "Americans do have a way of slaughtering most languages." Once again, the twins roared with laughter.

Through the rearview mirror, she felt their father's gaze. "As the ranch began to prosper, the Circle B stuck, but I must admit your fanciful version captures its true essence. Interestingly enough, the Sioux and Shoshone had two names for this area depending on the season. In winter they called it 'Walkway to the Clouds.'"

Kathryn felt a little shiver race across her skin. "How beautiful." He nodded. "And summer?"

"Valley of the Flowers."

Another Albion Basin. Just like home.

More stuff fantasies were made of, but she was through with those. Realizing the car had stopped, she undid her seat belt and leaned across to help Allie. "I bet bed sounds good about now."

"It does."

"I thought so."

Matt opened the door for Kathryn while their father picked up his daughter and carried her around the end of the house. Kathryn alighted from the car with her purse. "Thanks, Matt."

"Sure." He opened the trunk to get her parka and suitcase. "Follow me."

The two-story ranch house had been constructed of dark wood and local stone. At the back, there was a large covered veranda with picture windows facing an eastern exposure.

Matt showed her through the door into a room to wash hands and stow boots and parkas. He hung hers on a peg, then walked her down a hall that opened into a vaulted great room dominated by the rock fireplace. On either side were huge, tall picture windows looking out on the mountains. This had to be the heart of their home.

"I'll take your suitcase upstairs and be right back, Katy."

"Thanks, Matt."

The comfortable brown leather couches and chairs with colorful woven throws invited her to curl up. Framed family pictures covered one wall. Her eyes wandered over the floor-to-ceiling bookcase filled with books, games and an entertainment center. Dark honey-colored hardwood floors not covered by oriental rugs gleamed in the firelight.

She gravitated to the fire's warmth, eager to look at every photo and examine the titles.

"Welcome to the Circle B, Ms. McFarland. I'm Noreen Walters."

Kathryn swung around. The older brunette woman was probably in her fifties. Hearty-looking. Attractive. "How do you do." She shook hands with her. "From what I hear, nobody could get along without you and your husband."

"That's nice to know. How's my girl?"

"She's going to be fine, but needs bed rest and liquids with her medication. I'm really superfluous, except for checking her vitals. The one thing we don't want is to find she's getting respiratory problems or see her temperature elevate. It's been hovering between ninety-nine and a hundred since last night. I'm anticipating it will get back to normal by tomorrow."

"That little monkey fought her father about her cold."

"Isn't that why they call it the terrible teens?"

Noreen chuckled. "Do you have children?"

"No. I'm not married. What about you?"

A shadow marred her expression. "I had three miscarriages before we came to work for Colton."

Kathryn felt her pain. "Now you have two remarkable children."

The shadow disappeared. "Yes."

"I fear there are times when she thinks she has a stubborn third one." Her host's deep voice prompted Kathryn to turn around.

"You mean four," Noreen quipped. "You forgot Ed."

He smiled, then said, "I think we'll plan to eat dinner

around six. That should give Allie time for a good nap."

Noreen nodded. "If you're hungry now, Ms. McFarland, I'll send Matt up with a tray for you."

"Thank you, but I ate before we flew here. And please…call me Katy."

"I will," she said before leaving the room.

"While we're on the subject of names, mine is Colt."

It suited him down to the last irreverent tendril curling against his neck.

Kathryn had discovered that without the Stetson, he had a head of shocking black hair whose ends wanted to wave. The arrangement of hard-boned features made him a striking man. Brows of the same black shade framed his eyes. They were the color of spring grass and looked translucent in the fire's glow.

His eyes took swift inventory of her. She could hardly breathe.

Without conscious thought her gaze drifted over the rest of him. He wore a long-sleeved, plaid flannel shirt in blues and greens. The hem was tucked into jeans that molded powerful thighs. His hard-muscled physique revealed a man who kept fit in the outdoors.

There was an aura about him, a mental toughness and discipline she'd sensed beneath the male veneer. You didn't trifle with a man like him.

Allie knew it. She'd been raised by him.

Kathryn no longer questioned why his daughter had been afraid to call him from the hospital. Yet her reason for disappointing him had to have been so compelling that she'd been willing to risk it.

Though the subject hadn't been brought up by the twins or their father, Kathryn suspected this situation had everything to do with their mother. No one had talked about her or mentioned her, but it was clear Colt Brenner's woman—whether she'd been his wife or not, whether she was alive or not—was the elephant in the room.

"I need to take Allie's vitals. I'll just get the things I need out of my suitcase."

"The twins' bedrooms are on the next floor," Colt said. "The upstairs guest bedroom is between them. I'll show you."

She followed him to the foyer and up the staircase to the next floor. He moved with natural male grace. Aware her thoughts were too concentrated on him, she looked around her. The interior was an amalgamation of refined rustic and contemporary design. "You've created the perfect mountain home."

"Thank you. We used to live in the original house on the property. Now Noreen and Ed live there."

He opened the door to her room, which was decorated in earth tones with hardwood floors. She found her suitcase at the end of the queen-size bed covered with a patchwork quilt. After retrieving the bag inside it, she accompanied him to the bedroom on the left.

Matt was spread across the end of Allie's queen talking to his sister. It reminded her of the way Kathryn's brothers sometimes did that with her.

"Hi!" they said in unison. Matt stood up.

The sunny room with accents of blue and white delighted her. She moved to the side of the bed and sat down. "Shall we get this over with? Then you can rest."

Kathryn listened to her lungs with her stethoscope. They sounded clear. Her blood pressure was normal. Her pulse was a little fast; that didn't surprise her. Allie had expended extra energy for the flight.

She slipped the digital thermometer under her arm. After it beeped she read, "Ninety-nine!" Kathryn flashed her a smile. "You're going to live." She could tell her pronouncement relieved Colt.

Someone had put a pitcher of water and a glass on the side table. She got up and poured a full glass before handing her the pills she needed to take. "Drink all of it."

"Okay."

After she swallowed them, Kathryn asked, "Have you been to the bathroom?"

"Dad helped me." Her brown eyes darted to her father. "Could I call Jen first?"

He shook his dark head. "She phoned earlier today and I told her you'd get in touch with her tomorrow." In a surprise move, he reached into her bottom dresser drawer and pulled out a cell phone. "I'll turn this on in case you need to phone me." Colt put it on her side table.

If Kathryn wasn't mistaken, Allie looked guilty about her phone. She'd obviously hidden it before leaving for Salt Lake. At least the thief hadn't gotten hold of it when he'd taken her purse. "Is she mad at me?"

"I think it's more of a case of her being mad at herself for going along with you."

Allie averted her eyes. "I'll apologize to her."

"I think that better include her parents."

"I bet they hate me." Kathryn detected a tremor in her voice.

"Not their daughter's best friend," Colt assured her with a kiss on the cheek. "Sleep tight, honey."

Kathryn gathered up her bag and the three of them left the room. Colt turned to her. "There's an en suite bathroom in your room. After you've freshened up, feel free to come downstairs and watch TV or do whatever you'd like. I have work to do, but I'll ask Noreen to make you coffee or tea, whichever you prefer."

"If you have a cola, I'd like that."

"I'll get it for you," Matt offered.

"Thanks. I'll be down in a minute."

The second she found herself alone and closed the door, her breath came rushing out. Until just now she hadn't realized she'd been holding it. There was no one to blame but Colt Brenner for her body's uncharacteristic reaction.

Afraid to dwell on thoughts of him, she put her bag down and reached for the phone to call her mother because she'd promised. When her mom didn't answer, she left a message on her voice mail that she'd arrived safely.

After she hung up, she saw that she'd received several work messages and one from Maggie. Her pulse raced, fearing something might be wrong. Kathryn phoned her immediately, anxious to hear her sister's voice.

"Kathryn?"

"Maggie? What's happened?"

"Why nothing. I'm driving through Federal Heights right now, but couldn't wait to talk to you."

Kathryn frowned. "About what?"

"You know what. I was the one who opened the plane door. I stood right behind you when Mr. Tall, Dark and Handsome reached for his daughter. My jaw must have dropped a foot. It's a good thing Jake didn't see my reaction."

Heat crept into Kathryn's cheeks.

"Cat got your tongue? I thought so. When you find it, call me back."

Click.

Oh, Maggie. If only it were that simple...

He was spectacular all right, but there was layer after complicated layer to Colt Brenner, the man.

On the surface she understood the protective father and successful rancher, yet already Kathryn had picked up on negative vibes he sent out.

Her radar had been fine-tuned in Wisconsin. She was good at reading what was going on in other people's heads. She'd had to be after having been passed around to different homes month after month, year after year.

No one had wanted the little girl who'd been dumped on them at the farm, but they did their duty. She'd been tolerated and taken care of, but she'd been the proverbial rolling stone, gathering no moss.

The same thing was happening to her now, only this time it was Colt Brenner doing his duty. For his daughter's sake, he was tolerating Kathryn, taking care of her needs, but he didn't like being dumped on. Allie's behavior had placed him in an impossible position.

Allie had put Kathryn in an impossible position, too!

What Colt didn't realize was that Kathryn didn't

like it, either, but she didn't take his hostility personally. Through years of dealing with similar situations on the farm, she'd learned not to do that because she understood those families had no vested interest in her. She was a temporary encumbrance until the end of the month when she was happily shifted to someone else's household.

Her only comfort had come from playing with the youngest children, who were more accepting of her presence in their lives. Unlike the adults, they didn't see her as an intrusion. She knew Matt Brenner didn't see her that way.

During the rest of her stay here, she'd befriend him. If he was still downstairs, she'd ask him to help her do one of those puzzles she'd seen on the shelf. Besides hard work and her fantasizing, books and puzzles had helped save her life growing up.

IT HAD GROWN DARK on the way back from the lower pasture. Colt had driven there to haul more feed, but as it turned out, the trip hadn't been necessary. His stockmen had taken care of it.

He'd used the excuse of work to bolt from the house. Sixteen years ago, he'd been a naive twenty-year-old who'd gotten sidetracked by a woman's magic and didn't suspect the ugliness of what it masked until it was too late.

Never again.

The lights from the ranch house beckoned him. While he'd been gone, the wind had picked up. It brought snow flurries portending the storm that had moved in over the mountains. On nights like this, he always experienced a warm feeling of homecoming, but tonight he was aware of an added element because *she* was inside.

Colt ground his teeth. He wanted Ms. McFarland out of his house and off his land.

The scene that greeted him as he walked in the great room a few minutes later was so domestic and cozy, it caused an upheaval inside him.

"Hey, Dad? Come and look! Now that you're back you can help us put my puzzle of Brett Favre together." Favre was Matt's hero. Allie had bought him the thousand-piece version of the pro quarterback wearing his Vikings jersey and helmet after his football banquet. Colt had planned to work on it with the kids this weekend.

Their guest's hair gleamed like spun gold in the fire-light. She seemed to be concentrating hard. In fact, she didn't look up as he walked over to the card table Matt had set up in front of the fireplace. For some reason, it set off a rare burst of anger he needed to squelch. "First I need to check on Allie."

"Katy did it a little while ago. She was still asleep."

A pair of blue eyes flicked his way. They looked as hot as the fire, yet Kathryn's response was degrees cooler. "You don't need to be concerned. So far she's holding her own."

He took a fortifying breath. "That's good to hear. I'll let Noreen know I'm back so she can put dinner on."

"Allie shouldn't come downstairs before tomorrow. To save Noreen the trouble, maybe you and Matt could take a plate up to her room and eat with her?"

"What are you going to do?" Matt voiced the question on Colt's mind.

"I'll go up and get her ready, then I have some

business to do over the phone. Later on, I'll come down to the kitchen. But if it will put Noreen out…"

"Why would it?" Colt blurted before he realized he was sounding terse again. "While you're here, treat this house as your own."

"Thank you." She got up from the chair. "I'll help you finish this later, Matt."

"Great!"

Colt tried not to watch her leave the room, but the way she moved on those long legs mesmerized him. It didn't matter what she wore or the way she did her hair. She was a knockout, but he knew so much more lay beneath the surface of Ms. McFarland once you got past her initial beauty.

"She knows almost as much about football as a guy. She says her dad lives for the NFL games." Was that a fact. "She likes college football better, though. The Utes are her favorite team."

"Well, they would be, wouldn't they? Coming from Utah?" He headed for the kitchen. Matt followed.

"Yeah, except she says a lot of people like the BYU. They hate each other, especially because the Utes made the BCS twice. Her dad took her to the game they won against Alabama. Isn't that cool? She said her favorite player was Paul Kruger. He went to the NFL and plays for the Jets."

Colt couldn't remember the last time he'd heard his son this chatty. They found Noreen. "We're going to eat upstairs with Allie." He pulled three plates from the cupboard.

"What about Katy?"

"She'll come down for something later," Matt

explained before Colt could get a word in edgewise. "She's got work to do."

"What kind of work?"

"I don't know. She helps people."

Noreen was waiting for a more substantial answer. Colt started serving up the enchiladas. "Ms. McFarland works for the patient advocacy program at the hospital in Salt Lake."

"Imagine them flying her here with Allie. It's a huge expense."

Matt got some sodas out of the fridge. "She says she's a specialty nurse, kind of like some people have their own sports trainer."

Colt had trouble believing any of this had happened. "Have we got everything?"

"Yup. Let's go. I'm starving!"

"Thanks, Noreen," Colt murmured. "This looks delicious. Isn't Ed eating?"

"He'll be here in a minute. Let's hope Allie's hungry."

Colt put everything on a tray. Matt brought the drinks and they left the kitchen. At the top of the stairs he saw light beneath the closed door of the guest bedroom. He had to give Katy full marks for doing her job and being unobtrusive.

When he walked in Allie's room, she was sitting up in bed with the light on waiting for them. "Hi, honey. How are you feeling?"

"Good."

"Ready for dinner?"

Allie nodded as the two of them proceeded to wait on her. Finally they pulled up chairs and everyone started to eat. Colt was glad to see Allie finish off one of her enchiladas and dig into her salad. She was definitely getting better.

"Dad? While Katy's not in here, I want to ask you something."

"Go ahead."

"Thanksgiving's only four days away. Would it be all right if I asked her to stay with us until the weekend?"

He stopped chewing. His daughter didn't really just ask him that.

"Yeah, Dad," Matt chimed in. "In case I get sick she'll be here to take care of me. Besides, it'll take that long for us to finish the puzzle."

Putting down his fork before he made mincemeat of the rest of his enchilada, he said, "I'm afraid not, honey. Have you forgotten your uncle Bob and aunt Sherry have invited us to go to Butte for Thanksgiving? Your cousins are looking forward to it."

"They won't care if Katy comes. Aunt Sherry would really like her and she always has company stay over."

"Not this time. We have to think of Ms. McFarland, who's on loan from the hospital. No doubt she's in her room right now making plans for her next case. We can't expect to take advantage of her services like that, not after what she's done to help you."

His daughter's face fell. "I don't think I can eat any more."

Colt groaned. His daughter could manipulate when she wanted to, but this was going too far. He refused to fall for it. "That's all right. Tomorrow you'll probably be able to move around and work up more of an appetite."

In the silence that followed, he noticed his son had stopped chirping away. He'd chosen sides and had moved to Allie's corner. Colt continued to finish his meal. *Nip it in the bud.* That motto had served him well in the past.

His gaze flicked to Matt's plate. "Aren't you going to eat your apple pie?"

"Maybe later."

"Then I'll eat it now so we don't disappoint Noreen." So saying, he finished it off. While his children eyed him soulfully, he got up and put all the plates on the tray. "I'll be back in a few minutes."

Chapter Four

"Thanks for manning the desk for me, Donna. If my patient is better tomorrow, I'll fly to Salt Lake tomorrow evening and be at work Monday morning to give you a break. I know you want to get ready for Thanksgiving."

"That would great. If I can get all the shopping done Monday, then I'll cook a little at a time until the big day."

"How many are you having for dinner?"

"Twenty. Todd's brother and his wife and children are coming. What about you?"

"We're all getting together at Mom and Dad's." Thanksgiving at the McFarlands' was sacrosanct, not only for her family but for Kathryn. Until she'd been found, Thanksgiving and Christmas had been the most dreaded times of life to get through.

"I bet your family still can't believe you're home with them."

"Sometimes I can't, either."

"Not to change the subject, but you did ask. Another AMBER Alert has gone out. This time on a seven-year-old girl in Sandy named Whitney."

Kathryn's eyes closed tightly. She felt as if she'd been kicked in the stomach. "When?"

"About two hours ago. She got separated from her mother at a toy store in the South Towne Mall. It was packed with preseason shoppers. The woman's in agony."

Whitney would be in worse condition if she wasn't dead already. "Did you contact my mom?"

"Yes. She's already on it."

That was probably why her mother hadn't picked up earlier. "I wish I were there to help." But Allie had needed help, too. She still did, but not the kind Kathryn could provide.

The teen had serious issues only her father could work on with her once she found the courage to talk to him.

"You're just like your sister before she met Jake. She always wished she could be in ten places at once."

"She's still like that inside, but being a wife and mother has changed her life." Donna had started working for Maggie at the Foundation ten years ago and continued to be a good family friend, as well as an invaluable assistant, to Kathryn. "Keep me posted, will you?"

"When I hear anything new, I'll call you. Bye for now."

Kathryn hung up. If the little girl wasn't found, it could mean days, months, even years of unrelieved suffering. But she needed to set that care aside while she dealt with Allie.

When Kathryn entered the bedroom, the teen was

curled up on her side toward the window. Her shoulders were shaking beneath the covers. "Allie?"

She turned over. Kathryn could tell she was crying and rushed over to her. "Are you feeling worse?"

"No."

"Then what's wrong?"

"Everything."

Kathryn sank down on the side of the bed next to her, smoothing Allie's hair off her forehead. "Did you eat dinner?"

"Half of it." Half was better than nothing. "Katy? What are you doing for Thanksgiving?"

Where had that question come from? "I'm going to be with my family. What about you?"

"We're going to our aunt and uncle's in Butte to be with our cousins."

"That sounds fun."

Allie sat up in bed, wiping her eyes. "So you don't have to work?" Another question that had completely ignored Kathryn's comment.

"No."

"Then you could go with us, right? Dad said you'd be working with another patient so we couldn't ask you."

Her father had told Allie what any parent would have said in response, but in Colt Brenner's case there was much more to it than that. "What he meant was, I'd be busy with my work even if I stopped to have dinner with my family, and he'd be right."

"You mean you have to be at the hospital on Thanksgiving?"

"No. I do all kinds of jobs."

"Like what?"

"It's a long story. Where do you keep your brush? While I do your hair, I'll tell you."

"It's in the bathroom in the top left drawer."

"I'll be right back."

Kathryn slid off the bed and went to fetch it. After she came back, she said, "Turn your back toward me."

"Okay."

She gathered the glossy skein of hair in her hands and got started.

"That feels good."

"It's supposed to. Now to answer your question. I help my brother at the halfway house I told you about. Some of the homeless women have children. I do periodic health checks on all of them and work with him and his staff to help the adults find work and housing. Do you remember that brochure I gave you?"

She nodded.

"It talked about the McFarland Foundation. In the plaza where my condo is, there's a whole area on the ground floor where the foundation headquarters are located. My sister used to be in charge of it. Now I am, but of course I have people to help me.

"As soon as we receive word that a child has gone missing, we assist the police by sending out our own rescue people. We do ground and air searches and have resources to help find people who are lost to their families.

"When the hospital phoned me about you, it was because the police had brought you into the E.R. as a Jane Doe. That meant you couldn't be identified yet and could be a possible runaway or kidnap victim who'd either gotten away or had been let go. Every E.R. in every hospital in Salt Lake Valley knows to call the foundation if a Jane or John Doe is brought in."

Allie's turned her head. "Does it happen a lot?"

"More than you know."

"That's awful."

"I agree. After I was reunited with my family, I watched my sister doing all the things I do now. When I lived at Skwars Farm, I used to dream about becoming a doctor, but knew it was only a dream. But after I was found and was able to go to college, I changed my mind about being a doctor."

"How come?"

"Because then I wouldn't be able to be as free to do everything for the foundation that has to be done. So I became a nurse, but I'm on my own, so to speak."

"Is your sister a nurse, too?"

"No. She's an attorney who helps people who are trying to avoid bankruptcy." She was also a crack pilot.

"Does it make you feel bad you couldn't do the LSAT like she did?"

Kathryn broke into laughter. "Heavens, no. For one thing, I never wanted to be a lawyer. For another, I love what I do. As for my sister, she's superwoman and I adore her."

"I wish I had a sister."

"You've got Matt. That's even better. Think of all the cute guys he brings around."

A little laugh came out of her. "I'm glad you're my nurse."

"So am I."

"Your father must make a lot of money to pay for everything."

"Our family can thank my great-grandfather John McFarland four greats back for that. He was Utah's Copper King. He amassed a fortune worth hundreds of millions of dollars that he invested."

"I can't imagine that much money."

"Neither can I, Allie. He had mansions in London, France, New York and Salt Lake. My father makes sure it gets spent helping other people."

"Like that program you work for?"

"Exactly."

"No wonder you love him so much."

"He and my mother work together. They're awesome," she said, using the teenage vernacular.

"So's my dad." Suddenly Allie moved so her back rested against the headboard. She drew up her pajama-clad knees and locked her arms around them. "My mom left after Matt and I were born."

Ah...

Kathryn put the brush on the table and sank down on the side of the bed again. "How often do you see her?"

Allie stared at her out of pained brown eyes. "We've never met her."

An unseen hand squeezed Kathryn's heart. *Never?*

"Dad met her in Las Vegas when he was a big rodeo champion on the circuit, but they broke up after Matt and I were born. Dad thought she might have gone back to her aunt and uncle's in Salt Lake where she was raised, but he never saw or heard from her again."

"Allie…" Kathryn reached out and rocked her in her arms.

"At least when your family found you, you knew your mother loved you," Allie sobbed.

At least I knew that…

"All my friends have moms except me. Dad can't talk about it and Matt won't talk about it."

"So you decided to find your mother's aunt and uncle and talk to them." It made too much sense.

"Yes. Dad said they managed the Beehive Motel near the airport. I was going to take a taxi there, but then I got sick and that guy stole my purse with my money. I was hoping you'd stay through Thanksgiving and help me. Maybe phone them and talk to them for me since you do things like that all the time. Even if they don't know where she is, maybe they'll tell you something that would help and we could find my mom together. I just need to ask her why she didn't want me and Matt."

Good heavens. Kathryn slowly let go of her. From here on out, she had to be careful what she said to this fragile girl.

"The thing is," Allie added, "I don't want Dad to know."

"*What* don't you want me to know?" Colt's deep voice said.

Kathryn felt his commanding presence before she saw him walk around the other side of the bed. Allie flashed her a silent message of pleading not to give her away.

"About the present I'm getting you for your birthday next week."

Allie's explanation sounded convincing enough,

but Kathryn knew her father didn't believe it for an instant.

"My lips are sealed," Kathryn said to Colt with a playful smile.

"That makes two against one," he teased back without challenging Allie, but his light tone didn't reach his eyes. "I guess I'm going to have to settle for being surprised."

The tension emanating from him made it impossible to stay in the room. "If you two will excuse me, I'm going downstairs to work on that puzzle." Father and daughter needed to be alone. She eyed Allie. "I'll be up in an hour to take your vitals before you go to sleep."

"Okay."

COLT HATED SECRETS. He was glad Katy had chosen to leave the room because he had a few things to say to his daughter in private. After sitting down on the bed next to her, he grasped the hand closest to him. "Your hair looks pretty."

"She brushed it for me."

"Ms. McFarland appears to be an excellent nurse who no doubt will be in high demand for the coming holiday."

"You're wrong about that, Dad."

It looked as if they were going to talk about their guest whether he wanted to or not. "In what way?"

"She doesn't have another patient to take care of on Thanksgiving."

"In other words, she's willing to make herself at home here and at your aunt's, even though she thinks you'll be well enough to be up and around by tomorrow?"

His daughter studied him with a speculative expression. "You don't trust her, do you?" She removed her hand.

Her question jolted him. "We both owe her a debt of gratitude. Why can't you let it go at that?"

Allie didn't look away. "You act like she's taking advantage of us or something."

He breathed in deeply. "Let's put it this way. Even if the patient advocacy program provides this service, she's done something unprecedented by bringing you home. It's possible that now she's had a good look around, Ms. McFarland is a shrewd enough woman to play on your emotions hoping to extend her stay and see where it all leads."

Her eyes never left his. "I knew that was why you didn't like her, but Katy's not looking for a rich husband," she assured him.

He eyed her with incredulity. "Why would you say something like that?"

"I happened to overhear Michelle's mom on the phone to one of her friends. She said that with your looks and money, you would always be a woman magnet and that's probably why you haven't remarried yet."

Somehow when Colt wasn't watching, Allie had become an adult. His precocious fifteen-year-old daughter had thrown the gloves away. He didn't know her like this. "Allie—"

"I'll prove that you're wrong about Katy."

To his surprise she slid out the other side of the bed and walked to her closet. He saw her pull something out of her parka pocket. She scuttled back under the covers and handed him a brochure, of all things. "Here, Dad. Read this."

Colt had no idea what he thought he was going to see when he looked down at it. The picture staring back at him resembled the woman downstairs. He read the words beneath it.

Kathryn McFarland, lost for twenty-six years, has been FOUND!

McFarland… Suddenly it all came rushing back to him. The famous Utah kidnapping case involving the Copper King's family, whose wealth rivaled that of the Vanderbilts and the Carnegies.

He jumped to his feet.

Four years earlier there'd been breaking news on every television and radio station in America about the baby daughter stolen from four-time U.S. Senator Reed McFarland and his wife. After twenty-six years, she'd been found and was now back with her family.

Some newscasters had said the case was bigger, yet gruesomely similar to the Lindbergh kidnapping back in 1932 when the baby was stolen out of their home, but the McFarlands' story had a happy ending.

Katy was *that* Kathryn?

He stared at the picture again.

"That's the photo the FBI first released to the press. It was taken while she was still living at Skwars Farm."

Colt thought she looked like a deer caught in the headlights. Four years had wrought changes. She had a longer hairstyle now and a polish lacking in the photograph, but the facial features and beautiful bone structure couldn't be denied. When he tore his eyes from her picture, he read the information from front to back.

"That brochure only tells you about the foundation, Dad. Besides running it, you ought to hear all the other things she and her family do to help people."

For the next few minutes, he listened while Allie proceeded to enlighten him on the extraordinary way she'd carried on with her life since being reunited with her family. Each new revelation made him more shameful of his cynicism.

The McFarlands had lived through the horror of waking up to find their baby missing from her crib. Colt's panic when he'd first learned Allie had gone off and no one knew where she was had given him a small taste of their terror.

He reflected on Ms. McFarland's phone call to him and could only praise her for the calm way she'd let Colt know Allie was all right. That was because she knew how to talk to frantic parents.

She was no ordinary woman. Colt couldn't compare her to the other women he'd known over the years. In all fairness, probably some of them hadn't been out for all they could get from him, but he'd never let those relationships last long enough to prove him wrong. Allie hadn't been completely off in her assessment.

He rubbed the back of his neck, experiencing a new level of panic. All he had to do was look at his daughter. The telltale stars in her eyes when she talked about Katy bordered on hero worship. Allie could have searched the world over and not have found a more heroic person to idolize than the nurse who'd accompanied her to Bozeman.

Ms. McFarland needed to get back to her life. They needed to get back to theirs. Once Allie was better and

Colt was alone with his daughter again, he would confront her. He suspected why she'd gone to Salt Lake without telling him, but needed to hear it from her. When everything was out in the open and he could tell her he understood her reasons, then their lives could return to normal.

He handed Allie the brochure. "Keep this for your scrapbook. When you're old, you'll be able to tell your grandchildren that you were once taken care of by one of the most famous women in America, certainly the most altruistic."

"Altruistic? I never heard that word before."

"It means unselfish concern for the welfare of others. The McFarlands could have invented the word," he murmured. "We've encroached on her generosity long enough. She needs to get back to her other responsibilities."

"When is she leaving?" Allie cried out.

"If your temperature returns to normal by tomorrow, then I'll drive her to the airport." That was a given. If Allie's temperature shot up again, he'd ask Dr. Rawson to make a house call.

"But she said a couple of days—"

"Today and tomorrow represent a couple of days, honey. I'm going downstairs to do some work. I would imagine she'll be up soon to get you ready for bed. I'll peek in on you later to kiss you good night."

Her crushed expression was the last thing he saw before he almost bumped into Matt coming up the stairs. "Hey—where are you going so fast?"

"I'm getting the DVD they passed out at the football banquet from my room. Katy wants to watch it."

"Maybe you could visit your sister for a little while first? If we take turns, she won't be so bored."

Matt got that impatient look on his face, but he muttered, "Okay."

"Thanks. Who knows? Before long it might be you lying in bed with the flu, wishing someone would keep you company."

Colt found their guest seated on the couch in the great room. She was watching the national news while she talked to someone on her cell phone.

Illuminated by the fire, she made a riveting picture, Before her glance flicked to his, he'd picked up on the serious tone of her conversation. While he waited for her to hang up, he wandered over to the puzzle and fit in some pieces.

KATHRYN HAD EXPECTED MATT to come back into the room. The sight of his dark-haired father prompted her to tell her sister that unless something changed with Allie, she'd see her at the airport at noon tomorrow. She hung up and turned off the TV.

"Forgive me for ignoring you, Colt."

He looked across at her with his keen gaze. "You didn't have to do that for me."

No, but he'd brought a restless energy into the room that put her on edge. "There wasn't anything of interest to watch. I'm glad you came in so I could talk to you before I go upstairs. When you walked in on Allie and me earlier, she'd just told me something in confidence.

"For the sake of not upsetting her, I went along with her excuse about your birthday present. But I'm going up now to say good night to her. When I do, I'll tell her she mustn't keep secrets from you. Not that she needs any encouragement from me. She loves you too terribly to hold back much longer. What I'm hoping is that it will be sooner than later so you can have some peace. Good night."

More convinced than ever that he was only putting up with her presence for Allie's sake, she left the family room, anxious to separate herself from him. He probably wasn't aware he had that effect on her. The man was in hell with good reason.

Kathryn was so immersed in her troubled thoughts, she almost bumped into Matt at the top of the stairs with a DVD in his hand. She'd forgotten about that.

He slowed down. "I was just coming, but I had to talk to Allie first."

"Of course. Your sister has top priority." She looked at her watch. "I didn't realize how late it was getting and decided I'd better get my patient ready for bed. Tell you what. Leave the DVD downstairs and we'll watch it together in the morning. I really do want to see it." If his father hadn't been down there, she wouldn't have come up yet.

"Sure."

She felt his trail of disappointment as she went to her room to get her bag. Kathryn didn't like that her presence seemed to be creating a disturbance in Colt's household.

When she walked into Allie's room a moment later, the teen was listening to her iPod. She raised a sad face to Kathryn before removing the headset. "Hi."

"Hi, yourself. Looks like your brother's been taking care of you. That's nice."

Allie didn't say anything. "Let's check that temperature first."

After the beep went off, Kathryn checked the numbers. "Ninety-eight point eight. That's in the normal range. Tomorrow you'll be able to get dressed and go downstairs." She checked her lungs and blood pressure. Everything looked good.

"You're going home tomorrow, huh?"

Her mournful tone didn't escape Kathryn. She put everything back in her bag. "Unless you take a turn for the worse, which I don't believe will happen." She handed her a glass of water and the pills.

Tears glazed her brown eyes as she swallowed them. "Have you decided you can't help me find my mom?"

Kathryn had been expecting that question. "There's no such a thing as *can't,* Allie, but this is something you have to discuss with your father. I wouldn't dream of going behind his back to help you with something so painful and private for both of you. He's been such a wonderful father to you all these years, he deserves to know what you're thinking and feeling."

Allie bit her lip. "What if he gets mad at me?"

"You were grown up enough to go to Salt Lake on your own. At this point he realizes you're no longer a child incapable of relating to adult problems. Give him a chance and he'll surprise you with his understanding."

"You think?" Her eyes had fastened on Kathryn, she wanted to believe her.

"I *know.*" Kathryn couldn't say that about many things, but she'd felt Colt's deep love for Allie. So deep, in fact, she had an idea he was still in shock over what his daughter had done.

"Can I call you after you get back to Salt Lake? I'll use the phone number printed on the brochure."

Kathryn had to hang tough on this one. "Not unless you have his permission. You want to keep your father's trust, don't you?"

Allie's head was bowed. "Yes."

"So do I. You're very blessed to have a dad like him. I'll see you in the morning. Good night." She fought the impulse to hug her. Kathryn's strong compulsion to give in to Allie's wishes proved that this girl already meant more to her than she should.

After preparing for bed, she reached for her phone and got under the covers to call Donna. There was still no word on the abducted girl. Once they'd hung up, she phoned her parents and learned that her mother had been in contact with the missing girl's family.

The three of them commiserated over the tragic situation. Before she hung up, she told them that if she flew home tomorrow as planned, she expected them to come to her condo for dinner. They were always waiting on other people. Kathryn felt like waiting on them for a change.

This experience with Allie had made her more emotional than usual. Before falling asleep, she prayed that the little kidnapped girl would be found alive and that Allie would find the courage to confide in her father. She eventually fell asleep remembering the joy in Colt's voice and expression as he'd picked up his daughter and carried her to the car. Every parent should have such a happy reunion.

At eight the next morning, Kathryn showered and got ready for the day. She'd packed an oyster-colored silk blouse and dove-gray pants in fine wool, cinched with a wide leather belt. She caught her hair back with a tortoise shell clip and put pearl studs in her ears.

In a minute, she knocked on Allie's door and announced herself.

"Come in." The teen had already showered and looked terrific in a long-sleeved, navy-blue cotton pull-over teamed with Levi's and sneakers.

"Well, look at you. I don't think I need to take your vitals, but I'm going to anyway."

"First will you do my hair like you wore yours yesterday?" Allie handed her the brush.

"Of course. Have you got a scarf?"

"No, but will this neckerchief do?"

"Let me see it."

Allie pulled it out of her middle drawer. It was a Levi brand with a navy cowboy motif. She handed it to Kathryn.

"I think it's long enough to tie in a bow."

Kathryn brushed her hair back and made short work of it. She studied the teen. Whoever her mother was had to have been a beautiful woman. "You look lovely."

"Thanks."

"Now if you'll indulge me while I check you, then we can go downstairs for breakfast." A couple of minutes later and it was all over. "Your temperature is normal, Allie."

"That's what I was afraid of," she mumbled.

"You don't really mean that," Kathryn said, trying to be cheerful. "Although you still have some head congestion, your lungs are clear. Just take it easy for another day or two to get back your strength. Take your pills now, then we'll go."

"Okay."

Once that was accomplished, they left the bedroom and walked toward the staircase. Colt was coming up the steps two at a time, dressed in a plaid flannel shirt in reds and blues. He wore Levi's and cowboy boots.

By accident, his eyes lifted to Kathryn's, forcing her to swallow the cry in her throat. Beneath his inky-black hair and brows, those orbs had taken on the color of crystal green shards.

"Good morning, Ms. McFarland."

Kathryn found him the most attractive man she'd ever met in her life. "Good morning," she answered back, thankful she could speak.

Until she'd flown in yesterday, her brother-in-law Jake Halsey had been the only living male to merit that distinction. Considine lurked in her dreams. Who knew the day would come when a forbidding Montana cowboy who jealously guarded his mountain isolation would topple them both in an instant.

He switched his attention to Allie. "Hi, honey. Noreen has breakfast on the table. I was just coming up to get you. I guess I don't have to ask how you're feeling."

"Her temperature is normal," Kathryn volunteered when Allie only muttered something indistinct.

"That's the best news yet." He reached for her and carried her the rest of the way.

"Dad, put me down. I'm not a baby." But she said it with a giggle.

"Don't you know you'll always be my baby girl?" he teased before setting her on her feet with another hug.

When Kathryn imagined him hugging her like that, a shiver of delight raced through her body. She followed father and daughter through to the other side of their home, not having seen the vaulted living and dining room before. The same refined rustic decor and tall windows ran through the entire house.

So much daylight opened up the rooms to nature. The sight of new fallen snow from the night before was glorious. She almost blurted that this had to be one of the most beautiful spots on Earth, but she caught herself in time.

While Colt helped her and Allie to the table laden with scones and bacon, Matt came running in wearing a polo and jeans. He flashed Kathryn a smile before taking a seat next to their father. "I was hoping you guys would be up."

"After we eat, I want to see your video, Matt."

"Which one is that?" Allie wanted to know.

"My football banquet DVD."

Kathryn turned to her. "Have you seen it?"

Allie rolled her eyes. "About a dozen times."

"Then it must be good."

"Except we lost in the playoffs," he said.

"That doesn't matter, Matt. To think your team made it that far is terrific. Not every guy has the ability or the opportunity to even go out for football. Someday, you'll be able to show it to your children. Think how fun that will be for you and them."

Colt shot her an enigmatic glance. "Do you have a favorite sport besides football?"

Matt must have told his father what she'd confided to him. "Yes. It's skiing."

"We love it, too, don't we, Dad?"

"We do," he answered.

"Are you really going back to Salt Lake today?"

"Yes. At noon."

"Noon!" Both teens moaned aloud.

"Since your sister is on the mend, I'm needed elsewhere."

"But if you stayed until tomorrow, you could go skiing with us this afternoon."

"Matt! You heard Ms. McFarland. I'll be driving her to the airport shortly. There'll be no skiing for us today. We're staying in with Allie, and you have some homework to get busy on before school tomorrow."

"Can I at least go with you to take her to the airport?"

Kathryn heard Colt's hesitation before the answer came. "I don't see why not. Noreen will be here to keep an eye on Allie."

"I don't need her to watch me." His daughter's predictable response settled things for Kathryn.

Not wanting to get in the middle of a talk with his disgruntled children, she got up from the table. "Those scones were fabulous. Excuse me for a minute while I go in the kitchen and thank Noreen. Then I'll watch your video."

Colt wanted to see the back of Kathryn. She was doing her best to oblige him. Only another hour before he drove her to the airport and out of their lives.

Chapter Five

The snow had been heavier on the mountain, but last night's storm hadn't developed into anything ferocious. By the time Colt turned his car onto the highway, the plows had already been out to clear it for the rest of the drive into Bozeman. The clouds had opened up, allowing the sun to shine through.

Under normal circumstances, it was his favorite kind of winter day, but today had a different feel about it. An intangible gloom had descended over his household and none of his efforts could shake it. He'd left Allie seated in front of the fire to work on the puzzle with Ed. Between her red-rimmed eyes and his broken arm, they made quite a pair.

When Matt had brought Ms. McFarland's suitcase down to the Xterra, she'd moved ahead of him and had climbed in the backseat. His son got in front with him. So far Colt hadn't looked in the rearview mirror. He didn't want to meet a pair of blue eyes and be electrified by them again. It had happened with every chance glance since yesterday.

Matt turned his head toward her. "Katy? Are you going to the Utah-BYU football game on Saturday?"

"It's possible, especially because they'll be playing at the U, which is five minutes away from me. But I might have to work."

"Rich and I are going skiing, so I'm going to record it and then watch it after. Maybe I'll see you on TV."

She chuckled. "I'll probably end up having to tape it, too. I'm hoping we win. Last year we lost in overtime and it about killed everybody."

Colt listened while they talked about the flaws and virtues of both teams' quarterbacks. Once they passed the airport security check, he obtained permission to drive on through to the area where the white Cessna was parked on the tarmac.

"There's my ride. Have to run so I don't hold them up." She opened the back door and got out so fast with her suitcase, neither he nor Matt had time to assist her.

She eyed them without really looking at them, then smiled. "It's been a pleasure meeting Allie's family. Thank you for your hospitality. I won't forget." She extended her gloved hand, which they both shook. "Tell her to stay well, now."

Colt nodded, finally allowing himself to take in the sight of her shapely figure clad in the white parka. "I hope you know how indebted I am to you."

"I *do* know."

Yes, she did. The found Kathryn McFarland knew it better than most anyone else in the world.

"If I get sick, will you come and nurse me?"

Gentle laughter escaped her throat. "You've got a whole wonderful family to help you, Matt. Just take care you don't break a leg skiing on Saturday or you'll let your wrestling coach down."

He grinned. "You don't have to worry about me."

Still clutching her suitcase, she turned and started toward the open door of the plane. Colt watched her disappear inside. Disturbed by the odd sensation that swept through him, he wheeled around and strode back to his car. The second Matt got in, Colt started the motor and they took off.

On the way out of the airport he saw the Cessna gaining altitude. As it changed to a speck before vanishing from sight, he could suddenly put words to what was going on inside him.

Hell, hell and hell...

"Dad? Are you okay?"

Trust Matt's radar to detect the slightest irregularity. "Of course. Why do you ask?"

He hunched his shoulders. "I don't know. You've been acting kind of weird since Katy brought Allie home."

Colt drew in his breath. "That's because your sister has a lot of explaining to do. Now that Katy's gone, I'm going to get to the bottom of Allie's disappearing act."

Katy had taken his daughter's secret with her. Though he admired her integrity, he wished he hadn't been such a bad parent, that Allie didn't feel comfortable approaching him rather than turning to a stranger. Colt accepted total responsibility for this impasse. By a strange twist of circumstance, Ms. McFarland's unexpected intervention during Allie's crisis had underlined his need to deal with this problem head-on before the day was out.

"Are you mad?"

He made a gruff sound in his throat. What a question! Yes, he was mad, but not for the reasons his son was no doubt entertaining. "Let's just say she gave us both a scare I never want to live through again."

"Me, neither. What she did was *crazy.*"

"Not to her." Not to her.

"Katy was totally cool."

High praise, coming from his son. "I agree." To say anything more would encourage him. He didn't want to talk about her.

Colt turned at the entrance to the ranch where his tire tracks were still noticeable in the snow. They began the climb to the house.

"As soon as we get back, is it okay if I take Blackie on a short run? I want to see how his leg is doing now."

"Go ahead." Nothing like a ride to put life back into perspective.

Colt walked into the house expecting to find Allie in the living room, but Noreen told him she was in her bedroom on the phone. If he didn't miss his guess, she'd called Jen. "She's pretty broken up about Katy leaving."

Tell me something else I don't know, Noreen. "As long as I'm free for the moment, I might as well tackle the disposal." Anything to get his mind off the woman he'd thought of as Kathryn from the moment he'd read her full name on the brochure. He knew he hadn't liked the shortened version. It didn't suit her.

"Then I'll leave you to it. If you need me, I'll be at the other house."

"Thanks for all you do, Noreen."

Half an hour later, he'd finished the job and was

washing his hands when his cell phone rang. It was the bus depot telling him Allie's backpack had just been brought in on the bus from Salt Lake. He thanked them and let them know he'd be by for it later.

In case Allie was thirsty for something besides water, he grabbed a couple of colas out of the fridge and headed up to her room. He knocked on the door. "It's your dad."

"Come in," she answered in a flat voice.

He opened the door and found her sprawled on her stomach across the top of her bed with her shoes off and the phone in hand. She peered up at him with a crestfallen expression. "Is Katy gone?"

"Yes. By now she's been back in Salt Lake for a while." He moved a chair over to the side of the bed and sat down. "I brought you a drink."

"Thanks." She sat up cross-legged and took it from him. They both opened the tabs and drank. Colt liked the way Kathryn had done her hair with the neck scarf. "I apologized to Jen and her parents," she volunteered.

"That's good." After finishing off half the can, he put it on the floor. When he looked up, her eyes were swimming in tears.

"I'm sorry for what I did, Dad. I mean…about everything."

"Honey." He took her can from her and put it on the floor next to his. "I've the gut feeling this has to do with your mother, so before this talk goes any further, I want you to know I take full blame for what happened. This *is* about your mother, right?"

She nodded before burying her face in her hands.

"Dad?" Matt's voice sounded from the hallway.

"In your sister's room!" he called back. "Come on in."

Matt stood in the doorway staring at the two of them. "What's going on?"

"As I just told Allie, it's my fault she went to Salt Lake without telling anyone. It's time the three of us had the conversation I should have had with you years ago. Pull up the other chair."

He saw his twins exchange a private glance before Matt did his bidding.

"I've already told you my parents froze to death during a blizzard when I was four and your aunt Sherry was six. They didn't marry until their mid-thirties, so we came along late in their lives.

"What's interesting is that my grandfather didn't meet my grandmother until they were in their thirties. My father was their only child and he wasn't born until my grandmother was forty. I'm telling you all this because I was the dark horse in the Brenner family. I got married at twenty and had you two right off the bat." They both laughed.

"My grandparents loved you like you were their own children. They helped me raise you. I wish you could remember them, but you were too little when they passed away within a year of each other. I can tell you this much." Emotion almost closed his throat. "They were saints."

He eyed them with an ache in his heart because he was about to break his silence. When they heard the unvarnished truth, it would shatter them. His grandmother had warned him to tell them everything when they were old enough to understand, but for fear of hurting his children, he'd waited years too long. Now all three of them were going to be in a new kind of pain.

ON SATURDAY MORNING, Kathryn finished checking on one of the children at Renaissance House who needed to see a dentist, then went downstairs to make the appointment. When that was done, she let herself into her brother's office. While she waited for him to get off the phone, she wandered over to the windows overlooking the snow-dusted east gardens of the estate. The grounds became a fairyland of flowers in every season but winter.

It was cold out there this morning. Beneath an overcast sky, everything looked dead. Her thoughts flew to the Cloud Bottom Ranch, as she liked to think of it. Winter clothed the pines in a grandeur of pristine white.

Colt, astride his stallion, would be up on the mountain checking the herds. She could see the lone, tall cowboy in silhouette. He would be dressed in sheepskin and a cowboy hat covering midnight-black hair while he looked over his empire, making sure everything was in working order. His hard-boned feat—

"Yoo-hoo! Kathryn?" When she realized her brother was talking to her, she turned around, flush-faced. "Where were you?" he teased with a smile.

"I was wondering if it's going to snow before the football game this afternoon."

His blue eyes searched hers. "I don't think that was the only thing on your mind. You've been different since you got back from Montana. Everyone at Thanksgiving dinner noticed it."

She averted her gaze. "It's because that little girl hasn't been found yet."

"That and something else." Cord was psychic. "Whenever you want to talk about it, I'm your man."

"You think I don't know that?"

"Just checking. Are you going to the game with all of us?"

"That depends on what's happening at the foundation." She walked over to his closet for her parka and put it on. "I'm heading there now. If more volunteers are needed to continue the search, I'll be manning the phone."

"I'll save a seat for you in case you come late."

"Thanks."

"Do you know you work too hard? All the signs are there."

She leaned over the desk to peck his cheek without saying anything before leaving the mansion through the south entrance. The plaza was only a block down the street. Except for a few frozen spots, she accomplished her short jaunt on mostly dry pavement.

A group of people surrounded the "Blessed are the Children" sculpture that stood in the courtyard. She hurried past them to enter the doors and immediately heard the recording, "Welcome to the Kathryn McFarland Foundation. Take the time to come in and learn how to help us fight crime so the next kidnapping won't be your child."

Walking past the lobby screens showing the dates and times of the latest kidnap victims, Kathryn headed for the front desk. She could see several of the staff huddled together.

"What's going on?"

One of the new volunteer recruits named Melanie turned to her. "I was just going to phone you. We heard from a team of rescuers. They came across a little girl's unclothed remains up Millcreek Canyon."

A moan broke from Kathryn. It could be Whitney, but no one would know until the forensic expert got busy. Whatever the answer, someone's dear little child had been murdered.

"I'm going to my condo and calling home. My parents need to know what we've learned." They would want to be there for Whitney's family and wait for the news with them. "I'll be back."

"But I thought this was your day off."

"I don't always take one." Kathryn would rather be here. She was too restless. Work kept her from thinking. "See you in a while."

She walked out to the lobby and headed for the bank of elevators servicing the plaza tower. She took the private lift used exclusively for the penthouse. Only Kathryn and her family knew the code.

As soon as she walked into the living room, she removed her parka and sat down on the couch to phone her parents. As she knew they would, once she'd given them the update, they called off their plans to attend the game. No one could enjoy it right now.

After she hung up, she set the HD/DVR to record it. She'd left the condo without eating breakfast and knew she needed nourishment, but the news about a little girl's remains having been discovered hit her like a body slam. Her appetite was nonexistent.

Those poor parents.

Every time there was a watch-and-wait period, she thought about her own parents' agony of thirty years ago and got sick inside. Kathryn had assumed that after running the foundation since her graduation, she wouldn't react like this, but if anything her response to each new tragedy seemed to be affecting her more adversely than ever.

Her parents were so strong! Kathryn wasn't anything like them and would never be able to measure up. That distressed her so terribly she couldn't stand her own company. She freshened up, eager to get back to work. Working kept the demons at bay.

On her way through the living room for her purse, her cell rang, causing her stomach to clench. Kathryn didn't think it possible the child's body could be identified this quickly, but a comparison of dental records might have already been done.

She pulled out her phone and glanced at the caller ID. "Hi, Melanie. Has there been official word yet?"

"No." In a hushed voice she said, "I'm calling because this gorgeous—and I mean *gorgeous as in the extreme*—guy came over to the desk asking for you. I told him to stroll around and look at the exhibits while I tried to reach you."

Only one male on Earth fit that description, but he didn't venture outside his mountain kingdom unless it was a dire emergency.

Since Melanie was a twenty-year-old college student working for them part-time and a natural flirt, Kathryn could forgive her for the over-the-top exaggeration. "What's his name?"

"He said to tell you he was from the Circle B, but if you weren't available, he'd be back later."

Kathryn clutched the phone against her chest, hardly able to breathe. When she could find the words she said, "Tell him to wait for me. I'll be right down." She clicked off before Melanie could ask questions Kathryn had no intention of answering.

Right now her curiosity was on the verge of exploding, but she didn't have time to ponder his reason for being here. The fact that he knew where to come looking for her meant he'd talked in-depth with his daughter. All Kathryn could do was fly to the bedroom and change out of the work clothes she'd worn to Renaissance House.

Colt had only seen her in pants, so she donned a three-piece Pendleton wool suit in rich plum and slipped on her black dolly-pointed kidskin pumps. She put gold studs in her ears, then ran a brush through her hair. It had a natural wave and hung loose from a side part. A light spray of Fleurs d'Elle mist and she was ready. For *what* exactly she didn't know.

Maybe he'd brought the twins with him. Her pulse raced all the way to the plaza foyer. At the moment the only thing that mattered to her was that he'd either flown or driven to Salt Lake and had sought her out.

Slow down, Kathryn. Walk, don't run to him.

Reflecting back to her mid-teens, she'd always been the one to run from men who wanted a relationship with her. Yet a relationship was the last thing Colton Brenner had on his mind. He hadn't come here to pursue her. Far from it.

Your fantasizing days are over. Remember?

By the time she entered her workplace, she'd come to

her senses and could handle the sight of him standing at the counter, being chatted up by her staff. In his Stetson and black bomber jacket, every eye in the room, male or female, was riveted on him.

Gorgeous in the extreme, Melanie had said because there were no words, in any language, that came close to truly defining him.

She knew the moment he saw her. His head reared back like a Thoroughbred stallion's. He stepped away from the counter and started his long-legged stride toward her. As she saw him in the flesh once more, an unbidden thrill of excitement went through her.

"Hello, Colt." She rejoiced that her voice sounded so steady.

"Kathryn," he murmured. Not Katy. That meant he'd read her full name in the brochure and had chosen to use it.

Taking the initiative, she extended her hand. It got lost in his strong one.

"I hoped we might meet again one day, but didn't expect it to be this soon." She searched the green gaze focused on her. "Is Allie all right? Matt?"

"That depends on your definition of all right." His deep voice rumbled through her before he let go. "If you're talking about her physical condition, she's quite well thanks to you. So far, Matt hasn't come down with the flu." His eyes unexpectedly glinted in amusement, making him irresistible.

Her mouth went dry. "Did you come to Salt Lake alone?"

He nodded. "I flew in a little while ago and took a

taxi here hoping to catch you before you left for the football game with your family."

"I—I'm not going," she stammered.

"Why not?"

"I'll show you." She walked over to the screen with Whitney's picture. "This little girl has been missing for a week. Early this morning, a body was found up one of the canyons. My parents have gone to be with the girl's family while they await word from the police."

She tried to swallow, but the lump in her throat made it close to impossible. "This is a very hard time for everyone associated with the foundation."

"I think it must be hardest on you."

The compassion in his eyes drove her to avert her head. He'd managed to zero in on the troubling thoughts she'd been entertaining earlier. "How long are you planning to be here, Colt?"

"As long as it takes to talk to you, but obviously this isn't a good time."

To leave his children, she had to assume he wanted something specific from her.

"While we're in waiting mode, this is probably the best time. Have you eaten yet?"

"I had breakfast with the kids before I left."

"That was several hours ago. Come to my condo and I'll feed you while you tell me what's on your mind. It's just across the lobby in the tower. If I'm needed, one of the girls at the desk will phone me."

He studied her for a moment. "I don't believe you have a selfish bone in your body."

"That's because you don't know me."

They dodged a crowd of people shopping for Christ-

mas and took the elevator to the penthouse. During the
short ride, the warmth from his powerful body seeped
into hers. She could smell the scent of the soap he'd used
in the shower. Her awareness of him was so potent, it
unnerved her.

When the door opened and she stepped into the foyer,
she breathed more easily. "If you'll give me your coat,
I'll hang it in the closet."

Colt shrugged out of his jacket, then removed his hat
and put it on the hall table.

She walked him through the elegant living room with
its more traditional décor. "I'm sure you'd like to freshen
up. Go down that hall. The guest bathroom is the first
door on your left. When you want to find me, I'll be in
the kitchen. It's beyond the dining room you can see
from here."

"Thank you. I'll try not to get lost," he said in a wry
tone.

Kathryn had cooked for Steve several times, but
early on she'd realized her feelings for him tended to
be sisterly. She'd never known the kind of excitement
Colt engendered simply by being in the same room with
him.

After washing her hands, she got busy frying bacon
for the club sandwiches. He'd probably like soup and
a salad, too. When he walked in and lounged against
the wall looking fantastic in a white polo and jeans,
she almost cut her finger while she was slicing the
tomatoes.

"What can I do to help?"

She finished tossing the salad. "If you'll take the

plates into the dining room, I'll bring the coffee." Kathryn discovered she had an appetite after all.

"The view's incredible from up here," he said once they'd sat down at the table to eat. "Quite a change from Skwars Farm, Wisconsin." On that note, he devoured three quarters of his sandwich in one go while she ate her soup.

"Allie must have an excellent memory to recall that detail."

He eyed her over the rim of his coffee cup. "After being mesmerized by your extraordinary story, she wasn't bound to forget such an unusual name. The food's delicious, by the way."

"Thank you."

"I remember when you were found."

Reminding her of that day changed the tone of their conversation. "Even up on your mountain?"

Colt finished off the last of his sandwich. "News like that has long legs."

"I remember that day, too," she teased in order not to break down. There were two kinds of *found*. Whitney's unknown fate haunted her.

"It was a stunning development, the kind no one could believe. I'll be honest and tell you that since Allie showed me the brochure, I've been incredulous she would have ended up being the recipient of Kathryn McFarland's exceptional kindness. What are the odds of that happening?"

"Probably as great as the odds of your lovely daughter getting on a bus to come to Salt Lake one dark winter night without your knowledge."

His gaze sobered as it wandered over her features.

"What prompted you to take the time out from your heavy workload to accompany Allie all the way to Montana? If you performed that kind of service for everyone who needed help, there'd be nothing left of you."

Once again, Colt had asked a question that hit at the core of her growing distress. "I could say that your daughter is an exceptional girl and a real charmer. Both descriptions are true. But now that you've prompted me to think about it, I have to admit I was driven by an underlying anger."

He stopped munching on his salad. "Anger?"

Without realizing it, she'd crushed the paper napkin in her fist. "I have a lot of it inside me, Colt. When I first saw Allie lying there and went through her clothes looking for clues, I could see she came from a wonderful home. Everything about her screamed excellent health. She was well cared for."

Kathryn warmed to her subject. "It was obvious she'd been given every advantage in life. Once she spoke to me, she displayed good manners. In fact, she was so different from most of the troubled teens who end up at Renaissance House, I wanted to shake her for causing the most wonderful father in the world in her opinion so much grief. I knew you had to be in hell."

Their eyes met in silent understanding. To her chagrin, her lids began to prickle as emotion swamped her. "At her age I would have given anything on Earth to know my parents and swore that if I were ever united with them, I'd never leave their sight.

"I'd been told that my great-aunt Marie Buric had brought me to Skwars Farm because her grandson and his wife had abandoned me. After she died, her daughter

Olga took care of me until she died. From then on I was passed around the farming families. For years I prayed my parents would come and get me. I had no idea I'd been kidnapped by strangers and my real parents were looking for me. To have a home, an identity—you can't imagine what it's like not to have those things. But getting back to your question, I suppose a part of me felt compelled to see Allie home safely and *make* her realize how blessed she was to belong to you."

Colt's hand covered her fist clutching the napkin. "Thank God for you, Kathryn." His heartfelt touch filled her with warmth.

"Thank my remarkable parents." She put her other hand on top of his for a moment and squeezed gently before easing both away. "Their money started the foundation. They gave me this beautiful penthouse, paid my tuition so I could become a nurse. Without the patient advocacy program they set up, I would never have been called in on Allie's case. I'll never be able to repay them for giving me my life." Her voice shook as she spoke.

He sat forward, studying her with eyes so alive and green that she couldn't tear her own gaze away. "Don't you know that being united with their beautiful daughter was all the payment they could ever want? You're not a parent, but I am. Last Friday night when I couldn't find Allie, I had a brief taste of their terror. I never want to go through that again."

"No," she whispered.

"Your honesty has given me deeper insight into my daughter's soul. The powerful emotions that drove you all those years are driving my daughter. Though Matt's not vocal about it, both children need answers about the mother who abandoned them. What worries me is that without them, Allie's going to be stunted in ways I don't want to think about."

Kathryn stared at him. "You can't provide the answers?"

"After I got home from taking you to the airport, I sat down with the twins and told them as much truth as I felt they could handle. It's something I should have done years ago. My grandmother warned me that if I didn't explain things as soon as they could understand, there'd be repercussions."

A shadow darkened his eyes. "Considering Allie's behavior, my grandmother was a prophetess. Too late after the fact, the children now know their mother hated the ranch, hated being under my grandparents' thumb and hated me most of all for taking her away from the money and glitter of big-city life. Unfortunately that explanation isn't enough for Allie. She still wants to find her mother."

"Is that an impossibility?"

"Maybe. Maybe not. The twins were in the hospital a month. She never went in to hold or feed them. When I finally brought them home, she took off for long periods. After they'd been home a week, she went out one day and never returned. I knew she'd planned to leave me, so I can't say I was surprised."

Kathryn groaned. "Allie told me that prior to your marriage Natalie had been raised by her aunt and uncle in Salt Lake. Would she have gone there?"

Colt's eyes turned to flint. "No. During one of our fights, she admitted that her aunt and uncle were a tale of fiction. There was no Beehive Motel, but by that time

I'd figured as much because she never wanted to travel to Salt Lake to see them. It all came out that she'd lived in one foster home after another until she got a job in Las Vegas, where we met."

"Oh, Colt…"

"That's what you get for marrying a woman after only knowing her two weeks."

Two weeks? A stab of pain went through her. Colt had to have been besotted.

"Perhaps now you can understand why early on I maintained the story that she'd grown up in Salt Lake. I couldn't bring myself to tell the children their father's immaturity and poor lack of judgment had doomed them to a motherless existence. When you phoned me, I was horrified to think Allie had gone there on a wild-goose chase."

"It's only natural you wanted to protect them."

"Don't try to make it better, Kathryn, because you can't. I take full responsibility for being too drunk on the rodeo life to pay attention to what was really important until it was too late. The thing that alarms me now is that even though the twins know most of the truth, Allie's still wondering if Natalie might have been the object of foul play. In her mind, that would explain why she never came home that day."

"That's because she's heard *my* story," Kathryn lamented. On top of having been married to an irresponsible child, Colt was in real trouble because he had a daughter who was a big dreamer like Kathryn. Until presented with incontrovertible truth about her mother's character, Allie would cling to the possibility that something terrible had happened to her.

"You're right," Colt muttered. "My daughter would rather believe her mother's alive somewhere, unable to return home to her children rather than accept the alternative. In truth, Natalie tried several times to go in for an abortion, but I caught her in time."

Kathryn froze. "Do the children know about that?"

"No. I hope they never have to know. The fact is, I told Natalie I'd do anything for her if she would carry the babies to term. We made a bargain. I gave her all the savings I had and told her she could leave me after they were born, no questions asked." Colt stopped pacing. "She left with the money all right and made sure she stayed lost."

The revelations kept coming. "Was it a big sum?"

"No, but you don't have to worry about Natalie. She was resourceful. It took a while before I realized she'd stolen the world championship gold buckle I'd won at the NFR in Las Vegas. It was worth at least fifteen thousand dollars at the time. If she found the right buyer, she could have sold it for a great deal more money."

Kathryn got up from the table. "I'll pour us some more hot coffee." She needed a minute alone to absorb what he'd just told her. When she returned to the dining room, she put his cup and saucer in front of him. "I didn't give you cream or sugar, but maybe I should have asked the first time."

"As you figured out last week, I like it black."

"Having been raised on a farm, I learned to drink it with a lot of both. It's a habit I can't seem to break."

"We all need one or two of life's little pleasures to keep us going."

"I'm a chocolaholic, too," she confessed.

One corner of his compelling mouth lifted. "Aren't we all?" After he took a big swallow of the steaming liquid, he set the cup down. "How did your sister trace you to Wisconsin?"

His question told her exactly why he'd flown to Salt Lake. It didn't come as a shock, but she suffered the pang of disappointment to realize that where she was concerned, there was nothing personal about this visit.

She cleared her throat. "Maggie had the help of an undercover CIA agent named Jake Halsey who eventually became her husband. She'd gone to a genealogical firm hoping someone could research the name Buric. It was the only lead my family had to go on. Jake started working on it and cracked the case."

"Is he still with the CIA?"

"He has all the connections, but now that they're married and have a little boy, he works as a genealogist and gives the bureau help on certain difficult cases."

Her guest studied her for a moment. "I'd like to hire your brother-in-law to find Natalie. I'll pay any fee he charges."

"If he can do it, you couldn't find a better man for the job." She checked her watch. "I'm pretty sure he's already left for the game. Tell you what. If you're going to fly back today, I'll talk to him this evening and ask him to call you. Would that be all right?"

"I couldn't ask for more."

Gone in an instant was the hope that he'd be staying overnight in Salt Lake. Her spirits sank to another level.

He finished his coffee. "I know your coworkers are

waiting downstairs for you, so I'll leave and let you get back to your vigil. For what it's worth, I'm torn up over the little girl's kidnapping. At least if it's her body they found, the parents will be able to have a proper burial for her and try to cope with their loss."

She saw a glint of pain in his eyes before he added, "Unlike your family, who must have suffered hundreds of little deaths each time a body was found that might have been yours and then wasn't. Because of my own joy hearing from you that Allie was all right, I have some appreciation for your parents' joy when you were found."

Colt understood a lot.

"That was one incredible day." Kathryn put on a bright smile, pretending that his plan to fly back to Montana hadn't affected her. "Let me call for the limo to take you to the airport, then I'll go down in the elevator with you."

Chapter Six

Colt stomped the snow off his boots and entered the ranch house with Allie's backpack. He'd picked it up at the depot on his way home from the airport. Once he'd hung it on a peg, he removed his jacket and hat, before starting down the back hall. "Hello! I'm home!" he called out. "Doesn't anyone care?"

Noreen came in the great room. "I do, but I'm afraid Matt's still with Rich. The Carlisles are bringing Allie home from ice skating."

"It's looks like I got away with flying to Salt Lake undetected." He had no secrets from Noreen and Ed. After all these years, they were part of the family.

She flashed him a conspiratorial smile. "So far so good. I think they've been just as busy making plans for your birthday on Monday. Were you able to meet with Katy?"

Yes, he'd spent time with Kathryn McFarland, and it had gone by in such a flash he might have dreamed it. The last thing he'd wanted to do was leave her condo. If she hadn't been so consumed by her pain over the missing child, he would have planned to stay in Salt Lake overnight and ask her to dinner in order to be with her longer.

But it was just as well things had turned out the way they did. To spend more time with her would be a painful lesson in futility. They lived in different states, led different lives. She belonged to an extraordinary family and would never leave them or abandon her mission.

How to explain that to Matt and Allie who had a crush on her and could be hurt if he didn't squelch their burgeoning feelings for a woman who was already bigger than life to them?

That was why he'd flown to Salt Lake without telling them. If Jake Halsey could help him find Natalie, then progress would have been made without bringing Kathryn into the picture any more than was absolutely necessary.

"I not only met her, she fixed me an amazing lunch on no notice at all. Her penthouse overlooks the Great Salt Lake Valley in every direction. It's pretty spectacular."

"The McFarlands live spectacular lives."

Too spectacular. "Amen to that. I found out her brother-in-law traced her to Wisconsin and broke the case. He's former CIA. Hopefully he'll be able to track Natalie down. Kathryn's going to call me tonight and let me know one way or the other. If he can't do it, then I've got to find someone who can."

"That's got me worried, Colt. There's an old saying about being careful for what you wish for. You might get it."

Lines marred his features. "You try telling that to Allie."

"Oh, no. That's your department."

Meeting their mother face-to-face, if they could locate her, might be so traumatic for Allie and Matt that they'd never recover. But he'd made a promise to them and had to follow through. He heard the sound of footsteps coming down the back hall. "Dad?"

"I'm in here, Matt!"

He came rushing in. "Have you started watching the Utah game yet?"

"Not without you."

Noreen flashed him another smile. "Do you want your spaghetti in here?"

"We'll take care of it. You and Ed do what you want."

"I think we'll run into town and see that *Twilight* film Allie keeps talking about."

"You'll like it," Matt assured her.

Within a few minutes they'd planted themselves in front of the TV and started to watch the recorded game while they ate. By the end of the third quarter it looked like Utah would win if their defense stayed focused. Matt got totally into it, but Colt couldn't concentrate and went back to the kitchen with the empty plates to pour himself a cup of coffee.

While Matt whooped it up because Utah had just scored another touchdown, Colt's cell phone rang. He'd been waiting for the call, needing to hear Kathryn's voice.

It turned out to be her area code, but a different number.

"Hello?"

"Mr. Brenner? This is Jake Halsey."

"I appreciate your phoning me, Mr. Halsey."

"The name's Jake. Kathryn told me about the frightening incident with your daughter. I'm glad she's back home safe with you."

"Your sister-in-law had everything to do with a quick resolution and reunion. I'm indebted to her."

"I'm married to a McFarland. They're the most remarkable people I've ever known. To be honest, I'm still in awe of my wife, Maggie."

Jake had just described Colt's sentiments about Kathryn. Colt liked him for his frank speaking and gripped the phone tighter. "I'm assuming Kathryn explained I'd like to hire you to track down the children's mother, but only if you have the time and inclination."

"I'd do anything for Kathryn."

Jake Halsey appeared to be a remarkable man, too. "Thank you for your willingness to help. The last thing Natalie would want is to be found, but Allie's need to know more about her is so great, she went to Salt Lake without telling me. It's anyone's guess what happens if or when Natalie is located, but my daughter's in crisis."

"I agree," Jake murmured. "Tell you what. Since you're anxious to get going on this, Kathryn and I will make arrangements to take Monday off. Maggie will fly us to Bozeman and we'll brainstorm with you, but only if it's convenient."

As Colt's eyes closed tightly, he could hear Allie coming down the hall. His pulse shouldn't be racing at the thought of Kathryn coming with Jake. "It's an ideal time. Your wife's a pilot?"

"She's a brilliant attorney, too, and has access to resources we'll need." The sisters were superwomen.

"Between the four of us, we'll come up with a game plan."

"Only after we settle on a fee first."

"I wouldn't take your money. Maggie and I want to help."

"What about your son?"

"My stepmother will tend him while we're gone."

When you dealt with the McFarland family, every impediment was removed. "You have no idea how grateful I am. What time do you think you'll fly in? I'll meet your plane."

"Eight-thirty? It'll give us the better part of the day to strategize before we have to head back."

"Perfect." The kids would already have left for school.

"We'll see you on Monday then. If it looks like bad weather will delay our flight, Kathryn will keep you informed. I'm going to ask her to stay on in Bozeman for a few days to do some legwork for me. She has uncanny instincts. Any clue she picks up could be crucial to the case."

He ground his teeth unconsciously. The twins would be ecstatic. As for himself... "I look forward to meeting you, Jake."

"The feeling's mutual, Mr. Brenner."

"Call me Colt. See you Monday morning."

He hung up. Judging by all the noisy excitement coming from his kids in the other room, the Utes had won the game. But it couldn't compare to the conflicted emotions building inside Colt. To see her another time was only asking for trouble, the kind he couldn't afford.

Hell. He already felt like he did the time he'd picked the wrong bull at the Calgary Stampede. The legendary Genghis Kahn had taken him for the ride of his life. The rush had been beyond exhilarating until he found himself hurtling through space. When he woke up in the hospital, he realized a worse concussion would have cost him his life. It had taught him an important lesson.

Some rides you knew in advance to stay away from— like a ride with Kathryn McFarland—because you knew it couldn't last. Another world champion gold buckle was more attainable.

IT WASN'T UNTIL Sunday morning after Kathryn had gotten off the phone with Jake that she remembered Monday was Colt's birthday. She knew his children had to be planning something special for him. Kathryn didn't want to arrive at the ranch empty-handed, yet the wrong gift from her could send out the wrong signal to the elusive rancher.

Since the birth of the twins, he'd been guarding his space jealously against foolish, starry-eyed females. There had to have been an endless line of them over the years, but none had managed to break through the walls of defense he'd set up around his heart.

Maybe she could find something on the internet to do with the rodeo that would suggest a gift idea he wouldn't reject the moment she was out of sight. Ever since he'd told her about the children's mother stealing his gold buckle, she hadn't been able to get it off her mind.

After a half hour of searching, she found a sports memorabilia shop at one of the hotels in Las Vegas. They were auctioning off an officially authenticated, framed poster celebrating thirty-five years of world champion bull riding from the executive's private collection.

Represented were the sketches of four champions in their cowboy hats with their signatures to the side. To her delight she saw a younger Colt's likeness among the grouping, complete with his bold handwriting. It sent her heartbeat skittering off the charts. Beneath the four sketches was an enlarged picture of the gold buckle prize.

This twenty-four-by-thirty-two-inch poster was an absolute treasure.

Rather than go through the online bidding, she made several phone calls until she reached customer service and asked to speak to the manager. After offering him a price he couldn't refuse, he told her the framed poster was hers. She made the transaction with her credit card and told him she'd be in later to claim it.

After she'd clicked off, she called the airport and chartered a plane to Las Vegas. A few hours later, she flew in and picked up her precious purchase. The artist hadn't only caught Colt's chiseled profile, he'd captured his commanding presence and aura of focused energy requisite of a true champion.

While there, she made more enquiries about what other memorabilia she might find on Colt. The manager directed her to a poster shop along the Strip where she found four priceless posters of Colt, all the same picture.

Except for his chaps, he wore black from his Stetson to his boots. He'd been caught in motion on a bull during a championship ride. *Poetry in motion,* in her opinion. It was a spectacular photo.

Kathryn bought all four. One for each twin, one for Noreen and Ed, and one for herself. She would hang it on the library wall next to the bookcase that housed her Louis L'Amour collection.

Almost sick to her stomach with excitement, she flew back to Salt Lake with her secret stash, then drove over to her parents' home to have dinner. While they ate she told them her plans for the next few days. They ended up talking about Whitney's family, who were still waiting to hear something definitive from the police.

Kathryn left their house for the condo feeling guilty that so much pain for the little girl's parents didn't squelch the longing inside her to see Colt again.

After she entered the kitchen, she called Maggie to make final arrangements. Her sister indicated it would be clear weather for flying. They'd be by for her in their car at quarter to six in the morning. "There's no point in telling you to get a good sleep tonight because I know you won't," Maggie teased.

Since Kathryn knew she wouldn't, either, she didn't bother to argue with her sister. Once they said good-night, she pulled a poster from the tube and unfurled it against the fridge door. She used the French bread magnets one of her nieces had given her last Christmas to keep the corners in place.

Just looking at him sent a thrill through her body.

With her eyes glued on him, she phoned Donna so they could set up the schedule of volunteers at the foundation while Kathryn was away. Once that was accomplished, she called her psychiatrist and cancelled Monday's appointment. She would have to phone later to set another date.

While she was at it, she arranged for a rental car to be waiting for them at the Bozeman airport so Colt wouldn't see the presents she was bringing. Finally, she punched in his cell phone number, but this time she had to rein in her emotions to keep them from jumping all over the place.

Don't let him know what the mere thought of him does to you, Kathryn.

Swallowing her disappointment because he didn't pick up, she left a message on his voice mail. "Hi, Colt. I hope all is well with you. I just checked with Maggie. She said it will be good flying weather. One more thing. Jake asked me to let you know he's already arranged a rental car for us, so we should be at the ranch between eighty-thirty and—"

"Kathryn? Don't hang up!" Colt's deep, live voice arced through her, quickening her body.

"You sound out of breath." Would that he was in that condition because of her, but she knew it wasn't the case.

"I was riding in on Lightning when my phone rang, but when I pulled it out of my pocket, it slipped from my hands and fell down a snowy embankment. I had to hunt for it."

The image his words conjured made her smile. He'd made fast work to recover it before she'd clicked off. Colt wasn't a champion bull rider for nothing. "I'm glad it wasn't lost. You might have had to wait until next spring."

He made a low sound in his throat. "My last phone drowned when Matt's lemonade spilled into the cubbyhole of my dashboard."

"Uh-oh." It was her turn to chuckle. "Last summer I was leaning over a castle wall and mine fell into a moat. It's lying somewhere on the bottom, rusting out with all the swords."

A definite laugh rumbled out of him. "Neither of us seems to have had much luck."

Kathryn was having too much fun. *End it now.* "In case yours should short out, I'll make this fast. Maggie said it's good flying weather so we'll be there at eight-thirty, but just to let you know, Jake has arranged for a rental car. He likes to be independent." *Like you.*

"I can relate."

Yup. "We should be to the ranch by nine at the latest."

"Kathryn?"

"Yes?" she answered too breathlessly and could have kicked herself.

"I don't know how to thank you."

"Since Maggie and Jake literally found me, I tell them that all the time. It's a habit I can't break."

"I'm talking about you and what you did for Allie— what you and your family are prepared to do now to help find her mother."

If ever a person was thankful, it was this man, but Kathryn feared she'd never wring anything but gratitude from him.

"This is what we like to do, so enough said. Good night. See you in the morning."

"WHAT'S THIS?" Colt walked in the dining room and discovered Matt already seated at the table. That was a first on a school morning. There were only three places set. "Where are Noreen and Ed?"

"Since she's fixing a special birthday dinner for you tonight, we gave them the morning off to sleep in. I set the table and Allie's fixing your breakfast. We're going to do presents tonight."

On cue his daughter came through the door carrying two plates. "French toast and sausage coming up!" After she put his food in front of him, she gave him a kiss on the cheek. "Happy thirty-sixth, Dad."

A frown marred his features. "Did you have to remind me?" Then Colt grabbed her and gave her a bear hug. She laughed before coming through a second time, bringing her own plate and a mug of coffee for him. They settled down to eat.

Matt's brown eyes studied him. "You look nice, Dad."

"Meaning I usually don't?" he teased.

"Stop fishing for compliments," Allie scolded him. "You've got on a new shirt."

"It's the one your aunt Sherry gave me last Christmas."

"You look like a dude."

"Thanks, Matt. If I'd known I'd get a reaction like this, I'd have worn it before now."

"Black's your best color," his daughter informed him.

"Is that so?" He ate the last piece of toast.

"It makes your eyes look greener. They're really green this morning, like you're excited or something."

Nothing got past Allie. He downed the rest of his coffee. "That's because it's my birthday."

Matt scowled. "You've always said you wished we'd skip yours."

"Did I say that?"

"Yes!" they both answered in unison, exchanging a private glance Colt couldn't help but notice.

"Well, I take it all back. I've loved my surprise breakfast. It was delicious. Thank you both."

"You're welcome," Allie muttered, still staring at him with a puzzled expression.

His son nodded. "There'll be more surprises tonight."

Colt averted his eyes. His children didn't know the half of it. "Much as I hate to break this up, it's time to get you two down to the bus."

"I have to do the dishes first," Matt announced. He jumped up and started clearing the table.

"You stay put, Dad," Allie cautioned before helping her brother.

Together they made short work of it. In a few minutes they joined him in the truck. Colt headed down to the ranch entrance, relieved Kathryn wouldn't be arriving in a snowstorm.

After he pulled to a stop, he got out to give them both an extra hug. "Thanks for breakfast. Love you guys."

"Love you, too. Don't forget. We're coming straight home after school."

Allie nodded. "And don't go out on the range today because we're having your birthday dinner early!"

There was no fear of that. For once something else would be consuming Colt's time right here at home. "I can't wait."

He watched them get on the bus. Since he'd promised

the twins he'd look into finding someone who could try to locate Natalie, he was confident his daughter wouldn't be pulling another disappearance act.

After waving to the bus driver, he checked his watch. Seven-forty-five. Kathryn would be in the air by now. Colt started back. By the time he and Ed had nailed down today's work schedule for the hands, his guests would be arriving. Until then, the idea was to stay busy.

That wasn't a problem in the physical sense. At any given moment, there were tasks needing to be done on the ranch. It was his thoughts that made him restless, the same restlessness he used to get before trying out a new bull shipped up from Mexico.

No matter how prepared he was, some of its moves weren't what he'd anticipated. Kathryn had already knocked the wind out of him several times. The trick was to go the full eight seconds and avoid it administering him the *coup de grâce*.

"WHAT BEAUTIFUL country!" Maggie exclaimed from the front seat of the rental car. Jake had just turned onto the curving road leading up to the ranch. "Look at these walls of pines. They're breathtaking!"

Maggie echoed Kathryn's thoughts, but the feeling of homecoming was so intense she gripped the armrest tighter, unable to say a word.

Jake looked over his shoulder at her. "Are you all right, Kathryn? You're so quiet."

"I'm just remembering the first time I came here. The clouds hung heavy and hid the trees farther up the mountain. With the sun out this morning, you can see everything."

They eventually reached the vale where the ranch became visible. "Incredible," Jake murmured.

"It looks like a Christmas card," Maggie cried softly.

With all of the above, Kathryn concurred. Only this was one card you could drive into and find the ruler of this isolated kingdom at home. Her heart thudded too hard to be natural or healthy.

"Jake? Pull up around the side of the ranch house next to Colt's truck. We'll go in the back door. And one more thing. Leave the trunk popped. I'll take my suitcase in now. Later, when he's not looking, I'll come out to get the presents I brought."

He grinned. "Your wish is my command."

Kathryn let out a guilty sigh. "I'm sorry. I didn't mean to sound bossy."

"Not bossy. Nervous," Maggie said, sending her a secret smile.

Nervous didn't begin to cover what Kathryn was feeling. Every now and then she thought about her life back in Wisconsin and shuddered to think that if Maggie and Jake hadn't found her, she would never have met Colton Brenner. She scrambled out the backseat of the car and hurried to retrieve her bag from the trunk.

It was a good thing she'd moved fast because Colt had come out of the house, a tall dark figure in a black shirt and jeans bearing down on them with those powerful legs. Just in time she'd lowered the trunk lid so it looked closed, but wasn't.

"Welcome to the Circle B." He shook Jake's and

Maggie's hands before wresting Kathryn's suitcase from her. Their eyes met. The green of his irises matched the color of the pines.

"Hello, Colt," Somehow she'd managed to keep her voice from shaking. At the first sight of him, it was always an event that rearranged the atoms in her body. "It's nice to be back." Heavens, he looked so wonderful, she was in danger of falling straight into him.

"The children won't believe it when they get home from school and find you here."

"They didn't know we were coming?"

He smiled, making him irresistible. "If I'd told them, there would have been a war to get them to go to school and I would have lost."

She laughed. "I'm looking forward to seeing them, too."

"Let's get you inside so you can freshen up." Colt led them through the back entrance, where they removed their parkas. He turned to Jake. "If you want to use the guest bathroom down here, the women are welcome to go up to Kathryn's room."

He carried her suitcase upstairs and put it inside the guest-room door. His gaze locked with Kathryn's. "When you come down, Jake and I will be in the family room."

"We'll be there in a minute."

As soon as he left and shut the door, Maggie's brows lifted. "*Kathryn's* room? Sounds like you're already part of the family."

"Don't be ridiculous!"

"I'm only stating the obvious," she said before closing the bathroom door.

Taking advantage of the time, Kathryn zipped over to Allie's room and used her bathroom before rejoining her sister. "You've got the wrong idea about Colt," she said without preamble. "He's not interested in me personally. The complicated man has led an *un*complicated life for years and that's not going to change."

Maggie put her hands on Kathryn's shoulders. "Listen to me, little sister. It already has changed or he wouldn't have come to Salt Lake to see you. He has money. He could hire an army of people to look for his ex-wife. Why didn't he?"

"Because Allie asked *me* for help. And because a miracle happened to our family and she believes I'll be able to perform one for hers. I can tell you right now that after what Allie pulled, Colt's vulnerability over his children is so great, he'd do anything for them."

"That goes without saying, but why are you fighting me on this?"

"I'm not!"

"Yes, you are. What aren't you telling me?"

For once Maggie had made her cross. "He's grateful to me."

"Of course he is."

"But that's all!"

Maggie let go of her. "You're afraid of something. Tell me what it is."

She lowered her head. "I don't know exactly."

"I think you do."

"All right, then." She lifted her chin. "If you must know, I don't want to be like Steve."

Her sister blinked. "What do you mean?"

"He hung around you for years hoping for any crumbs

you would throw his way. But you never noticed him or any man until Jake came along and rocked your world." She swallowed hard. "I'm not like Steve. I'd rather die first," she whispered.

"Your situation is entirely different from mine. As for Colt Brenner, he's thrown you more than a crumb," her sister insisted.

"Wrong. Let me ask you a question. Who suggested I stay on a few days to do some of Jake's legwork here? Colt or Jake?"

"Jake."

"Don't you see? He didn't leave Colt a choice."

"I have a feeling he's secretly pleased the way things are turning out."

"No. He's been single sixteen years for a reason."

Maggie's expression sobered. "If you really believe that, then check into a motel in Bozeman after you drop us off at the airport and get busy running down evidence for Jake. You know I'll do my part. Once the objective has been accomplished and Colt doesn't need your services any longer, walk away from him and see what happens."

Nothing will happen. But no one gave sounder advice than Maggie. *Get the job done you've been asked you to do, then get out!*

On a gush of love for her sister, Kathryn hugged her hard. "You're brilliant! I'm ready to go downstairs and dig in."

"Good." With their arms around each other, they left the bedroom.

Kathryn knew the way to the family room, but the second she entered it, her heart rate went into hyperdrive at the sight of the two attractive males talking in deep concentration in front of the fire.

She felt a fresh stab of pain because she could sense Colt was anxious to catch up to his ex-wife. Natalie Brenner had to have been unforgettable for him to have married her within two weeks of meeting her and then go all these years without marrying again.

Chapter Seven

At noon, Jake closed the notebook he'd brought to keep a record. His steel-blue gaze shot to Colt's. "We've accomplished as much as we can for the moment."

Colt glanced at his watch. Two and a half hours of discussing strategies with these remarkable people had flown by. Once during their session around the dining-room table, Kathryn had excused herself for a few minutes. Except for Noreen who'd supplied food and coffee, they'd worked undisturbed.

"To tell you how grateful I am for your time and help wouldn't begin to cover how I feel."

Maggie smiled. Both women were so gorgeous, Colt could only marvel. "We'll all hope it doesn't take as long as it did to find my baby sister."

Kathryn got up from the table. "Twenty-six years will put Allie and Matt at forty-one." She'd done the math. "We can do better, right? I'll drop you at the airport so I can have a car." She looked at her family without including Colt.

If it was intentional, he didn't like it. "My Xterra's at your disposal while you're here, Kathryn."

She glanced at him. "I appreciate that, but I understand Noreen uses it to shop and pick up the kids from the school bus. Your routine shouldn't be interrupted because of me. I'll be scouting around talking to people on my own timetable."

"That's settled, then," Jake broke in. "I understand Noreen is over at her house. Please tell her how much we enjoyed the food."

"I'll be happy to."

"Shall we go, darling?" Jake rose to his feet to help his wife.

Colt followed the three of them through the house to the back entrance, where Kathryn put on her parka too fast for him to be of use. He decided it was a habit she'd developed over all the years she'd been forced to look out for herself.

"You live in paradise and have an absolutely beautiful home!" Maggie exclaimed on the way to the car. "This valley opens up like a stairway to heaven."

"Kathryn thinks it should be called the Cloud Bottom Ranch."

Laughter rippled out of Maggie. "That sounds like something my imaginative sister would say."

He stole a covert glance at Kathryn, whose cheeks looked flushed, before she climbed in the backseat behind Maggie. Jake shook his hand one more time before getting in the driver's seat.

Colt moved closer and tapped on Kathryn's window so she'd open it. He stared down into eyes as blue as Montana's big sky country. "The kids will be home by three-thirty. It'll make their day to find you here."

"I'll be back in time."

Not by a flicker of an eyelash or an inflection in her

voice could he detect what was going on inside her. To his irritation, she closed the window, putting a barrier between them when he wasn't ready for it. But as he turned away, he noticed the rapid throbbing of the pulse at her throat. It couldn't be the altitude doing all that to her.

He waved off his guests before heading back inside the house, but once at his desk in the den he couldn't concentrate on the accounts. After an hour, he gave up.

Damn if it wasn't happening to him…

That deep ache only the right woman could arouse, with her alluring scent and mysterious smile. How could he not crave the accidental brush of her hip against his or her sudden slight intake of breath in an unguarded moment?

Colt couldn't begin to count the ways the voluptuous shape of her mouth entranced him—or the way the unexpected compassion in those blue depths for someone else's stolen child could move him to tears.

When the phone rang, he clicked on without checking the caller ID and almost said her name. "Hello?"

"How does it feel to be another year older?"

"Sherry?"

She laughed. "Who else? You sound odd."

"I'm afraid my mind was on something else." *Someone else.*

"I thought I'd better get in a phone call before you start celebrating. Did our presents reach you in time?"

"They came two days ago, but after the great Thanksgiving you gave us, you shouldn't have sent anything."

"Colt! You're impossible!"

"Sorry. I didn't mean to sound ungrateful."

"I know," she murmured. "I wish we could be there to celebrate with you, but Bob couldn't get away. This is his busy time doing audits."

"But you'll be coming to our place for Christmas, right?" Except that he couldn't think that far ahead. He was still working on the countdown until Kathryn returned from town.

"You couldn't keep us away. Now tell me what's being planned for your birthday?"

"I'm not sure. The kids have been cooking up something with Noreen." *As for* my *surprise…*

"Then it's bound to be special because they love you to death. So do I."

"The feeling's mutual, Sherry. Thanks for making my day. I'll phone you tomorrow and give you the details."

"You'd better!"

After they rang off, he realized he couldn't stay in the house any longer without climbing walls knowing Kathryn wasn't far away. Why not surprise the kids and be there waiting for them when school was out? Pushing himself away from his desk, he strode through the house for his hat and jacket.

Once in the car, he phoned Noreen and told her to be on the watch for Kathryn. He was going to pick up the twins.

THE SILVER SPUR MOTEL on the outskirts of Bozeman provided exactly what Kathryn wanted. After seeing Maggie and Jake off at the airport, she registered at the front desk before driving around to Number Ten. The tiny room, with its log cabin walls, felt warm and she could park in front of it. No fuss, no bother.

While she'd been with her family and Colt earlier, she'd excused herself long enough to put her suitcase back in the trunk and bring in the presents for him. Once his birthday party was over, she'd tell the twins she had business in town and leave.

He'd hired Jake to track down Natalie. Though Kathryn would be helping her brother-in-law, she refused to use it as an excuse to stay at the ranch house. Colt didn't want her there, so the less interaction she had with his children the better. This was the best plan.

Before she drove back to the ranch, she took off her navy two-piece wool suit and changed into jeans and a café au lait long-sleeved blouse with a cream-colored crocheted vest. She'd already styled her hair in a French braid that morning and decided to leave the gold studs in her ears.

In deference to her cowboy mood, Kathryn pulled on the brown leather boots she always wore riding with her family. She liked the idea of being taller. It would put her at less of a disadvantage around Colt.

A fresh coat of coral frost lipstick, a little peach-scented lotion and she was ready to go.

With every mile that brought her closer to the ranch, she could feel more heat radiating from her body. By the time she'd parked the rental car at the side of the house, she was a trembling mass of emotions. The fact that the Xterra was missing only heightened her sense of anticipation.

Noreen greeted her at the back door. "I saw you

coming. Colt's gone for the twins. Come in and make yourself comfortable."

Kathryn followed her through the house to the dining room. "Something smells delicious."

"Matt asked me to make barbecued spareribs. It's one of Colt's favorite meals."

"It's one of mine, too. How can I help you?"

"Everything's ready except the decorations. Allie had visions of blue and white streamers hanging crisscross fashion above the table. Ed was going to do it, but he's been delayed. I brought in the ladder."

"I'm taller. Put me to work."

"That would be wonderful."

Kathryn eyed things critically. "Let's fasten them from the chandelier to the window frames. I'll twist them first."

Before long they'd transformed the room. She climbed back down. "There!"

Noreen beamed. "It's perfect."

"I think so, too. Where does the ladder go?"

"On a couple of hooks in the storeroom behind the kitchen. If you're going to do that, I'll run back to the other house and get changed."

"Go ahead."

Grabbing the leftover streamers and tape, Kathryn carried everything through the kitchen to a doorway at the other end. She turned on the light and found an empty space for the crepe paper on one of the shelves. There were hooks on the opposite wall. As she started for them, she heard Colt's voice coming from the kitchen. "Noreen?"

"She's at her house!"

The next thing Kathryn knew, he'd moved behind her and put the ladder in place. Her mouth went dry because she was trapped between his arms with her back against his chest. The strong pounding of his heart had already reset the rhythm of hers. Heat enveloped her body.

"Colt, you can let me go now."

"I could, but I don't want to," he whispered against the side of her neck. His hands slid around her waist, bringing her closer so there was no air between them. "It isn't often I find such a tempting morsel in my store-room. Surely you wouldn't deny me this simple pleasure on my birthday."

She sucked in her breath. "The twins will see us."

His warm breath at her nape sent sensation after ex-quisite sensation through her nervous system. "They dashed upstairs to do the last of their clandestine plotting."

"D-do they know I'm here?" she stammered helplessly.

"They saw the car, but assumed it was someone on ranch business waiting for me. Allie begged me to get rid of them fast."

"You should take her advice."

"Not until I've been given my birthday kiss."

"That wouldn't be a good idea." Her voice shook.

"I disagree." He turned her around so fast her head swam. While she was still reeling, he cupped her hot cheeks with his hands and lowered his mouth to hers.

Kathryn had wanted this for so long she melted against him, but his tender kiss was over before he'd allowed her to kiss him back. She moaned as he relinquished her lips. "That's for being an angel to my little girl. I'll never forget."

Gratitude. Colt had just bestowed the kiss of death.

They both heard excited voices that were growing louder. His hands slowly fell away from her face. "I guess it's time to reveal the mystery guest."

Struggling to recover from the pain, Kathryn rushed into the kitchen at the same time the twins made an appearance.

"Katy!" She saw them staring at her and Colt as if they couldn't believe their eyes.

"Your father hired my brother-in-law to track down your mother. Jake asked me to do some research for him in Bozeman, so I'm here for a day or two."

"Yes!" Allie squealed.

Realizing they needed more of an explanation, she said, "Since Ed was late, I volunteered to string up the decorations."

"I helped Kathryn put the ladder away," their father added in a wry tone.

At that remark, she might have blushed if Colt had kissed her with passion, but he wasn't capable of that emotion, at least not with her. The only way to handle this was to be a friend to him and his children.

"Thank goodness your dad arrived in time to prevent it from falling on my head!"

Matt let out a bark of laughter. Allie said, "The dining room looks awesome."

Kathryn smiled. "I can't take any credit. Noreen said the streamers were your idea."

"But you made everything beautiful. Will you come upstairs with me for a minute?"

"Sure. Excuse us," she called out to Colt without looking at him.

"Don't be long, ladies. It's my birthday and I'm ready to party."

Allie laughed. "I thought you were upset at being a year older! Come on, Katy."

Together they hurried through the house and up the stairs to Allie's bedroom. Kathryn eyed Colt's flushed-faced daughter. "You look fully recovered from your flu."

"I feel great!"

"That makes me very happy."

Her brown eyes glowed. "Your being here for Dad's party is perfect!"

"Jake took the day off from his work so my sister could fly us here this morning for a talk with your father. When I realized we would be arriving on his birthday, I brought a present that I thought you and Matt could give him along with your other gifts. It's guaranteed to be a hit. I'll get it."

Allie picked up a shopping bag full of presents and followed her to the guest bedroom.

"Here. Take this one in your other hand." Kathryn handed her the framed, gift-wrapped poster. "I'll bring my other presents." After putting the rolled-up posters beneath her arms, she said, "Let's go before your father gets too impatient."

They started down the stairs. "He's going to have a cow when he sees all this!"

Kathryn tried to keep a straight face. "Is that good or bad?"

"Definitely good," Colt answered for his daughter.

There was nothing wrong with his hearing. He stood in the foyer with Matt. His eyes locked with Kathryn's. She couldn't read what was behind that enigmatic gaze. If he feared she was hoping for a repeat performance of what had happened in the storeroom, he didn't need to worry. His grateful tribute had cured her.

Matt rocked on his cowboy boots. "Noreen's got everything ready."

They proceeded to the dining room. It was growing darker out. The addition of a lovely cloth, candlelight and a decorated chocolate cake forming the centerpiece provided the magical touches to the birthday feast. Kathryn read, "Happy 36, Dad."

"Here. Let me." Ed, the older, dark blond rancher now free of his cast, helped Allie spread her packages around the pile already visible on the hunt board. Both he and Colt gave Allie a curious stare as he lifted the framed poster and rested it against the wall.

While Matt helped Kathryn to the table, Colt helped his daughter. Noreen brought the ribs from the kitchen. Ed said grace and they were ready to eat.

For the next half hour, conversation centered around the twins and their latest activities. Kathryn mostly listened, only now and then asking a question. Throughout the delicious meal she avoided looking at Colt.

Once they'd sung "Happy Birthday" and had eaten cake, Matt and Allie took turns giving their dad a present to open. Every gift appeared to be a winner: a robe, sweats, cologne, socks, a Western shirt, leather gloves, ski gloves, new ski goggles, a couple of T-shirts…everything for the well-dressed rancher.

Kathryn finally dared to smile at Colt. "That's quite

a haul. I think it's time somebody else around here got a present." Five pairs of eyes blinked in surprise. "Matt? Will you hand one of those cylinders to Noreen and Ed? Then give one to Allie and take one for yourself."

While everyone started unwrapping their gifts, Colt stared at Kathryn with a bemused expression on his rugged face.

The responses were everything she could have hoped for. Cries of "Dad! Colt!" resounded as they unraveled the posters of the beloved man seated at the head of the table. "Oh, my gosh! You look so young!"

Allie ran over to Kathryn. "Where did you get this?" she cried out with tears in her eyes. "I *love* it! I can't wait to show all my friends! They're going to die!"

"You're so awesome, Dad!" Matt's voice croaked. "Rich has got to see this!" He stood in the corner of the room examining it.

Noreen and Ed's eyes grew misty as they handed their poster of the legendary rodeo champion to Colt for him to see. Ed handed him a pen. "I want your autograph. This could be worth a fortune someday."

Kathryn understood everyone's joy because she felt it herself, but it was time to make her exit. Otherwise she might never be able to pry herself away.

"Happy birthday, Colt." She got up from the table. "Thanks to all of you for letting me be part of this celebration. Noreen? The food was out of this world, but now I'm afraid I have to leave."

Allie looked stricken. "Where are you going?"

"Back to my motel in Bozeman."

"Motel?" the twins moaned together.

"Yes. While you people have a whole night of

celebrating ahead of you, I need to accomplish a day's worth of foundation work plus some business for Jake before tomorrow morning."

"But you *can't* go yet!"

"Kathryn said she had to leave," Colt reminded his daughter in a voice of understated authority. "She flew here from Salt Lake to help us find your mother, remember? Let's let her get on with her jobs. Matt? Would you bring down her suitcase, please?"

"Sure."

"Don't bother to go up, Matt. I left it at the motel." Avoiding Colt's piercing gaze, she looked at Allie. "I think there's one more gift your father hasn't opened yet. Right?"

"Yes," the girl whispered.

"Then have fun. I'll see myself out."

Kathryn hurried through the house to the back room, where she grabbed her purse and parka. Within a minute, she'd reached the car and was headed for town.

Colt didn't want her getting any more attached to his children and was glad she'd done the right thing by leaving. That was why he hadn't tried to stop her. Any goodbye had been said in the storeroom behind the kitchen.

Her pain went too deep for tears. Frozen-faced, she drove straight to her motel needing to talk to Maggie.

Maybe her sister had radar because the second she closed the door to the room, her cell phone rang. She pulled it from her purse and checked the caller ID. It was Donna.

Her stomach knotted because her assistant wouldn't call this late at night unless she had important news.

"Hello?"

"Kathryn?"

Just the way Donna said her name, she knew what she was about to say. "That body was Whitney's, wasn't it?"

"Yes."

Hot tears spurted from her eyes. "I have to get off the phone now and call my parents. Thank you for letting me know."

"Of course."

But the second Kathryn hung up, she threw herself across the bed and sobbed because a miracle hadn't happened for that little girl's family. She sobbed for all the helpless kidnapped children who this very night were being molested or killed somewhere in the world. Not even everything the McFarland Foundation could do had prevented this crime against Whitney.

Beyond heartsick, she lay there for a long time in such a deep sorrow, she didn't realize her phone was ringing. Finally stirring, she sat up and looked at the caller ID. It was her sister. She clicked on.

"Maggie?"

"I've been on the phone with the folks. Did you hear about Whitney?"

"Yes. I just got off the phone with Donna."

Neither of them spoke for a minute. There were no platitudes they could say to comfort each other. Another tragedy had befallen another child. Yet next to her grief lay her guilt for thinking of Colt right now and how incomprehensible it would have been if Allie had been lost to him forever.

"How was the birthday party?" her sister ventured. "You know what I mean."

"The surprise was everything I could have hoped for. Allie and Matt loved the posters, but I left before Colt opened the framed one."

"Why did you do that?"

"Because I got an answer earlier tonight."

"Translation please."

Knowing Maggie wouldn't let it go, Kathryn launched into an explanation of what had happened in the storeroom. "I was ready to explode like a volcano, but his brief, chaste thank-you kiss cooled everything down. He might as well have been the Pope giving me a benediction for my goodness."

Instead of her sister coming right back with the assurance that Kathryn had misread the situation, she said something entirely different. "You were right about him being a complicated man."

Maggie's quiet response set off an alarm bell. There was a message behind her words, otherwise she would have waited until Kathryn had returned to Salt Lake to talk about the little girl who'd been murdered. Kathryn gripped her phone tighter. "What do you know that I don't?"

"While you and I were upstairs at his ranch house this morning, Colt confided something to Jake. Maybe you already know what it is and have chosen not to tell me."

"Tell you what?" Her voice shook.

"He never divorced his wife."

"SEE, DAD? This looks perfect in here! Everyone who comes in will notice it before anything else!"

With Colt's children helping Ed and Noreen, a little rearranging had gone on and now the framed poster with protective glass hung on one of the walls in the family room. They'd wanted to put it in his den, but he'd ruled it out. Colt used that room to conduct business with the public and disliked the idea of his awards being on display. At least the family room was a little more private.

After Natalie had taken off years earlier, any of the stuff from his rodeo days he'd thrown in a box in the storage shed behind the old house. It was now covered with other boxes. Neither the twins nor the Walters had any idea of its existence. That was the way he'd wanted it. But he couldn't get away with doing the same thing to Kathryn's gift. His children wouldn't hear of it.

She'd transformed his birthday party into something else. The posters dredged up memories he'd suppressed for so long, he'd almost forgotten what those sweet days were like when he was single and hungry for a bull-riding title that would help make his fortune.

No one but Kathryn McFarland could have located that framed poster, let alone managed to get the collector to part with it. No doubt she'd been robbed of her money and had enriched the man's coffers by several thousand dollars, but money in and of itself meant nothing to her.

She'd go to any lengths without counting the cost in order to bring happiness to someone else. Except for disappearing to a motel this evening, she'd made Colt's twins ecstatic.

Though she was a flesh-and-blood woman whose mouth he could still taste on his lips, he didn't doubt he'd kissed an angel earlier. As anyone knew, angels went about doing good, especially this angel whose joy at being found after her long captivity might have turned her into another kind of captive. One who couldn't do enough for others. *One you might never be able to pin down, Brenner.*

That was Colt's new agony.

When he'd heard the children coming into the kitchen before dinner, it had almost killed him to let go of Kathryn, but what choice did he have when he was so on fire for her that he still trembled at the thought of holding her again?

"Dad? I thought you wanted to play Boggle."

His son's voice jerked him back to the present. "I do."

"Then let's get started."

Colt joined his children at the card table in front of the fire. A half hour later Allie said, "I win again! We need to play this on your birthday more often."

"Yeah," Matt chimed in. "You haven't won once. Usually you beat us by at least fifteen extra words."

"That's because you guys gave me such a great party I can't concentrate. Now it's time for bed." The twins protested, but he reminded them they had school in the morning.

Allie lingered on the stairs, holding her poster. "Do you think Katy will come over tomorrow?" It was the first time her name had been mentioned in the past hour.

He shook his head. "My guess is she'll do her work and fly back to Salt Lake. She's on a busy schedule trying to help you, honey."

Her downfallen expression didn't escape him. "I know. Well, good night."

Colt hugged her. "Thanks for a wonderful birthday."

Matt came loping into the foyer with his poster. "Hey, Dad. I just got off the phone with Rich. Would you be willing to train us how to ride a bull?"

Somehow Colt had known that question was coming. Kathryn had opened up the proverbial Pandora's box. "Why don't we talk about it tomorrow?"

His son grinned. "I'm holding you to it. 'Night." They high-fived each other before he bounded up the stairs after Allie.

The second he saw his son's boots disappear, Colt wheeled around and left the house, grabbing his hat and jacket on the way. Once in the truck, he phoned Noreen, letting her know he had an errand to run and would be back on the ranch in a couple of hours. There'd be no sleep for him until he'd dropped in on Kathryn and thanked her for her gifts in person.

At the third motel he spotted her rental car in front of Number Ten. Though the curtains were drawn, he could tell her light was on. He levered himself from the cab. A few steps to the door and he rapped on it. If he'd phoned her first, she would have put him off. This way she had to do it in person.

"Kathryn? It's Colt."

She didn't keep him waiting long, but when she opened the door fully dressed, she was on the phone and motioned for him to come in. Though he couldn't see tears, he knew she'd been crying and had a gut notion why. As he closed the door, he heard her say good-night to her mother before hanging up.

"Was it Whitney's body?" he whispered.

Her beautiful face crumpled in pain. She had no words. All he could do was pull her into his arms and try to comfort her, but he'd never felt so helpless in his life.

"Oh, Colt! This world can be so terrible, yet so wonderful, too."

He kissed the side of her temple. "It was wonderful tonight. I opened my last present and discovered that something I'd treasured and thought lost forever had been returned."

"I'm glad it made you happy."

"The children have hung it in the family room. That's twice Kathryn McFarland has restored something priceless to me."

She eased out of his arms. With a small smile she said, "I hear good things come in threes. Here's hoping we find your wife before long."

Colt heard her distinctly. She'd said *wife*—not ex, not Natalie, not the children's mother.

"So Jake has already told you."

"After they flew home, he started in on the investigation and mentioned it to Maggie. She didn't know if I knew or not, but it doesn't matter."

"What? That I'm still married?"

"That's your own business."

Chapter Eight

Her phone had started ringing. "Excuse me, Colt. I need to see who this is." She picked up. "Hi, Kit. It's good to hear your voice, but I've got someone with me. I'll call you back in a few minutes."

Kathryn gave him an inscrutable blue stare and the tension between them caused him to bite down hard. "What I have on my mind is going to take some time. If you'd like, I'll wait in the truck until you're through talking to your sister-in-law, even if it means I have to sit out there half the night." He wanted to let her know he meant business.

He was counting on her good manners not to tell him to get the hell out of her motel room *now*.

The fight going on inside her went on for a full minute before she said, "I'll phone Kit and tell her I'll talk to her tomorrow. She's as upset about Whitney as the rest of us."

Colt expelled the air from his lungs. While she called her sister-in-law back, he removed his hat and jacket and sat down on one of the two chairs propped near the table.

He liked it that the motel room was claustrophobic.

Kathryn only had two places to sit—the bed that took up most of the room or the other chair.

She chose the safer course, but it brought her close enough that their boots brushed. Much as he wanted to pull her onto his lap and kiss them both into oblivion, he turned in order to extend his long legs away from her. "I need to explain."

She shook her beautiful blond head. "It's not necessary."

Colt couldn't have felt more gutted if he'd been stomped unconscious by a bull. "It is to *me*," he fired back. "Jake needed to know about my marital status up front, but I preferred not to discuss it in front of you and your sister. Call it cowardice if you want. When he talked to me on the phone the other day, he told me he'd do anything for you, so I should have guessed he would start his investigation the minute he got back to Salt Lake. It's how you McFarlands operate."

Kathryn looked away.

"Whether you believe me or not, I came here tonight to talk to you about it in private. Until now, the time never seemed right."

"You don't have to tell me."

"You deserve the whole truth." He sat forward. "In the beginning, I was too involved in taking care of my premature babies and running the ranch to think about anything else. I figured that one day I'd hear from her through an attorney that she wanted a divorce. That suited me fine. I was in no hurry to rush into another ill-fated marriage."

Her pained eyes searched his. "No one would be."

"When she did make contact, I planned to get my

buckle back. The fact that I never heard from her again proved how much she didn't want to get caught."

"I don't know how you lived through that experience."

"The twins became my whole world."

She smiled. "Naturally. They're wonderful."

"After my grandparents died, I let go of my anger and made up my mind to be the best father I could. The ranch began to prosper and I found joy in my children. There were women, yet attractive as they were, I couldn't picture any of them being the kind of mother my twins needed."

"You'd lost a lot of trust," Kathryn murmured.

He nodded. "One or two of those women wanted to get married. I probably should have had Natalie declared legally dead so that could happen, but the desire wasn't strong enough to go to the trouble." He rubbed the back of his neck. "If Jake can't find her, then I'll go that route."

"Are the twins aware you're still married to their mother?"

Colt studied her through shuttered lids. "No. But if they raise that question, I'll tell them." After a pause, "Will you forgive me?"

She stirred in the chair. "There's nothing to forgive."

"Prove it and we'll go over to the Westerner for a drink and a dance. They have a good live band. It'll top off my birthday."

"That's right. It's your birthday." She glanced at her watch. "For another hour, anyway."

"Come on."

He stood up and reached for her parka in the closet. This time, she had to let him help her. The need to touch her had become paramount to his existence. She handed him his hat and they went out the door into the cold night.

Their arms and hips brushed as he opened the truck door for her, electrifying his body. It was a good thing the Westerner was only two miles away. The desire to have her in his arms was consuming him.

Colt hadn't been inside the bar for several years. The place was swinging. They'd heard the country music out in the parking lot.

"Hey, Colt!" several of his younger hands called out to him. He nodded to them. Every man's eyes had locked on to Kathryn while he ushered her through the crowd. With a packed dance floor, it was slow maneuvering. The wolf whistles and comments kept coming.

He whispered near her ear, "No one's seen anyone like you in here before. Stick close to me." His hands stayed on her shoulders from behind until he'd guided her to a free booth in the corner. He removed their parkas before sitting next to her.

A cheeky waitress came over to take their order. "Coffee for me," Kathryn said.

"Make that two coffees, one with cream and sugar." After the waitress left, the guy at the mike called for a round of line dancing. Colt eyed the gorgeous woman squeezed in the booth next to him. "Let's do it."

He grasped her hand and took her out on the floor to the end of the last row. For the next little while, he had the time of his life going through the motions with the best dancer in the room. Every male in the place envied him. *Eat your hearts out.*

Eventually they returned to the booth to drink their coffee. "Where did you learn to move like that?"

"Cord taught me and Kit. He's a cowboy at heart and would rather line dance than just about anything, but I think you could teach him a few steps."

"I got a lot of practice during my rodeo days. After an event, a bunch of us would head for the nearest bar to unwind."

"When did you start bull riding?"

"At Matt's age."

"Has he tried it yet?"

"My son's been making noises to learn, but after you showered your gifts on us tonight, he and his friend Rich have it all planned that I'm going to teach them the fundamentals starting this coming weekend."

She looked alarmed. "Does that bother you?"

"No. It's a great sport. If he wants to try to get good at it, there's nothing more challenging or exciting except maybe a slow dance with you." Color spilled into her cheeks. "Before this place closes, how about it?"

Dancing gave him a legitimate excuse to cling to her voluptuous body. They fit together as if they'd been made for each other. Way too soon, the band played their last song, bringing an end to the enchantment.

Colt protested inwardly as he helped Kathryn back into the truck. He'd wanted to keep her in his arms all night. Out on that floor he'd forgotten he was still legally married. For a while, nothing mattered but the physical and mental closeness they shared.

"Did you just say something?" he asked as they headed for the motel.

"Yes. I was thinking about your gold buckle. I have a hunch it could be the key to putting us on Natalie's trail. What exact time frame are we talking about from the moment you won the world championship until she left?"

They were back to the investigation. "The twins were premature and born in July. She left in August. Approximately eight and a half months."

"Did you go straight to Montana after you'd won?"

"We stayed in Las Vegas for another two days, then drove to the ranch in my old pickup truck."

"So before you even left Las Vegas, she could have gone behind your back and talked to a contact about selling your gold buckle to some collector for a big price?"

"It's possible. Knowing what I know now, Natalie was capable of anything." He didn't want to talk about her.

"Did you still have it when you reached the ranch?"

How could Kathryn be talking like this after what they'd been doing for the past hour? "It doesn't work that way. I was presented my award, but they sent it back to Montana Silversmiths to have my name hand-lettered in gold on it. I received it by overnight courier a month later."

"Did it come with a special belt?"

"There's no belt. My grandparents kept it in a place of honor on the mantel along with my other awards. My grandmother was the first to notice it was missing.

Natalie must have taken it the day she left the house for good."

By now they'd reached the Silver Spur and she'd already opened the truck door. Colt climbed out to help her down, but he didn't know how he was going to leave her. For sixteen years he'd existed without her. Now she'd started a fire in him that would never go out. Every second with her made it burn hotter.

When she opened the motel-room door, he went inside with her, ostensibly to make sure she was safe. He checked the bathroom and the closet. "I wish you'd come back to the ranch with me tonight. I'd feel better."

"Thank you for caring, but I'll be fine."

He'd been studying her appealing features all night and couldn't get enough of them. "What's your agenda tomorrow?"

"A dozen different things. I plan to get an early start."

"I'll take you to dinner."

"That would be lovely, but I might not be here."

"Why?" he demanded.

"If I've accomplished everything Jake wants, I'll fly home in the afternoon."

"With Maggie?"

She nodded.

His hands balled into fists. "Don't you ever stop to enjoy yourself?"

She flashed him a breezy smile. "I've been doing that all day. Thank you for a wonderful night of dancing. For thirty-six years, you're remarkably good. It must be the bull rider in you. Good night, Colt. I'll be in touch."

KATHRYN ENTERED her psychiatrist's empty reception room at nine and waited until he appeared at the door of his private office, telling her to come in. She sat down opposite his desk. He was a short, balding man who wore steel-rimmed glasses.

"I'm sorry I couldn't come in last week. I've had to go out of town several times on child advocacy business."

He smiled. "These appointments are for you, not me."

"I realize that." She'd been coming to Dr. Morrow's office for over four years. He was a friend who knew her inside and out, but one of these days he would retire. She couldn't imagine not having him in her life. Lately it seemed her problems were getting worse, not better. What would she do without him? The thought sent her into a panic.

"I happened to see you on last night's news."

She nodded. "Our family attended Whitney's funeral yesterday morning. I think half the city must have been there." The intrusion of the TV networks had been too much.

Her doctor sat with his elbows on the desk, tapping his fingertips together. "Why did you go?"

His question stunned her. "You mean our family?"

"No. *You.*"

Kathryn frowned. "Because I run the foundation."

"Besides that. I want you to think very hard. Before our session ends, I'd like an answer." He sat back in the chair. "What are you doing for fun these days?"

"Fun?"

Her brother had asked her the same question the other day.

"You don't have any," he commented. "When you first came to me and described Anna Buric's life in Wisconsin, this is what you said." He opened a folder on his desk. "I'm going to read from my notes.

"Some days were good when Nelly brought me books to read. We had fun cooking in the bakery. Sometimes she would take me driving around the farm. Those were good times. On my days off I climbed trees in the apple orchard with the younger children. I liked reading stories to the littlest ones. It was like I was their mother. I used to pretend they were my children. That was fun."

Kathryn averted her eyes.

"Isn't it interesting that my notes on Kathryn Mc-Farland—once all the joy of reunion had finally died down—don't mention anything about having fun."

"That's not true!" she protested. She'd had so much fun with Colt on his birthday that she'd come close to begging him to stay the night with her.

"I'm afraid it is. Your life is all about work. Why?"

"Because it's what my family does."

"You mean to tell me your brothers and sister don't ever have any fun?"

"No. Of course not. They do all kinds of fun things. They ski and ride horses. They recently went to the Utah football game together."

"Did you go to the last one?"

"No."

"Why not?"

"I had foundation business."

"Let me ask you another question. You were planning

to move out of the McFarland Tower and get your own house. Have you done that yet?"

"No."

"Why?"

"Because there's no place more convenient to my work."

"Have you joined that book club your friend suggested?"

"No. I never have the time."

"What about a pet? We talked about that before, too."

"Much as I'd like one, with my schedule I decided I wouldn't be able to give it the love and attention it deserves."

He took off his glasses and rubbed his eyes. "Have you done any dating since you turned down Steve's proposal?"

"No."

"I see. Have you formulated an answer to my initial question?"

In a rare show of temper she said, "Is this really necessary? You know very well I want to give back what my parents sacrificed for me during all those years I was missing."

"That's a lofty goal, but one that's quite impossible. You're not your parents. It isn't the same situation."

"I know that."

"No, I don't think you do. They carved out a life for themselves. Now it's up to you to live the one destiny intended for you, not the one you assume you have to live in order to make up for all their pain."

There'd been occasions when Dr. Morrow had made

her angry, but never more so than now. She felt the blood heat her cheeks.

"Guilt has a lot to answer for in this world, Kathryn. You feel more guilt than most people because of the new life you don't think you deserve since you were found. That's why it rips you apart whenever another child is kidnapped and killed."

Her eyes stung with salty tears.

"Guilt is driving you to be all things to all people. Unfortunately if you're not careful, it's going to break you."

Colt had said virtually the same thing when she'd accompanied Allie home from Salt Lake.

"You're a healthy, lovely woman who, since your kidnapping, has taken on the senseless obligation of owing your parents your life. I don't believe for a second that's what they want. This crusade to be like them and live up to the model they established through the Kathryn McFarland Foundation has overtaken your life."

She lowered her head. "You make me sound like a freak."

"That's one description for a hopeless workaholic. You spent the first twenty-six years wishing you could find your parents. Once you did, you've spent the past four years trying to make it up to them. It's past time you thought outside the box and did something that has nothing to do with the past thirty years. Otherwise, you'll remain single and burn out early. Is that what you really want?"

"No."

"*No?* That's the first time you've ever admitted it to me. What's happened since our last session?"

She squirmed. "I'd rather not talk about it."

"If not to me, then who?"

"It's not that, Dr. Morrow."

"You've met a man."

Heat crept through her body. "Colt's married with teenage children and owns a cattle ranch in Montana."

"At least he's flesh and blood, not your fantasy outlaw. I do believe you're making progress. Since we've run out of time, we'll talk more about this rancher at our next appointment."

Kathryn left his office tied up in knots and got into her Jeep. While she'd been in her session, Jake had left a message on her voice mail asking her to call him as soon as she could. She phoned him on the way back to her condo.

"Jake? Did you get a break in the case?"

"Let's just say your hunch paid off. When that collector in Bozeman gave you a list of serious collectors of Western memorabilia, one of your phone calls to them produced results. A Jonathon Dix from Omaha, Nebraska, phoned me an hour ago asking for you. He's in possession of Colt's gold buckle he bought four months ago off another collector."

The blood pounded in her ears. "You're kidding!" She could hardly breathe. "How does he know if it's authentic?"

"Colt's name is there in gold letters. If you still want to buy it, the price is thirty thousand dollars."

She couldn't hold back her cry of excitement. "Have you told Colt?"

"No. I'm leaving that up to you. This is our first big lead. A word of advice from a man who married a

McFarland? Let him buy his own prize back so he can feel like a man."

Whoa. Her brother-in-law hadn't minced words. She supposed she deserved that reminder.

"Message received." Once she surprised Colt with the news, she'd let him run the show from here on out. *Talk about fun!*

"Good girl. When you get to Omaha, pick that collector's brains. Depending on how long Natalie kept his award and how many collectors have purchased it since, we might be closer to her than we think."

"I pray we are. Love you, Jake."

"Ditto."

It was Friday noon. Without a moment to lose, she chartered a flight to Bozeman, then flew through the condo to pack a bag. On the way to the airport she would arrange for a rental car. No more asking favors from Maggie. Jake was probably sick and tired of that, too.

By quarter to three that afternoon, she drove up to the side of the ranch house. Though it was partly sunny, fresh snow had fallen during the night. She saw tire tracks but no sign of the truck or Xterra.

Not about to be defeated, she drove on to the barn in the distance where she could make out a couple of hands. She drew up to them. They eyed her with male interest as she stepped into fresh snow. The younger one tipped his hat. "Hi! I remember seeing you with the boss at the Westerner."

She nodded. That was last Monday night, but it seemed like a century ago. "Do you know where I might find Colt?"

"Sure. He's at the far pen with the vet. If you keep following this road, you'll come to it."

"Thank you very much."

She got back in the car and drove on. The knowledge that she'd be seeing him in a few minutes was causing her temperature to spike.

"DON'T LOOK NOW, Colt, but there's this knockout golden filly I'd sell my soul for approaching the pen."

"What are you talking about?"

"Turn around and find out, but don't say I didn't warn you."

Colt moved his boot-clad foot off the bottom rung of the fence and looked over his shoulder. When he saw the same vision, he felt a quickening in his blood real enough to convince him he'd just survived a powerful earth tremor.

As Kathryn walked toward him in her cowboy boots, the sight of her blond hair beneath a chocolate-brown cowboy hat blew him away. Neither he nor Tom, who was very married with four children, could tear their eyes from her hourglass figure outfitted in jeans and a dark brown fitted jacket. The fringe swayed with every movement.

"I probably should have phoned you I was coming, but I wanted to surprise you." She sounded a trifle out of breath.

Tom nudged him hard in the back.

"It's a fact you've done that," Colt said in a husky voice. Her hot blue eyes had a vaguely imploring quality that sucked him in. "Kathryn McFarland, meet Dr. Tom Sutton, my vet."

She extended her hand. "How do you, Dr. Sutton."

"I'm doing better than one of Colt's foals."

"Oh, dear."

He chuckled. "But she'll live." Tom turned to Colt. "Call me if you don't see improvement in a couple of days." After winking at him, he gave Kathryn a smile and walked around the pen to his truck, but Colt only had eyes for the stunning female standing in front of him. The urge to carry her off to his secret place on the mountain was so strong, it alarmed him.

"Please forgive me for interrupting, Colt, but this couldn't wait."

He cocked his head. "Don't you know you can always bother me?" His question caused color to creep into her face. It felt like years instead of days since he'd molded her to him while they were dancing. Colt's need for her was so acute, he'd planned to fly to Salt Lake tomorrow because he couldn't stand to be apart from her any longer. "What's happened?"

"Jake called me with some good news this morning. He hasn't found Natalie yet, but one of the collectors I contacted this week phoned him from Omaha. His last name is Dix. Four months ago, he bought your gold buckle from another dealer. It's there if you want to buy it."

She could have phoned him with that news, but she chose to deliver it in person. Now was the time to find out if he was just dreaming this up. "Then I think we ought to fly to Nebraska tomorrow."

To his shock, she didn't give him a reason why she couldn't. Instead she said, "If we're going that soon, we'd better make flight reservations."

So Maggie wouldn't be doing the honors. Another good shock.

"Did you already check into the Silver Spur?"

"No. I came straight here."

Maybe he really was hallucinating, otherwise why wasn't she fighting him? There was a catch here somewhere. "That's good because I wouldn't let you stay in town again. Tomorrow we'll take the twins with us."

At the same time her eyes lit up with emotion, she bit her lip. "Do they know Natalie took it?"

He shook his head. "I told them someone stole it a long time ago."

"They'll be so excited for you."

"That won't even cover it when they find out you're staying over. Follow me back to the house and we'll surprise them."

It seemed the most natural thing in the world to grasp her hand. They walked through the snow in a kind of companionable silence he'd never known with any woman. Before helping her into the rental car, he gave her fingers a squeeze. "I'm glad you came," he whispered.

She avoided his glance. "This was an important find for you."

Colt lowered his head. "I'm glad you came," he repeated forcefully against her lips and felt her body tremble.

"So am I."

What he heard helped him find the strength to shut her door. They had all night after the twins went to bed. Colt could be patient a little longer. Barely.

On the way back to the house, he watched her through

the rearview mirror. It reminded him of the day she'd brought Allie home from Salt Lake. He couldn't take his eyes off her then, either, but at that point in time he was terrified that if he let his guard down for an instant, he would fall irrevocably in love with her.

They reached the house just as the twins were getting out of the Xterra with Noreen. He had the impression that if his daughter's brown eyes opened any wider, they'd pop.

Matt found his voice first. "Katy!"

Their guest walked over and gave them both a hug, backpacks and all.

Allie eyed her father curiously. "Did you know she was coming, Dad?"

"Nope. She surprised me."

Noreen smiled at Kathryn. "Will you be staying for dinner?"

"She's here for the weekend," Colt announced before Kathryn could. "I think steak fajitas sound good. We'll all help." He walked over to pull her suitcase out of the back of the car. More shock because she let him do it.

"How's the bull riding coming, Matt?" she asked as they all went in the back door of the house.

"Dad drove me and Rich over to the Thorntons' ranch this morning. They have practice bulls and an indoor arena. We watched Billy Thornton for a while. He's a year older than I am."

"Is he good?" she queried as Colt helped her off with her jacket. Beneath it she wore a silky brown blouse tucked in at the waist. She removed her hat and put it on the shelf above the pegs. Every move she made captivated him.

Matt laughed. "He's terrible, isn't he, Dad?"

"We're all terrible at first."

"It probably made him nervous with your famous father looking on." They moved down the hall to the family room. Allie led the way.

"Look, Katy. We hung Dad's poster in here."

"So I see. It's what this room needed." She smiled at Allie. "Now it's complete."

Colt's daughter beamed. "I think so, too."

"No, it's not," Matt piped up in a serious tone. Everyone looked at him in surprise. "His gold buckle should be on the mantel. When I told Billy that Dad's got stolen, he acted all weird like he couldn't believe he'd really won it."

Kathryn darted Colt a heart-stopping smile. "How long are you going to keep your children in suspense?"

He studied her enticing features before his gaze swerved to the twins. "We'll have to prove Billy wrong and fly to Omaha in the morning to pick it up."

Matt stared at him with uncomprehending eyes. "What do you mean?"

"I mean someone found it."

After a long silence, Allie turned to Kathryn. "*You* did it."

"I located a collector who knew another collector."

"Oh, Katy!" Colt watched his daughter throw her arms around Kathryn.

"Would that I could find your mother as easily, darling."

An excited yelp came out of Matt, who was oblivious to the emotional byplay going on around him. "Rich has got to hear this!" He plopped down on the couch and pulled out his cell phone.

While Kathryn continued to work her magic on his children, Colt slipped into his den to make online reservations to Nebraska for four people. When he went back to the family room, he discovered the three of them had gone upstairs with her suitcase. He could hear their heightened chatter, the kind that had been missing in his home without a mother.

Colt had tried to do everything for his twins, but he couldn't give them that. As for being a husband to Natalie, how could he have done that when she'd never had any intention of being a wife?

What would it be like to have both?

AFTER DINNER, Kathryn delighted in the videos of the twins taken at different times and seasons of their lives. Now Colt had sent them to bed.

Since she'd arrived at the ranch earlier in the day, it felt as if she'd been playing house. There was a mommy and a daddy and a boy and a girl. The perfect family except for one flaw. The real mommy was missing, just as Kathryn's real mommy had been missing for the first twenty-six years of her life.

How odd that when Kathryn was a young girl on the farm, she fantasized about the people in her make-believe house—her real parents and siblings. She never once saw herself as the mommy, only the child. Then in her fantasies about Considine, she was simply his woman. Kids didn't enter into the picture in her fantasy.

Her childhood was so abnormal, she didn't play like

a normal child, or plan realistically for the future. She never once thought about dating or getting married. Frankly, to belong to a man after her long captivity was anathema to her.

Until Colt.

But he wasn't free. It wasn't just the legality of it. What Natalie had done to him had left emotional scars. How could he honestly ever trust a woman again? There was no violence in him. The shield he'd erected was much more powerful to keep him safe. Today he'd let his guard down a little, but one wrong move on Kathryn's part and the ice around his heart would never melt.

"I'm going to say good-night, too." She started to get up from the couch, but he pulled her onto his lap.

"Not yet. I need this first."

In a lightning move his mouth closed over hers. The hunger of it caused her to gasp. This was no benediction. He didn't pretend to coax a response from her. His blatant longing was unmistakable. They were crossing a line here where fun had been left behind and the real stuff of life was happening.

To deny him now could cause permanent damage. She didn't *want* to deny him anything, but it meant exposing the heart she'd been guarding for years, too. It gave him power to inflict joy and pain in equal or unequal amounts.

"Colt—" she whispered before she gave up the battle and began kissing him back with a passion she hadn't known herself capable of.

He lay down and pulled her on top of him. Kathryn wasn't prepared for the rapture he created. They drank deeply and fully, producing a moan from her. Every kiss sent exquisite sensations through her body. She forgot time and place as his possessive lips roamed her features relentlessly.

"There are no words." He sounded drugged before his mouth devoured hers with barely disguised ferocity.

She couldn't speak, either. To talk meant to interrupt something she never wanted to stop, not even for a second. Between the pleasure of his hands and mouth, she realized a person could die of ecstasy.

Much later, he murmured, "If we were alone in the house, I'd take you to my room."

If they were alone, she'd go with him, unable to help herself. The reminder that Allie or Matt could make an unexpected appearance did what nothing else could. She tore her lips from his and got to her feet, but she staggered. If Colt hadn't been right there to catch her, she would have fallen over.

"It's late," she cried as he crushed her against him, drawing another kiss from her mouth.

"Don't leave me yet."

"You think I want to?"

He buried his face in her hair. "I'm afraid."

"Of what?"

"That I'll wake up and discover this whole day and night have been a dream."

She chuckled. "When I get up in the morning and have to hide swollen lips and the rash on my face from your children, you'll know this was real."

He lifted his dark head and examined her. Using his index finger, he trailed it over her bottom lip. His eyes kindled with light. "You're right. I've left my brand on you."

"Yup. I'm a marked woman." *Colt's woman.* "See you in the morning."

Chapter Nine

"Here's your buckle. I understand it was stolen."

Colt nodded to the owner before hanging back so his twins could crowd around the counter to look at it. Kathryn stood next to them.

The dealer handed it to Matt. "Feel that?"

"Whoa. It weighs a ton."

"More like a pound." The older man smiled at Colt.

Allie took hold of it. "Is it solid gold?"

"No. The base is sterling silver made by Montana Silversmiths."

"Hey, Dad? Did you hear that?"

"Montana's the best."

The collector pointed out the features. "See these ribbons, letters and cast figures?" Allie nodded. "They're made of 24-carat gold. Did you know it took 110 hours to produce this?"

"You're kidding!" his daughter cried in wonder.

"And thousands of hours of practice for your father to win it," Kathryn pointed out.

"I'll make you a deal. I was hoping to sell it for thirty

thousand dollars, but since it's rightly yours, I'll let you buy it back for twenty thousand dollars."

"I appreciate that, but fair is fair." He pulled out his credit card. "If you don't charge me the full amount, I won't buy it."

"Very well, but I won't add on tax." He swiped the card and Colt signed the slip.

"The buckle's yours, Mr. Brenner. Shall I wrap it up in a box?"

"No!" Allie cried. "Put it on your belt, Dad."

"Yeah," Matt seconded.

Colt turned to Kathryn. "You think?"

Her eyes had gone so fiery a blue, they made his water. "Do it."

He undid the one from his belt and snapped in the gold buckle.

Allie grinned. "You look hot, Dad."

"You're the man!" his son exclaimed.

Kathryn sent him a private smile before she turned to the other man. "Will you give me the name of the collector who sold it to you? That person might have other rodeo memorabilia we'd like to buy."

The buckle was stolen property. Colt understood the man's hesitation, but she had a way of allaying his fears.

"Just a minute." He disappeared in the back room of his store.

While he was gone, Kathryn eyed the twins. "Let's show off your dad and take him to that ice cream parlor we passed. The sign said the Cornhusker superduper sundae is supposed to serve six. I would imagine you can finish off what we can't eat," she teased Matt.

In the midst of the joviality, the owner came out with a card he handed to Kathryn. He smiled at Colt. "I'm glad you have your buckle back."

"So am I. Thank you."

"You really have earned it the hard way," Kathryn said when they left the store. "If I were you, I'd always wear it. With it on your person rather than sitting on the mantel or framed against a wall, someone would have to steal it off you and we know that couldn't possibly happen. Don't we, kids?"

"Yup. Dad would annihilate them."

"Is that so?"

"Yes." Allie put her arm through Colt's.

The idea of Kathryn trying to wrestle it away from him filled his mind all the way to the ice cream store.

When they were halfway through their mammoth dessert, Kathryn's cell phone rang. Since yesterday when she'd surprised him at the pen, he'd been in a different world and resented the slightest interference. They had plans to stay over in Omaha tonight.

Whatever the news, she paled and got up from the chair, turning her back to them. Colt felt shredded. The twins' crestfallen expressions said it all.

He joined her and waited until she'd hung up. "What's wrong?"

Her face was a study in pain. "That was Maggie. She said our father slipped on some ice and fell while he was shoveling. Oh, Colt! It knocked him unconscious and he hasn't come out of it yet. Mother's freaking out!"

News of that kind would shake anyone, but this was Kathryn's father, the man she worshipped.

"She's chartered a plane. It's waiting for me at the

airport. I have to go." She looked at him, but he knew she wasn't seeing him. That terrible foreboding he'd experienced twice in his life crept over him once more. Kathryn had ties she could never give up for him. He sensed in his soul she was slipping away from him. It had been a dream, after all.

"Of course. Let's go, kids."

The twins heard what she said and hurried out the door with them. Colt braced her arm as they ran toward the rental car.

KATHRYN FLEW DOWN the hall of North Avenues Hospital to her father's private room. Fearing the worst, she opened the door to discover all her siblings had assembled, yet she sensed at once there was a festive mood with a lot of talking going on.

Her mother sat on the far side of the bed with a happy expression on her face. Kathryn's anxious gaze shot to her father. He was awake!

"Darling girl! Come over here and let me give you a hug."

"Dad!" she cried for joy and hurried to the side of the bed.

"Kind of reminds me of when you were in the hospital and we all walked in to find our Kathryn lying there with your leg in a cast."

"I'll never forget." When she felt his arms go around her shoulders, she started to sob and couldn't stop.

"It's okay, sweetheart. I just took a little longer to wake up, but the scan says everything's fine."

"Thank heaven. If I'd lost you…"

He looked at her mother. "No one's going to lose me

yet. Maggie said you were in Omaha with Mr. Brenner and his family."

She wiped her eyes. "Yes." She felt Jake's gaze on her. "H-he bought back the gold buckle that was stolen from him," she stammered. "When I left him, he was wearing it."

"I'd like to see one of those up close. When are we going to meet him and his twins?"

The family had done a lot of talking. "He has no reason to come to Salt Lake. Right now Jake's trying to find his wife for him." There was no sense hiding anything when they all probably knew everything anyway. She clutched his hand. "What does the doctor say about you?"

"Provided there are no complications, I'll be able to go home in the morning."

"I'll stay with you tonight."

"There's no need for that, honey," her mother spoke. "They'll bring in a cot for me."

Maggie put an arm around Kathryn. "You're coming home with Jake and me tonight. You haven't been over in ages. Robbie's been missing his aunt."

As long as her father was going to be all right, Kathryn needed to be alone, but she refrained from telling Maggie in front of everyone.

She kissed her father once more. "No matter how good you feel, Dad, you look tired. We'd better leave so you can get the rest you need." The nurse in her had come out.

Kathryn went around the bed to kiss her mother. "I'll come to the house tomorrow to help."

"Thank you, honey. We'll love it."

The room slowly emptied. Maggie waited for her at the door to the staircase. "Walk down with me so we can talk in private and not be bombarded by reporters wanting to know about Dad." Kathryn gladly agreed. "If he'd awakened an hour sooner, I wouldn't have called and ruined your trip."

"I'd still rather be here with him until I know he's out of the woods. As for Colt, I get the impression he doesn't take many weekend trips away from the ranch with his children. They had a lot of plans after I left, so the timing was perfect."

"Not for you."

"Don't read more into this than there is, Maggie. I went to Omaha in the hope of picking up a lead on Natalie. The collector gave me the name and number of the person who sold the buckle to him, so the trip wasn't in vain."

They paused on the next landing. "What do you mean 'in vain'?"

"Maggie…he's *married*."

"For heaven sake's, Kathryn. That's something easily dissolved."

"He told me he could've had her declared legally dead a long time ago, but the desire wasn't strong enough to bother. I think he wants to see her again because he's never been able to let go of her memory."

"That sounds sick. Colt Brenner doesn't strike me as a sick man. I think he meant exactly what he said. It would take an exceptional woman for him to get interested in marriage again enough to do something about his marital status. Whether Natalie is located or not, if that special woman comes along, you can bet he'll make sure he's single a second time."

Kathryn hurried down the next flight of stairs. Her sister was faster and blocked her from further movement.

"Stop looking at me like that, Maggie. *I'm* not that special woman."

"There's something you need to know."

When her sister got that look in her eye, Kathryn felt the hairs lift on the back of her neck. "What?"

"This is classified. Jake would kill me if he knew I told you," she admitted.

"That's the last thing you have to worry about. My brother-in-law's so in love with you it's sickening." She walked around Maggie and started down the last set of stairs to the parking level.

"What if I told you Colt told Jake he was going to start proceedings?"

Kathryn almost tripped on the steps and had to grab hold of the railing.

"I thought that might give you something to think about, considering he could still put it off *until* or *if* she's found," Maggie said in a tone of satisfaction.

When they opened the door to the underground garage, Jake was waiting for them. They walked her to her Jeep and helped her in. "We'll see you at home."

"Actually I'm going to the condo. But thanks for the offer, you two. I have a lot of foundation business to catch up on. If I do it tonight, then I'll have time to spend with Mom and Dad tomorrow. Good night."

On the way home she checked her voice mail. Her heart raced when she saw that Colt had left a message.

I phoned Jake a little while ago. He told me your father gained consciousness with no complications and could be going home as early as tomorrow. I can only imagine your joy. If you have a minute tomorrow, call me and give me an update. The twins are very anxious to hear from you.

Colt, Colt. Was it true what Maggie said? She was terrified to believe it, but more terrified not to.

With the phone still in her hand, she realized Donna had also left her a message.

I received a call from Allie Brenner through the foundation hotline. She says it's urgent she get in touch with you. I knew you'd want to know.

Kathryn had just parked in the plaza garage. She briefly closed her eyes. She'd always been completely honest with Colt and honored his wishes, but she couldn't ignore his daughter's plea. Without hesitation, she phoned Donna.

"Hi. I just listened to your message. Did Allie leave her cell phone number?"

"Yes."

"Then will you text her with my number so she can call me direct?" Where Colt was concerned, the need to keep everything aboveboard was paramount.

"Of course. I'll do it right now. I heard about your

father on the news. They said he's gained consciousness. Is he going to be all right?"

"Yes, thank heaven. He'll go home tomorrow."

"That's wonderful news. Talk to you later."

Kathryn hung up and dashed inside the tower. As she walked out of the elevator into her condo, the phone rang. She checked the caller ID and clicked on.

"Hi, Allie."

"I know I'm not supposed to call you, but I couldn't help it," she began before she started to cry.

"It's all right, darling. I'm glad you phoned."

She heard sniffing. "You are?"

"Of course."

"Dad said your father was going to be okay."

"Yes. It's the best news."

"I know you love your father the way I love mine. If anything happened to Dad, I'd want to die."

"Nothing's going to happen to either of our dads, Allie. Mine still has years of living to do yet, and yours is going to see you and Matt grow up, go to college, get married, have children and be a grandpa to them. As Matt says, he's such a dude he'll be showing your sons how to bull ride."

Allie's laughter between the tears was music to her ears.

"What was that frontier museum at the hotel like?"

"I don't know. We're back home. Dad didn't want to stay in Omaha. None of us did without you." Those words melted Kathryn's heart. "Uh-oh. I've got to go."

That meant Colt had walked in on his daughter. Kathryn hung up the phone and removed her coat, reliving the moment when Maggie had called to tell her about their father.

One day they would lose their dad, yet she had the conviction she'd be able to handle it. But when she boarded the plane taking her to Salt Lake and looked back at Colt, a paralyzing chill went through because she knew it would be a different story if he went out of her life.

COLT SAT DOWN at the side of Allie's bed. She'd hidden herself beneath the covers. "I thought I heard you talking to someone. Isn't it rather late for you to be on the phone with friends?"

In a minute she pushed back the quilt and sat up. "I phoned the foundation hotline and left a message for Katy. She called me back. Are you mad at me?"

"No," he said. "Thank you for being honest."

"I know you said her dad was getting better, but I just had to talk to her for a minute."

"I understand."

Her eyes filled with tears. "I love her."

He could hardly swallow. "I'm aware of that."

She drew her knees up to her chest. "Dad? You know that promise you made to find our mom?"

"How could I forget?"

"While you were on the phone with Ed, Matt and I talked about it and we've decided we don't want you to look for her."

Colt hadn't seen that one coming. "Why not?"

"B-because," she stammered, "if she'd been like Katy, she wouldn't have left. I also know you don't want to see her again."

Nope. Natalie had been dead to him since the moment she'd told him she wanted to abort their children.

"Even if you find her, she won't want to see us, otherwise she would have come years ago. We don't want her to come if it isn't her own idea."

His children were growing up so fast, it took his breath away.

She bowed her head. "You know when I was in the hospital?"

"Yes?"

"Katy took care of me the way Mrs. Wagner takes care of Jen when she's sick, only Katy's different and clever and smarter and a lot more exciting and so kind she makes me cry. Oh, Dad, I—I feel so ashamed." Her voice caught.

"What are you talking about?"

Allie unexpectedly threw her arms around his neck and sobbed. Her words came out in spurts. "All those years she didn't have a mother or a father to love her, but Matt and I have always had you. You're the most wonderful father in the whole world."

Colt could hear Kathryn's voice as she'd imitated those exact words of Allie's to him over the phone.

"Will you forgive me for putting you through so much pain?"

He hugged her close. "Allie sweetheart, we've been through this before. There's nothing to forgive."

"Yes, there is. Because of me, you hired Katy's brother-in-law and it has put him and her sister out. Please call him and tell him to stop looking for her. To be honest, I'm afraid he might find her and it will all have been for nothing because Matt and I never want to see her or know her. Matt never really did, but he went along with me."

Well, well…nothing could be any plainer than that.

He kissed the top of her head before letting her go. "I'll call him tonight to let him know."

"Thanks." She wiped the moisture off her face with the sheet.

Colt got up from the bed. He paused at the door to look back at her. "You want to know something?"

"What?"

"If you hadn't gone to Salt Lake and met Kathryn, I wouldn't be wearing my gold buckle. How happy do you think that makes me?"

A smile broke out on her face. "Pretty happy."

"Yup. Good night, honey."

He stopped by Matt's room. His son was on the computer looking up bull-riding trivia. "As far as I can tell, no one's ever had better scores than you, Dad."

"Keep looking. You'll find them." He put a hand on his shoulder. "I was just speaking with your sister. She asked me to call off the search for your mother."

Matt looked up at him. "Yeah. Is that okay with you?"

"It was always okay with me."

He smiled. "That's what I thought."

"Then we're good?" Colt asked.

"Yeah." They high-fived each other. "Dad?" Matt called out as he started to leave the room.

Pausing mid-stride, Colt turned to him. "What is it?"

"It was fun flying to Omaha with Katy. She's awesome."

Awesome didn't begin to cover it.

BESIDES WORRYING about her father, Kathryn spent a restless night waiting for morning to come so she could phone Colt. Her abrupt departure from them in Omaha, coupled with Allie's brief call last night, had left her hanging. She'd hoped to make contact before she had to leave for the Grand America Hotel this morning to give a talk.

At seven, she received a call from her Donna. "I thought I'd phone in case there's anything you need before you take off."

"No. I'm as ready as I'll ever be."

"Good. The Salt Lake County sheriff's chief deputy just phoned for verification that things were lined up on our end. I told him we'd sent our brochures and a video clip to the conference chair a week ago."

"Bless you, Donna. I don't know what I'd do without you. Talk to you later." She hung up and fixed herself a cup of coffee and some toast before getting in the shower. After arranging her hair in a French roll, she phoned her mother. At five to eight, Kathryn could count on her being up.

"Mom? How's Dad this morning?"

"Other than a sore bump on his forehead, he's fine. You know him. He's already eaten breakfast and showered. Now he's dressed and wants to go home."

"I bet you didn't get any sleep."

She laughed. "No, but I didn't mind. They've taken such wonderful care of him, it's a relief."

"I'm glad. Has the doctor been in?"

"Not yet, but when he comes, I'm sure he'll release him. Ben and Cord will be here to drive us home. How soon will you be coming to the house?"

"I have a conference at ten. My part will be over by noon."

"Which one is that?"

"The Great Salt Lake Valley Metropolitan Area Kidnapping Summit. My talk follows the keynote address."

"Now I remember. It's the first one ever to be held in Salt Lake. They're lucky to have you on the program. I know you'll be wonderful!"

"Thanks, Mom. Expect me before one. If there's any different news about Dad, call me no matter what. Love you."

Kathryn had an hour before she needed to leave for the hotel. Though she disliked calling Colt this early, she suspected he was already out on the ranch working. In his message he'd asked her to phone him when she found a minute, so hopefully he wouldn't mind.

To her disappointment it rang several times and went to his voice mail. All she could do was let him know she'd called and would try again later. In a restless mood, she left the kitchen and walked back to her bedroom to get dressed and do her makeup.

With the kind of media coverage this meeting would get, she decided to wear her black wool suit. The tailored two-piece with the long sleeves was simple, yet sophisticated. A strand of pearls with her pearl studs would add the right touch.

While she got ready, she kept her cell next to her in case Colt phoned, but by twenty after nine he still hadn't returned her call. After putting on her closed-toe black pumps, she slipped into her knee-length camel-hair coat and called for a limo.

It didn't take long to reach the hotel. After turning off her phone, she got out and had to face a barrage of photojournalists on her way in to the conference room. Dozens of security people had converged because the governor and one of the state senators had arrived before her. As all of them were friends with her and her family, they got up to give her a quick hug and ask about her dad's accident.

FBI Special Agent Larry Forsythe, the keynote speaker, and other law enforcement dignitaries she knew clustered around her before the meeting started. The room had filled to capacity with local police and federal agents. There were even some CIA. Jake had planned to come, but she hadn't seen him yet.

Once the chief of police had helped her off with her coat, she sat down and tried to collect her thoughts. It was difficult because she kept checking her voice mail to see if Colt had sent her a message yet. So far, nothing.

As soon as the meeting got under way and all the dignitaries were recognized, she put the phone back in her bag and concentrated on Larry's speech. His thoughts echoed the same cry heard from the political arena. He urged local police and federal agents who investigated kidnapping cases to work together and not let bureaucratic red tape slow them down.

In summation, he said, "Utah and Idaho have had arguably the nation's two most high-profile kidnapping cases in half a century. The courageous woman on the stand needs no introduction. Twenty-six years after being kidnapped, she was returned alive to the Senator Reed McFarland family of Salt Lake City.

"May I present Kathryn McFarland, who now runs

the McFarland Foundation, a cause established by her parents in her honor to help fight the terrible crime of kidnapping.

"For the past four years this remarkable, selfless woman has been giving our community everything she possesses in terms of self, time and money to protect our children from suffering her fate. In the coming year she has agreed to be a part of this summit conference as we take it to the western states. She will now address you."

Kathryn rose to her feet accompanied by a thunderous ovation. When it finally quieted down and everyone was seated, she looked out at her audience. "That lasted so long I felt embarrassed *until* I realized something. Your outpouring came from the joy of knowing that law enforcement was triumphant in cracking my particular case, cold though it was for a quarter of a century."

A hush fell over the audience.

"My circumstance and that of my sister-in-law Kit, who was also kidnapped and lost for twenty-six years, were unique. Though today we have the technology in place to catch these godless criminals faster than ever before, it still requires good old-fashioned police work.

"We need more cable news channels that will run whole hour feature programs and get the pictures out there. Our communities have the manpower, but it needs to be harnessed into an army of volunteers who will assist law enforcement in doing house-to-house searches, combing beaches, mountains and forests.

"Unfortunately we have a problem. As Agent Forsythe just warned, we must get rid of the red tape and share every bit of information possible if we're going to do better. To that end you've been given a brochure the foundation puts out. We're trying to work with every hospital, soup kitchen, school, law enforcement agency and media outlet to battle this evil force together. Our goal is to get the citizenry actively involved.

"In view of this, my dear mother and father, who've been the life force of this great cause, have pledged more funds to augment existing law enforcement funds and payrolls already in place in the Salt Lake Valley to fight this war. Together we can win."

She walked back to her seat while the whole room exploded in cheers. Agent Forsythe went back to the podium and waited for the din to subside. "If you'll all make your way to the banquet room, we'll eat lunch while we hear from the governor."

Kathryn put her coat back on and left through the same exit with the other dignitaries. A few yards off she caught sight of Jake and another dark-haired agent, equally tall and well honed, dressed in a charcoal suit and tie. She assumed he was CIA, too, until her gaze lifted to his hard-boned face. Her legs went weak as jelly.

Colt!

"Well done," her brother-in-law whispered, giving her a hug. "Maggie's waiting for me. Your dad just got home. I'll see you at your parents' house later." He disappeared into the crowd, leaving her alone with Colt.

His stare was fiercely intense. "Do you have to attend the lunch here?"

Her heart throbbed in her throat making it hard to

find her voice. "No. My part's done. In fact, I was on my way out. Come with me."

"Kathryn?" Agent Forsythe interrupted. "I'll see you at the conference in St. George on Friday?" She nodded. "Without you, we could never have assembled such a huge crowd. Thank you."

"You're welcome."

As he walked away, Colt cupped her elbow and ushered her out of the hotel past half a dozen journalists with cameras.

"Sorry about that," she said once they were safely inside the limo. She told the driver to take her to her parents' home, then said, "For someone as private as you, this kind of thing must feel like a huge intrusion on your life."

His gaze swept over her features. "You handle it like you don't even see them."

"I've had four years to deal with it. You get used to it."

"The camera has to love you. You look very beautiful today. Cool, like a mountain stream."

So cool she didn't seem touchable to him? What had happened to the man who'd kissed her senseless the other night? Colt sounded so far away just then she shivered.

"Thank you. When you're a public figure, everyone wants a piece of you. It's a facade I've created to distance myself."

"Your speech was inspiring, but then so is your whole life. When I think what you did for Allie, yet she's only one of the many you've helped in the same way."

"Careful, Colt. You're giving me a swelled head."

His sober expression alarmed her. "Not you. You're the antithesis of a narcissist. Someone with a destiny like yours doesn't think of herself."

Why did she get the impression he was backing away from her? What had she done? Pain made her daring. "I see no sign of the Montana rancher today. How come?"

He smiled, but it didn't reach his eyes. "Obviously my facade doesn't ring true."

"Colt?" she cried softly. "What's wrong?"

"Why, nothing."

The tension was palpable. "We're almost to the house. My father said he'd like to meet you and see your gold buckle up close."

"Before I left home this morning, Matt asked if he could wear it to school."

"Did you say yes?" He nodded. "Your son idolizes you. Your daughter, too, but you already know that."

He didn't respond, leaving her more empty than ever.

The limo turned and drove up the winding drive to her parents' Tudor-styled home. It stopped behind the cars parked in the courtyard.

She needed something clarified before they got out. "Why didn't you phone and let me know you were coming?"

"I had to call Jake last night about something important and he suggested I fly to Salt Lake. By the time I made arrangements, it was too late to reach you. He thought I might find the conference of interest. Maggie drove us straight from the airport to the hotel so we wouldn't miss your talk."

"I see." She clasped her hands in a death grip. "Can't you tell me what it is before we go in?"

"I'd prefer to wait until you've seen your father and know he's all right."

His shield had gone back up. Sensing something ominous, she scrambled out of the car before he could come around to help her.

Chapter Ten

An hour later, after a delicious lunch, Kathryn broke in on Colt's conversation with her brother McCord, whom everyone called Cord. The two of them had been talking horses and rodeos, subjects it turned out were close to both their hearts.

She'd put her coat on, looking too gorgeous to be real. "I'm ready to leave when you are."

Cord grinned at her. "What's the hurry?"

Colt didn't give her a chance to answer. "If you'd heard your sister at the kidnapping summit, you would know she has a list of things to do most people couldn't accomplish in a lifetime."

Her brother hugged her. "That's our Kathryn. She's so busy these days, she hasn't even been skiing with me."

"I'm afraid that's my daughter's fault, Cord, but Allie is fully recovered from the flu now and understands Kathryn's attention is needed elsewhere." He shook Cord's hand. "It's been a privilege to meet you and your family."

"The pleasure was all ours, believe me. How soon are you going back to Montana?"

"My flight leaves at five. The twins have plans for us." He looked across the living room at the family seated around Kathryn's parents. Exceptional, gracious people, all of them, but she was definitely the shining star in their family tree. "I'm glad your father is on the mend."

"Thank you. So are we. None of us is ready to lose him yet, especially not his baby girl who wouldn't be able to handle it after only recently finding him. She's his favorite," he teased his sister.

Throughout the conversation there'd been total silence from Kathryn. Colt expected her cheeks would flush at her brother's comment, but the opposite happened. She was acting so different from the warm woman who'd filled his arms the night they'd gone dancing.

Cord walked them to the door. Kathryn hurried outside and got in the limo without waiting for Colt. When he climbed in behind her, she said, "If it's all right with you, I've told the driver to take us to my condo. Whatever you have to tell me, I'd rather talk there."

In less than five minutes they reached the McFarland Plaza and rode the elevator to the penthouse. After they walked into the foyer, she looked over her shoulder. "I'll only be a minute. Make yourself comfortable."

Once she'd vanished, he removed his suit jacket and tie. He walked through the rooms enjoying the sights of the valley from each angle. The fast-moving clouds made for fascinating viewing. When he reached the kitchen, he saw the poster of himself taking up the greater part of her fridge. He'd be a liar if he didn't admit he was flattered.

By the time he'd walked back to the living room,

she'd joined him. Gone were the pearls, the fabulous black suit and cashmere coat, the black high heels. In their place she wore navy sweats and sneakers, but it changed nothing about her.

The energy she brought into a room made everything around her pale. He'd never forget the way she'd kept today's audience spellbound. It wasn't just her looks. It was her spirit, that intangible life force unique to her.

She sat down on one end of the couch, tucking her legs beneath her. "Whatever you had to tell me and Jake must have been important for you to have flown here this morning."

Colt moved closer to her without taking a seat. He put his hands on his hips. "Last night the twins asked me to put a stop to the search for their mother."

Her eyes widened in shock. She shook her head. "Why?"

"I'll quote my daughter the best I can. 'Matt and I have decided we don't want to see her or know her. If she'd been like Katy, she wouldn't have left.'"

Colt had the satisfaction of watching color seep back into her cheeks.

"'Even if you find her, Dad, she won't want to see us, otherwise she would have come years ago. We don't want her to come if it isn't her own idea.'"

Allie had said a lot of other things, too, but Colt chose to keep those to himself.

Kathryn sat straighter. "Your daughter's made a complete turnaround."

He nodded. "She's done a lot of growing up over the past few weeks. Naturally I phoned Jake right away. It wouldn't have been fair to keep him or you on the job another minute."

"My brother-in-law doesn't look at life that way."

"It's because he's crazy about you."

She got to her feet. "Being Maggie's sister helps."

Colt couldn't reach her. "Nevertheless the Brenner family has intruded on the McFarlands' time and generosity long enough. You all have your own busy lives to lead."

"You didn't have to come to Salt Lake to deliver that message."

He took a deep breath. "You didn't need to accompany Allie to the ranch."

Kathryn averted her eyes. "I told you my reasons. Why don't you tell me yours?"

"To thank you in person for what you've done for my kids, especially Allie. Your influence has helped her to resolve a problem that has caused her pain since her first recollections of life. For that I'll be eternally grateful to you."

She shifted her weight. "Whatever small part I played, the real praise goes to you. After I met my father and lived with him, I thought there couldn't be another father in the world to match him. All those years to have gone without, then I was handed the royal prize.

"I was very smug about it. In truth, I felt sorry for everyone else who didn't have him for their parent. Four years went by, then I met Allie. When she told me about you, I realized I wasn't the only person in the world who'd been handed the royal prize. It came as a stunning revelation, believe me. So you see, she was good for me, too."

Colt didn't dare stay to listen to any more. He fastened his tie and slipped on his jacket. "We'll never forget you. Now I'd better get going. I'm supposed to be at the airport an hour and a half before boarding."

She followed him to the foyer. "Have a safe flight home and give the twins my best."

"I'll do that." He stepped into the elevator. "I have no doubts your speech in St. George will have the same electrifying effect on law enforcement there."

KATHRYN WATCHED the door close.

Something horrible had just happened to her world and she didn't understand why. On autopilot she ran into the bedroom for her cell and called Dr. Morrow. She had to leave a message, which meant he was with a patient. "Please call me. This is an emergency!"

With phone still in hand, she rushed over to the bedroom window. It looked out on South Temple. She strained to see if she could see Colt getting into a taxi, but she searched in vain for him. He'd probably used another exit out of the Plaza.

Her body was in so much pain, she couldn't move. When her phone rang, she saw that it was Donna. Though she didn't want to get it, she had to.

"Donna?"

"Hi. Sorry to bother you, but since the conference at least twenty-five calls have come in on the hotline wanting you to phone them back. How shall I handle it?"

Kathryn pressed her head against the glass. "Ask the volunteers to return the calls with the message that I'm temporarily unable to deal with any requests. I'll talk to you later." She hung up, too filled with anguish to function.

What if she drove out to the airport to have a gut talk with Colt? Would he consider it an invasion of his privacy? Disgust him?

Her inner voice screamed yes because Natalie was the only woman who'd ever managed to turn him from a bachelor into a married man and that was sixtee—

A ringing phone interrupted her thoughts. "Dr. Morrow? Thank you for calling me. I have to talk to you."

"My last appointment will be over at ten to five. You come in at five."

"I can't thank you enough."

Kathryn hung up and checked her watch. It was ten to four. The walls were already closing in on her. She had to get out of the condo and made the decision to leave for his office in Olympus Cove now.

Grabbing her red cable-knit cardigan, she rode the elevator down to the car park, not having bothered to change out of her sweats. The trip would only take her twenty minutes. She'd wait in the Jeep until it was time.

On the dot of five, Dr. Morrow opened the door and told her to come in.

"I did what you advised," she said the minute she sat down. "I went to Bozeman on Friday, not only to do business but to have fun. I felt Colt and I were getting closer. In fact I *know* we were, but then today everything changed."

"How?"

"He flew here. I was speaking at a conference and

he slipped in with Jake. Afterward he treated me like an…acquaintance. When he left my condo, he made no overture to see me again. I don't know what I did wrong. I—I think it's over and I can't bear it."

Dr. Morrow sat back in his chair and studied her until she felt like squirming. "You didn't do anything wrong, but you *are* Utah's Joan of Arc celebrity on what appears to be a lifetime mission. Remember our last session. You've been modeling your life after your parents.

"This Colt on the other hand is a born and bred Montana cattle rancher, raising teenagers no less. Try to separate yourself from the facts for a moment. How do you see these two people getting together in a significant relationship? Honestly."

She didn't have to think long about it. "I don't."

He pressed his fingers together. "Neither does Colt. Worse, you're the Anne Frank of our nation who survived. Everyone wants a piece of you. There's the answer to your first question."

Kathryn frowned. "My first?"

"That's right. The second and more important question is, what do you want to do about it?" He removed his glasses and rubbed his eyes. "That's all the time I can give you for now. I'll see you at your regular appointment next week."

COLT SHONE HIS POWER flashlight around the shed. The place was a mess. It had been the catchall since his grandparents had died. Before that, his grandmother had kept everything organized.

He moved between the clutter until he came to the boxes he'd stacked on top of his rodeo stuff. With only five days to go until Christmas, he realized he'd better sort through it if he wanted to give his son a meaningful present.

Allie had been easier to buy for. A private chat with Jen had produced a long list of items his daughter wanted. He'd already taken care of her gifts and those for his sister and her family.

For Noreen and Ed, he'd ordered a Winnebago. They'd always talked about going sightseeing in a camper but never did anything about it. Colt was always encouraging them to take more vacations. Somehow they never did. It was long past time they enjoyed more of life. The camper would provide the incentive and was being delivered Christmas Eve.

As for Matt, he needed something special.

Colt made space in order to set the offending boxes on the floor. In a minute, he pulled a hammer from his hip pocket and pried open the big crate. Using his flashlight he peered inside. It was like finding buried treasure.

"Well, would you look at that," Ed spoke, startling the daylights out of Colt.

His head reared back. "Where did you come from?"

"I was locking up the house when I thought I saw a light coming from the shed, so I came out to investigate. It's after midnight! You sure pick a hell of a time to rummage."

"I only got the idea tonight, but I had to be sure the twins were asleep before I sneaked out. Think he'll like any of this junk?"

Ed snorted. "There's junk, and then there's junk. Are you daft?"

"I was only asking. If I wrap up this stuff, I hope it'll give him some fun opening it. I think I'm ready for Christmas now." He glanced at his foreman. "What about you?"

"Noreen has everything under control. What did you get Kathryn?"

Colt's eyes slid away. "Who in the hell is that?"

"That bad, huh?"

His jaw hardened. "Don't start in, Ed. The twins do enough of it."

"Somebody needs to get to you. Since you flew back from Salt Lake ten days ago, you've been ornerier than Lightning before you broke him in. The hands around here have been forced to keep wide berth. That's something that's never happened before."

Shut up, Ed.

"What did that sensational woman ever do to you except transform your kids and remind you that you were once a great champion?"

"You said it first," Colt snapped. "*Sensational* puts her outside the realm of possibility."

"What are you talking about?"

"You weren't there when she learned that the body the volunteers from the McFarland Foundation found was that of the missing girl. Kathryn has a need to comfort others that goes beyond the normal person's capacity. It's what drives her.

"At that kidnapping conference, she was such an inspiration the FBI has years of speaking engagements and commitments lined up for her all over the West." The veins stood out in Colt's neck. "You didn't see how she reacted when she thought her father might be dying. Hell, Ed, he's her *life!*"

"I hear you, Colt."

He shuddered. "Being kidnapped did things to her I can't fight. You didn't hear her tell Allie how at her age, she swore that if she were ever united with her parents, she'd never leave their sight again."

Silence filled the shed. His outburst left him with nothing but a gnawing hunger that would haunt him to the grave.

"Funny how with all that going on in her life, she left their sight several times to fly to Montana."

"On business for Allie and me!" Colt thundered. "But you haven't seen her pop up around here lately because that business is over."

"If you say so. Why don't I help you take all this junk into my house where it will be hidden? Noreen and I will wrap it for you so Matt doesn't suspect anything."

Colt wheeled around and clasped his best friend on the shoulder. "Thanks for putting up with me."

Ed's expression grew solemn. "You know I'd do anything for you if I could."

"I do. But the truth is, Kathryn McFarland is destined to belong to the world." He looked down at the things in the crate. "Shall we get started?"

KATHRYN WROTE DOWN the number of Colt's ranch house phone before coaching the poor salesgirl on what to say. It was Christmas Eve and all the clerks looked frazzled. But Kathryn had bought enough things to make it worth the college girl's time.

"No matter who answers, just identify yourself and ask for Mrs. Walters. If she's on the phone, tell her just a minute and hand the phone to me. If she's not available, give them your extension number and ask that she phone you back ASAP. Got it?"

The redhead nodded and pressed the digits of the store phone. "Hello. This is Julie at Macy's Gallatin Valley Mall. I need to speak to Mrs. Walters. Oh, good. Just a minute please." She passed the phone to Kathryn, who clutched it in nervous excitement.

"Noreen? It's Kathryn." She heard the woman's slight gasp. "Please don't give me away. Are you alone?"

"For the moment. Colt's sister and family arrived a few minutes ago. We'll be eating at six-thirty."

It was four o'clock now. "Will anyone else be there?"

"Just us."

Perfect.

"I'm in Bozeman and I've brought gifts for everyone, but I want my presence to be a secret for now. When it gets dark, could I come to your house first?"

"I was just going to suggest it. Park around back. I'll leave the door unlocked."

"Bless you."

She handed the phone to the clerk. "Thank you so much. Merry Christmas."

"Merry Christmas to you, too."

Kathryn left the department store with her packages and headed for the rental car. Earlier, after flying into Bozeman on a charter, she'd driven straight to the Silver Spur with her load. Now that her shopping was done, she had to finish wrapping presents.

On the way back to the motel she stopped at a drive-through for a hamburger and fries. She needed fortification for what lay ahead. Since talking to Dr. Morrow, she'd suffered agony hoping Colt would call or fly to Salt Lake to see her. It didn't happen.

Deep down, she knew nothing would happen if she didn't act on her feelings. Maybe nothing would even if she *did* act, but she loved him too desperately not to prove it to him in the only way she knew how.

At six-fifteen, she stepped out of her motel room and felt snowflakes on her nose and eyelashes. Hastened by a gusting wind, the predicted storm had moved in.

By the time she reached the ranch entrance, she could hardly see a foot in front of her. Luckily she'd come here enough that she knew where to drive and anticipated the wide curve up the mountain.

Needing the momentum so she wouldn't get mired, she kept on going when she reached the vale. Ed and Noreen's house stood nestled in a stand of pines near the new ranch house. She could see a glimmer of light and headed in that direction, not daring to stop until she'd driven as close to the back door as possible.

Grateful to have arrived in one piece, she dashed inside the kitchen of the comfortable 1940s vintage home toting two heavy laundry bags. She thanked Noreen silently for leaving the lights on.

Aware that everyone was at the other house enjoying their Christmas Eve dinner, she took a calming breath and undressed down to her underwear. Laying everything aside in a pile, she opened the red laundry bags with their rope drawstrings and started getting into the padded red Santa suit.

The costume was made of beautiful red velvet with white fur trim. She'd bought the full works! It took forever to put everything on, especially the wig and beard, but finally she was ready.

When she went back outside with the two empty bags, more snow had built up on the car. If she couldn't make it over to Colt's house, she would have to call Noreen for help and it would ruin her surprise.

Luckily the ground was level and inch by inch she managed to make progress, but there was no way she'd manage the slight rise around the side of his house. At one point, the car just couldn't go any further, which meant she'd have to use the front door.

That was okay. In fact it was probably better because she could ring the front doorbell. She got this fluttery feeling in her stomach wondering what kind of reaction she'd get from Colt.

Please don't be too angry.

All her gifts were in two big bags. She had to get out of the car and stand there in the snow while she put them into the red laundry bags. The car clock said quarter to eight. Their meal would be over by now.

Once her red hat with its white fur trim was in place, she was ready and started trudging through the snow with her packs. This experience gave her a whole new appreciation for department-store Santas.

The going was slow because she felt clumsy in the big black boots. She'd practiced wearing everything at home, but doing this in a Montana blizzard was something else again.

Kathryn finally reached the front porch and tugged

the bags up the steps to the door. She hesitated for a moment. Maybe it was unlocked. That would be much better. Then she could make her big entrance and really shock everyone.

When she tried the handle and pressed the lever, it gave. More of Noreen's work?

Please understand why I'm doing this, Colt. Please.

With as much stealth as she could muster, she eased her way into the foyer with the bags. She could hear voices coming from the dining room. Someone had arranged a garland around the entry to the living room. The magic of Christmas filled the house.

To her left she saw a beautifully decorated tree standing in front of the tall living-room windows. Beneath it were a ton of presents. The smell of pine and Christmas scented candles filled her nostrils. A nativity scene had been set up on the coffee table. Emotion brought tears to her eyes.

Before she did another thing, she opened the pack and pulled out her cowboy hat. If everything went off the way she hoped, Colt would think Santa was a neighbor. But to give him a hint, she purposely walked over to the staircase and left the calling card of her Stetson on the end of the banister where he wouldn't be able to miss it.

What he wanted to do about it after discovering it would decide her fate. Fearing the worst, she almost lost her nerve. But when she considered what she could gain, she fought off her demons and reached in the pack for the last item to complete her outfit.

Once she'd fastened the belt around her fat belly, she grabbed the necks of the bags with her padded gloves and moved into the living room. Too late to back out now.

Chapter Eleven

"Dad?" Allie cut in on Colt, who'd been talking to Tom. "Listen! That sounds like sleigh bells."

No sooner had his daughter spoken than he heard "Ho! Ho! Ho!" It was coming from the living room.

"It's Santa!" the kids all cried at once.

"I think they're right," Sherry murmured in surprise.

Colt couldn't believe it. His gaze flicked to Ed's, who shook his head in bewilderment. Noreen looked equally stunned.

The kids leaped out of their chairs and ran into the other room with Matt leading the way.

"Merry Christmas! Ho! Ho! Ho!" sounded the booming voice.

Colt brought up the rear in time to see the jolly fat man in red standing in front of the tree pulling out presents from his packs. One of his neighbors had gone to a lot of trouble for this unprecedented visit and looked the personification of Santa. Incredible.

This year, the joy of Christmas wasn't in his soul. Colt wished he weren't so empty inside, but the knowledge that Kathryn could never be a part of his life had darkened his world. He honestly didn't know how he was going to get through it.

"Have you all been good?"

"Yes!" the kids answered.

"Then there's plenty for all!" Santa boomed as he motioned with his arms for the adults to come all the way in. Colt ran a list of all his friends through his mind, but he didn't recognize one of their voices.

When he lumbered over to the children, his body jingled. He handed each one a present. The kid's noisy excitement turned to oohs as they opened their gifts and discovered a large, hand-painted nutcracker.

Amazed by such extravagant generosity, Colt almost forgot to open his gift. It was a chocolate ball arranged in sections and smelled like an orange. He turned to Sherry just as she put a chocolate-covered strawberry in her mouth.

"I'll come back next year if you kids promise to be good!" Santa grabbed his packs and headed for the foyer.

"We will." They followed him to the foyer. "Thanks for the presents, Santa!"

"Ho! Ho! Ho!" Colt heard him call out. "Merry Christmas to all and to all a good night!" When the front door closed, you could still hear his sleigh bells.

Allie came back in to show Colt her splendid-looking nutcracker prince. "I love this! You planned it, didn't you, Dad?"

He shook his head. "I wish I could take the credit."

"That was fun!" Sherry's kids ran to their parents to show them their nutcrackers.

"This is so cool." Matt wandered over to Colt while

he opened and shut the mouth of his mouse king. Colt handed him a wedge of chocolate. "Umm. That's good. I bet it was Roger's dad. He likes to do stuff like that."

"His father isn't that tall," Allie argued. "I've always wanted one of these." She looked at the bottom. "They're made in Germany. Thanks, Dad." She kissed his cheek. "I know you did it."

There was no convincing her otherwise. Colt couldn't imagine who'd played the part—maybe one of the hands—but he knew it was the work of Ed and Noreen. Tomorrow he'd get them to admit it.

He glanced at Sherry. "As long as we're in here already, shall we let the kids open one present before bed?" She nodded. "Who wants to go first?"

Tom suggested they start with the youngest.

"Go on," Colt encouraged Sarah.

While the children took turns, he exchanged a glance with Ed, who was munching happily on chocolate truffles. He held one up. "Mint." So far, he hadn't given anything away.

After the kids opened another gift, Colt went to the kitchen for a plastic bag and came back to the living room to help Noreen clean up.

He found himself counting the minutes until everyone went to bed. Tonight he intended to hibernate in his room and find forgetfulness with some of the Jack Daniels Tom had brought him.

"Dad? Paul and I are going to listen to our new CDs in my room."

Good. "Have fun. We'll see you guys in the morning when more fun stuff begins."

"Yeah." They high-fived each other.

Colt walked over to Allie. "I think it's time you and Sarah went up, too."

"We're going." They gathered up their things.

"Thanks for my nutcracker," Sarah told Colt. "It says on the bottom she's the sugar plum fairy."

Noreen's choice of gift for the kids was a huge hit. Hopefully the new Winnebago would be a hit, too. "Good night, girls."

"Hey, Dad!"

The level of excitement in Matt's voice caused him to turn. His son came running back in the living room sounding out of breath. He was carrying something else in his other hand. The instant Colt saw the chocolate-brown Stetson, everything became crystal clear. His heart gave a resounding clap.

Forgetting everything, he made a dash for the front door and hurried into the snow. It had fallen continually since dinner. His eyes made out faint track marks in the drive. Without a moment to lose, he raced around to his truck and followed them. They led to Ed and Noreen's.

A car had pulled up in the drive, covered in snow. Hardly able to breathe, he jumped out and rushed around to the back door of the house.

"Kathryn?" He charged into the kitchen.

"I've been wondering how long it would take you."

Colt swung around. She was sitting on the counter in a Christmas-red skirt and sweater. Her gorgeous, nylon-clad legs were crossed at the knee. The transformation from Santa back to flesh-and-blood woman wearing high heels left his senses reeling.

"When it seemed like you would never come, I was afraid you didn't want to."

Didn't want to?

"I came the second Matt discovered your hat on his way up to bed." He took a step closer. "I guess you know you turned a regular Christmas Eve into something magical for the kids. They think they're way past believing in miracles. You should have seen Allie's eyes light up at the sight of the nutcracker prince."

"I'm glad. While she was in the hospital, we had long talks. I told her the Ballet West put on the *Nutcracker* every winter and hoped one day she'd be able to see it."

"She loves you, Kathryn. So does Matt."

"I love both your children." Her smile charmed him down to his core. "Tonight I had more fun than you can imagine. I've never played Santa before, but I was afraid in case you resented the intrusion."

He drew in a sharp breath. "You were superb, like you are at everything. I think I might be in the middle of another dream."

She cocked her head, sending the mass of blond silk to one shoulder. "Why do you say that?"

"How long can you stay this time?"

"It depends on this blizzard."

"That's what I thought," he sighed.

"Colt!" Her eyes glinted with pain. "It's impossible to reach you, isn't it?"

His head reared. "What do you mean?"

"Do you honestly think I came all the way here in this storm on the most wonderful night of the year to suddenly take off again? Don't you know I'm here for as long as you want me?"

She couldn't know what she was saying. The muscles in his throat constricted. "No more pretense."

"When did I ever do that?"

"Maybe not, but I need an honest answer from you."

"I've never given you anything else."

Maybe he was cracking from the strain of wanting her so terribly. "It's Christmas. You missed twenty-six of them with your family. Why aren't you home with them tonight?"

"Because I wanted to be here with you."

"Why?"

"You know why! Oh, sometimes you drive me crazy! I love you, Colton Brenner. I'm so madly in love with you it's disgusting."

"Kathryn..."

"You still don't believe me?" she cried.

"It's not that," he murmured. "I saw you speak at that conference. It's clear you're needed by the world to keep other people inspired."

"I'd like to think I'm needed elsewhere. Come here and let me convince you I'd be good for you."

He held back. "I'm afraid to touch you. Tomorrow— the day after tomorrow—you'll have to leave on another noble cause that requires your particular gifts. It's what you do because you're Kathryn McFarland."

"Not anymore."

The blood pounded in his ears. "Say that again?"

She moved off the counter. "That was the old Kathryn who has served her thirty years trying to find out who she really is. Now it's someone else's turn to do that job. Since meeting you, I'm not the same person."

Colt wanted to believe her so much. "Who are you, then?" he whispered.

In the next breath, she wrapped her arms around his chest. "Promise you won't laugh if I tell you something?"

"I swear."

"For quite a while now I've thought of myself as Colt's woman, hiding out on the Cloud Bottom Ranch."

He'd promised not to laugh, but he couldn't help it. Happiness flooded his being.

"I'm tired of being the Lost and Found McFarland. I want to settle down with my own man on our own mountain where nobody knows our business. I want to help you keep raising our children—because that's how I think of Matt and Allie—and hopefully give you another baby. I have such dreams, you can't imagine. If that terrifies you, I'll go away and never bother you again."

Colt crushed her against him. He buried his face in her hair, relishing its fine texture. "How does your family feel about it?"

"Didn't I ever tell you how great they are? They want me to be happy. Imagine that. Of course, they'll be happier if you make an honest woman out of me first."

"You don't have to worry about that. Two days ago I became a single man."

Her head flew back. "You did? You *are?*" He saw heaven in those blue eyes devouring him.

"You don't know the battle I had not to come and get you and drag you away to my secret hideout."

"I want to see it."

"When the snow melts, we'll ride up there. Marry me, Kathryn."

"What do you think I've been trying to tell you? Don't you know you didn't even need to ask? I'm yours for the taking, Colt. I was from the minute I heard your love for Allie over the phone. I've already told you the reason why I accompanied her back here, but it was also because I had to find out if you lived up to the image that had filled my mind."

"I couldn't wait to meet you, either. There was something about you…"

She kissed him all around his mouth without kissing him dead center, driving him crazy. "Tell me about it. All it took was stepping off the plane with your daughter. There was this gorgeous hunk of Western male striding toward me with purpose and that was it. I swear it was like being hit by a bolt of ligh—"

Colt smothered her words, needing her kiss more than he needed air. When he finally lifted his mouth from hers he said, "I love you, Kathryn, but it's going to take all night to even begin to tell you what you mean to me.

"Unfortunately we've left my house full of family who won't be able to settle down for a long winter's nap until we make an appearance. Let's go. The sooner we get this over with, the sooner I can concentrate on you."

He picked her up and carried her to the door. She opened it and they walked out into a white wonderland toward the truck. The snow had stopped falling.

"Oh, Colt! This is the most beautiful place on Earth."

"It is now."

Unable to keep their hands off each other, it took him longer to get her home. "They're back!" he heard Matt shout from the front door as he lifted her out of the truck.

Colt swept her inside the foyer where everyone had gathered. Unwilling to put her down, he couldn't refrain from kissing her in front of them.

"Whoa, Dad!"

He eventually lifted his head and smiled at the family he loved. "I've already got the Christmas present I want. Kathryn has agreed to marry me. It's all settled. Now you don't have to worry about me anymore, Sherry."

His sister had broken down in happy tears.

"Awesome," Matt whispered. His brown eyes had grown suspiciously bright.

"Put me down, darling," Kathryn whispered against his jaw.

As he lowered her, his Allie came running and quietly sobbed as she hugged both of them. "I'm so happy. I've wanted you to be my mom forever."

"I've wanted to belong to all of you forever. Come here, Matt."

While Noreen wiped her eyes, Ed smiled at Colt. "Life doesn't get better than this."

"Nope."

"Who is she?" Sarah asked. She looked as bewildered as Paul.

Their father flashed Colt a broad grin. "Santa Claus. Didn't you guys know Santa's a girl?"

Circle B Ranch, six months later

"MOM? WHERE ARE YOU?"

"In the den, Matt!"

"Good! I need you and Dad to sign this." He hurried in the room and handed her a form.

Kathryn took a look at it. "Did this just come in the mail?" It was the National Junior Bull Riders Association Membership and Release to Ride.

"Yeah. There's some other mail, too, and a postcard from Ed and Noreen. They love the Winnebago. This was sent from Mount Rushmore."

She glanced at it before getting back to the business at hand. "I can see you've filled everything out." It was the parents' consent and release form.

"Yeah." He was so excited he was bouncing with energy. Matt had grown taller since Christmas. His body had filled out more. When he was an adult, he'd be a heartbreaker like his father.

His father. Kathryn's husband. She loved him too much. To wake up in his arms every morning constituted the greatest happiness she'd ever known.

She signed her name. *Kathryn Brenner.* "If you want to get this in the mail by five, then we need to find your dad. Let's drive up to the north forty and look for him."

Colt hadn't known about her doctor's appointment this morning. Now she had news that couldn't wait and she wanted to deliver it in person. Matt's timing was perfect.

"Let's go." She put the letter marked Personal in her pocket for Colt, then grabbed her purse. They left the house through the back door and headed for the new Ford truck Colt had bought her. "You drive."

She tossed Matt the keys. Next month, he'd turn sixteen and would take his driver's test, but she let him drive everywhere on the ranch. He was a good driver; Allie was not as good yet. Under Colt's tutelage he was becoming a pretty good bull rider. Maybe a champion one day like his dad.

"Thanks."

On the way up to the range she phoned Allie. She'd stayed overnight at Michelle's. Kathryn planned to pick her up when she drove Matt into town later. As they climbed higher, she breathed in air perfumed by the wildflowers. The sight of cattle grazing beneath a blue sky made the experience surreal.

Colt was easy to pick out in his black Stetson. He must have seen them coming because he separated himself from the men and galloped toward the truck on Lightning. Like the poster of him, he represented the quintessential cowboy, at home in his element.

They both got out to wait for him. He rode straight up to them. His green gaze bored into hers. "Is everything all right?" Their vigilant protector never took time off worrying about them. That was one of the reasons she loved him with a passion.

"Everything's wonderful." She smiled to reassure him.

"I need you to sign my junior bull-riding release form, Dad."

Kathryn felt her husband's relief. Before he dismounted, she could tell he was trying hard not to laugh.

To his son, this constituted an emergency. Matt handed him the form.

Colt walked over to the truck and signed it against the fender. "You'll need to send the forty-dollar fee."

"I'll write him a check," Kathryn volunteered.

"Here's the money I earned helping Ed." He pulled two twenties from his pocket.

Colt took them and put them in his shirt pocket. "Now you're really official. I'm proud of you."

"If it gets there in time, can we go to Oklahoma's junior rodeo in July?"

"A bargain's a bargain. We'll all go and make a vacation out of it." He gave Matt a bear hug.

"So…" Her husband's eyes traveled to Kathryn. Through veiled lashes he looked her up and down the way he'd done early this morning before they'd made love. Just being near him turned her insides to mush. "Anything I can do for you?"

"I would say you already have."

They were so in tune with each other, Colt picked up on her message and turned to Matt. "Do you mind if I to talk to your mother for a minute?"

"Heck, no. Just don't make it too long," he teased. He walked around the truck and got in behind the wheel.

Colt looked down at her. "Our son's in no doubt how I feel about you. Now talk to me."

"Darling!" She couldn't hold it in any longer. "We're going to have a baby. I hope you meant what you said about having one with me because it's too late to change your mind now."

His eyes blazed with new light before he caught her in

his arms. "Kathryn," he cried softly. "I've been hoping for this since our wedding night. Lately I've worried that maybe something was wrong with me and I couldn't give you the thing you wanted most."

"Oh, I got everything I wanted when I married you. To have your baby is one of those added blessings you hope for but don't always get."

"I wish we weren't standing out in the open where all the hands can see us."

"I know. I picked the worst time to tell you, but as soon as I left the doctor's office this morning, I had to come. I could never keep anything from you. When you get home tonight, we'll celebrate."

"What's that little worry line on your face?"

"I hope the twins will be happy about it."

"How can you even say that when all they do is hint?"

"I know. I'm being paranoid."

His white smile thrilled her. "That's your prerogative as an expectant mother. But I tell you what. I'll bring Chinese home so you don't have to cook. We'll tell the twins together. We'll all want to know everything the doctor said."

"That sounds wonderful. Oh! I brought you a letter marked confidential that might be important." She pulled it out of her back pocket and handed it to him. "Now I'd better go. Matt is already antsy about getting his form in the mail. See you tonight."

He gave her a hungry kiss before helping her into the passenger side of the truck. "Drive safely, son."

Colt waited until the truck disappeared down the slope before he opened the envelope. A small note fell out.

Colt: I sent you this the second it came to my house. I was afraid a phone call would alert Kathryn. Let me know if you want to talk. Jake.

He looked at the letter. It had been typed on paper with a Sahara Hotel, Las Vegas, Nevada, letterhead.

Dear Agent Halsey:
    Re: Natalie Brenner
    Your inquiry prompted an investigation of a cold case concerning the death of a former employee working here sixteen years ago. The DNA sample you sent matched the DNA sample of the estimated twenty-year-old woman hired by the name of Vicky Adams who was found dead in the employees' bathroom on the fourth floor. I've included the Clark County coroner's report with the death certificate. She died from a mixture of alcohol and drugs. No foul play was suspected. The remains are on mortuary rotation.
    If I can be of further assistance, don't hesitate to call.
Office of Internal Affairs

Colt blinked. Natalie was dead.

He bowed his head. Later he would phone Jake to thank him for a masterful investigation. As for Natalie's body, he'd pay for it to be buried at one of the local Las Vegas cemeteries under the name Vicky Adams.

There was no decision to make where the children were concerned. They'd already said they wanted to leave the past in the past. That was what Colt intended to do.

With a new sense of peace that life had come full circle, he mounted Lightning and started down the mountain to find Kathryn. She was his future. Filled with exhilaration that they'd created a new life, he broke into a gallop.

"Hey, Colt!" one of the men called after him, but he was already too far away to answer.

* * * * *

The Sheriff's Christmas Surprise

MARIE FERRARELLA

Marie Ferrarella is a *USA TODAY* bestselling and RITA® Award-winning author who has written more than two hundred books, some under the name of Marie Nicole. Her romances are beloved by fans worldwide. Visit her website at www.marieferrarella.com.

Chapter One

It was a nice little town, as far as relatively small towns went. Hardly any trouble at all.

Which, when he came right down to it, was the problem. The town was nice; it was little and it was peaceful.

And Sheriff Enrique Santiago was restless.

Rick's people had lived in and around Forever, Texas, as far back as anyone could remember. This was especially true of the Mexican and the Apache branches of his family. The Black Irish contingent came later, but still far back enough to be only slightly less old than the veritable hills.

All three branches had left their indelible mark on Rick, found in his gaunt cheekbones, his blue-black, thick straight hair and his exceedingly vivid green eyes, which could look right through a man's lies.

He was a walking embodiment of the nationalities that called Forever their home. But he wanted something different, something that would make his adrenaline accelerate, at least once in a while. The need to feel alive was why he'd taken the post of sheriff to begin with.

But being sheriff in Forever meant breaking up an

occasional fistfight when the weather was too hot and tempers were too short. It meant making sure Miss Irene wasn't wandering around town in the middle of the night in her nightgown, sleepwalking again. Or worse, driving through the center of town in her vintage Mustang while sound asleep.

It wasn't that he hankered after dead bodies piled up on top of each other, but he did yearn for days that weren't all stamped with a sameness that had the capacity to drive a sane man crazy.

And that was why these days he was thinking about moving north. Specifically, Dallas. Not just looking, but doing something about it. He had a friend on the Dallas police force, Sam Rogers, a born and bred native of Forever. Sam had let him know that the Dallas police force was hiring again. So he'd filled out an application and requested an interview.

And waited.

A Captain Amos Rutherford had called him Wednesday and told him that they liked what they read and were interested. The man promised to get back to him about a time and place that was convenient for them both for the interview.

The promise of an interview had put a bounce in his step this morning, the day after Thanksgiving. Never one to dawdle, he got ready even more quickly than usual. Moving fast, he threw open the front door and his size-eleven boot came a hairbreadth away from kicking what appeared to be an infant seat that was smack in the middle of his doorstep.

An occupied infant seat.

The occupant of the infant seat made a noise just

before the toe of Rick's boot made contact with said infant seat. His hands flying out to the doorjamb in an effort to keep from pitching forward, Rick managed to catch himself just in time.

"What the—?"

Stunned and surprised but ever mindful of the five-foot nothing, formidable grandmother who had raised him, Rick bit off the curse that shot to his lips. He gazed down at the infant seat and the baby he very nearly had wound up punting across his front yard.

As if sensing the attention, the infant, all waving arms and gurgling noises, swaddled in blue, looked right back up at him. Intense blue eyes met green.

The baby was smiling.

Rick was not.

This had to be somebody's really poor idea of a joke, Rick thought, although the point of it eluded him.

Immediately, his deputies came to mind. He'd said more than once that nothing ever happened in Forever and his three-man team, which contained one woman, had also heard him say more than once that he was seriously thinking about leaving the small town because the boredom was getting to him.

This was undoubtedly their idea of "excitement."

Rick glanced around the immediate vicinity. He lived approximately five miles out of town, on a small plot that was barely half an acre. The terrain was as flat as an opened bottle of last week's ginger ale and if there was someone hanging around to witness his immediate reaction to the baby, they would have been hard-pressed to find a hiding place.

There was no one around.

Rick frowned and squatted down to get a close look at the baby. It didn't help. He didn't recognize the infant.

With a sigh, he picked up the infant seat and rose to his feet.

The baby was blowing bubbles, drooling on everything and appeared unfazed by the fact that he was out here, apparently all by himself for who knew how long.

Rick touched the baby's hand to see if it was cold. The temperature had dropped down to the upper forties during the night. The tiny, curled fist was warm. The baby had to have been dropped off in the past hour.

He scanned the area again. Still no one.

Rick had always had an eye for detail and for faces. His only requirement was that the faces had to belong to someone who was at least two years old. Prior to that, one baby looked pretty much like another to him.

Which was why he didn't recognize the infant he was holding.

"This someone's idea of a joke?" he asked out loud, raising his voice.

Only the wind answered.

Holding the infant seat against him with one arm, Rick gingerly felt around the baby to see if a note had been left and slipped in between the baby and the seat. As he disturbed the blanket in his search, an overwhelming, pungent odor rose up.

"Oh, you've got to be kidding me," he muttered, his nose wrinkling automatically.

His uninvited visitor made another, louder grunting noise, doing away with any doubts about what was going on. There was a full diaper to be reckoned with.

"Okay, enough's enough," Rick called out. "Take your kid back."

But no one materialized. Whoever had dropped the child off on his doorstep was gone.

Rick's frown deepened. "You didn't come with your own set of diapers, did you?" The baby gurgled in response.

"Yeah, I didn't think so," Rick muttered, shaking his head. "Hope you like dish towels," he told the baby as he walked back into the house.

Rick knew without having to raid his medicine cabinet that he had no powder to use on the baby, but because his Mexican grandmother had been adamant about his learning how to cook when he was a boy, he knew he had cornstarch in the pantry. Cornstarch was fairly good at absorbing moisture.

"Beggars can't be choosers," he told the infant as he appropriated the box of cornstarch off the shelf.

With nothing faintly resembling a diaper and only one set of extra sheets, which he was *not* about to rip up, Rick was forced to press a couple of clean dish towels into service.

Armed with the towels and box of cornstarch, he laid the baby down on the kitchen table and proceeded to change him.

He had no problem with getting dirty and more than once had sunk his hands into mud when the situation called for it. But when it came to this task, he proceeded gingerly.

And with good reason.

When he opened the diaper, he almost stumbled backward.

"What are you, hollow?" he demanded, stunned at just how much of a "deposit" he found. "How can something so cute be so full of…that?" he asked.

The baby responded by trying to stuff both fists into his mouth.

He was hungry, Rick thought. "Well, no wonder you're hungry," he commented. "You emptied everything out." As quickly as possible, he got rid of the dirty diaper, cleaned up his tiny visitor and put on the clean, makeshift replacement. "Let's get you back to your mama," he told the baby, laying him back down into the infant seat and strapping him in.

Within five minutes, Rick was in his four-wheel-drive vehicle, his unwanted companion secured in the back-seat, and on his way into town.

"You brought us something to eat?" Deputy Larry Conroy asked, perking up when he glanced toward the man who signed his paychecks as the latter came through the front door.

From where Conroy sat, he could see that the sheriff was carrying something. Given an appetite that never seemed to be sated, nine times out of ten, Larry's mind immediately went to thoughts of food.

"Not unless you're a cannibal," Alma Rodriguez commented, looking around Rick's arm and into the basket. "What a cute baby." She eyed her boss and asked, "Whose is it?"

Rick marched over to the desk closest to the door—it happened to belong to his third deputy, Joe Lone Wolf—and set the infant seat down.

Long, lean and lanky, Joe jumped to his feet and

looked down at the occupant of the infant seat as if he expected the baby to suddenly turn into a nest of snakes.

"I was just about to ask you three that," Rick answered, his glance sweeping over the deputies.

"Us?" Larry exchanged glances with the other two deputies, then looked back at his boss. "Why us? What do we have to do with it?" He nodded at the baby, who was obviously "it."

Hope dwindled that this was just a prank. "Because I figured that one of you left him on my doorstep."

Alma had a weakness for babies and a biological clock that was ticking louder and louder these days. She was making funny faces at the baby, trying to get the infant to laugh. "It's a he?" she asked.

"Well, yeah," Larry said, as if she should have figured that part out quickly. "He's wearing blue."

Joe slid back into his chair, pushing it slightly away from his desk and the baby on it. "Doesn't mean anything."

"It's a he," Rick confirmed, his tone indicating that the baby's gender was *not* the important issue. "And I want to know where he came from. Any of you ever seen him before?"

Forever had not yet cracked the thousand-occupant mark. Be that as it may, he wasn't familiar with everyone who called the small town home. In addition, Forever stood right in the path of a well-traveled highway and had more than its share of people passing through. For all he knew, this little guy belonged to someone who had made a pit stop in Forever for a meal and had gotten separated from his family for some reason.

Larry looked at the baby again and shook his head. "Nope, don't recognize him."

Joe had already scrutinized his temporary desktop ornament. "Never saw him before."

"How can you be so sure?" Rick asked. "They all look alike at this age."

"No, they don't," Alma protested. "Look at that personality. It's all over his face." She realized that the others were watching her as if she'd taken leave of her senses. "What? Just because you're all blind doesn't mean I have to be."

"So you recognize him?" Rick asked, relieved.

"I didn't say that," she countered. Turning back to the baby, she studied him one last time and then shook her head sadly. "No, I never saw him before. This baby's not from around Forever."

"You know every baby in Forever?" Larry asked skeptically.

"Pretty much," she answered matter-of-factly. "Hey, I'm a law enforcement officer. It's my job to notice things," she added defensively. Alma had to raise her voice to be heard above the baby, who had begun fussing. Loudly.

Joe looked at him. "I think the kid wants you to hold him."

"Since when did you become such an expert on babies?" Larry asked.

Wide shoulders rose and fell in a careless manner. "Just seemed logical, that's all," Joe responded.

"I'll hold him," Alma volunteered. But when she took the baby into her arms, he only cried louder.

Reluctantly, Rick took the baby from her. The infant instantly quieted down.

"Looks like you've got the knack, Sheriff," Larry chuckled.

If he had it, Rick thought, he didn't want it. People this small made him nervous. He could easily see himself dropping the baby.

"Why don't you take him to Miss Joan's?" Alma suggested. "Everyone who comes through town stops there to eat. Maybe she remembers seeing him with his parents."

"Or if he does belong to someone in town, she'd recognize him," Larry added, "just in case you *don't* know every kid in town, Alma."

Rick looked at his three deputies one by one, his deep green, penetrating eyes locking with each pair in turn. He knew them, knew their habits. Neither Larry nor Alma could maintain a straight face if this was a hoax. Joe, he wasn't so sure about.

But to his disappointment, not one of his deputies was grinning. Or looking guilty. This was on the level. Someone had left a baby on his doorstep.

Why?

Rick sighed, placed the baby back into the infant seat, strapped him in again and then picked up the infant seat. He looked down at the baby. The little boy was smiling again.

At least the kid had something to smile about, he thought.

"Anybody wants me," he murmured as he left, "I'll be at the diner."

JOAN RANDALL, fondly referred to as "Miss Joan" by everyone, had run the local diner for as long as anyone in town could remember. Five foot five, with rounded curves and hair that looked to be just a wee bit too strawberry in color, the years had been kind to her. For the most part, she'd kept the wrinkles at bay despite her advancing age. Her eyes were quick to smile and she had an earth-mother quality about her that coaxed complete strangers to suddenly open up and share their life stories with her.

She had the same effect on the people she rubbed elbows with on a daily basis.

Rick had once ventured that Miss Joan had heard more confessions than all the priests within a fifty-mile radius put together.

The older woman lit up when she saw Rick walk through the door, a fond smile growing fonder when she saw that he was not alone.

"Whatcha got there, Sheriff Santiago," she teased, coming around the counter to come closer to him. "A new deputy?"

"I was hoping you could tell me," Rick answered. He carefully placed the infant seat on top of the counter, making sure that the baby was secure and that the seat didn't wobble.

No longer being lulled by the soothing constant motion of Rick walking, the baby began to fuss and complain again.

Having come over on the other side of the counter, Miss Joan peered into the infant seat. She studied the infant for a moment, then raised her eyes to Rick's.

"Looks like the little guy who was in here yesterday," she told him.

"Do you remember what the people with him looked like?" Rick realized that the question had come out a bit testily. He was quick to apologize. "Sorry." He kept one hand on the infant seat; the other he dragged through his hair. "This hasn't exactly been one of my better mornings."

Miss Joan smiled understandingly, then her brown eyes shifted toward the baby.

"I'm sure this little guy could say the same thing." Leaning in closer, she cooed at the infant. "Where's your mama, honey?"

"You remember what his parents looked like?" Rick pressed again, hoping that he would be able to get to the bottom of this fairly soon.

If the boy's parents had really abandoned him, then there were consequences to face, but he was hoping a logical reason was behind this.

"I sure do, they were the only strangers here on Thanksgiving. They looked like two sticks," Miss Joan told him. "One thinner than the other." She frowned, recalling. "The guy hardly looked old enough to shave and he had one short temper. Kept complaining and telling the little bit of a thing with him to shut the baby up. The little guy kept fussing." She smiled as she nodded at the infant. "Like the way he is now."

"The baby's mama seemed kinda tense," Guadalupe Lopez, one of Miss Joan's three waitresses and the only one who worked part-time, volunteered as she set down the sugar dispenser she was refilling and crossed over to them. "I thought she was going to cry a couple of times.

I wanted to say something, but it wasn't my place. The customer's always right." She raised her eyes to her boss. "Right, Miss Joan?"

"Most of the time," Miss Joan amended. She turned her attention toward Rick. "I felt sorry for the baby and for his mama, but can't rightly say I was sorry to see them all go. That baby's daddy had a mean streak a mile wide. Didn't want any trouble—" Her knowing eyes shifted to Rick's face. "Unless it means that it would keep you hanging around here—and us—a little longer," Miss Joan said, looking at Rick significantly.

So what happened between yesterday and this morning to separate thin parents from chubby baby? Rick wondered. "Did you happen to see if his parents were leaving town or if they were visiting someone?"

"Looked as if they were headed out of Forever to me. I heard the guy saying something about wanting to burn rubber." Miss Joan slid her forefinger along the baby's cheek. Her smile deepened. "So where did you find this little guy?"

"On my doorstep."

The two women looked surprised. "Huh," Lupe uttered, looking amused. "Don't that beat all."

"Not hardly," Rick muttered. This didn't make any sense. He definitely didn't know anyone who resembled sticks. Why had they picked him to be the one they left their son with? Or had they picked him? Maybe it was just a random choice. "Look, I've got to go see if I can find these people and find out what the—" he glanced at the baby and switched words "—heck is going on. Would you look after him for me?"

He deliberately didn't address either woman, leaving

it up to them which one would say yes. When there was no immediate taker, he added, "I can't take him with me while I'm running down his parents. No telling how long I'll be out and I think the little guy's hungry."

The infant was back to shoving his fists into his mouth.

"I can see your point," Miss Joan agreed. She pursed her lips as she looked at the infant. "I've got a diner to run and I don't have much experience with short people." Her eyes shifted over to the petite waitress. Lupe came from a large family. Eleven kids in all and she was the oldest. "Don't you have a bunch of little brothers and sisters, Lupe?"

"Too many," Lupe said with a sigh. "Why? You want one?"

"No, but…" Miss Joan's voice trailed off, but her meaning was quite clear.

Lupe seemed to know better than to resist. Besides, it was obvious she thought the little guy was cute.

"I can take care of him for you, Sheriff," she volunteered. She turned the infant seat around toward her and began to unfasten the straps securing the baby. Freeing the infant, she picked him up. "But make sure you come back."

"Don't worry, I will," he promised. With that, he made his way to the door.

Rick was back faster than he intended.

Strictly speaking, he was back before he left. Opening the door, he was about to walk out of the diner when a statuesque blonde all but knocked him over. Contact was hard, jarring, and oddly electric as their bodies slammed together, then sprang apart.

Stunned, with some of the wind knocked out of her, the woman staggered, somehow managing to keep from falling, but just barely.

"I'm sorry, I didn't mean to run into you like that," she apologized in a deeply melodic voice that reminded him of aged whiskey sliding down the side of a thick glass on a chilled winter morning.

His badge and uniform seemed to register belatedly in her brain and she added, "But you're the man I need to see—" The baby made another noise, pulling her attention over to where Lupe stood holding the baby. Her eyes widened.

"Bobby!" she cried, appearing stunned and thrilled all at the same time.

Chapter Two

Trial attorney Olivia Blayne was seven steps beyond bone tired.

The twenty-nine-year-old had been on the road for more hours than she cared to think about, taking off the second she finally managed to get a lead on her younger sister's location. That was thanks to an ex-boyfriend who knew someone who could track down the coordinates of her last cell-phone call, a service which, ironically, she paid for.

In reality, she'd been paying for her sister since the day their parents had been killed, victims of a senseless robbery at the small jewelry store they owned and operated.

From the moment she'd left Dallas behind in her rearview mirror two days before Thanksgiving, Olivia had haunted every roadside diner from there to here—a small town two steps away from the border—in hopes of finding her sister and her three-month-old nephew, Bobby.

Ordinarily extremely law-abiding, she had driven like a woman possessed, determined to bring both of them back to Dallas—preferably over Don Norman's dead body, she thought bitterly.

But as the hours peeled away—and her stomach protested more frequently that she'd put off eating—Olivia started to despair that she was on a fool's errand and was never going to find either her sister or the baby.

Robert Blayne, her father and ever the pragmatic one, had taught her to rely on logic; Diana, her mother, to believe in miracles. In Olivia's estimation, she needed the latter, not the former. The former was far too daunting to think about now.

When she all but collided with the six-foot-something rugged officer in a khaki uniform, she found her miracle. Or at least half of it.

It took Olivia less than a second to recover and rush over to the young, fresh-faced Hispanic woman holding her nephew.

Her heart, all but bursting with joy, leaped into her throat.

"Bobby," she cried again, tears smarting her eyes. She blinked twice, refusing to let them escape. She'd always hated women who broke down and cried. Crying was a sign of weakness and she couldn't allow herself to be weak, not even for a moment. Far too much depended on her being strong.

Olivia stretched out her arms to the infant, eager to take him from the petite, dark-eyed waitress.

Hesitating, Lupe looked toward Rick for guidance and he nodded. Only then did she let the baby be taken from her by the woman in the deep blue—and somewhat dusty—power suit.

Bobby felt like heaven in her arms. For a second,

Olivia pressed her cheek against his, just savoring the moment, the contact.

"Oh, Bobby, I was beginning to think I'd never see you again," she whispered to him.

Bobby wriggled, making a noise and seeking freedom. Reluctantly, Olivia loosened her hold on him, resting him against her shoulder. She'd discovered that, at least for now, it was his favorite position.

"So 'Bobby' is yours?" In Rick's estimation, the question was a needless one, but he still had to ask it. There were rules to follow, even in a town as small and laid-back as Forever.

The question indicated that the sheriff thought Bobby was her son, so she said, "No." The second the word was out, she negated her response, afraid that the man might think she was just some crazy woman, jumping at the chance to grab a baby.

God knew she probably looked the part, she thought, catching a glimpse of her reflection in the aluminum-covered bread box.

"Yes."

The woman in the expensive suit looked just a bit flustered, her pinned-up hair coming loose in different sections. Rick allowed his amusement to show. "Is this like some kind of a Solomon thing?"

For a moment, Olivia didn't answer. She hadn't realized how good it would feel to have this little bundle of humanity in her arms again until she'd begun to believe that she never would.

"No." Swaying just a little to lull the baby, Olivia continued to hold him against her shoulder as she looked at the man with the rock-solid chest and the annoying questions. "Bobby's my nephew." One hand cupping the back of Bobby's downy head, she turned and scanned the all-but-empty diner. A sinking feeling was setting in again. Tina wasn't here. "Where's my sister?" she asked.

Rick had a question of his own for her. "I take it that's the baby's mother?"

At twenty-four, Tina had turned out to be much too young to be a mother. Or at least, much too immature. But, for better or for worse, Tina was still Bobby's mother.

"Yes."

Rick nodded, leaning back against the counter. "I was hoping *you* could tell me where she was."

Damn.

Olivia focused on the small-town sheriff for the first time, her eyebrows drawing together as she did a quick assessment of the man, a skill she found useful in the context of her present vocation. She could tell if a man was being sincere, or if he was lying. The only time her ability seemed to fail her was when it came to Tina. But maybe that was because the thought of her sister lying to her, after all that they'd been through, was particularly hurtful.

She wanted to believe that Tina was better than that. Wanted to, but really couldn't. Not any longer. Not after the disappearing act she'd pulled.

"Sheriff, I've been trying to find Tina and the lowlife who forced her to run off with him for the last forty-eight hours. All I know is that she should be somewhere around here."

As she spoke, Olivia became aware that the matronly

looking woman behind the counter, who was quite blatantly listening intently to every word, had placed a cup
of coffee and a powdered bun on a small plate practically directly in front of her.

Olivia raised her eyes to the woman's, an unspoken
question in them.

The woman was quick to smile. "Thought you might
need that right about now, honey," the older woman said.
"You look like you're running on empty."

Admitting a weakness, or even that she was human,
was not something Olivia did readily, even to someone
she'd never see again. But she had been turned so inside
out these past few days, what with one thing and another,
that the protest that quickly rose to her lips turned into
a simple "Thank you."

The next moment, giving in to her tightening stomach, she look a long sip of the inky coffee. And felt
human again. Almost.

Watching, Miss Joan slanted a quick look toward
Rick and then chuckled, pleased that, once again, her
intuition had been right.

"I was gonna ask if you wanted cream and sugar with
that, but I guess not."

"Better?" Rick asked the baby's aunt when she came
up for air and set down the cup.

Olivia nodded. "Better." Her eyes shifted toward the
woman behind the counter. "How much do I owe you?"
she asked, setting her purse on the counter and attempting to angle into it with one hand while still holding
Bobby.

Miss Joan waved away the gesture. "It's on the house,
honey." And then she winked. "It's my good deed for

the day. Everyone should do one good deed every day. World would be a whole lot nicer," she declared with a finality that left no invitation for debate.

Rick had waited patiently for the almost criminally attractive woman to finish her coffee. He figured it would help her pull herself together. He wasn't going anywhere and there was no hurry, but he did want some answers. Most of all, he wanted to know why the infant had been left on his doorstep. Was it happenstance, or was there some reason he'd been singled out?

"Is your sister an underage runaway?" he asked the baby's aunt.

Olivia sighed. "Tina's not underage, she's twenty-four and technically, she's not a runaway." She set her mouth hard as she thought of her sister's boyfriend. She had tried, really tried, to make him feel welcome—she should have had her head examined—and drop-kicked the jerk into the middle of next year. "He forced her to go with him."

Rick raised an eyebrow. First things first. "Who's *he?*"

Olivia laughed shortly. The sheriff had inadvertently echoed her own sentiments. Just who *was* the tall, gangly, brooding individual who looked like a poor, dark-haired version of a James Dean wannabe? Or maybe it was that new sensation, the actor who was playing a vampire, that Don fancied himself to resemble? Whoever Don Norman envisioned himself to be, he had managed to brainwash her sister, turning Tina into some kind of mindless lemming who would follow this worthless human being off the edge of a cliff.

Well, not while she was around, Olivia silently vowed.

Not while there was a breath left in her body. If she had to, she would drag Tina back kicking and screaming and sit on her sister until she came to her senses.

But none of this did she want to share with a virtual stranger no matter *how* good-looking he was. Her sister's insanely poor judgment was her business. It was *not* up for public scrutiny.

"*He* is Don Norman," she told the sheriff. The moment stretched out and she knew the man was waiting for more. "And ever since he came into my sister's life, Norman has turned it upside down, and turned my sister into some pathetic, mindless groupie."

"Groupie," Rick repeated. The word had a definite connotation. He made the only logical connection. "This Norman's a musician?"

Olivia laughed shortly again. Don thought of himself as a musician, but as far as she knew, he'd never gotten paid and was currently part of no band.

"Among other things, or so he says," she replied crisply. "Mostly he's just a waste of human skin." She looked down at the baby in her arms.

Please don't take after your father, she implored Bobby silently.

"Sounds like you don't like him much," Miss Joan speculated, wiping down the same spot on the counter that she'd been massaging for the past few minutes.

"No, that's not true. I don't like him *at all*," Olivia corrected. "I tried, for Tina's sake." She patted the baby's back, moving her hand in slow, small concentric circles. The repetitive movement tended to soothe him. "And for Bobby's. But it's really hard to like someone who repays you for putting him up for six months by stealing your jewelry."

"He stole your jewelry?" Rick asked, his interest in the case piquing. "You're sure that he was the one who took it and not—"

Olivia saw where the sheriff was going with this and cut him off.

"Tina didn't have to steal anything from me. All she had to do was ask and I'd give her whatever she needed. I *have* been giving her everything she's needed." Olivia pressed her lips together. *And how's that working out for you?* a voice in her head jeered. "Norman's the thief," Olivia insisted. "He stole the jewelry, he stole my sister. I don't care about the jewelry, that's replaceable," she told the sheriff, struggling to hold on to her temper. It wasn't easy. Just thinking of Don pushed all her buttons. "My sister is not. And I am really afraid that something terrible is going to happen to her if she stays with the man."

She raised her eyes to the sheriff's. It killed her to ask a stranger for help, but she knew when she was out of her element. Tina's welfare took precedence over her pride.

"Can you help me find them, Sheriff?"

He'd always been a fairly decent judge of character. He had a feeling that the woman before him was used to taking charge of a situation. Was this actually nothing more than a glorified matter of power play? Did she resent the fact that her sister had run off with a boyfriend she disapproved of?

"If your sister left with this Norman guy of her own free will—" Rick began.

Olivia knew a refusal when she saw it coming. Quickly, she changed strategies. "All right, then go after him for stealing my jewelry. I'll press charges. Whatever it takes to get him out of my sister's life and mine, I'll do it."

"I'd be careful how I phrase that if I were you," Rick warned her.

Olivia felt her back going up. She'd been through a lot these past few days and there was precious little left to her patience. "I'm a lawyer, I don't get careless with words, Sheriff."

"And there's abandonment," Lupe chimed in, speaking up for the first time. "You could get this guy for that."

The word "abandonment" suddenly sank in. Olivia realized that with her mind racing a hundred miles an hour and going off in all different directions at once, she'd gotten so caught up in finding the baby, she hadn't asked the sheriff a very basic question. There was a huge chunk of information she was missing.

"What are you doing with my nephew in the first place, Sheriff? Why do you even have him?"

"I found your nephew on my doorstep this morning when I was leaving for work," he informed her matter-of-factly.

"On your doorstep?" Olivia echoed, stunned. "That's impossible. Tina would have *never* let Bobby out of her sight." She paled as a possible explanation came to her. "Unless something's happened to her." Her eyes widened as she caught hold of the sheriff's arm, a sense of urgency telegraphing itself from her to him. "Sheriff, you've got to help me find—"

"Don't go getting ahead of yourself," Rick told her. He thought of one plausible explanation, although it was a stretch. "Maybe your sister figured that what was ahead was too dangerous for the little guy."

He was being kind, making up an excuse to calm the blonde with the ice-blue eyes. In his heart, though, he believed that perhaps the woman's sister had gotten bored with playing house and had decided to abandon her latest toy, leaving him in the first place that came up. Maybe they'd passed his place on their way out of town and impulsively decided to drop the baby off on his doorstep.

Technically, his mother had done that, Rick thought, leaving him and his younger sister, Ramona, with her mother-in-law. He could still remember what she'd looked like as she'd promised to be "back soon."

"Soon" had turned into close to eighteen years. By the time she actually *had* returned, he didn't need her, or her lies, in his life. She'd come back too late. He'd grown up with a substitute mother, his tough-as-nails grandmother, molding his life and Mona's. Maria Elena had been a hard taskmaster, but her heart had been in the right place and she had made him the man he was today. And for that, he would always be grateful to the pint-size martinet.

"Or maybe Don felt that the baby was dragging them down and he told my sister to get rid of Bobby—or else," Olivia said.

"But he is the baby's father, isn't he?" Lupe asked, horrified.

"The baby's his," Olivia allowed slowly. "But it takes

more than getting a woman pregnant to make a man a father," she said with feeling, raising her chin.

Rick saw the anger in her eyes and found the sparks oddly fascinating.

"That vermin has no more of an idea on how to be a father than a panther knows how to walk around in high heels," Olivia declared angrily.

"Interesting imagery," Rick commented. He glanced down at her feet and saw that she was wearing fashionable shoes whose heels could have doubled as stilts. They had to be around five inches. How did she manage to walk around in them?

"Feet hurt?" he guessed.

They did, but that was something else she wasn't about to admit. Besides, she'd gotten used to the dull ache.

"No," she denied. "Why do you ask?"

"Haven't seen heels that high since the circus came through a couple of years ago." He glanced at her shoes again, shaking his head. The women he knew were given to jeans and boots. But on the other hand, he had to admit the woman had a great set of legs. Best he'd seen in a very long time. "They just look like they might hurt."

She lifted the shoulder the baby wasn't leaning against in a partial shrug. Bobby'd fallen asleep and she wasn't about to disturb him. Olivia lowered her voice. "That all depends on what you get used to," she told him, the inflection in her voice distant.

The woman wasn't kidding when she said she knew her way around words. "I suppose you have a point. By the way," he said, and extended his hand toward her. "I'm Sheriff Enrique Santiago—Rick for short."

There was no way this man came up short in any category, Olivia caught herself thinking before she blocked any more personal observations.

Where was her mind?

Impatient with her oversight—names should have been exchanged immediately—rather than put her hand into his, she wrapped her fingers around his hand, automatically assuming the dominant position. "Olivia Blayne."

"Olivia?" he echoed. She couldn't tell if the sheriff was amused or charmed. "Now there's a name you don't hear every day." Amused, she decided, he definitely sounded amused. Why? "What do they call you?" he asked.

Undoubtedly he was waiting for her to render up a nickname, something along the lines of "Livy," or maybe "Livia." He couldn't possibly be thinking of "Olive," she thought in horror. That name conjured up the image of a certain tall, skinny cartoon character from her childhood days.

There'd been a boy in the neighborhood, an older boy—nine to her seven—Sloan something-or-other, who'd teased her mercilessly. He'd called her Olive because she had been that skinny back then. The nickname had turned into the driving force that motivated her to not only put some meat on her bones, but to get fit as well. She'd been relentless about the latter in her teens.

"Olivia," she informed him tersely. Only Tina got to call her something else. Tina called her Livy, but right now, Olivia didn't know if she was up to hearing that name.

Many thoughts crowded her head. She was far too worried that something had happened to her sister. She was absolutely certain that Tina would have *never* just left Bobby like that. Not unless she wasn't around to prevent it.

Don't go there!

If it turned out, mercifully, that Tina was all right, she was going to kill her sister with her bare hands for putting her through this, Olivia thought angrily.

She took a deep breath, forcing the dark thoughts into the background. Instead, she focused on the infant sleeping on her shoulder. Focused on how good, how soothing that felt, to know that he was safe and that he was here, with her. It allowed her to pretend, just for the moment, that everything would be all right. That Tina was all right.

"Where are you from?" Rick asked.

"Dallas," she told him. A look she couldn't read came into his eyes. "We're both from Dallas."

That was over four hundred miles away. She was a long way from home. "How did you happen to track them to Forever?"

"Luck," she replied. Because she could feel his eyes on her, waiting, she elaborated. "Tina called a friend of hers, Rachel. She told Rachel that she thought she'd made a mistake, but it was too late to change things. Rachel knew I was looking for Tina so she kept Tina on as long as she could. I have a…" Olivia hesitated for a moment, looking for the right word, then settled on "friend at the cell phone's service center."

There was no need to say that Warner had also been someone she'd once cared about until things got too serious, spooking her. For now, maybe forever, she was committed to her career and her sister—and Bobby— and that was more than enough.

"He managed to get the location of Tina's last call to Rachel triangulated. I used the coordinates and came here instead of Nuevo Laredo," she said, mentioning another small town in the area. And then an idea occurred to her as she said the name. "Maybe that's where they went," she said hopefully.

"Easy enough to check out," he told her. "You have a picture of your sister?"

Olivia smiled in response. It was a confident smile, the kind that lit up a room, and a man if he happened to be in the path of it, Rick speculated.

Shifting slowly so that she didn't wake the baby, she told Rick, "I can do better than that."

Yes, he thought, *I'm sure you can.*

The next second, he upbraided himself for his lack of focus.

She put her hand into her purse, rifling around, searching for the copy of the picture she'd almost forgotten to bring with her. She'd had to double back to the condo in order to pick it up. Finally locating the object of her search, she pulled it out and held it up for him to see.

"It's a picture of my sister with the slime."

Rick bit the inside of his mouth to keep from laughing. He had a feeling that Olivia Blayne would interpret it as laughing at her and wouldn't appreciate it.

Chapter Three

Rick studied the photograph he'd been handed.

"Not bad looking, as far as slime goes," he commented.

The woman in the photograph looked more like a girl, really, and clearly resembled her older sister. They had the same golden-color hair, like a spring sunrise in the desert. The same bone structure as well, but while on the girl, it appeared almost too delicate, on the woman in the diner, it seemed far more classic and refined. He could see her moving with ease through influential circles in high society.

Indicating the photograph, he looked back at Olivia. "Mind if I hang on to this for a bit? I'd like to send it out with the APB." Realizing that he was guilty of just tossing around initials that she might not be familiar with, he began to explain, "That's an—"

"All points bulletin," she concluded for him. "Yes I know. You don't have to stop to break things down to their lowest level for me, Sheriff. I am familiar with some of the terms used in law enforcement." And then, because she needed something to hang on to, something to reassure her, despite her facade of confidence and bravado, that Tina was all right, she asked, "Did you happen to see my sister when she was in town?"

Rick took another glance at the photograph. Though he sensed she wanted to ask him questions about her sister, about her condition and how she'd seemed to him, he'd seen neither of the two individuals she attempted to locate.

He shook his head. "Sorry, I didn't."

Miss Joan ceased overcleaning the counter and spoke up. "I did."

Olivia instantly gravitated toward the owner of the diner. "How did she look? Was she all right?" Though Olivia had never seen any firsthand evidence of it, she strongly suspected that Don had a temper. Without a hovering older sister, he'd be free to treat Tina any way that he wanted to.

The very thought brought a numbing chill down her spine.

An intuitive look came into Miss Joan's kind hazel eyes. "I didn't see any bruises, if that's what you're asking," the older woman told her. "But your sister did look like she could do with a decent meal and about a day's sleep. I felt sorry for her, but there wasn't anything anyone could do." There was more than a trace of regret in Miss Joan's voice. "The guy she was with kept her on a real short leash. And he didn't seem too happy about this little fella fussing and crying," she added, nodding toward Bobby. "In my opinion, someone needs to take that boy behind the barn for a good whopping."

Rick could see the woman beside him growing progressively tenser. Olivia's hands fisted, even as they held the sleeping baby against her, and her expression hardened.

"Shooting him would be better," Olivia murmured with feeling.

He had a feeling she meant it. The woman certainly wasn't the squeamish type, he thought. The sooner he tracked down the missing pair and sent them all on their way, the better.

Sliding off the stool, he saw the question in her eyes. "I'm going to go post that APB, see if anyone's seen your sister and her boyfriend. You wouldn't happen to know the kind of car they were driving, would you?"

Not only did she know the kind of car they were driving, she rattled off the make, the model, the color and the license plate for him in a single breath, right down to the long scratch on the driver's side bumper.

"You've got a good eye," Rick commented, impressed. In his experience, women who looked like Olivia Blayne didn't know their way around cars, much less absorb that much about them.

"I've got a good memory," she corrected. "Don doesn't have two nickels to rub together. The car belongs to Tina. I bought it for her when she graduated high school."

"Wish I had a sister like you," Lupe said wistfully. A look from Miss Joan had her going back to filling sugar dispensers.

Rick hadn't heard what Lupe said. He was busy studying Olivia, trying to get a handle on her. She sounded more like an indulgent parent than an older sister.

Aware of the sheriff's penetrating scrutiny, Olivia called him on it. "What?"

"Let me get this straight. You bought your sister a car. If I understood correctly what you said, she lives with you and you took in her no-account boyfriend even when you didn't want to." Most women Olivia's age either lived on their own or with a lover, not a younger sister and that sister's deadbeat boyfriend. At least not if they could afford a place of their own, as she so obviously could.

Olivia seemed impatient for him to get to the point. "Yes?"

"Well, looking at those kinds of facts, I'd guess that you were compensating for something." His eyes held hers. She knew she could turn away at any time, but she decided to face him down. "Were you?" he pressed.

Her first impulse was to indignantly say no, but she wouldn't cut this short. She'd always zealously guarded her privacy, hers and Tina's. Her second impulse was to tell this would-be Columbo in boots and a Stetson that it was none of his damn business and just walk away. But she couldn't.

She needed him.

Finding Tina would take a lot longer if she went about it on her own and the man had resources he could tap. Those resources could prove very useful and time saving in the long run.

Besides, she assumed that he was familiar with the area. She definitely wasn't. That all added up in his favor, even if he was too nosy for her own good.

Since the sheriff continued watching her, quietly waiting for a response, she had to tell him something. Otherwise, she ran the risk of alienating the man. And while alienating people normally didn't bother her, this time it might prove to be a liability.

Oh, damn it, Tina, why couldn't you just stay put? Why are you such a flake? What would Mom and Dad say if they were alive now?

If they were alive now, none of this would have happened. Tina had adored their father and would never have done anything to incur his disapproval.

Instead, Tina had become involved with someone who had no redeeming qualities whatsoever, gotten pregnant and then irresponsibly run off. And on top of that, from at least outward appearances, she'd abandoned her baby. Something like that could get her locked up for a long time in a place like this, Olivia thought.

After a moment's debate, she decided to tell the sheriff something she didn't normally share. None of the people at the firm where she worked were aware of this. But maybe if Santiago knew, it would make him go easier on Tina.

Right now, she could see that he wasn't about to nominate her sister for Mother of the Year, or even of the hour. And she just wanted to take Tina and the baby home, not hang around to do battle over any kind of charges he would want to bring against her sister.

Taking a breath and mentally bracing herself for the words she was about to say, Olivia began. "Ten years ago, my parents were gunned down in the jewelry store they operated." The corners of her mouth curved in a humorless smile. "Gunned down for two hundred twenty-three dollars and seventeen cents. That was all the money that was in the register. The rest were credit card receipts that did the thieves no good.

"My sister," Olivia continued grimly, "was in the store at the time, in the back, doing her homework. The gunmen never saw her, but she saw them and what they did. I couldn't get her to talk for a week."

She remembered rushing home from college. Remembered the awful, empty feeling inside her as she'd identified the lifeless bodies of the people who had once filled the corners of her world so richly, so lovingly.

"Tina started acting out shortly after that, getting into fights at school. Crying at the drop of a hat. She was always afraid to go out by herself, always looking over her shoulder." Olivia looked up at him and lifted one shoulder in an almost hapless shrug. "I did what I could to make her feel safe."

Rick didn't follow her reasoning. "By giving her things?" he asked.

Olivia inclined her head. "Among other things," she allowed. She could see the sheriff didn't understand. Most men wouldn't, she supposed. "Possessions give you a feeling of stability, of continuity. Owning something *feels* good."

Rick laughed shortly. The sideways logic interested him, not that he bought into it.

"Then Ed Murphy must feel really stable," he commented. When she raised a quizzical eyebrow in response, he told her, "Ed's one of Forever's more eccentric citizens. He's always pawing through things other people throw out. A lot of that stuff finds its way into Ed's one-bedroom house. I hear it's like a rat's nest in there these days."

She didn't know if he was just relating a quaint story or subtly ridiculing her. Sheriff Enrique Santiago looked like a simple man on the surface—sexy as all hell, but simple—but she had a strong suspicion that beneath those prominent cheekbones was a rather shrewd, logical man.

For now, she decided to reserve her final judgment, at least for a little while. She hadn't gotten to the position of junior partner in her rather highly regarded, high-profile firm so quickly by making hasty decisions and snap judgments.

"About that APB," she prodded.

"On it," he assured her. With that, he turned on his heel and started for the door. When she followed him, shadowing him step for step to the door, he stopped short. "Are you coming with me?"

She smiled. "Can't put anything over on you, can I?" she asked in what she hoped he'd take to be a teasing manner. She had to keep reminding herself not to get on his wrong side and that she needed him.

He glanced at Miss Joan. "I figured you'd be more comfortable staying here." And he would be more comfortable going about his job without having her less than five feet away.

"Comfort isn't my main priority," she informed him, her voice growing more serious. "If you don't mind, I'd like to go with you, see what you do."

Having a beautiful woman around was way down on his list of things he minded. But, in this case, he knew it wasn't just to keep him company. "Don't trust me to send out that APB?"

He *was* sharp, she thought. He seemed a little too laid-back for her taste and she just wanted to make sure that he did everything he could to locate Tina. But she knew that admitting as much would be a tactical mistake, male egos being what they were, so she forced another smile to her lips, one that was a little sensual around the edges, and said, "No, I just like leaving myself open to new experiences."

The amused smile that came to his lips told her that she could have phrased that considerably better.

She was tired, Olivia thought, and there was no denying that emotionally she'd been through the ringer these past forty-eight hours. That was the reason she wasn't at the top of her game.

"Nice to know," he responded.

She could have sworn a twinkle had entered those incredible green eyes.

Or what could have passed for one, she amended silently. Seeing as how she'd never encountered a "twinkle" before that wasn't captured within an old-fashioned string of Christmas lights. Like the ones her father used to string up around the house during the holidays, she remembered fondly.

The next moment, Olivia felt a pang in the center of her chest. That she missed her parents went without saying, but she missed them the most around this time of year. Thanksgiving this year had been spent with her searching for Tina, an emptiness eating away at her as she stopped at one diner after another, encountering dead ends and pitying looks.

She didn't even want to think about what Christmas might be like if she didn't find Tina.

Decorations had started going up all over Dallas right after the pumpkins had been put away. That only prolonged her nostalgia and the sadness that inevitably overtook her. There was a very real chance that this year, she would wind up spending Christmas alone. Alone because she'd lost touch with all her friends in her drive to succeed, to give Tina a sense of stability and try to meet her every need. Alone because Tina wouldn't be there.

Damn it, since when did you turn into this maudlin, self-pitying creature? Your life is what you make it, so make it good, Livy, make it good.

Besides, she wouldn't be alone. If nothing else, Bobby would be there and Bobby needed her.

She hugged the baby to her a little tighter.

"Hey, aren't you forgetting something?" Miss Joan called out after them.

Olivia turned around, reaching into her purse with her free hand. Obviously the woman had changed her mind about being generous. Just as well.

"I offered to pay you," Olivia reminded the woman, crossing back to the counter.

Miss Joan merely shook her head, a patient, tolerant expression on her face.

"I was talking about the baby's infant seat," she said, pointedly holding it up. Olivia had left it on the counter after taking her nephew into her arms.

Rick was at her side in two steps, picking up the seat.

He nodded at Miss Joan. "Thanks." With that, he was back at the front door in time to open it for Olivia and the baby. The latter began to rouse from his all-too-short nap.

"I think he might be hungry," Miss Joan speculated,

raising her voice so that they would hear her as they walked out of the diner.

Stopping again, Rick looked at Olivia. He hadn't thought of that. For the most part, babies were beyond his realm of expertise. "She has a point. I could swing by the grocery store," he volunteered. "Pick up some milk and a baby bottle—"

"Or we could go to the backseat of my car," Olivia interjected, stopping him before he could go any further. "I packed a few bottles and some formula for Bobby before I left. Tina only took one bottle with her." A smile that was equal parts affectionate and long-suffering resignation came over her lips. "Tina doesn't exactly plan things out."

But Olivia wasn't like her sister, Rick observed. She came prepared. He found that to be an attractive quality in a woman.

"She's not alone," he told her. "I see that a lot as sheriff."

Olivia unlocked her car. "You can put the seat in the back," she told him.

Seeing as how the diner was barely five feet away, he found the fact that she'd locked her vehicle before leaving it amusing. People didn't lock their doors in Forever, much less their cars. In part that was because people trusted one another around here. In part it was because there wasn't all that much worth taking. It all worked out in the end.

And all that did was remind him that his job was superfluous. A halfway intelligent monkey could handle it. He needed something more challenging.

No sooner had he deposited the seat into the back

than Rick found himself on the receiving end of Olivia's nephew, who was now fully awake and not in the best of moods.

"Hold him for a second," she said after the fact.

He cradled the infant in the crook of his arm. "You asking me or telling me?"

"Whichever works," she answered glibly, then inclined her head in a semiapology as her tone replayed itself in her head. He undoubtedly thought she was being too bossy. God knew Tina had accused her of that often enough. "I'm sorry. I have a habit of issuing orders. Comes from taking charge so much, I guess. I didn't mean to offend you."

Secure in his manhood and comfortable in his own skin, it would take a great deal more than a petite blonde in expensive high heels and a designer suit to rattle his confidence. Her apology, however, did surprise him. He would have put money on her never actually apologizing for anything she did.

Maybe you *couldn't* always tell a book by its cover. "No offense taken," he answered. "I was just being curious."

Shifting the baby to his other arm, Rick peered over Olivia's shoulder into her vehicle. He was about to ask if she wasn't worried that the formula might have spoiled in the car, but he had his answer before he got to ask the question. She'd brought along a large cooler filled with ice and baby formula. He noticed that she'd also brought along several packages of disposable diapers. They were piled up on one side.

Rick laughed to himself. Olivia Blayne struck him as the kind of person others gravitated to during a natural disaster. She obviously knew how to think on her feet and was prepared for anything.

Except a runaway sister.

But then, if he was being honest with himself, he still wasn't a hundred percent convinced that her sister hadn't opted to run off rather than have every moment of her life planned out by a well-intentioned but highly dictatorial older sister.

Or at least that was what he would have surmised Tina's feelings to be on the matter.

If it wasn't for the fact that the baby had been left on his doorstep, Rick had to admit that he would have been inclined to just let the whole matter go, even if the woman making the charge was, hands down, the most gut-tightening attractive woman he'd laid eyes on in a very long time.

Beauty-contest-winner pretty or not, though, that still didn't make Olivia Blayne right, he thought.

Bottle in hand, Olivia straightened up, hit the lock on the rear door and closed it.

"Do you have a microwave or a stove where I could warm this up?" she asked, indicating the chilled bottle in her hand.

"We have a microwave," he assured her. There was one in the small room where he and the others took their lunch and occasionally, when he had someone sleeping it off in their only cell, their dinner. "We got it just after we learned how to make fire by rubbing two sticks together," he couldn't resist adding.

Olivia opened her mouth to respond, then shut it again. She would have to be more careful how she phrased things around this small-town sheriff, she chided herself. There was obviously a vein of sensitivity beneath the rock-solid pectorals.

Taking her nephew back from his arms, she flushed slightly. "I'm sorry, I didn't mean to sound as if I thought you were backward in Forever."

"But you do, don't you?" he asked knowingly. There was no indication that he took offense at that, or even that he found it irritating. "Think it," he added when she looked at him quizzically.

"No," Olivia denied with feeling, then, as he continued to look at her knowingly, she relented. "Well, maybe just a little. This *is* a small town," she said by way of what she hoped he'd accept as an explanation.

"Little or not, progress finds us all," he assured her, then confided in a conspiratorial whisper, "We've even got one of them there newfangled com-pew-ters. Now if we could only figure out how to make it work."

"All right, all right," she surrendered, "point taken. I'm sorry. I'm really not trying to be condescending. Having to track down my sister and Bobby has thrown me off track. I'm usually a lot better than this."

"Looking forward to seeing that," he told her with a wide smile that somehow found its way into her belly a moment before it unfurled.

The next moment, she quickly blocked the feeling that flowed out through her. Olivia deliberately shifted her eyes away from him and wound up looking at the single-story building that housed Forever's police department.

The only thing that mattered, she told herself as she

followed the sheriff inside, was finding Tina and taking her home.

She didn't have time to think about anything else.

At least, not now.

Chapter Four

Humming a bastardized version of "Here Comes Santa Claus," Alma emerged from the back storage closet carrying a huge, somewhat worn cardboard box that looked to be almost half as big as she was. Written across the side in big, block letters, were the words *Christmas decorations*. With a dramatic sigh, the female deputy set the box down on the small table against the wall that functioned as the catchall for everything that didn't have an assigned place within the office. During the holidays, it housed the pint-size Christmas tree as well as any baked goods that generous citizens—or Alma—wanted to send the sheriff's department's way.

Only when she set her burden down did Alma see the sheriff and the person and a half who were with him in the office.

Olivia felt a definite chill as the woman regarded her.

"I see you found the baby's mother." The expression on the deputy's face was far from friendly. It wasn't hard to see what she thought of a woman who left her baby on someone's doorstep.

"No, this is his aunt, Olivia Blayne," Rick told Alma.

Alma's expression softened a degree. "She's been looking for the baby. And for her sister."

"Her sister, the mother?" Alma asked, still eyeing Olivia.

"Got it on the second try," Rick congratulated the woman drily. He glanced at the teeming box the deputy had set down. Once Alma got caught up decorating, there was no stopping her. "Look, I need you to stop decorating the office for a minute and put out an APB for me."

"Haven't started decorating yet," Alma informed him. Resigned that the decorating would have to wait, she held her hand out. "Give me the information." Rick gave her both the paper he'd written on and the photograph of the missing duo. Alma glanced at the photograph first, then looked at the description of the car. Raising her eyes to her boss, she shook her head. "You should've been a doctor, Sheriff. Medical people appreciate handwriting that looks like a chicken did a war dance after stumbling over a bottle of ink."

Joe glanced up from the book he was studying. He'd been taking classes online, intent on eventually getting a degree in criminology. His face remained expressionless as he told her, "You can't say that," in his low, rumbling voice.

They'd been together so long, they were like siblings, she, Joe and Larry, with a sibling's penchant for squabbling.

"Say what?" Alma asked.

"'War dance,'" Joe told her.

Alma pressed her lips together, annoyed. "Why not? You say things like that all the time."

Joe went back to reading. "I'm a full-blood Apache, I can make any reference to Indians I want to. One of the few pleasures that your government forgot to take away from us," he deadpanned.

Alma's eyes shifted toward the sheriff.

Rick raised his hand before she could speak, waving away anything that might have risen to her lips. Friendly squabble or not, he was not about to get pulled into this.

"Just get that APB out for me," he told Alma. "Now."

She sat down at her desk and looked at the paper again. Her brow furrowed as she turned the paper upside down, pretending to try to make sense of what was on the page. But she really couldn't decipher what Rick had written down.

"What kind of a car are we talking about?" she finally asked.

"It's a red Mustang, 2004," Olivia filled in, moving over toward the woman's desk.

"Red Mustang, huh? Shouldn't be too hard to spot," she commented. She moved the keyboard closer and began to type. "How long have they been gone?" she asked conversationally.

"They took off several days ago. This is the closest I've gotten to finding them." Despite the fact that she was swaying slightly in an attempt to soothe her nephew, Bobby was becoming more audible about his displeasure. Olivia turned toward the sheriff and held up the bottle she had in her other hand. "You said there was a microwave around here?"

About to point her in the direction of the back room, Rick decided he might as well take her there himself.

Alma, who was far better at the computer than he, was taking care of putting out the APB. So right now, nothing was on tap except some annoying paperwork that required his attention. The paperwork wasn't going anywhere.

"This way," Rick said, walking in front of the woman and her fussing nephew.

The room that did double duty as a kitchen/break area and storage facility was only slightly larger than a walk-in closet. The window on the opposite wall gave it the illusion of being larger than it was.

Rick pointed out the microwave. It sat in the middle of a table that looked only a fraction more sturdy than a folding card table. The microwave itself had seen better days. It had come to them, a second-hand donation from Miss Joan, who had upgraded the one in her diner.

Olivia shifted the baby to her other side, trying to prop him up on her hip. The boy was still too small for that and she didn't want to have to juggle him while testing the milk. Putting the bottle inside the microwave, she selected a time, then pressed Start. When the oven dinged, she turned to the sheriff and held the baby out to him.

"Hold him, please," she requested,

Now what? Rick eyed her uncertainly. Why was she giving him the boy? "You want me to feed him?"

She opened the microwave and took the bottle out again. "No, I need to test the milk to make sure that it's not too hot for Bobby."

Olivia shook out a few drops on her wrist. Then, because she didn't want to just let the milk slide down her skin onto the floor, she quickly licked the drops up.

Why he found that simple act so sensual and arousing was something Rick told himself he'd have to explore at a later time. Right now, he figured it was best not to go there.

"What's the verdict?" he asked.

She smiled, setting the bottle down on the table for a moment and holding out her arms. "It's warm, but not too hot."

"Like the fairy tale," Rick commented, handing the baby back to her.

"Fairy tale?" Olivia asked, curious. Sitting down, she tucked Bobby against her and started feeding him. The moment she placed the nipple near his lips, he started sucking greedily.

"Goldilocks and the Three Bears," Rick told her, resting a hip against the table as he watched the baby eat. "You know," he elaborated, "too hot, too cold, just right."

"Oh, right." Her mind hadn't gone in that direction for a reason, which she explained. "I didn't take you for the type to know fairy tales."

Rick laughed shortly. "I didn't just appear one day, wearing a badge and a gun belt. I was a kid once, just like you were."

The smile that came to her lips was sad, distant, as if she was trying to access something and wasn't quite successful. She looked down at her nephew, taking comfort in just watching him. "I don't remember ever being a kid. It feels like I was always an adult."

He read between the lines, remembering what Olivia had said to him earlier. "How long have you been at it?"

Her eyes met his. "'It'?"

He nodded. "Taking care of your sister."

She didn't even have to stop to think. She could have told him the figure in months if he'd wanted it that way. "Ten and a half years."

No wonder she didn't remember having a childhood. She practically hadn't. She had to have been in her teens when she'd taken on the responsibility. "That's a long stretch."

She smiled at his choice of words. "You make it sound like a prison sentence."

He paused for a moment, his eyes on hers. The woman didn't sound bitter about it, which he found impressive. "Is it?"

"No," Olivia said with feeling. "I love my sister." She didn't want him thinking she was being a martyr about this. Nothing could be further from the truth. "Do I wish that Tina was a little more responsible? Yes, of course I do, but that doesn't mean I don't love her."

"Didn't say you didn't." Finished with his bottle, the baby's mouth had traces of formula all over it. Rick took out his handkerchief and gently wiped away the milky substance. "But life's a complicated thing. You can love someone and still find that there are times you don't like them very much."

To be honest, he expected more denials. He was surprised to see that he'd evoked a smile from the woman instead.

Her eyes crinkled a little as she said, "You have siblings." It wasn't a question.

Rick began to tuck the handkerchief back into his pocket and was surprised when Olivia put out her hand for it. He surrendered it to her and watched as she spread it over her left shoulder.

"One," he told her. "A younger sister."

"We have that in common then." Placing Bobby against her shoulder, Olivia gently began to pat the baby's back, waiting for the obligatory burp. "Except that your sister is probably one of those superresponsible types."

He had no idea how she had guessed that. "She is." Then he explained, "Abuela wouldn't have allowed her to be anything else."

"Abuela," Olivia repeated slowly, searching for a match in her memory banks. And then she brightened just as Bobby burped. She kept him there a little longer, in case more was going to come up. She didn't want to risk her suit getting more stained than it already was. Her dry cleaner would probably tear out what little hair he had left when he saw what she wanted him to clean this time.

"That's 'grandmother' in Spanish," she said, pleased that she remembered.

He had no idea why it would matter to him one way or another that she spoke Spanish. After all, it wasn't exactly that unusual. For more than half the population of the state, Spanish was either a first or second language. But it did.

"That it is."

Olivia gleaned a few things from his tone, putting her own interpretation to it. "Your grandmother raised you, didn't she?"

He was ordinarily the one asking the questions, not

answering them, but he indulged her. For now. "She did."

If his grandmother had raised him, that meant that his parents hadn't been around to do it. Did she have more in common with him than she thought?

"Did your parents pass away, too?" she asked quietly, as if the occurrence demanded reverence.

For a moment Rick thought of ignoring the question, or acting as if he hadn't heard her. But she'd probably only ask again. Besides, he wasn't ashamed of his background and everyone around town knew his history anyway. That was both the good thing and the bad thing about living in a town the size of a small, above-ground pool. Everyone knew everyone else's business.

That being the case, there didn't seem to be much point to being secretive. Even if this woman was just passing through.

"I haven't the slightest idea," he answered.

Olivia was quiet for a moment, digesting his answer and taking it apart. She was right, she thought. The sheriff *had* looked particularly incensed when he thought her sister had willfully abandoned Bobby. Undoubtedly that was because he'd been abandoned himself.

Though her expression didn't change, she found herself feeling for him. Her parents had had no choice in the matter. What kind of a mother willingly walks out on her child?

Olivia lowered her eyes, cradling Bobby in her arms. "Oh."

For reasons he didn't quite fathom, he wasn't annoyed, he was amused. "That was a really pregnant 'oh.'"

Olivia shrugged, pretending to be engrossed in cleaning away the telltale signs of Bobby's last burp from his little round face. "Sorry. I didn't mean to pry."

The hell she didn't. "You said you were a lawyer, right?"

This time, she did raise her eyes and look at him. "Yes."

"Isn't that inherent in your nature, then? To pry?" He rephrased it to seem less hostile. "To find things out?"

"I'm not being a lawyer right now," she told him, letting down her guard. His sharing something private with her had stirred her compassion. "I'm just a worried aunt and sister." She paused for a moment. "And I'm sorry about your parents."

He eyed her quizzically. "What about my parents?"

Maybe she shouldn't have ventured onto this ground, but for a moment, there had been a connection, a kindred feeling. And, since she had opened this door, she might as well walk through the doorway with dignity.

"About them not being there for you," she told him. "I know what that feels like."

He didn't doubt that she *thought* she knew what that felt like. But their situations were ultimately very different. "How old were you when your parents—"

"Nineteen," Olivia answered quickly.

"Then you don't know," he said matter-of-factly. "I was eleven." The world looked a lot different to an eleven-year-old than it did to someone who was mostly grown. "My sister was six. My father had been long gone by then. One day my mother dropped us off with her mother-in-law, saying she'd be back soon," he recounted, trying his best to separate himself from his words. "Turns out that she and my grandmother had a difference of opinion when it came to the meaning of the word 'soon.' To my grandmother it meant a couple of days at the most." Rick shrugged. "Probably less."

"And to your mother?" She had a feeling she knew the answer.

He set his mouth grimly. His eyes were steely as he said, "Fourteen years."

That was still less time than she'd thought, Olivia said to herself.

"Hey, Sheriff," Alma called from the next room.

Rick straightened, moving away from the table. He was glad for the interruption. He wasn't sure what had come over him, but he'd shared far too much with this woman who'd been a complete stranger to him an hour ago. Shared a hell of a lot more than he normally did with people he actually knew.

He had no idea what had compelled him to run off at the mouth like that, except that there was something about her eyes, something that transcended rules and decorum and seemed to pull the words out of him.

Though it sounded absurd, it was as if the woman was looking right into his soul.

Asking him to look into hers.

He was applying for this job in Dallas just in time. A few more months in Forever and he'd be ready for the loony bin. Maybe sooner. There was absolutely no earthly reason for him to be waxing philosophical like this.

People who sat around spinning theories about why someone did or didn't do something ordinarily annoyed

the hell out of him—and here he was, voluntarily joining the ranks.

Definitely time for a change of scenery, a change of
venue.

Rick got his mind back on business and away from
wondering what other threads he and the woman with
the hypnotic blue eyes had in common.

"Coming," he called back to Alma.

Before he could cross to her, Alma told him, "I think
I found a match."

Olivia's heart leaped into her throat. She had no idea
why a feeling of dread suddenly washed over her. This
was what she wanted, to find her sister. Why then was
she afraid to hear what the sheriff's female deputy had
to say?

Feeling as if she was getting up on borrowed legs,
Olivia rose to her feet and followed the sheriff into the
main room, every step she took resounding in her head
and body.

"That was fast," Rick commented to Alma. He glanced
at the monitor beside her computer.

"People remember a red Mustang," Alma said. "Especially one that crashed into a utility pole."

"Crashed?" Olivia cried, struggling to rein in the
deep fear that seized her heart.

For a second, she couldn't breathe. That was the anxi-
ety kicking in, she told herself, trying to work her way
out of the terror that threatened to overwhelm her.

She wasn't going to pass out, she told herself firmly.
She *wasn't*.

All she needed to do was just hang on for a second
and the room would stop spinning and settle back into

place. Silently, she talked to herself the way she did to a nervous witness when she was taking a deposition. Calmly. Soothingly.

"Yeah," Alma said in response to the single-word question. The deputy shifted her chair so that both Rick and the woman with him could clearly see what was on her monitor. She pointed to the bottom of the monitor, where the short notification started. "It says here that there was an accident." She began to read. "A 2004 red Mustang, heading northwest, was clocked going about ninety-five miles an hour when it suddenly swerved and careened into a utility pole."

Holding Bobby tightly against her, Olivia stared at the screen. She tried to read, but none of the words sank in.

"Does it say if they—if they—"

Olivia couldn't bring herself to say the words that were tantamount to ushering in death. Instead, she went at the information from another angle.

"Does it say if they're all right?"

Standing behind her, Rick had quickly scanned the report himself. It wasn't very long.

Turning toward her, he said, "Looks like you're not going to be having any more trouble with your sister's boyfriend."

She knew what that meant, but she needed to hear him say it. "Don's dead?"

The sheriff nodded. "Says here he died instantly at the scene."

Oh God, oh God, oh God. She couldn't stand the man, but she hadn't wanted to see him dead—just gone.

Her mouth felt utterly dry as she pushed the next words out. "And my sister? Tina? Was she—"

He spared her the agony of finishing the question. "She was badly injured. They took her to Pine Ridge."

She didn't understand. "But it says here that the accident happened in Beaumont."

"It did," he told her. "But Pine Ridge is the site of the closest hospital."

That meant that her sister was alive. They didn't transport dead people to the hospital; they took them to the morgue.

She looked at the sheriff, her heart pounding. "But she's alive, isn't she?" she asked in a whisper. If she raised her voice she knew it would crack.

He nodded, and his voice was gentle as he answered, "According to the feedback."

It was a noncommittal answer, but she'd take it. She desperately needed to hang on to something while she pulled all the threads together—again.

"Okay," Olivia said, trying to center herself, to gather the thoughts that were scattered in all different directions. "Okay," she repeated. "We'll go to Pine Ridge. Bobby and I will," she clarified.

"You'll need directions," he told her.

No, she thought, she'd need strength, but there was no handy dispenser lying around to give her some of that. She had to dig it up and tap into it.

In response to his observation, she shook her head. "No, I don't need directions, I've got a GPS. I'll be all right." *And, please God, let Tina be the same.* "Thanks for all your help," she said as she quickly hurried out of the office.

Chapter Five

Rick wouldn't have been able to say why he followed her outside. Maybe it was a sense of duty mingled with curiosity. He'd already decided that she was a stubborn woman and, for the most part, stubborn people both irritated him and turned him off.

But not her.

And if asked, he wouldn't have been able to explain exactly why.

Maybe that was where the curiosity part came in.

She looked around, as if to decide which direction to take in order to find the diner. It was obvious that she wasn't exactly a tracker.

Amusement pulled at the corners of his mouth. Common sense kept it from surfacing. "At least let me drive you over to the diner," he offered.

She would have wanted to say no, but that would be living up to the old adage about cutting off her nose to spite her face. She wasn't sure which way to go to get to the diner and she didn't want to ask the sheriff because it would make her seem stupid. The people around here were probably born tracking.

"That would be very nice of you," Olivia said. "Thank you."

"No problem." He opened the rear passenger door so she could deposit the infant seat and then the infant.

Ultimately it took almost less time for him to drive back to the diner than it did for Olivia to secure the infant seat in the rear of the police car. She remained in the back with her nephew for the short hop back.

He glanced in the rearview mirror, his eyes meeting hers. "She's going to be all right," he assured her with quiet confidence.

Had there been something in the report he hadn't mentioned? "How do you know that?" she asked.

"I don't," he admitted. She felt her spirits dip drastically. "I just know it helps to keep a positive thought."

"Right," she murmured, looking out the window. All the positive thoughts in the world hadn't kept her sister from running off with that lowlife.

Bringing the vehicle to a stop, he was quick to get out. Rick rounded the hood and was at the rear passenger door, opening it for her before she had a chance to remove the seat belt she'd secured around Bobby's infant seat.

He stuck his head in and nodded toward the baby. "Let me take him for you."

She was about to say that she didn't need his help. The words rose automatically to her lips. But while that might be true in this instance, letting the sheriff take the baby allowed her to exit the vehicle with some semblance of modesty, rather than just sliding out with the baby in her arms and her skirt up somewhere between her thighs and her waist.

Once she was out, rather than hand over the baby to her, Rick walked to her car. There were now several other cars parked in front of the diner, but he had no trouble finding hers. Even if he hadn't seen her retrieving the bottle and formula from the cooler, he would have known the vehicle was hers. They tended toward practical cars around here, mostly four-wheel drive and all-terrain vehicles.

No one in Forever had an expensive car that was just for show. Certainly not a Mercedes.

A sense of practicality didn't keep him from admiring her car, though. It was a beauty.

Like the woman who drove it.

Where the hell had that snuck in from? he wondered, caught off guard. It seemed to him that he was paying a hell of a lot of attention to someone who was, at best, just passing through. It wasn't like him.

Still, he was a servant of the people. Or so it said somewhere in his job description. The term that was used was "people" not "just the citizens of Forever." That meant, in an odd sort of way, he was her "servant" as well.

So he asked the kind of question a concerned servant was wont to ask.

"Are you sure you don't want me to take you to Pine Ridge? It's easy to get lost around these parts. Some of the towns around here never even make it to a map. Just a cluster of a few buildings with a handful of people in them."

Having opened the rear passenger door, Olivia was trying to secure the infant seat to the cushion and having less than complete success. Why was she all thumbs like this?

The sharp pain in her heart told her that she knew the answer to that. Olivia didn't want to go there. She did anyway, albeit involuntarily. She wasn't thinking straight because she was worried about Tina. Worried that, even now, it might be too late. That Tina was dying this very minute.

Olivia banished the notion from her mind. Instead, she addressed the sheriff's offer. Maybe another time, she might have let him drive her. But right now, she wanted to be alone. In case she cried. She didn't want any witnesses.

"Pine Ridge is large enough for a hospital, right?" she asked, tossing the words over her shoulder as, kneeling on the backseat, she continued to struggle with the infant seat.

Rick found that he had to exercise extreme control to keep from staring at what might have been the best well rounded posterior he had seen in a very long time. Forcing himself to blink, he raised his eyes up toward the back of her head.

He was in time to witness part of her hair coming undone as she hit her head against the inside of the roof. Several bobby pins came raining down, as did another section of her hair.

Still on her knees, she stopped what she was doing and turned around in the car to look at him. "Right?" she asked again.

It took him a second to vaguely recall the initial question. Something about Pine Ridge and being big enough for a hospital. "Right."

"Then it should be on the map." She sighed, wiggling back out again. "That seems pretty secure," she said, more to herself than to him.

She'd drive just under the speed limit, she told herself. The infant seat—and its precious cargo—would be fine if she kept a steady pace.

Even so, for good measure she stuck the cooler on the floor just beneath where the infant seat was. That should keep it wedged in, even without the belts.

"If I could have my nephew back," she said, the corners of her mouth curving just a little. The sheriff looked rather comfortable holding Bobby. She caught herself wondering if he was married and how many children he had. Not that it mattered.

Rick surrendered the baby, placing Bobby in her arms.

"Hang in there, sweetie," she said to Bobby.

Turning, she ducked back into the rear seat, this time to secure her nephew into his seat. And once again, Rick found himself captivated, staring at her shapely anatomy and trying very hard not to let his imagination take over. He reminded himself that, after all, he *was* the sheriff. But then again, sheriffs were not plaster saints.

Out of the corner of his eye, he saw Miss Joan at the diner window, looking out on to the parking area. Observing him with a knowing smile.

That old woman needed a hobby, Rick thought. One that didn't involve turning everything she saw into gossip.

As Olivia ducked back out of the rear of the vehicle, he reached into his breast pocket and retrieved a business card. He'd had fifty printed up when he first took the position some four years ago. He still had close to that number left. The phone number to the sheriff's department was a matter of record. Other than numbers taking the place of the initial two call letters, the department's number hadn't changed. People knew it by heart.

But she didn't.

"Here." He held the beige card out to her. "It's the department's number," he explained. "In case you find you need help with getting your sister home."

She dealt better with adversity and challenges than with kindness. Kindness threatened to undo the barriers she'd worked so hard to construct around herself. Threatened to make her vulnerable. He was offering something that went above and beyond the call of duty.

She tried to give the card back. "Thank you," she said stiffly. "But I won't need it."

"Take it anyway," he urged. He surprised her by placing his hand over hers and urging her fingers to close around the card. "You never know."

"But I do," she contradicted. "I know my limits and my capabilities and I'm perfectly capable of finding this particular needle in the haystack." Again she held the card out to him.

But he wouldn't take it back. "Humor me."

She sighed softly and, because he was so close to her, he felt a little of her breath against his cheek.

The reaction was automatic.

His gut tightened in response. Accompanied by an unnerving tingle.

"All right," she murmured. "If it makes you feel better—"

"It does," he assured her. A beat later, an easy smile underscored his words.

Olivia placed the card on the dashboard of her immaculate Mercedes and got in behind the wheel.

"Thanks again," she said, shutting the driver's side door. Placing her key into the ignition, she turned it.

And heard absolutely nothing.

Frowning, she repeated the process.

With the exact same results.

Her frowned deepened. Olivia removed the key and then reinserted it in the ignition, hoping that the third time would be the charm.

It wasn't.

This time, however, there was a small whimper coming from what sounded like the front end of her car. When she tried turning the ignition on for a fourth time, the small whimper suddenly turned into the very grating sound of metal on metal, and from every indication, neither piece of metal was faring very well in this screeching, unexpected confrontation.

The last go-round had set Rick's teeth on edge. It was infinitely worse than nails being dragged along a chalkboard. He squatted down so that he was level with the open window on the driver's side and asked mildly, "Problem?"

Frustrated, Olivia pressed her lips together. The man knew damn well there was a problem. A problem she couldn't fix. All she knew about cars was where to put the gas. She was willing to bet that men around this area were born with a torque wrench in one hand and a can of motor oil in the other.

With effort, she forced herself to sound civil and not stressed out. "It seems that way."

She didn't have time for this. Every moment she wasted here was a moment that—God forbid—she might not have with Tina.

Though she hated resorting to this, Olivia raised her eyes innocently to his and asked in the most helpless female voice she could muster, "Can you fix it?"

The question amused him. He wondered if the big-city attorney just assumed he could lay hands on the hood and bring it back from the dead.

"Depends on what 'it' is," he told her. "Pop the hood."

"All right," she said gamely, then looked around for an icon on the dashboard that would point her in the right direction. There wasn't any. Though it bothered her to admit ignorance, if she sat there any longer, the sheriff would figure it out on his own. "And how do I do that?"

He congratulated himself on not laughing. "Here, let me pop it for you," he offered.

She slid out and he slid in, taking her place. The seat felt pleasantly warm against the back of his legs, the warmth working its way through the fabric of his uniform. He did his best not to dwell on that, or on the woman who had warmed the seat with her own.

Finding the hood release on the lower left side of the dashboard, just below the steering column, Rick pulled the handle up. The hood made a slight rumbling noise as if it were attempting to separate itself from the rest of the car. Satisfied, Rick got out again.

He raised the hood and looked down into the belly

of the car. Doing so yielded no insight for him. There was no telltale smoke rising up, no cracks that he could readily see. A quick check of the dipstick told him that at least her oil was full and running clean. He let the hood drop back into place, then pushed it down so that the latch would catch.

"Well?" Olivia pressed impatiently. "Do you think you can fix it?"

He shook his head. "I'm afraid this is a job for the mechanic."

"All right," she said. Hands resting on her hips, she looked around for a garage with the appropriate sign hanging out front. She didn't see one, but that only meant that this mechanic the sheriff was referring to had to be located in the heart of this postage-stamp-size town. "Where is he?"

"Fishing."

"Fishing?" she echoed incredulously. This was becoming a nightmare.

"That's what I said," he answered easily. Taking out his handkerchief, he swiftly wiped his hands, then tucked the handkerchief back in his pocket.

"And he's the only mechanic around here?" she questioned.

"Only one we've got. He should be back Monday," he assured her.

"Monday?" Olivia rolled her eyes. "What am I supposed to do until Monday?" She had hoped that everything would be resolved by Monday. That Tina and the baby would be back home and she could be where she belonged. At the firm. "How am I supposed to get to Tina if he doesn't come back until Monday?"

He was as laid-back as she was frazzled. "We could go back to my original suggestion," he said in an even, unhurried voice. "I could take you up to Pine Ridge myself."

There was that, she supposed. But she hated being in anyone's debt, no matter what that debt was. If you were in debt, they could call it in at any time, collect at any time. She didn't like what that implied. Constantly waiting for the other shoe to drop wasn't the way she wanted to live her life.

But in this case, she didn't appear to have a choice. Not if she wanted to be there for Tina—and to see with her own eyes that her sister was really all right.

So she nodded, none too happily. "I guess I don't have any choice."

"No," he contradicted, "you have a choice. You could wait here until Mick comes back on Monday."

With her luck, the mechanic would fall off the fishing boat and drown. But she had another idea, a better idea than having the sheriff as her chauffeur. "Is there anywhere around here where I could rent a car?"

He shot down her hopes with a single word. "Nope. No reason to have one of those. Everyone's got their own car around here."

"Whether it's running or not," Olivia muttered under her breath in disgust. She took a breath and tried to put her best face on. "If the offer's still open, I'd like to take you up on it." God, she thought, it almost sounded as if she was begging.

"The offer never closed," he said mildly.

Apparently tired of playing a passive part and watching through the window, Miss Joan opened the door and walked out of the diner. She stood on the first step, a force to be reckoned with.

"You two can leave the baby with me," she called. "This way, you won't have to be stopping every half hour or so to feed him, or change him, or to keep him from crying."

Stunned, Olivia glanced from the owner of the diner to the sheriff. "How did she—"

"Miss Joan reads lips," Rick explained, clearing up the mystery. "Her parents were both deaf and she wanted to be able to relate to them, see what life was like for them with their challenges."

"No law against readin' people's lips," Miss Joan said cheerfully. She crossed to the Mercedes and looked into the back, where the baby was still strapped into his infant seat. "It's not like invadin' their privacy and readin' their mail," she added with a toss of her head, her bright red hair bouncing about.

"Oh, but it is if they're talking in low voices and have a reasonable expectation of privacy," Olivia countered deliberately.

Miss Joan stopped and awarded her with a long, sweeping look. Olivia felt as if she was being x-rayed. "I forgot, you're one of those lawyer types." The older woman definitely didn't seem impressed.

Startled, Olivia looked at the sheriff. He had obviously told her. When had he had the opportunity to talk to the diner owner about what she did for a living? And what else had he said to the old crone?

As if reading her mind, Rick raised his hands, fingers spread, shoulder level, a man surrendering before the shooting started.

"Don't look at me. Miss Joan has this knack of just knowing things." He smiled at the older woman fondly. "There's some talk that she might be a bit clairvoyant." He said it to humor Miss Joan, not because he believed it for a minute.

She would have opted for the woman being a witch, Olivia thought darkly. Or, more likely, someone who eavesdropped a lot. Whatever the explanation, she didn't like the woman presuming things and just taking over. She liked the idea of leaving her nephew with a stranger even less, especially since she'd come so close to losing him. She was having a real problem with the idea of letting him out of her sight.

Miss Joan had already removed all the straps and freed Bobby from his seat. Taking him into her arms, she was cooing something unintelligible to the little boy and Olivia could have sworn he was giggling. That was gas, correct? she thought.

"She's right," Rick was saying. "We can make better time without bringing your nephew along." The way he saw it, the boy would be better off in one place. "And he couldn't be in better hands than Miss Joan's."

How did she really know that? Olivia wondered. She just had the sheriff's word for it. He was a stranger to her. For all she knew, he could be a serial killer. The diner owner could be one as well. Experts were only now discovering that there were a lot more women serial killers than they had initially believed.

Stop it, she silently shouted at herself. *You're making yourself crazy. For once in your life, take something at face value and be done with it. Graciously accept the woman's offer. You'll be back soon enough to pick up the boy. What are they going to do, sell him into a white slavery ring before you get back?*

Olivia set her mouth grimly. She had no choice, really. If she took Bobby along, she knew the sheriff was right. Bobby would slow them down and she had this uneasy feeling—most likely paranoia, but it was there nonetheless—that she really didn't have time to waste. She needed to get to Tina's bedside as soon as possible. And, with any luck, get to the bottom of why her sister had left Bobby on the sheriff's doorstep. There *had* to be a reason, she silently argued. Tina wasn't *that* much of a flake. She absolutely refused to believe that she was.

So, summoning her best courtroom smile, the one she flashed to telegraph confidence to the people sitting in the jury box, Olivia looked at the diner owner and said to the older woman, "Thank you, Miss Joan. I appreciate the help."

Miss Joan chuckled knowingly as she cuddled the baby against her. "You don't right now, but you will. In time."

Olivia had no idea what the woman meant by that, but she had a feeling that she might regret asking for an explanation, especially given the condition of her nerves. So she merely nodded and let the comment pass, chalking it up to something that only another native of Forever would understand.

Chapter Six

As she opened the passenger-side door and started to get into the sheriff's car, Olivia stopped and looked over her shoulder at her own car. The sports car appeared completely out of place beside the other vehicles, like a debutante who had unwittingly wandered into a soup kitchen.

She glared uncertainly at the sheriff. "Um, is it all right to just leave my car in front of the diner like that?"

The sheriff smiled and Olivia instantly felt her back going up. Was he laughing at her, or at the question? Either way, she felt foolish.

"If you're asking me if anyone's going to strip your car for all those pretty little parts it has, no, they're not. We tend to respect property around here. Besides, Miss Joan's got a dog, Bruiser. Big dog," he added. "Just the thought of Miss Joan letting him loose keeps those with a little larceny in their hearts on the straight and narrow. I wouldn't worry if I were you," he assured her.

Rick got in, put his seat belt on and suppressed a sigh. Olivia was still standing outside the passenger side. Had she changed her mind about going?

He leaned over to the right so that his voice would project better. "Something wrong?"

Olivia unconsciously bit her lower lip. Something new to worry about, she thought. She peered into the car and asked, "Is it safe to leave Bobby here with that dog around?"

Hindsight told him that maybe he shouldn't have mentioned Bruiser. The lumbering, part Labrador, part German shepherd and all puppy despite his advancing age, was exceeding gentle around children, as if he instinctively knew that he could accidentally hurt them if he wasn't careful.

"Bruiser's a lovable lamb when it comes to kids," Rick assured her. "Miss Joan has to yell, 'Go get 'em' for Bruiser to go after someone. And even when he 'gets' them, he doesn't hurt them—much," he couldn't resist adding with a grin.

"Then he *has* gone after someone?" Olivia asked uneasily, looking back at the diner.

"So legend has it," he replied patiently. "It was a trucker, passing through. Didn't think he had to pay for his supper. Bruiser made him change his mind. And it was just the one incident. But that was enough to put the fear of God into any would-be thief." That was the point of the whole story. "Your car's safe. And so's your nephew."

Trying to put a lid on her uneasiness, Olivia slowly sank down onto the passenger seat. She didn't bother with the seat belt. Rick waited, leaving the key in the ignition, untouched. After a beat, she realized he was waiting for her to buckle up, which she did. With a nod of approval, he turned on the ignition.

She felt testy and argumentative and annoyed with herself for being that way, but she couldn't help it. "Tell me, if this place is so law-abiding, why does it need a sheriff?"

Rick laughed quietly under his breath. In private, there'd been times he'd asked himself the same question. The short answer was that it made the people in town feel safe to know someone official was looking out for them.

Out loud, he said, "To make sure Miss Irene isn't sleepwalking through the middle of town at midnight, or thereabout, in her nightgown. Or worse, driving while she's asleep. And there's the occasional drunk who needs to be locked up for the night for his own good."

"Is Miss Irene Miss Joan's sister?" she asked. Just how polite were these people? If she lived here, would she automatically become Miss Olivia?

And why the hell was she thinking about that? She'd rather be marooned on a desert island than live in a place like this.

"The term's a sign of respect for ladies who've seen close to seventy years or so," Rick answered, turning the vehicle toward the right.

Olivia's lips pulled into a thoughtful frown. For all intents and purposes, it sounded as if she'd fallen, head-first, into an old *Andy Griffith Show* rerun. Places like this didn't really exist, did they? Was Forever really this simple, this uncomplicated, full of kind souls, or was it just a veneer under which was a cauldron of bubbling darkness, of secrets that were eventually going to erupt?

Since she wasn't saying anything, Rick glanced in her

direction and saw the frown. In his opinion, he hadn't said anything that was frown-worthy.

"What?" he asked.

"I was just wondering about what you said. About guiding old women in their nightclothes back to their homes and locking up the occasional drunk for his own good." She looked at him, trying to get a handle on the man beside her. He didn't appear to be particularly sleepy eyed. What was he doing in a place like this? "Is that enough for you?"

She knew that it certainly wouldn't have been enough for her. The description he'd given her sounded downright boring and, if nothing else, he appeared to be a very vital man in the prime of his life. Didn't he want to achieve something? *Make* something of himself?

Her question rang in his head. No, it wasn't enough for him. Which was why, he thought, he'd sent in the application to the Dallas police department. Because he kept thinking there had to be something more.

But the topic was personal as far as he was concerned and she was a stranger, albeit a hell of a sexy one. He didn't share personal feelings with strangers—not without a good reason, at any rate.

"It was," Rick said evasively.

Olivia was quick to pick up on the keyword. "Was," she repeated. She studied his profile. "But it's not anymore?"

He turned down another street. "I thought you said you were a lawyer."

"I am."

Olivia noticed that when he took information in, he

nodded. Like now. "Do the lawyers from where you come from dabble in psychology as well?"

She responded to the question with a laugh and a careless shrug. "Sheriff, we *all* dabble in psychology, whether we realize it or not. You do," she pointed out, turning the tables on him.

"Me?" he asked a tad too innocently.

The sheriff's tone told her all she needed to know. That not only was he aware of using psychology, but that he thought he already had her pegged.

Not by a long shot, Sheriff.

Most men she ran into these days thought they had her pegged. In her company only for a few minutes and they began to assume she was ambitious to the point of being driven. They didn't realize that ambition had nothing to do with it. She was carving out a place for herself at the firm for one reason and one reason only.

Security.

She'd had to take care of herself and Tina for all these years. And now there was another little mouth to feed— and to send off to college someday. That took more and more money—money that, it had sadly been proved over and over again, didn't grow on trees. Money that was only generated—if she was lucky—by the sweat of a hardworking brow.

Her brow.

If everything went well and there were no upsets, perhaps Tina would add a little something to the bank account in time, but right now, the real responsibility for taking care of everyone fell on her shoulders and would continue to in the foreseeable future.

So she worked her proverbial tail off and sacrificed.

Predominantly what she sacrificed was her social life. Other than attending office functions, she had no social life to speak of.

In the beginning, when she'd begun to work at the firm of Norvil and Tyler, the friends she'd once had made attempts to include her in their gatherings. But she always had to beg off for one reason or another, because she was working twice as hard as anyone else at the law firm. She was trying to become indispensable.

After a while, her friends stopped asking her to go out with them. By now they'd gone on to live their lives without her.

All she had in her life was her work and Tina. It was enough, she told herself.

"You," she assured him, answering his question. "I'm sure you size up everyone who happens to pass through your town."

"Only if they require my services," the sheriff told her.

There was just a touch of humor about his mouth, enough for her to momentarily wonder just what those services he was referring to were.

Oh, damn, Liv, you are overwrought, aren't you? Stop having R-rated thoughts about Rick Santiago and focus on what's important. Getting to Tina. Bringing her and Bobby home. Who cares what kind of "services" the cowboy with a badge renders?

She was roused abruptly out of her wandering thoughts when she realized that they weren't leaving town. They were going back to his office.

He pulled his vehicle up in front of the squat building. "Why are we stopping?" Olivia asked. Had he changed his mind about driving her to Pine Ridge after offering to do it? Was this payback for her asking him questions? He didn't seem like the vengeful type, but then, how much did she actually know about this man with the sexy smile? Next to nothing, really.

Rick got out and closed his door. "Just want to tell Alma where I'm going and let her know that she's in charge."

"You're putting a woman in charge?" Maybe the man was more progressive than she thought.

The look the sheriff gave her was patiently tolerant. Olivia could feel herself bristling—and becoming embarrassed at the same time.

"Why not? Alma's good at her job," Rick told her. "Besides, I know I can count on her to give me the biggest bribe." He saw Olivia's eyes darken with disappointment. "That was a joke," he told her drily. "I guess I better not quit my day job any time soon." He paused for a moment and looked into the vehicle. "You might want to make use of the facilities," he suggested, motioning toward the building with his head. "It's going to take us a few hours to get to Pine Ridge."

Olivia pursed her lips, struggling not to take offense. Did he think she was ten? Or the flip side of the coin, did he think she was a doddering old woman who needed to be reminded that she had to go to the bathroom periodically?

"I'm fine, thank you," she said tersely.

Rick shrugged at what he saw as her stubborn refusal. Made no difference to him one way or the other.

"Suit yourself. You don't strike me as the type to

relieve yourself on the roadside, that's all. And the land's pretty flat from here to there. We'll be lucky to see any brush at all, much less find it just when you might have a need—"

"I said I was fine," she repeated, quickly cutting him off before he could get too explicit.

Rick stood where he was for a moment, his eyes sliding over her slowly, as if assessing what she'd just declared.

"Yes, I'd say you are," he agreed. Straightening, he began walking toward his office. "I won't be long."

"I'll wait here," she assured him in case he was going to ask.

"I expect you will," he replied without bothering to turn in her direction.

SHE WISHED THAT THE SHERIFF hadn't made such a big deal about going to the bathroom before they left Forever. She silently blamed him for the fact that she was unusually preoccupied with the thought that she had to go, and that she would *really* have to go before they reached civilization again.

Suppressing a sigh, Olivia stared out the window at the desolation that stretched before them. Granted, as a native Texan, she was more than aware that this was, for the most part, what her home state looked like. But living in Dallas was like living in any large city. A person tended to forget that the world beyond the sophisticated urban boundaries was mostly rural. And when she was jockeying for position on one of the main highways threading through Dallas, desolation like this slipped her mind.

But here it was, miles of nothing with more miles of nothing just beyond that.

Without her trusty GPS or even a map, she had no idea where they were or how far they'd come. Unable to hold back the question any longer, she turned toward the sheriff and raised her voice to be heard above the country and western music playing on the radio. "How much farther?" Olivia asked.

Rick hid his smile and congratulated himself on pulling it off. "To Pine Ridge?" he asked innocently.

Olivia lost her slender hold on her temper. "No, to Disneyland. Of course to Pine Ridge."

The look on his face told her that he thought he saw right through her. "Anyone ever tell you that you've got the personality of a rattlesnake when you're uptight? I told you to use the facilities," he reminded her matter-of-factly.

She made up her mind right there and then that she would rather die before she would own up to needing to use the great outdoors as a not-so-great bathroom. "I'm fine," she insisted. "And for your information, I *don't* have the personality of a rattlesnake. I'm just anxious about Tina."

"Being anxious isn't going to change anything," he told her. Someone on the radio was hawking a contest for tickets to the latest country and western touring concert. Rick turned the radio down. "Might as well just think positive thoughts."

She wondered if the man practiced what he preached. "That's very Zen of you."

One shoulder lifted and fell in a careless shrug. "Don't know about Zen, but I find it helps me cope."

He glanced at her for more than a fleeting second. With nothing up ahead to hit, he could spare the time. "You have bad feelings about something and it doesn't come true, you've wasted a lot of time and energy worrying about something that didn't happen."

"What if it does come true?" she countered. "If you're having all these positive thoughts and they couldn't be further from the truth?"

Her question didn't change his position. "Way I see it, you've got all the time in the world to be upset and mourn over something bad. No need to rush it. And maybe, taking on a happy frame of mind might just help you cope."

Maybe the man never had to deal with anything more tragic than getting jelly doughnut stains off his uniform. He was in no position to give her "helpful" advice. "All this wisdom, maybe you missed your calling. Maybe you should be stuffing fortune cookies."

Rather than take offense, he seemed amused. "Something to think about for my retirement days," he quipped. Rick nodded toward the sign that was coming into view. "You can get yourself more comfortable," he proposed delicately, "over there."

Her eyes widened. "Behind the sign?"

Rick had to bite down on his lower lip to keep from laughing out loud. "No, in the town the sign says we're coming to."

Relieved that they were at journey's end, she looked more closely at what she'd assumed was a billboard ad. Reading it now, Olivia frowned again. What was going on here?

"That sign says we're approaching the town of Beaumont."

"And so we are," he said drily. "Guess that means you pass your eye test."

She was getting really annoyed with his folksy manner. She liked getting results, not the runaround.

"Why are we stopping in Beaumont?" she asked. "You told me that my sister's in the hospital in Pine Ridge. Did they switch her?" she demanded. And if they had, why hadn't he told her before this?

But the sheriff shook his head. "No place to switch her to," he reminded Olivia. "Unless the good people of Beaumont built themselves a hospital in the last few hours."

Olivia dug deep for patience. When she spoke, she said each word slowly and separately, as if she was talking to someone who was mentally challenged. "My question again is why are we stopping in Beaumont?"

Again, rather than be annoyed, he appeared tickled by her bad mood, which only annoyed her further.

"Because, Livy, you need to relieve yourself before you start turning funny colors, and I need to talk to the sheriff to get all the information I can about your sister's accident and also find out the whereabouts of the body."

She was about to snap at him for calling her by the nickname, but the second half of his statement stopped her cold.

"Body?" Olivia echoed as he slowed down and made a right turn down a street. "What body?"

The sheriff's office—a building that made the one back in Forever look as if it was constructed to be state of the art—was in the center of the street. Rick pulled his vehicle up before it.

He looked surprised that she seemed to have forgotten. "The guy your sister was with when the utility pole jumped in front of the car," he replied with just a touch of sarcasm. "Bobby's father," he prompted when she didn't say anything.

Don.

With everything going on, she'd forgotten about Don. Or maybe that was just wishful thinking on her part. In either case, she was relieved all over again that the small-time con artist and would-be musician was never going to be the source of her sister's grief—and thus hers by proxy—again.

She just prayed that there wasn't going to be some other "Don Norman" waiting in the wings to pounce on her vulnerable sister. That Tina would finally come to her senses and select the next man in her life for his personality and better qualities, not the fact that he looked good in a pair of jeans and had seductive, bedroom eyes.

She could only hope, Olivia thought, mentally crossing her fingers.

Kindness and understanding is worth a boatload of sexy, she told herself fiercely.

So why did the sheriff in the little backward town appear to have both going for him? He seemed kind and understanding on the one hand and had sexy, bedroom eyes coupled with one damn fine seat on the other.

Where was she going with this?

A hot shiver ran up her spine.

If she didn't get some rest soon, she would wind up

doing something or at least saying something that would ultimately embarrass her beyond words.

"I'll stay in the car," she told him stubbornly.

She was well aware that this would backfire on her. Maybe, if he stayed in the sheriff's office long enough, she would be able to find a diner or some public place that believed in bathrooms and not outhouses.

Rick got out. "Sun's directly overhead," he pointed out, his index finger indicating where she might glance to find the fiery orb. "You might not want to stay in the car right about now."

He didn't think she had enough sense to come out of the rain, she thought resentfully. Or the hot sun. And it *was* hot despite being the tail end of November. If her car hadn't decided to give up the ghost and play dead, she would have absolutely no reason to be in this predicament. Stupid vehicle was just out of warranty, too. It figured.

Olivia blew out a long, frustrated breath. So far, this had not been one of her better weeks. She just hoped that the worst was behind her and not, God forbid, just ahead.

"I changed my mind," she informed him, getting out and slamming the car door behind her. "I want to hear what the sheriff has to say as much as you do. More," she underscored, "because you don't have a personal stake in this case, and I do."

"I take a personal interest in every case I get," he said evenly, contradicting her assumption as he walked up to the building's front door. He held it open for her and gestured. "After you."

With a quick nod of her head, Olivia walked in front

of him and entered the building. And as she did, Olivia decided that the man was just a tad too laid-back to be real.

She didn't trust the sheriff any further than she could throw him.

Maybe less.

Chapter Seven

If she were to guess, Olivia would have estimated that the small building that housed the Beaumont sheriff's department was somewhere around seventy-five years old, if not more.

The wooden floor creaked in protest beneath their feet as she and Rick walked into the tiny office.

The faint smell of cigarettes mingled with another, mysterious smell that Olivia couldn't readily identify. Maybe that was for the best. Whatever it was, was musty. The office itself was shrouded in semishadow. The midafternoon sun had completely bypassed it, apparently having better places to be. There was a certain chill about the room. And, except for the sound of breathing, it was eerily quiet.

There was only one occupant in the room, presumably the town's sheriff. The heavyset man appeared to be dozing. He had his boots, drastically worn down at the heel, propped up comfortably on his scarred desk. Olivia couldn't help thinking that the man was a portrait of contentment, sleeping the sleep of the just, seemingly without a care in the world.

An amused smile playing on his lips, Rick crouched

down close to the sandy-haired man's ear and loudly cleared his throat.

The older sheriff started abruptly, roused out of a dream he obviously was enjoying a great deal more than the reality he was forced to wake up to.

Rising back to his feet, Rick grinned as he looked down at the other man. "Working hard as usual, I see, Josh."

Swinging his sizable legs down to the floor, Sheriff Joshua Hudson cleared his throat, stalling for time as his brain cleared itself of the cobwebs that had imprisoned it. He appeared only slightly embarrassed to be caught this way. Obviously, it wasn't the first time.

He lifted his chin defensively. "I was just resting my eyes."

"Well, they certainly look well rested," Rick assured him. He stepped back slightly, in order for the man to be able to get a clear view of Olivia, and then made the necessary introduction. "Olivia Blayne, this is Sheriff Joshua Hudson. Josh, this is Olivia Blayne."

The sheriff leaped to his feet, his boots thudding heavily on the wooden floor. After quickly wiping his right hand against his pant leg, Josh extended it to Olivia as he beamed at her.

"Pleased to make your acquaintance," he said, sounding, in her estimation, as if he genuinely meant it.

Her mind on the reason they were here, Olivia had to force a smile to her lips. "Hello."

Rick spoke up for her before Hudson could ask what brought them to Beaumont. "Olivia's here about that car accident that happened on the outskirts of town earlier today."

The sheriff's deep-set, small brown eyes slid over his visitor quickly, making an educated guess as to the exact purpose of her visit.

"You're an insurance investigator?"

"No, she's the sister," Rick said before she had a chance to answer.

She wasn't accustomed to having someone speak for her. The look she shot Rick said as much. From what she could see, the man ignored it.

Olivia noted that Rick's revelation made the heavyset sheriff uncomfortable. Had he a hat in his hands, she had a feeling that he'd be running the brim nervously through his moist fingers. And then she found out why he looked so uneasy.

"Not the boy's sister?" he asked hesitantly in a voice that was far too small for him.

Olivia shook her head. "No, I'm Tina's sister."

"Oh. The girl in the hospital." Hudson didn't look all that relieved over the clarification. It was obvious that he felt badly for her, as well as for Tina. "What can I do for you?" The question was directed at Olivia rather than at Rick. And then, as if his brain was slowly coming around and engaging, he gestured toward the chair next to his desk. "Please, take a seat, Miss Blayne."

"That's all right, I'll stand." Olivia felt far too restless to sit. Coming here, she'd had all she could do just to remain seated in the car. Off and on she had the completely unrealistic urge to leap out and just run to her destination, despite the fact that she had no idea where it was. Blessed with a great many skills, she freely admitted that a sense of direction was not one of them.

The older sheriff bobbed his exceedingly round head

up and down a number of times as he digested her words. The next question he asked momentarily floored Olivia. "Do you want to see the boy's body?"

She never wanted to see Don again, and to view him enshrouded in death was absolutely the last thing she needed. But she knew that Tina would ask after him and her sister would want her to make sure that he was indeed dead.

Olivia knew how Tina thought. Most likely, now that Don was dead, her sister would wind up making some kind of hero out of him, glossing over his shortcomings and focusing on his few semigood points, reminiscing over the one or two actual good moments they'd shared.

If she didn't go to the morgue to see the body, worse, if she didn't verify that Don was really dead, Tina would live out the next few years, if not more, waiting for him to come walking through the door again. She would have bet money on it. Olivia suppressed a sigh. She had no choice in the matter. She had to see him.

Gritting her teeth, she forced the word "yes" out.

Her stomach tightened and she did her best not to succumb to the sick feeling the thought of seeing the man generated. With all her heart—and not for the first time—she sincerely wished that Tina had never gotten involved with Don.

She tried not to dwell on the fact that he could have easily killed Tina in the accident. Hell, maybe that was even what he was trying to do. She wouldn't have put the idea of a suicide pact beyond him. His mind had been twisted enough to savor something like that.

Sheriff Hudson pulled up his sagging khaki trousers,

mumbling something about the weight of the gun belt dragging them down, and gestured for Rick and Olivia to follow him out of the office.

"Doc Moore's got 'im on ice, so to speak." He looked over his shoulder at Olivia. "Didn't know what else to do with him. Nobody to claim him until you came along," he told her. "First dead stranger we've had in these parts in a decade or so. 'Fore my time, anyway. I can take you to the car after you see him," he volunteered. "Harry towed it to his shop. Not that it can be fixed," he confided. "But Harry figures maybe some of the parts can be salvaged. Unless you want the car, of course," he qualified. Slanting a glance in her direction.

"No, Harry can have it," she assured Josh, freely giving up any claim to her sister's car. "I just need to check out the glove compartment."

She wanted to make sure she had the registration and insurance information before the car was stripped down. Someone in the family had to be practical, she thought. And the job always fell to her.

"Sure thing," Josh said cheerfully.

"Thank you," she murmured.

Hudson beamed. Turning to his other side, he slanted a look toward Rick, as if to silently call attention to the fact that the woman had just thanked him. They didn't often see a woman as classy as this one.

"Hey, no problem," Josh assured her.

It occurred to Olivia that this man was the last one to have seen her sister. Any details he could volunteer were more than welcomed. She needed something to cling to, to fuel those so-called optimistic thoughts that Santiago kept pushing.

"And my sister?" she asked. "What can you tell me about her?"

"She was bleeding pretty badly," Hudson said. "But she was definitely breathing. I checked. The ambulance from Pine Ridge came right quick enough and the medical guys took her to the hospital there. Doc Moore said she was pretty banged up, but he thought that she'd make it if they got her to the hospital in time." There was sympathy in Hudson's eyes as he concluded, "Dunno any more than that."

His small eyes shifted from her to Rick and then back again.

"We appreciate the information, Josh," Rick told the older man when Olivia said nothing.

Rick could see that she was having trouble dealing with all this and wordlessly placed his hand to the small of her back, silently communicating his support. In response, he felt her stiffen against his palm, but she didn't pull away.

Rick thought of it as progress.

"I'LL LEAVE YOU alone with him," Dr. Evan Moore volunteered after introductions and explanations had been made.

Olivia raised her eyes to the friendly physician. She appreciated his thoughtful gesture, but there was no need for it. She shook her head.

"No need, Doctor. I've seen all I need to see." And what she needed to see was that the man who had all but literally destroyed her sister's life was truly dead. He couldn't hurt Tina—or Bobby—anymore. And for that she was truly grateful. "Thank you," she added belatedly. With that, she turned away from the body on the table and walked away.

The doctor's next question stopped her in her tracks. "What do you want me to do with the body?"

Olivia set her mouth grimly. She supposed telling the man to feel free to cut Don's lifeless body up for fish food sounded a little too harsh. But there was absolutely no way she intended to go through the time and expense—not to mention mental distress—of having Don's body transported back to Dallas. She wanted him permanently flushed out of Tina's life—and as far away as possible. She'd figure out what to tell Tina later.

"Bury him," Olivia instructed tersely. Turning around, she placed one of her business cards on a nearby table. "Send the bill to me at this address. I'll mail you a check."

"Maybe you could give the doc a partial payment?" Rick suggested tactfully. "As a sign of good faith. Times are hard," he reminded her.

He was right, but she couldn't help resenting it. She should have thought of that herself. She didn't like having her shortcomings pointed out to her.

Wordlessly, without looking in Rick's direction, she took out her checkbook and wrote a check for five hundred dollars. Tearing it off, she crossed back to the doctor and handed it to him.

"If that's not enough," she told him, "let me know. I'll send you the rest." And then, as if reading the man's mind, she added, "Nothing fancy. He doesn't deserve it."

The doctor nodded knowingly. "Nothing fancy," he echoed. He put the check and his hands deep into the pockets of his lab coat. "Consider it taken care of, Miss Blayne."

Before making their way back to Hudson's office, the older sheriff took them to the town's only garage to see what was left of Tina's car.

The air in Olivia's lungs backed up when she first saw the wreckage. The entire front end was pushed in, looking like a crumpled accordion. Seeing it, she couldn't understand how her sister hadn't met the same fate as Don. Or how either one of them had managed to avoid becoming one with the twisted metal.

"You okay?" Rick asked.

She nodded numbly, not trusting her voice to answer him.

The glove compartment door had been knocked off and she could see some things inside the narrowed space. Olivia took out the papers she needed and tucked them into her purse.

All she wanted now was to leave this behind her and see Tina.

"Can we get going now, please?" she asked Rick.

"Absolutely." There was no reason to stay any longer. He'd already exchanged a few words with Josh and satisfied himself that the other man had relayed all the details of the accident. As they passed Josh's office, Rick said with a grin, "You can get back to that dream you were having, Josh."

"Got a better one in mind now, Santiago," Hudson told him, staring unabashedly at the woman his fellow sheriff had brought with him.

Rick didn't have to guess the subject of the other sheriff's new dream. His grin widened.

The grin remained even as he got back into his car. Olivia was already inside, buckled up and ready to go. When she saw Rick's expression, she couldn't help questioning it.

"What?"

Rick started up the car and pulled out. "Nothing," he said, diminishing its importance. Then, because she continued watching him, he said, "Josh's got something new to dream about."

Olivia sighed. The man talked in riddles, giving her bits and pieces instead of a whole answer. What little patience she had was all but gone. "What?"

"You."

He got a kick out of saying that, even though he had a feeling it wasn't being received in the same spirit. The woman needed to learn how to laugh at herself. How to lighten up a little bit.

"Unlike Forever, Beaumont doesn't get all that many people passing through," he said. "It's usually a while between new faces."

From what she'd seen, the town looked to be the size of a postage stamp. And it was off the beaten path, which was probably why Don had chosen to pass through it on the way to who-knew-where. She had no doubt that the town enjoyed very little variety. One day, most likely, was pretty much like another.

"How do they stand it?" she asked.

Not only did the good people of Beaumont "stand it," they seemed to thrive on it, he observed. "They find ways to entertain themselves. I suspect they'll be talking about your sister and her boyfriend and the accident for some time to come."

Olivia couldn't imagine a life like that. Couldn't imagine submitting to it willingly. She suppressed a shiver that threatened to dart down her spine.

"The boredom would kill me."

Rick laughed. "Everybody's gotta die of something." He spared her a long, appreciative glance. "You look like you'd be pretty hearty to me."

Just how deeply had this man analyzed her? And why? She wanted to ask, to have him explain himself and what he meant by some of the things he'd said. But she told herself not to go there. Knowing would only lead to more dialogue and, just possibly, more insight into the man in the driver's seat. She didn't want more insight; she just wanted to find Tina and get the hell out of Dodge, or, in this case, Forever.

Olivia shifted restlessly. "How much farther is it to Pine Ridge?"

He did a quick calculation, glancing at his odometer. "Ten miles as the crow flies."

That would be a straight line. Almost nothing worked out to be a straight line when it came to traveling. Paths were always comprised of twists and turns. "And if the crow is driving a sheriff's car?"

He grinned. "Depends on whether or not he can reach the gas pedal." He saw that his response aggravated her. The lady had a short fuse. He wondered if she erupted for other reasons as well.

Why was he thinking about that? He hadn't had those kinds of thoughts, or questions, since his fiancée had died a week before their wedding. Why now?

"Same amount," he finally told her. "The land's flat."

"I hadn't noticed," Olivia cracked.

The monotony of the road was enough to put a driver to sleep, she thought. Was that what happened? Had Don fallen asleep behind the wheel and crashed into the utility pole?

She needed answers.

"I doubt if there's very much you don't notice, Olivia," Rick commented without looking in her direction.

As a trial lawyer, she'd learned to question everything, to hold everything suspect. Nothing was ever taken at face value, which was both her loss and her strength.

"Trying to flatter me, Sheriff?"

Someone else might have taken offense at that, but he didn't. "Calling it the way I see it, that's all. Besides," he pointed out, "in case it hasn't occurred to you, there's nothing to be gained by flattering you, Olivia."

Impatience ate away at her. Theirs was the only vehicle on the road. And he was going just under sixty. What was the purpose of staying under the speed limit out here?

"Can this thing go any faster?" she asked shortly.

"It can," he replied, continuing to drive at the same speed.

You would think the man could take a hint, she thought, her frustration growing. "In this lifetime?" she prodded.

He glanced in her direction. "Are you asking me to speed?"

Was everything black and white for this man? She hadn't thought that men like Rick Santiago still existed. Law-abiding to a damn fault.

"I'm asking you to get to the hospital before I start collecting social security checks."

"Don't worry, your sister's stable."

She frowned. "More positive thinking?" Olivia asked sarcastically.

He made no comment about her tone, simply said what he felt she needed to know. "Just before we left for Beaumont, when I went into the office, I had Alma call Pine Ridge Memorial and ask about your sister."

"Why didn't you say something?" she demanded.

She had that edge to her voice again, he noted. "I thought I just did."

"I mean sooner," she stressed.

He lifted the shoulder closer to her in a half shrug. "If I did, you might've thought I was making it up just to get you to calm down."

She supposed that he had a point, but if she followed that line of reasoning, why had he picked now to tell her? "And now?"

"Now we're pretty much almost there. It'll help you hang on for the last leg of the trip." He paused, debating. But she would find out this part, too. She might as well be prepared for it. "There is one thing, though."

Olivia braced herself. "What?"

"According to the hospital, your sister hasn't regained consciousness yet."

"She's in a coma?" Olivia cried incredulously. All she could think of was that some people *never* woke up from a coma. "Why didn't you at least tell me that sooner?" she demanded.

"Because it would upset you—just like it's doing

now," he said. "And I figured you had enough to deal with."

She began getting a claustrophobic feeling. "So you decided to appoint yourself my guardian?" she demanded.

He sounded as low-key as she was uptight. "Just trying to help," he told her mildly.

"I don't need any help," Olivia snapped.

He shrugged, letting her declaration slide. "Whatever you say."

She took a deep breath, struggling for control. Struggling to keep from feeling overwhelmed. God, but she wished there was someone to turn to. But there hadn't been anyone there for her for more than ten years now.

She should be used to this by now, used to soldiering on alone. And, for the most part, she was. But that didn't make times like this any easier. And it didn't keep her from longing, every once in a while, for a handy pair of shoulders to lean on....

And what's the sheriff? Chopped liver? He just tried to help and instead of thanking him, you bit his head off and handed it to him.

Taking another deep breath, she let it out slowly, then glanced in the sheriff's direction. She turned her face forward before she spoke. "I'm sorry, I do appreciate everything you're doing, Sheriff. I didn't mean to lose my temper."

Yeah, you did, he thought, but he left that unsaid. "Apology accepted," he told her. "By the way, that's Pine Ridge just up ahead."

A sense of excitement and foreboding mingled inside

her as Olivia sat up straighter, straining to get her first glimpse of Pine Ridge. With any luck, maybe her sister had come out of the coma and she could take her back home.

Startled, she realized that Santiago's optimism was infectious after all.

Chapter Eight

For a relatively small town—Olivia judged that it was perhaps a shade or two larger than Forever—Pine Ridge's hospital was surprisingly modern in appearance. The inside of the building looked fresh and crisp, as if it had been recently renovated. Two storied, it boasted of "over eighty beds," six of which were dedicated to the intensive care unit.

The ICU was where the attending physician, a general surgeon named Dr. Owen Baker, had placed her sister after he and another surgeon had finished operating on Tina for close to five hours.

Feeling increasingly agitated and stressed, Olivia forced herself to let Rick take over. He was the one who approached the woman at the admissions registration desk to ask about her sister. She knew that had she been more clearheaded, she would have resented his acting on her behalf. But now a part of her was grateful to him.

Dr. Baker had to be paged more than once before he finally came to the ICU area to speak to them. Or rather, to her, Olivia silently amended since she sincerely doubted that Santiago was even mildly interested in her sister's condition, despite his disclaimer about taking a personal interest in the people he found himself dealing with.

Narrating a quick synopsis for them—the six-foot-four, prematurely gray surgeon was obviously anxious to be on his way—Dr. Baker concluded by saying, "And now we just have to wait and see. It's out of our hands. We've done everything humanly possible for your sister."

She wanted to ask if he was referring specifically to himself and the other surgeon, or lumping together the staff as well. And was he thus stepping away from the situation, leaving it "in God's hands," the catchall phrase she felt people used to absolve themselves of any guilt.

Personally, she had decided at her parents' funeral that God had better things to do than to dabble in her life. Whatever happened to her—and to Tina—was on her, and she was the one responsible for their lives.

And how's that working out for you?

She wanted to ask Baker more questions, to ask him how well he and the other surgeon fared in their surgeries. Were they usually successful? But questions like that often sounded bitter and, at the very least, antagonistic. It would have sounded as if she was taking out her helpless frustration on the surgeon when the man had probably done his best.

She wanted to get back to familiar ground, take Tina home.

"I'd like to take my sister back to Dallas. Can she be moved?" Olivia asked, fully expecting the man to say yes.

Maybe it came off sounding condescending, but there

were top surgeons in Dallas. No doubt any one of them was better equipped to help Tina than a doctor in this one-and-a-half-horse town.

To her surprise, Dr. Baker shook his head and said firmly, "Absolutely not—unless your goal is to kill your sister. She's definitely not strong enough to be moved. There were serious internal injuries. She has several cracked ribs, we barely saved her right lung, her liver was badly bruised and we had to remove her spleen— among other things."

She could feel Rick watching her. He probably thought she was crazy, too. It didn't matter. She just wanted what was best for Tina, what would give her sister the best chance at recovery.

"Even by helicopter?" Olivia pressed, determined to get Tina the best of care, not have her sister languish here.

A half smile curved the surgeon's thin lips. "Not even by a transporter beam."

Great, the man's a science fiction aficionado. Just the quality she was looking for in a physician. "When *can* I move her?" she asked, not bothering to bite back her impatience.

"When she gets stronger," Baker answered simply, then glanced at his watch.

She knew that was for her benefit, but she still had questions. "And when do you think that'll be?"

"A few days, a week, a month—"

"A month?" Olivia echoed incredulously, staring at the man.

Dr. Baker seemed unmoved by her distress. "Everyone gets well at their own pace." His pager went off and he looked relieved to be able to turn his attention away from his patient's pushy sister.

"Sorry, I *really* have to get back to the emergency room. I should have been back there already," Baker said.

Not waiting for her to say anything further, Tina's surgeon turned on his heel and hurried away. He nodded at Rick before he left.

"He's not sorry at all," Olivia commented to Rick, annoyed, as she watched Dr. Baker disappear around a corner.

Rick's response surprised her. "Can't say I really blame him, the way you were grilling him."

His comment stung. But then, why would she expect loyalty from a man who was little more than a stranger to her?

"I wasn't grilling him," she protested.

Rick laughed shortly. "If you'd grilled him any more, you could've put barbecue sauce on the man and called him done."

Olivia frowned at his interpretation. "Very colorful."

"Accurate," he countered. This wasn't going to turn out well and he had no desire to argue with her. "Why don't we go and see your sister instead of picking fights with the people who are helping her?"

She noticed that he said "helping" rather than "trying to help." More optimism on his part? She found herself wishing she could share in his take on things. It might go a long way in reassuring her. Because, at the moment, all she was feeling was exceedingly nervous. And seriously worried.

"Okay," she agreed.

She did want to see Tina, no matter what condition her sister was in. If nothing else, she wanted Tina to know she was there for her. She'd read somewhere that even when people were in comas they were aware of their surroundings. She could only hope that was true.

"For the record, I wasn't trying to pick a fight," she told Rick. "I just wanted to light a fire under the good doctor, get him moving."

"Looked to me like he'd been moving all day. You're being too hard on the man." The sheriff looked at her significantly. "Not everyone is a streak of lightning across the sky."

Was that how he saw her? Like a streak of lightning across the sky? She knew if she asked him, it would sound as if she was flirting with him and she didn't want to plant any ideas in Santiago's head. She was definitely *not* interested in flirting with him. Maybe, at another time, in another place—and if he wasn't the sheriff of a hick town—

She silently laughed at herself. Basically, she was saying that it would never happen. She was just burying it in conditions. Just as well. She did better alone.

The line echoed in her head as they went to find Tina.

IT WASN'T DIFFICULT locating ICU. Once there, they found that Tina was the only one in the small, isolated area.

Obviously a slow day for traumas, Olivia thought sarcastically.

She was using sarcasm in a desperate attempt to

shield her exposed feelings, even within the confines of her own mind. If she didn't, it was just a matter of time—maybe even minutes—before she wound up breaking down. And if that happened, she wasn't sure she could pull herself back together again.

For a moment, Olivia stood where she was, hesitant to approach her sister, to see Tina up close.

Even at this distance, her heart twisted at what she saw.

"She looks so pale," Olivia murmured.

"I'll be right outside if you need me," Rick told her softly. And with that, he stepped out of the room.

Sensitivity. The sheriff was displaying sensitivity. The next thing she'd be finding out that Forever was the town where Santa Claus and his elves took their summer vacations, she thought.

Taking a deep breath, Olivia slowly approached Tina's bed. Every step literally vibrated through her, echoing a warning, or putting her on some sort of notice.

She wanted to run, but she didn't dare.

The sun came into the room, but all she felt was a darkness that threatened to swallow her and Tina up. Whole.

"Tina?" she whispered once she was at her sister's bedside.

There was no reaction from Tina, no noise at all. Just the sounds of the machines that were attached to Tina, keeping track of her vital signs, feeding her and fighting off whatever infections lurked in the wings, waiting for a chance to envelope her weakened body.

"Tina, it's me, Livy," Olivia whispered. "I came as soon as I could. This was one hell of a hide-and-seek game you played this time." That had been Tina's favorite game as a child. God, but she wished they could go back to that time. "You definitely weren't easy to track down," she told the still figure. "Not like when you were little. But then, you always wanted to be found back then." Olivia took a breath, her voice quavering. "I got the feeling that you didn't this time."

Olivia could feel the tears in her throat, threatening to choke her. She took Tina's hand in hers, wrapping her fingers tightly around it.

Willing her sister awake. Willing her to be well.

Tina's eyes remained closed.

"I found Bobby." She went on talking as if Tina had responded to her. Praying that she would, that her words would penetrate this thick curtain that separated them and bring her sister back to her. "He's okay." She pressed her lips together as she looked down at her little sister. "Why did you leave him like that, Tina, on a stranger's doorstep? Did you know this was going to happen? Was Don threatening to kill you both for some twisted, screwed-up reason?"

The question echoed around the small area, mocking her.

"Oh Tina, wake up, please wake up," she begged, squeezing her sister's hand a little harder. "Talk to me. Tell me what happened. Tell me how to make it all better for you. Give me a clue. I'll take care of you," she promised, her voice cracking, "but you have to give me a clue what you need. I can't keep doing this all by myself."

Olivia gazed down at her sister. There was no indication that any of her words had penetrated, or that Tina was any closer to coming around than she had been a few minutes ago.

No indication that she would *ever* come around.

Overwhelmed and close to the breaking point, Olivia began to softly cry. Once she allowed herself to stray from the rigid path she'd set down, she couldn't quite manage to find her way back.

The tears, the sobs, just kept coming, threatening never to stop.

Olivia felt as overwhelmed now as she had when the police had come to the dorm that bleak, horrible evening to notify her that her parents had been murdered.

The floor beneath her feet had been slowly disintegrating since she'd walked into the ICU and she now found herself free-falling through space with no signs of being able to stop.

Her heart was breaking.

While plummeting down into this blindingly dark abyss, she became vaguely aware of a pair of strong hands gently taking hold of her. Turning her around. And then she was enfolded in warm, comforting arms.

Instinctively, Olivia buried her face against her comforter's chest. She shook as she cried herself out.

She lost track of time.

A minute, an hour, a day, Olivia had no idea how long she stood there, allowing herself to be held, sobbing out her pain.

Gradually, she became aware of a scent. It wasn't the scent of cologne or aftershave or even shampoo. The scent teased her memory, making her think of shaving cream. Familiar shaving cream.

And then she knew who had wordlessly offered his

support, held her while she temporarily ceased being "the responsible one" and just gave in to the hurt, the pain, to the frustration and the sorrow swirling inside her.

The man whose chest became more and more soggy from her tears was Rick.

Olivia struggled against the very strong desire to sink further into the abyss. Taking a deep breath, she raised her head. Her eyes met his.

"I must look terrible," she mumbled.

Rick fished out a handkerchief from his pocket and offered it to her. She was surprised to see that it was neatly folded in four rather than just crumpled and bearing signs of being shoved haphazardly in his back pocket.

"You look like someone who's been through a lot," he contradicted. There was an understanding, encouraging smile on his lips. "Nothing wrong with that."

Nobody would accuse the sheriff of being a smooth talker, Olivia thought, but there was no denying that the man knew how to be kind. She searched for something cryptic to say, something flippant to use as a shield, which would effectively draw attention away from her anguish.

Nothing came to her.

All she could do was whisper a faint thank-you, and surrender the handkerchief once she'd wiped away the tears from her cheeks.

He shook his head, closing his hand over hers and gently pushing it back. "Keep it," he told her. "In case you need it again."

Olivia wadded the handkerchief up in her hand,

sternly telling herself she wasn't going to cry anymore. She'd had her momentary breakdown, now it was time to get a grip.

Tears never solved anything.

"I thought you were going to wait outside," she said, her voice still hardly above a whisper. She was afraid that if she raised it, it would crack noticeably. She still had a ways to go before she was back in control of herself and she knew it.

"I thought so, too," he acknowledged, then nodded toward the wall next to Tina's bed. "But the walls are kind of thin here and I heard you talking to your sister." For her benefit, he lowered his voice. "And I heard her not answering you."

A hint of a smile curved the corners of her mouth. "You know that's not possible, right? You can't 'hear' something that isn't being said."

Rick merely smiled indulgently. "We've got a different set of skills out here," he told her. To her surprise, he took her hand, not like a lover but like a friend. He gave it a gentle tug, encouraging her to come with him. "C'mon."

She didn't have the strength to oppose him, didn't even have the strength to ask him where he was taking her. Because if it was to the car, she wasn't ready to leave, not yet. But rather than offer any opposition, she waited to see where he was going.

When Rick brought her over to the elevator, she allowed a sigh of relief to escape. They weren't leaving. The ICU was on the first floor and all they had to do to get to the parking lot was to walk through the front doors.

The elevator arrived within seconds of his pressing the down button. Ushering her into the elevator car, Rick pushed the button with the glowing B for the basement on it.

With effort, Olivia finally managed to pull herself together enough in order to begin framing a question. She got to utter only the first word.

"Where—"

"Cafeteria," he replied simply, anticipating the rest of her question. "By my reckoning, you haven't had anything to eat in quite some time."

She raised her eyes to his, her brain slowly engaging again. "Neither have you," she pointed out. They hadn't stopped at a single take-out place since they'd left Forever.

"Exactly. I figure we both need to fuel up. The world always looks a little more manageable on a full stomach," he told her.

Olivia didn't quite see it that way. Food was usually grabbed as she made her way to another destination, nibbled on every so often as she toiled over briefs and opening statements. She never sought out food for its own sake, or consumed it for the sheer pleasure of it the way she once had. This was why she'd never bothered to learn how to really cook.

Right now, she could feel her stomach churning in turmoil, tightening to the point that breathing became difficult. She was clearly running on empty, she thought, but she was far too agitated to sit down for a meal.

"I'm not sure I can keep anything down," she confided.

"Well, this is a hospital. I'm sure I can get someone

to scare up an IV for you if you refuse to eat," he told her matter-of-factly. Obviously he intended for her to eat and was prepared to wait her out until she gave in and ate.

She was about to protest his taking charge this way, acting as if she was some wayward, willful child who couldn't fend for herself. As if she'd suddenly been deemed incompetent.

For a moment, her back was up and she was ready to get into it with him.

But a part of her, a more grounded, clear-thinking part, annoyingly reminded her how badly she wanted someone to lean on, to share a little of the burden that she struggled with. And it was clear this sheriff, from that tiny spec-on-the-map town, was doing just that. He was taking charge, relieving her, just for a moment, of the burden she'd voluntarily picked up over ten years ago.

Sighing, Olivia walked in ahead of him as he held the swinging double doors open.

At first glance, the cafeteria dining area appeared to be only a little bigger than the kitchen in her apartment back home. An elderly woman nursing a cup of coffee sat at one of the seven tables. The other tables were empty.

It was obviously between meals, Olivia thought. A glance toward the food service revealed some things to choose from. A few platters planted on beds of ice maintained their positions behind glass partitions.

"Maybe I can try to keep something down," she told him.

"Every success starts out with someone trying," Rick said, handing her a tray.

One look at his face told her that the sheriff actually believed in the simplistic adage.

Because she was still clutching the handkerchief he'd given her, Olivia kept her negative retort to herself. But she felt relieved that she was beginning to return to her old self again.

Chapter Nine

Olivia discovered that she was hungrier than she'd realized. The moment she put a forkful of the beef stew that the sheriff had insisted on paying for into her mouth, she could feel her taste buds cheer. She ate with gusto, something she couldn't remember doing in the recent past.

She was almost finished when she became aware of Rick observing her. His eyes almost seemed to be smiling as he watched her.

Lowering her fork and raising her guard, she met his gaze. "What?"

"Just nice watching you enjoy something," Rick replied.

She thought of how he'd insisted that she eat. He was the one who had put the stew on her tray, guaranteeing that she'd like it. "You just like being right."

"That, too."

He finished the cup of coffee he'd been nursing. The roast beef sandwich he'd ordered had become history quickly. The dispute over payment of the tab was taking longer to die.

She was accustomed to paying for everything or, at

the very least, her own way. For the past ten years, she'd been adamant about not being in anyone's debt in any manner, shape or form. "I still feel I should pay for my meal."

He wasn't about to get roped into another discussion about this. The price of the stew and her soft drink was not going to break him. Besides, when he came right down to it, he kind of liked sitting across from her at the small table.

"That horse has already been ridden and put away," Rick told her. "A person who really feels in control lets other people do a few things once in a while." She put down her fork, finished. Rick nodded his approval. "Now then, you want dessert or are you ready to go?"

"Go?" The way he asked made her feel that he wasn't referring to making their way back to the ICU and Tina.

"Back to Forever."

That was what she was afraid he was saying. She shook her head. "I can't leave Tina." Not when her sister was like this, unconscious and vulnerable.

The woman was overprotective, he thought. Could be why her sister ran off the way she had. But it wasn't his place to say that. Besides, he had the feeling Olivia would only get her back up if he did. "Seems to me that your sister's in good hands. Her son needs you more than she does right now."

Bobby.

Oh God, she'd forgotten all about him. A huge wave of guilt washed over her, drenching her as it momentarily stole her breath away. How could she have forgotten about the baby?

Olivia pressed her lips together, vacillating, trying to sort things out in her head. The fact that the little boy was some sixty plus miles away presented a definite problem in logistics. She knew she couldn't be in two places at once, but where was she most needed? Tina had always been her first priority, but now there was Bobby. Bobby had no one to take care of him except for her. And to complicate matters more, she didn't even have a running car.

"Don't worry about not being able to come back," Rick said, as if he was reading her mind. "I'll bring you here tomorrow."

She'd assumed that this was a one-shot deal. "But aren't you busy?"

An amused smile played on his lips. "As it happens, I'm in between crime waves, so I've got a little down-time." The smile widened as he added, "You might have noticed that."

He was essentially offering to be her chauffeur. The man didn't know her from Adam—or Eve. Why was he being so nice to her? She'd never liked things she didn't understand.

"It's not that I'm not grateful," she began slowly, "it's just that I can't impose on you like this."

"Nobody said anything about imposing," he pointed out. "In Forever, we take care of our own."

"But I'm not from Forever."

He laughed softly. "Your car's parked in front of the diner. That's close enough."

"I'll pay you for your services."

Ordinarily, stubbornness to this degree irritated him,

but he had to admit that this woman did fascinate him. "No need. Besides, I wouldn't know what to charge."

She had a solution for that. Her whole life was built around finding solutions. "I could make a donation to your favorite charity."

He had a better suggestion. "How about you just pass it on when the time comes?"

She eyed him quizzically. "Pass it on?"

He nodded. "The next time you come across someone in need, help them."

Olivia opened her mouth to protest that she wasn't in need, but she realized that would have been a lie. Because she was. Just because she didn't meet the stereotypical definition of a needy person did not negate the fact that she really was a person in need.

For the moment, she underscored, to make herself feel better.

"Okay," Olivia finally agreed, knowing that any further arguing would be futile and it would make her out to be an ungrateful snob to boot. She balked at the image even as she began to wonder if that was the way she came across. And if so, underneath it all, *was* she actually a snob?

The idea bothered her. A great deal.

She *wasn't* a snob, Olivia insisted silently. She didn't think of herself as better than the next person. But if that "next person" happened to be standing in the middle of Forever, Texas, well, she did feel she was more sophisticated, more polished.

Did that ultimately make her a snob?

Maybe she was a snob. She was also very confused and torn.

In the end, she agreed with the good-looking sheriff. Bobby was her responsibility and right now, he needed her more.

THEY WERE BACK ON THE ROAD within fifteen minutes. And Olivia wound up dozing off within thirty. The monotony of the open road, bathed in approaching twilight, lulled her to sleep.

Hearing her soft, even breathing, Rick glanced in Olivia's direction. He smiled to himself when he realized that she had nodded off. Asleep, she couldn't talk, couldn't argue and he had to admit that, for now, he found her more attractive that way. But then, he was attracted to her no matter what the circumstance. She was a damn fine looking woman by anyone's standards.

He'd already noted that she didn't wear a ring. She hadn't mentioned anything about a husband or significant other waiting for her back home. So, as far as he knew, she was unattached. It made him wonder. An intelligent woman who looked the way she did was one hell of a package. Yet as far as he could tell, no one had taken her home to unwrap.

Was that by choice? And if so, why?

Was there something in her background the way there was in his?

He felt his stomach muscles tighten the way they always did whenever he thought of Alycia. Alycia Banderas. He had been one week away from marrying her when a cross-country moving van had flipped over on its side, crushing not just her car but all of his dreams in one awful moment. That kind of event made a man step back and wonder about how fragile life really was.

He was getting philosophical in his old age.

Well, once he got that job on the police force in Dallas, he doubted he'd have time for philosophical conjecture. His friend Sam had confided that he had trouble finding *any* time to himself. The job claimed the man 24/7. From where he sat, Rick couldn't help thinking that he really liked the sound of that.

OLIVIA SLEPT THE ENTIRE trip back.

She had to have been really drained, he thought, his sympathy aroused. Too bad he couldn't let her go on sleeping, but even if he was so inclined, he wouldn't be doing her any favors. Her neck would be killing her tomorrow.

Forever was just up ahead.

Rick decided not to stop at his office and go straight to the diner to pick up the baby. As he drove past the city limits, Olivia stirred beside him. The next moment, she bolted upright, apparently startled that she'd fallen asleep in his car.

Her neck hurt and the corners of her mouth felt moist. Oh God, she hoped she hadn't drooled, she suddenly thought.

Embarrassed, she mumbled, "I must have fallen asleep."

"Must have," he agreed.

She didn't have to look, she could hear the grin in his voice. Had she talked in her sleep? Or worse, snored? Olivia felt uncomfortable as well as really vulnerable.

"Why didn't you wake me?" she asked, an accusing edge to her question.

Rick shrugged. "Didn't see the point. You were tired. I thought you could do with the rest."

"I should take my turn behind the wheel," she told him. "It's only fair."

The amusement reflected in his expression only deepened. She couldn't shake the feeling that he was laughing at her.

"To you or to me?" he asked.

She barely heard the question. As she looked through the windshield, it suddenly dawned on her where they were, in front of a diner.

The diner.

The one she'd left Bobby in. And that was her car on the right. How long had she been asleep?

"We're here?" she questioned.

"We're here," he confirmed, turning off the ignition. He got out, rounding the hood to open the door for her. But as he drew closer to her car, he glanced in its direction.

What he saw stopped him in his tracks.

An uneasiness undulated over her. What was Santiago staring at?

Opening the passenger side door, she struggled to shake off the last layers of sleep. She needed to be on her toes, to be able to think. She needed—

Olivia's mouth dropped open as she saw what the sheriff was looking at.

"Oh my God," she cried, horror stricken. "My car. What happened to my car?" she asked. She'd left the top down and the upholstery on the front passenger side looked as if a wild animal had gotten in and attacked it.

Stunned, she ran her hand along the jagged fabric. "It's all ripped up inside."

"Not all," he qualified. "Just that section," he said, pointing to the damaged area. "But it does look pretty bad."

The door to the diner opened just then and Miss Joan, holding Bobby in her arms, appeared. For a moment, she simply stood there, as if taking the scene in. And then Rick saw a pink hue of embarrassment across the diner owner's face.

Miss Joan raised her chin, ready to own up to her part in what had happened. She faced it the same way she faced any and all events in her life, good or bad: head-on, showing no fear.

"I'll pay for it," she told Olivia.

Fully awake now, Olivia turned in the older woman's direction. Stunned, shaken up, she didn't know whether to laugh or cry.

What she did do was cross to the woman and take Bobby from her. She needed to touch something that linked her to her life and not this Alice in Wonderland place she had unwillingly found herself in.

Olivia struggled to wrap her head around this latest twist, still confused about what had happened to her beautiful car. "You did this?"

"Not personally," Miss Joan answered, stretching out her words as she searched for the right ones to say next. "Bruiser did. His chew toys are leather," she explained quickly. "He likes the smell."

"He likes more than the smell," Olivia declared, clearly distressed. "He obviously likes the taste, too."

Holding Bobby to her, Olivia inspected the damage

more closely. It was as if expensive upholstery had met with the blades of a blender head-on—and come out the obvious loser.

"Bruiser likes to patrol the area," Miss Joan said haplessly. "He thinks he's keeping me safe."

Olivia stared incredulously at the woman. "And he thought my car was going to attack you?"

"I'm sorry," Miss Joan apologized. "Like I said, I'll pay for it. Shouldn't take Mick more than a week to get it fixed."

"A week?" Olivia echoed.

She didn't have a week. She barely had a couple more days. She'd taken a specific leave of absence from her firm to search for her sister and her nephew. And while the senior partners at Norvil and Tyler indicated that they valued her and viewed her as an asset to the company, Olivia was not naive. She was well aware of the way things worked. A whole slew of second-tier attorneys waited in the wings for the first glimpse of an opening. They would all be willing and eager to fill her space.

Suddenly overwhelmingly weary, Olivia felt as though the two halves of her life were on a collision course. On the one hand, she needed to be back at work, to keep building her career. On the other, she needed to be here for Tina and for Bobby. She couldn't abandon either one of them. She couldn't just pick up and leave with the baby, waiting until such time as the doctor who'd operated on Tina gave her the go-ahead to take her sister back home to Dallas. And maintaining a vigil for Tina while keeping Bobby with her came with its own set of problems as well.

Okay, first things first, she told herself. One step at a time. "I need a place to stay tonight," she said to Miss Joan.

"There's the motel on the outskirts of town," Lupe told her, coming out of the diner to join the small gathering. The few customers inside the diner were either eating or relaxing after a meal. No one was in any hurry. The regulars never were.

Miss Joan frowned at the waitress's suggestion, vetoing it.

"You don't want to go there," she said, shaking her head. "They got bugs and snakes in every room. You'll be putting the baby at risk, not to mention yourself."

Olivia shivered. She wasn't exactly open to sharing space with bugs and snakes. She began thinking that she and Bobby were going to have to spend the night in her chewed-up car—once she got the top up. *If* she could get the top up, she qualified.

"Are there any other options?" she asked.

Again, Miss Joan seemed embarrassed, as if she had once more dropped the ball. "I'd put you up, except that I'm having the house painted and I'm staying with my sister right now." Her brown eyes shifted toward Rick. "How about you, Sheriff? You've got that big ol' spare bedroom just sitting there, going to waste. You could put her and the baby up."

Oh no, Olivia thought. Staying with the sheriff was not a good idea. It was just asking for trouble and from where she stood, she had more than her share of that right now.

She shook her head, rejecting the suggestion. "I don't think—"

Miss Joan didn't let her finish. "Sure, you do," she contradicted. "The alternative's either sleeping in your car, or with vermin. You might not mind it, but you've got to think of the baby. In the motel, he could get bit. In your car, he could catch a chill. It's settled then," Miss Joan declared, seeming pleased with herself. "Why don't I put together some dinner for the two of you—on the house," she added quickly, "seeing as how Bruiser made lunch out of the inside of your car. Not that I'm trying to get out of paying for that, but dinner's the least I can do to show you how really sorry I am." With that, the woman turned on her heel and hurried back into the diner. "I'll have it ready in a jiffy," she promised.

Olivia blinked, trying to focus. She felt as if she'd just been run over by a steamroller, one that used words like "jiffy." Without realizing it, she tightened her arms around the baby, and Bobby squealed in protest. Startled, Olivia loosened her hold just enough. Sniffing, Bobby settled down.

"Look, if you don't feel comfortable about this," Rick began, choosing his words carefully, "I can ask around, see if I can find someone willing to put the two of you up."

She was beginning to feel like a charity case. She didn't want him supplicating on her behalf. If she had to make a choice, she'd rather stay with him than a stranger. At least she knew the sheriff. Sort of.

Olivia forced a smile to her lips. "I don't feel uncomfortable," she lied. And then it dawned on her. Maybe it wasn't her he was concerned about. Maybe there was a girlfriend, a lover, who wouldn't take kindly to her staying at his house.

"Unless you'd rather that we went somewhere el—"

"I'm fine with it," he told Olivia, cutting her off abruptly.

Olivia was far from convinced he meant what he said. Maybe there was a back room at the diner she and Bobby could use. They had to close down sometime, right? "You're sure?"

"I'm sure." He said it so firmly, he left no room for doubt—or argument.

"All right," she murmured, even though it was against her better judgment.

She wasn't afraid of Santiago. It was more a case of being afraid of being alone with him. Throughout this whole day, she'd felt something…something shimmering between them. Tension, electricity, attraction.

Something.

Suddenly, Olivia stifled a scream as Bobby grabbed her hair and yanked hard. Every single hair seemed to separate from her scalp. He'd managed to bring tears of pain to her eyes.

"Here, let me get that," Rick offered. Very carefully, he loosened the chubby little fingers just enough to remove the strand of hair caught in the baby's grasp. "Better?" he asked once he'd freed her hair.

"Better," she breathed. The next moment, she thrust the baby at him. "Could you hold Bobby for me for a minute? I want to get my suitcase out of the trunk."

"Sure thing." Rick took the infant from her before she could finish her question.

Bobby instantly lit up. It was not lost on Olivia. "He really seems to like you," she observed, pulling the trunk release on the driver's side floor. The trunk popped open.

"The feeling," Rick told her as he looked at the little person in his arms, "is mutual."

Rick turned so that he could watch as she took out the suitcase, then fished out the other, larger case from the inside of the car. The latter was filled with supplies she'd brought along for her nephew—disposable diapers and a few changes of clothing. She'd even packed one of the boy's toys, he noted. The woman was nothing if not prepared, an admirable quality. Along with all her other admirable qualities.

"Here," Rick said, offering the baby to her. "Why don't you take Bobby and I'll just deposit these things in my car. Along with the food," he added, seeing Miss Joan headed for them.

Olivia caught herself thinking that she could get used to this.

Immediately, she warned herself against trusting someone's kindness. Good things never lasted. The only person she could rely on was herself. She had to remember that. To think anything else was to leave herself open to disappointment and disaster. The sooner she remembered that, the better off she would be.

Chapter Ten

It looked like a home that had seen its share of happiness. Olivia felt it the moment she saw it. She didn't have to be told that this was Rick's house. She just knew.

Single story with a white stucco exterior, the house had a paint job old enough to have witnessed several winters, but not so old that it showed signs of suffering from the effects of a merciless summer sun.

When Rick pulled his car up in the driveway and turned off the ignition, Olivia hesitated about getting out. There were lights on in the house.

"Maybe you should have called ahead and checked if it was all right to bring home houseguests." She glanced into the back of the car at her nephew. Lulled by the drive, he was sound asleep. A condition subject to change at the drop of a hat. "Especially one who cries."

"You'll just have to work on that," he quipped, humor curving his mouth. And then he saw that she was serious. "And called ahead to check with who?" he asked.

A girlfriend? A wife? A friend? She shrugged, at a loss as to specifics. "With whoever's in the house."

Rick watched her. "There's no one in the house," he told her.

His sister was away at college—her last year—so there was no one to greet him when he came home at night, a fact he was acutely aware of. He was seriously thinking of getting a dog, except it wouldn't be fair to the dog to leave him alone all day. Conditions at the sheriff's office were fairly relaxed, but not enough to accommodate a dog.

Olivia got out and began to remove the infant seat restraints holding Bobby in place. Bobby continued sleeping.

She nodded toward the house. "The lights are on," she pointed out.

Was that it? He laughed, shaking his head. "Automatic timer. Makes it seem less empty when I come home."

"That bothers you? The emptiness," she added when he didn't answer. He didn't strike her as the lonely type.

"Sometimes," he allowed. He took out the cooler filled with baby bottles and formula that she'd transferred into his vehicle, as well as her suitcase. "My sister lives here when she's not away at college. After an entire summer of Mona's chatter, the house feels unnaturally quiet when she's gone."

"You get along with your sister?" she asked, following him to the front door.

"Better now that she's outgrown her bratty stage," he quipped.

He paused to unlock the front door, then picked up the cooler and suitcase again, only to park both just inside the door. Rick waited as she looked around, wondering what she thought of his home. He assumed that she was accustomed to fancier digs, but this suited him. Even though he would most likely take that job in Dallas, this would always be home to him.

"Let me show you to your room," he offered.

He led Olivia and the baby down a very short hall. He opened the door to the first room on the left. It was a very feminine bedroom. The double bed had a canopy overhead. The canopy matched the white eyelet bedspread which, in turn, matched the shams on the pillows.

Bobby began to stir. She automatically started to sway, attempting to lull him back to sleep. "Let me guess, this is your sister's room?" Olivia didn't exactly like the idea of invading someone else's space, even if they weren't there to witness it.

"No, my grandmother's." He looked at her, amused. So far, both guesses she'd made about the house had been wrong. "You're not very good at this game, are you, Olivia?"

Because he was putting them up, she bit back the first retort that rose to her lips. Instead, she looked around again. He'd said that no one was home. That didn't mean that someone wasn't due back. "Your grandmother, where is she?"

A fond look came into his eyes. "Probably bossing the angels around, telling them how to play their harps if I know her."

"Then she's—?"

"Yes," Rick answered quickly, cutting her short before she could say the word he really didn't care to hear.

"I'm sorry."

"Yeah, so was I." His grandmother had been gruff and strict, but both he and his sister knew she loved them. That was never in question. "This is her house. She left it to me and to Mona. Abuelita said it was all she could give us." There was irony in his smile. "She didn't realize that she'd given us so much more than just a building. She gave us a home."

Aware that his voice had become softer when he spoke about the old woman, Rick cleared his throat, as if that could erase outward signs of sentiment. He became all business.

"Listen, I might be able to find Mona's old playpen in the attic. It would give you someplace to put your nephew when he's sleeping." He nodded over toward the bed. "That way you don't have to worry about him rolling off and hurting himself."

He really was more thoughtful than she'd given him credit for, she thought, impressed.

"Thank you," she murmured. If there was a playpen in the attic, they had to have lived in the house a long time. "How long have you and your sister lived here?"

"Mona was six when my grandmother took us in. I was eleven, but she took care of us off and on—mostly on—right from the beginning." His eyes met hers. "Why?"

"Just curious," she answered evasively. It occurred to her that she was asking too many personal questions.

Olivia had a feeling he felt the same way when he replied, "Uh-huh."

When she turned to ask him what he meant by that, Rick had already left the room. A couple of minutes later, she could hear the sheriff walking around in the attic, just above her head.

That was when Bobby woke up fully and began to fuss. Like any three-month-old who hadn't eaten in a couple of hours, he was hungry. He let her know the only way he knew how. He cried.

"Message delivered, loud and clear," she assured him. The next moment, she began to sing softly, hoping to distract him. She made her way back to the front of the house and the cooler. Bending down carefully, still singing, she extracted a bottle. "Now all I need to do is find a microwave," she told her nephew. Bobby cried again. "You don't want to know the logistics, you just want your bottle, right?"

She shifted the baby to her other side, took the bottle and went in search of the kitchen.

It wasn't much of a search. By the time Rick came back downstairs, carrying the slightly scarred playpen— folded in fourths—in his hands, she had just finished warming Bobby's bottle and was testing its warmth on the inside of her wrist.

"I see you found the kitchen," he noted.

"Wasn't hard. It was the only room with a stove," she cracked. Sitting down with the baby, she began feeding him. "And you found the playpen."

He leaned the playpen against a wall and went to the sink to retrieve a dish towel. After running water over it, he crossed back to the playpen.

"It's a bit dusty," he told her, "but nothing a little water won't fix. There's even a mattress for it." That, too, was folded in fourths inside the playpen. "It's kind of thin," he admitted, "but I can fold up a couple of

blankets and put them on top of it. That should keep
him comfortable."

Bobby made greedy sucking noises as he ate. She
smiled at him. She'd never thought about having children—taking care of Tina had filled that void, or so she
thought. But Bobby had stirred things up, made longings
emerge. Longings that probably didn't have a chance in
hell of being fulfilled. That didn't make them any less
intense.

"Why are you going to all this trouble?" she asked
Rick suddenly. After all, they were nothing to him.

"Because he needs a place to sleep. And so do you,"
he added. "And Miss Joan was right, that motel is too
vermin infested. You'd probably catch something, sleeping there."

It wasn't that she wasn't grateful, she was just trying
to understand. "But we're perfect strangers."

One side of his mouth rose a little higher than the
other, giving him an oddly endearing appearance that
instantly shot a salvo through her gut. She tried not to
notice, but it was too late.

"I don't know about perfect," Rick said, "but as for
being a stranger, my grandmother always said that a
stranger was just a friend you haven't made yet." And
then he laughed quietly. "Of course, she said it in Spanish, but I think the translation might be lost on you."

Olivia vaguely recalled taking Spanish in high
school, but right now, that seemed like another lifetime. Her sense of competition goaded her to answer
him in Spanish, some small, trite phrase she could fit
her tongue around. But with her luck, he'd think that she
was fluent and start rattling off at a mile a minute. If

that happened, she'd only be able to marginally follow maybe a few key words. And maybe not even that. She didn't want to amuse him, she wanted to impress him.

Why? In a couple of days, you're never going to see him again. Why does impressing him matter?

She didn't know why, it just did.

"You're right," she agreed, "it would be. I only remember a few words in Spanish, none of which would work their way into a regular conversation."

She had him wondering what those words were.

Olivia focused her attention on her nephew. The greediness had abated and his pace had slowed. He'd only consumed half his bottle. Thinking it best not to force him to drink any more, Olivia placed the bottle on the table and then lifted Bobby up, placing the infant against her shoulder. In a routine that had become second nature to her, especially in the middle of the night, she began patting the baby's back, coaxing a burp from him.

For once, the burp didn't come with a soggy deposit of formula on her shoulder. The small eyes drifted shut and he dozed off again. With any luck, she would be able to put him down for a few hours.

Very softly, she tiptoed back into the bedroom where Rick had put the playpen. She laid her nephew down very carefully, afraid of waking him up. She needn't have worried. Tonight, he slept like a rock. She thanked God for small favors.

She paused over the playpen for a moment longer, looking down at this small, perfect human being. For the most part, Bobby led an uneventful life and right now, she had to admit she envied him for it. Her own life seemed to be going at ninety miles an hour with no signs of slowing down.

As she turned away from the playpen she almost walked right into Rick, who was standing in the doorway observing her. He stepped back at the last minute, preventing a collision.

How was it, she wondered, that she could feel the heat radiating from his body? Feel it against her own skin.

"I'm going to warm up a little of what Miss Joan sent over. You interested?" he asked.

Yes, she was interested. Definitely interested. But not in anything that could be warmed up on a plate. The thought had come at her from left field, startling her. She shook her head, trying to extinguish the thought.

"No?" he questioned when she simply shook her head.

That hadn't been to answer him, that was to clear her head. "No—yes. A little," she qualified.

"That wasn't a multiple-choice question." He studied her for a minute. "You okay?"

"Yes," she answered a tad too quickly. "Just punchy, I think. I'm going to stay here a few minutes longer, just to make sure he stays asleep."

"Okay."

As he walked out of the room, heading for the kitchen, he could hear her singing softly under her breath. Some sort of lullaby, he guessed.

She had a nice voice.

RICK HAD JUST FINISHED heating up the food and putting it on the table when Olivia walked into the kitchen. "He still asleep?" he asked.

Just for a moment, she'd debated using Bobby as an excuse, as a shield to hide behind. But she refused to behave like a coward. What was she afraid of? Eating? Sitting opposite a good-looking man and talking? It sounded very silly, putting it that way.

"Still asleep," she echoed. "For now." She took a deep breath and smiled. "Smells good."

"I added a few things," he confessed. That was when she noticed a collection of small jars of herbs and spices scattered along the counter like partying soldiers. "We can eat in the kitchen, or on the patio. It's fairly warm tonight."

And there was a blanket of stars out tonight. She'd noticed that when she'd gotten out of the car. The thought of sitting with him in such a blatantly romantic setting made her feel uneasy.

She seized the first excuse she could think of. "I think we should stay in the kitchen. I won't be able to hear Bobby if he cries if we're outside."

"Good point. Kitchen it is." He gestured toward the table. "Have a seat."

She sank down in the closest chair. Picking up a fork, she took a tentative bite of what he'd prepared. And then another, and another. The food tasted progressively better with each bite she took.

Olivia glanced over to the counter beside the stove. More than a few containers had been left out. She recalled Rick telling her that his grandmother had taught him how to cook.

Good-looking, sensitive and he knew how to cook. As far as she could see, that made him a triple threat and damn near perfect.

There had to be something wrong with Rick. What was the deal breaker here? Was the man a closet serial killer? As she slanted a look at him, she had a pretty good feeling that wasn't it.

Rick could feel her eyes on him. Was she trying to find a polite way to tell him that she didn't like his augmentations to the meal?

Rather than speculate, he asked. "What?"

"Why aren't you married?"

He didn't know what he expected her to say, or ask, but this didn't even remotely come close. But two could play at this game. "Why aren't you?"

A fair question, she supposed. She told him what she told herself. "I've been too busy."

Rick laughed shortly. "Right. The weight-of-the-world-on-your-shoulders thing."

Just what was he implying? That she was using her busy schedule as an excuse not to get into any serious relationships?

Well, aren't you?

Lots of people had thriving careers and still had the wherewithal and time to find love. She didn't have a relationship because she was afraid. Afraid of losing someone else the way she'd lost her parents. Without any warning. In the blink of an eye. To lose a spouse like that, someone you loved with your whole being, would be completely devastating. She honestly didn't know if she could survive that. The only solution was not to put herself in that position in the first place. If she kept out of the minefield, she wouldn't run the risk of blowing up.

"Well, you certainly can't use that excuse," she retorted defensively. Then she suggested, with a trace of sarcasm, "How about the other tried and true one? The one that goes 'I never met the right girl'?"

Rick pulled his shoulders back. She'd struck a nerve without realizing it. If he flippantly agreed just to terminate this line of dialogue, it would be dishonoring Alycia's memory. Dishonoring it because she *had* been the right girl. And he would have been happy spending the rest of his life loving her.

Taking a deep breath, his eyes met hers. "Oh, I met her all right."

"And? What happened?"

When he spoke, his voice was completely devoid of emotion. Because he couldn't allow himself to feel anything. It hurt too much.

"She died."

For a moment, Olivia thought he was pulling her leg. But then she looked into his eyes and knew that he wasn't. He was serious, and she felt terrible. The man had voluntarily acted as her chauffeur, driving her to the hospital when he didn't have to. He'd literally taken her and Bobby in and she was repaying him by callously digging up memories best left untouched. Not once but twice.

What was the matter with her?

She knew she should be apologizing, backing away from the painful subject as quickly as she could. That was the way she normally handled an uncomfortable situation.

That wasn't the way she handled it now.

All sorts of questions buzzed in her head, looking for answers. "What was her name?"

"Alycia."

"Alycia," she repeated. "That's a beautiful name."

The smile was sad. "She was a beautiful woman."

An emotion she seldom experienced reared its head. Jealous. She was jealous.

How could she be feeling jealous? Jealous of a dead woman?

Because no one had ever felt that way about her; no one had ever said her name with such sorrow echoing in his voice.

Olivia pressed her lips together, her mind ordering her to drop the subject. She didn't listen, of course. Instead, she heard herself asking, "What happened to her?" And for the life of her, she wouldn't have been able to explain why she was asking. She just needed to know.

He recited the circumstances to her the way he had to her parents, struggling to distance himself from the words. "One of those cross-country moving vans lost control and jackknifed on the highway, crushing her car. Doctor said she died instantly."

How devastatingly awful for him. She felt his pain. Felt that terrible hole widening in her gut. "I don't know what to say."

He shrugged carelessly, looking away. "Nothing to say."

The ensuing silence seemed to separate them.

This would have been a good time for Bobby to wake up crying. But he didn't wake up. He continued sleeping. "Is it true?" she asked.

"Is what true?"

"That saying about it being better to have loved and

lost than never to have loved at all." She had no idea why it was suddenly important for her to know.

"You mean if I had a choice between losing her and never having had her at all, which would I pick?" She nodded in response. "That's easy. I'm glad I had her for whatever short time we shared together."

It made her realize how empty her own life was, despite the turmoil and the breakneck pace she kept. The thought negated her tired feeling and made her restless instead.

"Let me get the dishes for you," she offered. She needed to do something with her hands.

"No need," he told her. "I usually just stack them in the sink until I run out of plates and glasses. I've got a few days to go."

"I can't sleep with dirty dishes in the sink," she said.

As she reached for his plate, he put his hand out to stop her and nearly wound up knocking over his glass. He made a grab for it and so did she. The result was that her fingers went around the glass and his went around her hand.

Something basic and raw, and very, very vulnerable telegraphed itself back and forth between them.

It was hard to pinpoint the source, whether it originated with her, or with him. The only thing that was clear was what pulsated between them. Waiting for a chance to explode.

Chapter Eleven

For one isolated, tense moment, Olivia was almost certain that the man was going to kiss her. And, if she was being honest with herself, *hoped* he would kiss her.

But the moment slowly passed and nothing happened.

Embarrassed and determined not to show it, Olivia cleared her throat and nodded toward the glass that they were both keeping upright. "I think you can let go. I've got it."

"Yes," Rick agreed quietly, the timbre of his voice softly slipping along her skin, sending her body temperature up by several degrees, "you do."

The erratic electricity rushing up and down her spine made her oblivious to everything else in the room.

Everything but Rick.

She couldn't help wondering if this man had a clue as to how sexy he was, and that he just seemed to radiate sensual appeal simply by breathing. He couldn't be oblivious to it, but he acted as if he didn't realize that he was tall, dark and bone-meltingly handsome.

Were the women in this town blind?

One by one, his fingers left her hand. She became

aware of the fact that she'd stopped breathing for the duration of the contact.

"Maybe you're right about those dishes," Olivia murmured, tearing her eyes away from his. "Maybe I'd better get to bed and get some rest. It's been a very long day and there's no telling how long Bobby's going to be asleep."

Rick nodded, as if he didn't see through the thin excuse. As if he didn't know that she was running for dear life, running from something that had flared to life. Something that, given the present situation, had absolutely no chance of longevity.

"See you in the morning," he said.

"Right."

Instantly on her feet, Olivia got out of the kitchen—and away from him—as fast as possible without running. She needed to get away before she regretted her actions and consequently had him thinking she was the kind of woman she wasn't. The kind of woman who enjoyed having casual, fleeting hookups.

She wasn't that kind of a woman.

Olivia couldn't remember the last time she'd been alone with a man who wasn't engaged in giving her a deposition.

Get a grip, she silently lectured, leaning against the bedroom door she'd just closed.

Lectures not withstanding, it took a while for her heart to settle down and stop pounding.

RICK HAD ALWAYS THOUGHT of himself as a light sleeper. But apparently, there was light and then there was *light*. Although he thought he'd been listening for the baby's cries, when morning broke he hadn't heard any sounds coming from his miniature houseguest—or the baby's aunt.

There was no other reason why, when he made his way to the kitchen, Rick was caught by surprise when he found her in the room ahead of him.

But there she was, in the center of a homey scene that looked straight out of some Family Channel Christmas celebration. She was making breakfast with the scent of fresh brewed coffee—strong, just the way he liked it—filling the air, along with other delicious aromas.

What really completed the picture for him was Olivia, standing there with her hair down about her shoulders. She looked younger, softer. Approachable. And damn embraceable.

Shoving his hands into the pockets of his jeans, Rick masked his surprise. "You cook?" It turned out he wasn't the only one who was surprised that morning.

When Olivia glanced over her shoulder at him, about to confirm his query, she almost dropped the spatula. She *did* drop her jaw. Last night, she hadn't thought it was humanly possible for Sheriff Enrique Santiago to look any sexier than he did.

But she was wrong.

Barefoot and with his hair tousled, he was sexier than any living creature had a right to be. Especially since he'd neglected to button the shirt he'd carelessly thrown on. It hung open, testifying to the fact that the good sheriff was either the recipient of some incredibly fantastic genes from his family tree, or that he worked out religiously. She could count all his rigidly displayed abdominal muscles.

It took her too long to find her tongue, although she congratulated herself for not swallowing it.

"I cook," she finally replied in a voice that was only a shade less than breathless.

Turning away because she was afraid of melting on the spot, Olivia drew in a long breath and tried to access her brain.

Her first attempt failed.

This would have been a good time for Bobby to start crying, rescuing her from an awkward moment. She glanced over to where she'd relocated the playpen. But the little boy had suddenly developed an overwhelming fascination with his hands, which he held up in the air and twisted in every conceivable direction, obviously marveling at their dexterity by cooing and gurgling.

With no small relief, Olivia could feel her brain function again. "I thought that making you breakfast was the very least I could do to say thank you for putting us up like this." She hadn't cooked in years, not once there'd been enough money for takeout from one of the better Dallas restaurants, but, like riding a bike, it had come back to her.

"Nothing to thank me for," Rick assured her, taking a seat. She placed a steaming cup of black coffee before him. He smiled appreciatively. The aroma was enough to kick-start his day and get him going. "The room was there whether or not you used it." He took a slow sip, letting the inky liquid wind its way through him, waking up every cell it came in contact with. "You sleep well?" he asked her.

She had slept like a woman anticipating an earthquake, but no way could she have admitted that and not had him asking embarrassing questions. "I have a lot on my mind and Bobby was restless, but under the circumstances, yes, I think I slept pretty well."

The sheriff's deep green eyes held hers for a moment and she had the impression that she hadn't fooled him at all, but that could have been her own paranoia.

Turning back to the stove, Olivia quickly slid the omelet and the warm slice of Texas toast from the griddle onto a plate and placed the latter before him next to his coffee cup.

He sampled the omelet first. The next moment, he was smiling and nodding his approval. "This is really good. I didn't think you knew how to cook," he confessed. She hadn't struck him as the type who would have taken the time to learn.

They were both guilty of typecasting each other, she thought, amused.

"Had to," she told him. "It's a lot cheaper than takeout and when you're on a tight budget, every penny counts." That he seemed to understand. "These days I don't have to worry about living from paycheck to paycheck. But that doesn't mean I can't whip something up if I have to. I actually like cooking."

"Lucky for me I got to be around when you started whipping," Rick commented, doing justice to the serving she'd given him. He was almost half finished. "This is *really* good."

Maybe it had something to do with having all her nerve endings so close to the surface. Whatever the reason, Olivia hadn't thought a simple compliment could please her so much. But it did.

"Thank you."

"Aren't you going to have any?"

"I never seem to be able to eat anything I make, at least, not until it reaches the leftover stage." She'd always cooked for Tina and wound up nibbling a little of the meal later on.

"That would explain the killer figure," he observed, "but you really should have something."

She barely heard the second part of his statement. The first had caught her up short, even though he'd uttered it as if it was just a throwaway line. And telling herself that he probably handed out kind words a lot more than he handed out tickets didn't temper the effect the compliment had on her. For a moment, she reveled in the words, smiling, Olivia had no doubt, like some village idiot.

"I'll have some coffee," she said, taking down another cup from the cupboard and filling it three-quarters of the way up.

"That'll put meat on your bones," he quipped.

She didn't have to look at Rick to know that he was grinning. She could hear it in his voice. Was he teasing her, or being sarcastic? And why should it matter either way? Once Tina was conscious, she was out of here. More than likely, she'd never see Santiago again.

Even so, she couldn't let his comment go. "Do I look that skinny to you?"

She wasn't fishing for another compliment, but it had been a long while since she'd actually looked at her reflection and maybe she'd lost touch with the woman she had become. Her life, in the past year, had been one great big blur of briefs, trials—and coming to grips with Tina getting pregnant and giving birth to Bobby.

Having Don in the mix hadn't exactly helped with clarity, either.

"No," Rick replied honestly. "You don't. But you will if you just run on liquids. You really should eat something. Didn't your mother ever tell you that breakfast was the most important meal of the day?"

"I vaguely recall something like that," she admitted. "Point noted." She nodded her head as she held the steaming cup of black coffee with both hands, drawing in comfort from the heat.

Olivia glanced over his shoulder and out the window. The world outside hadn't lightened up any and, at this hour, it should have. Instead, it was growing progressively darker.

"Looks like rain," she observed.

There was concern in her voice. He knew what she was thinking. That if it rained, he might use that as an excuse not to take her back to the hospital. She needn't have worried. He'd never seen rain as a deterrent.

"The crops could do with some rain," he told her. "Ground's been getting parched."

She took a breath, inching toward her subject slowly. She needed him so she was careful not to be too blunt. "Do you have flash floods around here?"

"Don't worry, I'll take you back up. Barring a daring bank robbery taking place here, of course."

Rick sounded so serious, it took her a moment to realize he was kidding.

And then she smiled. "I take it you don't have robberies out here."

"Oh, every once in a while, theft does rear its head. Usually it's some school kid being threatened by the class bully for his lunch money or something along those lines. Most of the time, though, Forever's pretty much safe as safe can be." He was rather proud of that, even though Forever's tranquility added to his general boredom and ultimately had caused him to apply to the Dallas PD.

Can't have it both ways, Santiago, he silently lectured. *Either be content with the peace or go where the action is.*

The baby began to fuss. Her rest period over, Olivia was on her feet in an instant. "He wants his bottle," she said.

In anticipation of Bobby's next feeding—she'd already updated a schedule for the infant—she'd prepared the bottle just before Rick had walked into the kitchen. After taking Bobby out of the playpen, she sat down and fed him.

Rick was surprised that watching her with the baby could stir such warm feelings within him. After all, neither one was anything to him. There was no reason for him to be experiencing this kind of a reaction.

And yet, he was.

Further proof, he decided, that he really did need a change. To move on and find a new place for himself. A new, rewarding place. Who knew what that would bring with it?

MICK HENLEY CUT his long weekend short and returned a day early, grumbling to anyone within earshot that it was raining "cats and dogs" at his favorite fishing hole some fifty miles southeast of Forever. Being soaked to the skin clearly took away some of the pleasure generated by pitting himself against nature.

On his stop by the diner for some much needed hot coffee, Mick was informed by Miss Joan that the "chewed up, overpriced piece of machinery sittin' outside" her place was in desperate need of his skills.

Those were the words he used when he showed up on Rick's doorstep that morning just as Rick was finishing up his breakfast.

"Miss Joan said that the lady who's got the keys to that sorry vehicle's staying here," said the tall, almost painfully thin mechanic. He raised himself up on his toes in order to peer into the sheriff's house, most likely to see if he could spot the woman in question. Rick was six-two, but Henley was approximately two inches taller, seeming even taller because he was so rail-thin.

Drawn by the sound of voices, Olivia came up behind Rick, holding Bobby in her arms. She heard the stranger's last sentence.

"It won't start," she told the mechanic. She looked at him a little uncertainly. This was the town mechanic? The man looked more like a wild-eyed prophet out of some poorly cast movie set in biblical times. All he needed was a flowing robe and rope sandals to go with his long, straggly gray hair and the three-day stubble on his gaunt face.

"So Miss Joan tells me. She also tells me that Bruiser used your car as a big teething ring." He laughed shortly. The noise sounded more like a cackle to Olivia. "I always did say that dog was a decent judge of machinery."

She didn't feel overly optimistic about leaving her car's fate in the hands of a mechanic who took his lead from a dog, but, since Henley was the only mechanic in town, she had no choice.

"Do you think that you can fix the problem?" she asked, trying to sound as upbeat as she could.

"Can't rightly say," he told her honestly. "Haven't figured out what the problem is yet. Well, since I ain't got nothing else to do, I'll tow your car to my garage and have a look-see." About to leave, he paused. "You got the keys?"

"Not on me, but I'll go get them," she said, debating whether she should add, "don't go anywhere," or if that was understood. The man didn't seem overly bright, but she decided not to state the obvious. She was counting on Rick to keep the man there until she retrieved the car keys. "I'll be just a minute," she promised.

With that, Olivia hurried off to the bedroom, where she'd left her purse. She was back within moments. Bobby gurgled, obviously enjoying the quick sprint to the rear of the house and back.

Returning, she was just in time to see the semi-amused, utterly envious look that the older mechanic was giving Rick. Curious, she instinctively knew to keep her question to herself.

"Here they are," she said, rejoining the two men. She held out the car keys to Henley.

Long, sun-browned and permanently stained fingers wrapped themselves around the keys. Henley nodded. "We'll talk again," he promised, taking his leave.

About the car, or about something else? An uneasy feeling slid up and down her spine. But then, if the old man had meant anything sinister, Rick would have called him out on it, right? The latter was the law around here, she reminded herself, for whatever that was worth.

She was beginning to feel as if she'd gotten trapped in an episode of *The Twilight Zone*. How else could she explain this sudden, strong attraction for Rick? It just wasn't like her and yet, every time she came within close proximity of the man, her system suddenly and loudly declared: Go!

"And he's the only mechanic in town?" she questioned Rick again, watching Henley's back as he retreated to his vehicle, a fifteen-year-old truck that had definitely seen better days.

"Yes." Rick added for her benefit, "Don't worry, Mick's good at what he does."

"I certainly hope so," Olivia murmured. Any further exchange was curtailed as they both became aware of the fact that Bobby had pungently recycled his breakfast. "I'd better go change him," she said with a sigh.

"Not a bad idea," Rick agreed as she turned to hurry back to the bedroom.

WHEN RICK TOOK her to the hospital later that day, her hopes that Tina had regained consciousness quickly died. Her sister was no better. On the bright side, the surgeon told her, when she caught up to him, that Tina was no worse, either.

"You've got to understand, Ms. Blayne," he told her, "This is a process that doesn't have a specific timetable. It doesn't punch a time clock that says it'll be gone in a certain amount of hours or days. We just have to wait and see how she responds. And you're going to have to stay patient," he added.

That was easy for the doctor to say. His whole life was here. He didn't have a job waiting for him back in Dallas. A job that came with a very impatient boss who, when she'd asked for some time off, had looked as if it physically pained him to give her even a short leave of absence.

A leave of absence that might not be nearly long enough.

She would have to call Norvil tomorrow to request an extension. She definitely wasn't looking forward to that. All things considered, she would rather go before Susan Reems, known as the district's "hanging judge" to plead a case rather than ask Harris Norvil for a favor.

She stayed with Tina for several hours, talking to her, reading to her, hoping to bring her sister around, if only just a little.

But nothing changed and, finally, she asked Rick to take her back to Forever.

"At least there was no bad news," Rick said as they drove back, trying to be encouraging. And he was right, she thought. Things could have been a lot worse.

The bad news waited for them once they got back to Forever. They stopped to pick up the baby at the diner and returned to Rick's house. No sooner did they walk through the door than the phone rang.

"It's for you," Rick said, holding out the receiver. "It's Mick. Here, I'll take the baby," he offered, trading her the receiver for the infant.

She had a bad feeling about this. "Hello?"

Mick started talking immediately. "It ain't a death sentence or nothing like that," he assured her. "But your car needs parts I don't carry—don't usually work on fancy, pricey cars—but I can order them. Shouldn't be but a couple of days—"

"A couple of days?" she echoed. She'd hoped it was something simple, like a new battery.

"If we're lucky," Henley tacked on. "Now, you want me to send for 'em, or just forget the whole thing?"

That wasn't an option and she had a feeling this skinny highwayman knew it. "Send for them," she instructed, biting back a sigh.

"First thing in the morning," he promised.

The connection went dead. She stood there holding the receiver, fighting the urge to throw it across the room. Olivia hung it up instead.

She went in search of Bobby and found him in the guest room. Rick was playing peekaboo with him and Bobby was laughing a funny belly laugh that had already become part of his personality.

Standing there, watching them for a couple of minutes, she could feel the knot in her stomach unclenching. The child wasn't really hers. Neither was the man. But it didn't matter. For one isolated moment in time, she looked upon it as a family scene, something she was part of by virtue of simply *being* there and it made her feel good.

She found that she could even smile.

Chapter Twelve

For the next three days, as the threat of rain hung in the air, so prevalent that Olivia could almost taste the drops, the sheriff-with-the-heart-of-gold drove her to see her sister every morning and then drove her back to Forever and her nephew at the end of the day. In between, Rick would disappear, leaving her to stay with her sister and pray for a miracle as she kept up almost a steady stream of conversation, interspersed with reading the local newspaper out loud to Tina.

It made no difference.

Tina remained in a coma, out of reach. It was getting harder and harder to see her sister that way.

As her mind searched for positive things to dwell on, Olivia began to wonder where Rick went during the day after he left her at the hospital. Was he visiting friends he knew in town? Going to the movies? What?

When he came to Tina's room to pick her up the evening of the third day, Olivia decided to ask him outright. She knew that he had every right to his privacy and she had no right to pry.

But knowing that didn't diminish her curiosity.

However, before she could open her mouth to ask,

Rick handed her an umbrella. That was when she noticed that his hat and jacket were wet. Not damp from accumulated drizzle, but wet, *really* wet.

"You're going to need this," he told her. "It's raining like there's no tomorrow." The sheriff glanced over Olivia's shoulder at the unconscious young woman in the bed, then back at her. "No change?"

"No change." God, but she hated the sound of those words. They were the same two words the nurses told her every morning as she walked into the ICU, asking how Tina was doing.

Rick gave her an encouraging smile as he led the way toward the front entrance. "Maybe tomorrow."

"Yes, maybe tomorrow," Olivia echoed, wishing she could actually believe that.

Whether Tina regained consciousness or not, once her car was back among the running, she was going back to Dallas to talk to their family physician to find out what it took to get Tina airlifted from Pine Ridge Memorial and brought to Parkland Memorial Hospital, one of the outstanding hospitals in the state. The doctors there must be able to bring Tina around. Parkland Memorial attracted a more gifted class of surgeon, she thought, tamping down the desperate feeling within her.

It wasn't raining when she walked through the door and went outside. It was pouring. Relentlessly.

"Here, take this," Rick said, opening the umbrella and thrusting it into her hand. Before she could protest that he needed it more than she did, he was gone, weaving through the parking lot to retrieve his vehicle.

The wind came from all angles, driving the rain almost at a slant on one side, then shifting positions and sending it lashing at her from the other side. She found herself shifting the umbrella from one side to the other in an attempt to keep at least semidry.

It was a losing battle.

When he drove the car up to the hospital's front entrance several minutes later, she saw once again that Rick looked absolutely soaked to the bone. Shutting the umbrella as swiftly as she could, she dived into the front passenger seat and quickly shut the door. Despite her efforts, she was almost as wet as Rick.

"Why didn't you take the umbrella?" she asked.

The shrug was dismissive and careless. "It would have just held me up."

It was a lie and they both knew it. He'd left it with her in hopes that it would keep her relatively dry. Apparently chivalry was not dead, at least not in Forever, Texas. She didn't realize she was smiling.

Shifting in her seat and looking at his profile, she could barely make it out in the encroaching darkness and rain. "Where do you go every day?"

That struck him as an odd question. The most logical answer would have been to say "to Pine Ridge," but she wasn't simpleminded. He could tell that she assumed he didn't hang around town.

"When?"

"When you drop me off at the hospital. You never stay," she pointed out, not that he was under any obligation to stay with her. "Do you go visit friends, or…?" She let her voice trail off, waiting for him to fill in the blank.

"Or…" Rick responded, his lips curving in amusement.

Reaching over to the side, he turned on the rear window defroster and switched on the window defogger.

The windshield was clouding up. Impatient, he wiped the mist away with the palm of his hand. It didn't exactly improve visibility.

"Or," she repeated. "And that would be?" Olivia pressed, waiting.

"I go back to Forever and deal with whatever comes up during the day," he told her simply.

The heater wasn't helping all that much. Visibility was going from bad to worse. He slowed the car down to a crawl.

She must have missed something, Olivia thought. Good Samaritans were only found in Bible passages and movies of the week. "You drive all the way over here, drop me off then drive back and in the evening you repeat the whole process all over again?"

He slanted her an amused look, sparing only a second. The road needed his undivided attention. "Nothing gets by you, does it?"

"Why?"

"Why doesn't anything get by you?" he speculated as to the nature of her question. "If I had to guess, I'd say it's because you're sharp."

She wanted answers. She desperately wanted clarity for a change. And he was having fun at her expense. "Don't mock me, Rick, you know what I mean. Why are you going out of your way like this for me?"

He would have thought that it was evident. But then, life in a large city tended to make people suspicious of random acts of kindness. He spelled it out for her.

"Because your car's dead in Mick Henley's garage and your sister's in a coma in Pine Ridge Memorial and you have no way to get there," he said.

"Yes, but none of that is your problem. It's mine."

"While you're in my town, I see it differently."

Olivia watched him for a long moment as the windshield wipers rhythmically dueled with the wind-driven rain that crashed against the windshield. They were equally matched.

"Thank you," she finally managed to say. "I don't know if I remembered to tell you, but I'm very grateful to you for everything you've done for Bobby and me—and my sister."

Taking credit always made him feel awkward. Taking credit that wasn't due him only made it that much worse. "Didn't do anything for your sister except manage to locate her," he said.

He was taking modesty to a whole new level. The people she associated with in the firm would have torn him apart in a matter of moments. "But don't you understand? That was the important part. I wouldn't have found Tina if not for you."

"You would have found her," he guaranteed. "You're too stubborn not to."

Whatever she was going to say in response was swallowed up as they suddenly hit what felt like a giant pothole or, in this case, just a plain hole in the ground. The car listed to the right, her side dropping about half a foot. Olivia screamed as she slammed against the door.

"We're fine, we'll be fine," Rick insisted, raising his voice above the howl of the wind so that she could hear him.

His forearms strained and then ached as he hung on to the steering wheel, fighting for control of the vehicle.

It swerved, sliding first one way, then the other as he tried to compensate.

Struggling, he finally managed to get them beyond the sinkhole and to the side of the road. He pulled over and stopped to catch his breath.

"Do you charge extra for that?" Olivia quipped, trying to sound unfazed as she waited for her heart to stop racing.

"No extra charge," he told her.

The rain continued to get worse as they drove on. Rick began to talk, trying to take her mind off what was going on beyond the windshield, but it was futile. Visibility had gone to practically zero.

He blew out a long breath. "I think we're going to have to stop somewhere for the night. If the rain keeps up like this, I might wind up driving off the road again, or into some swollen creek."

As it was, the rain was seeping into the car via the doors. The floor had already accumulated half an inch of water and it promised to only get worse.

"*Is* there anywhere out here to stop?" Olivia asked skeptically. She didn't remember seeing a hotel.

Rick glanced at the car's navigational system. For now, it was still working, but he didn't know how much longer he was going to be able to say that. He hit the square that said "hotels." Only one name and address popped up. It barely qualified.

"There's this run-down motel about two miles from here. It doesn't look like much, but the rooms have got roofs and it's a place to stay dry while waiting for the storm to break, or for morning, whichever comes first." He glanced in her direction. "From the looks of it, some of the roads going back home are going to be flooded. They tend to flood when it really rains hard," he explained, then began to drive again, going very slowly. "Staying at The Sunshine Inn's going to be our best bet."

"IF THIS IS THE BEST BET, I'd hate to see the worst," Olivia commented some twenty minutes later, after she'd called Miss Joan to explain that they were temporarily delayed until morning and the desk clerk, a tired little man with sleepy eyes, had handed them the keys to the last available vacant room. According to what he told them, stranded travelers had flocked to the motel, the only port in the storm for miles around. His drooping eyelids covered eyes that came close to lighting up as he referred to the fact that this was the first time since he had taken over as manager that every room in the motel was rented.

The last available vacant room was the picture of neglect. The first thing Olivia noticed was the dust. It had gathered and formed a thin layer across the scarred dark bureau and on both the head and footboards of the double bed.

The bed was the second thing she noticed. There was only one.

And there were two of them.

Rick saw the concern on her face as she regarded the bed. "Don't worry, I'll take the floor," he told her. Since there was no sofa or even an upholstered chair in the room, that left only the floor for him to stretch out on. He supposed that it was a step up from camping.

Olivia was shaking her head. "No, that's not fair," she

told him. "I've put you out enough. You take the bed, I'll take the floor." It was the only decent thing to do, she thought.

The threadbare carpet was peeling back in places and looked far from sanitary. The bed at least appeared clean, Rick judged.

"Look, we're both adults. No reason we can't share a bed," he told her. He saw the leery expression in her eyes. "One of us stays under the covers, the other sleeps on top of them. Good enough?" he asked.

If she protested, she knew he was going to think that sex was foremost on her mind and it wasn't—at least, not exactly. Left with no choice, Olivia nodded, and echoed, "Good enough," and went to see how bad the bathroom was.

She discovered that it was surprisingly clean, under the circumstances. There was even a set of bath towels that looked as if they'd been recently purchased. The pile still felt relatively fluffy.

"I'm going to take a quick shower," she said, sticking her head out of the bathroom. "Unless you want to go first."

He declined, saying, "I take my showers in the morning."

Ordinarily, so did she, but she was tense and wet from the rain. Knots the size of small boulders resided in her shoulders and she hoped a hot shower would help undo them.

"I'll be right out," she promised.

"Take your time. We're not going anywhere," he answered.

Olivia went in and closed the bathroom door. He

heard the click as she turned the lock. Definitely not a trusting woman, he thought. And in this case, maybe it was just as well. She surely represented temptation. His reaction to her all along had been a surprise to him. He hadn't been more than fleetingly attracted to a woman since he'd lost Alycia. And he *meant* fleetingly. As in a matter of minutes at best.

This, he had to admit, was something different. So having a locked door between them when she was showering wasn't the worst idea.

Looking for a diversion, Rick turned on the antiquated TV set that just barely fit on the wobbly cart. As he flipped from one channel to another, he found himself watching either static or snow. Or nothing. Apparently the weather had dealt a fatal blow to the reception in the area. Bracing himself for a long, drawn-out evening, he shut off the TV.

Just in time to hear the bloodcurdling scream coming from the bathroom.

Olivia.

He had his gun out immediately.

"Olivia, are you all right?" he shouted through the door.

When all he got was another scream in reply, he tried the doorknob. It wouldn't give. But the door itself was just barely mounted in its frame, a victim of age and time and perhaps a few rowdy parties. Rick kicked it in on his first try.

The water in the shower stall was running full blast, the shower stall door hanging open. Olivia had jumped out right after her first scream. She was dripping wet, trembling and completely heart-stoppingly naked.

And then he saw why she'd screamed and run out of the stall.

There was a rat in the stall and at first glance, the rodent looked to be just a shade smaller than a miniature pony.

As if aware of his audience, the rat ran out of the stall and scurried over in Olivia's direction. Jumping back, she screamed for a third time.

Wanting to stop the rat before it reached Olivia, Rick looked around for something to hit it with. There was nothing. He did the only thing he could. Taking aim, he shot the rat.

Stifling a scream, Olivia began to sob. She was still trembling. Ordinarily, she would have held together, but the encounter with the rat had been the catalyst, the proverbial final straw. Everything that she had been struggling with to keep under wraps, to keep bottled up inside her just came pouring out.

Confronted by this gut-twisting pain and anguish, Rick did what anyone else would have done. He did what came naturally. Murmuring words meant to soothe, he took Olivia into his arms to reassure her and to offer her comfort.

"It's okay," he said, repeating the two words over and over again like a healing mantra. "It's okay. The rat's dead. He can't get at you anymore." Holding her close to him, acutely aware that only one of them was dressed, he tried not to allow his mind to make the most of that input. Instead, he focused on what had transpired and what needed to be ascertained. "Did he bite you?"

"No."

Rick was afraid she might have gone into shock, but

he couldn't very well begin a detailed exam, searching her body for bite marks. All he could do was press home the point. "Are you sure?"

Shaken, she nodded. "I'm sure."

He felt the words vibrating into his shoulder, accompanied by warm breath that seemed to brand his very skin.

"I'm sorry," Olivia apologized, in between the sobs she was trying to stifle. "I don't usually fall apart like this. It was just a stupid rat. But he climbed right into the stall and his face was inches from mine and I—I—"

She couldn't stop sobbing. Very gently, Rick stroked her hair, telling her over and over again that it was all right, that she'd had a lot to deal with and it wasn't the rat that she was crying about, but everything else.

"But it's going to be all right. I promise."

The words he said got to her. They made her feel defenseless and vulnerable. And yet, at the same time, they made her feel safe, because he understood, understood maybe better than she did what she was going through.

She clung to him, trying to hang on to his strength, trying desperately to get her own back.

And then somehow, somewhere in the middle of the sobs and the soothing words, she lost herself.

Looking back later, Olivia wouldn't be able to say with any certainty just what steps came next and who really was responsible for what.

One moment, she was crying her heart out, damning her poor self-control for breaking down this way. The next moment, she'd turned up her face to his and found herself kissing him.

Or maybe he was kissing her.

Whichever way it started, several seconds into it they were kissing each other. Kissing with a passion and a longing that both surprised and frightened her even as she reveled in the feel of it. Reveled in the wondrous heat that the kiss was generating. It flowed to every part of her starting from the center on out.

She felt alive and vibrant for the first time in years.

Olivia clung to him, digging her fingers into his shoulders as if to reassure herself that he was real, that this was happening. As the kiss grew, deepening, making her feel as if she was sinking inside of it, she became completely disoriented and lost. But it was a good lost. At least for now.

Damn it, what the hell was he doing?

He'd broken down the door and burst into the room to help her, thinking to possibly save her from whatever had made her scream like that. He hadn't come running to the rescue like that simply to have his own turn with her. He had no intention of taking advantage of her.

The woman was naked. And he had seen every single magnificent curve, even as he went to offer her comfort.

Offer her comfort, he silently jeered. He should be giving her something to put on, not draping her on himself as if she were some sort of human shirt.

What the hell was the matter with him? What was he thinking?

That was just the problem, he realized. He wasn't thinking, wasn't thinking at all, just feeling and react-ing. And savoring one of the sweetest kisses, one of the sultriest bodies he had *ever* come across in his thirty-one years on this planet.

Let go of her, damn it. Let go of her.

But he couldn't.

Not when everything inside of him had suddenly gone on tactical alert, responding to the incredible stimuli he had right before him.

He could feel himself losing ground. Giving in by inches. Giving in to the attraction that had been building within him ever since he'd first seen Olivia come striding into Miss Joan's diner, fire in her eyes and all but literally loaded for bear.

There was no excuse for what he was doing. No excuse for savoring her kiss, her nearness. No excuse for holding on to her so tightly, feeling her body heat penetrate his own.

Anger and disappointment struggled for possession of him, trying to wrench the thin strands of control away from the rest of him. The part that didn't have the same moral code as he had been instilled with, obviously.

And he discovered that the longer the kiss went on, the more he wanted to build on the emotion that it kicked up. Build on it and make love with this woman who'd come into his life out of the blue like an unexpected hurricane.

Being with her here in this fleabag of a motel, kissing her and feeling the burn from within only served to remind him just how very empty his life had become.

Chapter Thirteen

Rick honestly had no idea where he ultimately found the inner resolve and strength, but he did and he was able to force himself to pull back before anything happened.

Pausing for a moment to pull himself together, he made sure that he looked only into Olivia's eyes when he spoke to her. If he looked elsewhere, the words just wouldn't come out. The woman's body left him all but completely speechless.

He nodded his head toward the towel rack. "Maybe you should put a towel on."

Had she done something wrong? Why was he backing away?

Embarrassed, horribly uncomfortable, Olivia tried to cover by resorting to a wisecrack. "I would have expected you to ask me to put on high heels, not a towel."

The image of Olivia, her supple body completely nude except for a pair of black stilettos nearly made him swallow his own tongue. He could feel the heat rushing over his body, the almost insurmountable desire to pull her back into his arms and lose himself in her all over again. That he didn't, that he held himself in check, made him superhuman.

"I'm sorry," she began, quickly reaching for the lone towel that hung on the rack.

But as she pulled the towel to her, the rack, barely attached to the wall by badly rusted screws, came flying away and fell to the floor. It landed within a hairbreadth from her foot, and would have hit her if she hadn't jumped. But that threw her off balance and she wound up bumping up against Rick.

Instincts had him closing his arms around her to keep Olivia upright.

And then they were back to square one, with his hormones raging, begging for release. The scent in her hair filled his head, further lowering his resistance. "You know, there's only so many times that I can pull away," he told her.

Olivia turned around in the circle of his arms, facing him, her body tingling. Eager. She had to know. "Why do you want to pull away?"

"Want to?" he echoed incredulously. "Is that what you think? I *don't* want to," he assured her. "I'm doing it for you. I don't want you making a mistake."

Her heart all but melted right there in her chest. "Maybe I don't think it is a mistake." She searched his face, trying to read what was on his mind. But she couldn't. She could only hope. "Do you?"

His eyes held hers. "I don't know what to think," he said honestly.

"Then maybe you and I shouldn't think at all. Maybe," she continued, raising herself up on her toes, her lips achingly close to his, "we should just let things happen and see where it goes."

Straight to hell on a toboggan, Rick couldn't help thinking. But he couldn't very well tell himself that he was being noble and shielding Olivia if she didn't want to be shielded. And heaven knew he was hungry, as hungry as a man coming off a forty-day fast.

He couldn't remember the last time he'd been with a woman. The last time being with a woman had mattered to him, he'd been with Alycia. The night before she'd died in the crash.

Although he didn't want it to, Rick had the feeling this time would matter. Making love with this woman would leave a lasting impression on him. It would change him.

But it was far too late to put on the brakes, too late to walk away. Because she'd turned her face up to his, offering him something he wanted more than anything else in the world.

He wanted her.

As gently as if she was in danger of shattering, Rick took her into his arms and drew her to him. He softly touched his lips to hers. The sweetness of her kiss took his breath away and his heart began to hammer wildly.

As did hers.

He could feel the way it beat against his chest. Could feel her heartbeat echoing within him until two hearts had somehow melded into a single one.

He wasn't quite sure when the frenzy took hold, but the tempo of the inner music between them increased and the gentle kiss deepened until there was nothing gentle about it.

He kissed her over and over again, finding that the more he kissed her, the more he wanted to. She put a fire in his belly the likes of which he hadn't experienced in a long, long time.

All of her life, she had measured twice before cutting once. She had always been so cautious, so careful that she'd earned the teasing nickname of "Grandmother Olivia" when she was just in junior high school. The nickname followed her all the way to college.

She didn't care, because reckless actions had consequences and would have gotten in the way of her making something of herself. And even if she were given to reckless behavior, she didn't have that luxury, because there wasn't just herself to think of. There was Tina, always Tina. Even if she had wanted to be wild, she couldn't take the risk because she always had to be there for Tina.

But being there for Tina hadn't exactly worked out all that well, had it? All those years of behaving, of being restrained, of thinking everything through to its conclusion not once but several times, that all seemed wasted now. Tina had rebelled and not only gotten pregnant, but then run off with the father of her baby, leaving her to rattle around alone in her expensive, empty high-rise apartment.

With all that in her background, Olivia saw no reason not to give in to this incredible pull, the overwhelming attraction to this man that surged in her veins.

Her mouth sealed to his, Olivia fumbled with the buttons on his shirt, working them through the holes until the material hung freely about his torso. She eagerly yanked the shirt from his shoulders, from his body, wanting to touch him.

Olivia ran her palms over his hard torso, gliding her fingers over the ridges of his abdominal muscles the way she'd longed to do ever since she'd seen Rick walk into his kitchen with his shirt hanging open.

The hardness she discovered sent a jolting electric current zipping through her veins, at the same time that it moistened her very core.

She wanted him, wanted him to make love with her, to kiss her until she was mindless. Their lips locked in a kiss, they somehow managed to stumble their way out of the bathroom, working their way into the bedroom. The path was marked with clothing that had been shed.

With each new frontier she crossed—taking off his shirt, his jeans, sliding her hands along his underwear and tugging at it, teasing herself as well as him—her breathing grew progressively labored. Maintaining focus became difficult. Her mind was spiraling out of control.

She bit her lower lip to keep from crying out as he trailed his lips along the side of her neck, nibbling at her sensitized skin. He set off fireworks within her. Showers of blues, reds, golds, greens and so many more exquisite, indescribable colors danced through her mind's eye as Rick lowered her to the bed.

She felt as weak as a thin thread and as resiliently strong as a steel wire as Rick brushed his lips along the more sensitive areas of her body, bringing about a quickening that was equal to nothing she'd ever experienced before.

As he explored, caressed, suckled, the excitement within her grew until she almost couldn't breathe, couldn't pull in enough air to sustain herself. A cry of ecstasy escaped as she felt his tongue taking possession of her, inciting a mini-riot within her very core.

She gasped, bucking, arching, trying to follow the feeling, to frame it and hang on in order to prolong the climax.

When it was done, when she couldn't hold on to even a sliver of it a second longer, Olivia fell back on the bed, exhausted and all but disoriented. In a haze, she thought she heard Rick laugh softly and then felt the warmth beginning all over again as he started to take her on a second journey, the route different, the result identical.

This time, she cried out his name, clutching at his shoulders like a woman about to go spinning off the edge of the earth and desperately trying to anchor herself before that happened.

Before she disappeared into space and became nothing more than a speck in the heavens.

And then, suddenly, he was there, just above her, distributing his weight equally between his arms, his hands firmly planted on the mattress on either side of her.

A heartbeat earlier, she'd felt the hard contours of his body as he'd pulled himself up along hers. The quickening within her core began just on the promise of what was to come. She was more than ready for him, more than ready to share the moment rather than to experience its wonders alone, the way she'd just been doing thanks to his clever actions.

Or she *thought* she was ready for him.

There was no way she could have been prepared for this. For the crackling rhythm that flashed through her body over and over again as he entered her and then began to move his hips. She breathlessly hurried to synchronize her movements to his.

They went faster and faster, racing to catch the ride of their lives.

She heard him make a sound as he was swept up in the moment and heard her own voice blending with his as the whirlpool seized them both at the same time, lifting them up, freezing in the moment and then, slowly, receding again.

She couldn't catch her breath. And quite possibly, she would *never* catch her breath again. But it had been worth it because this, she knew, was going to be the one precious experience of a lifetime.

Her lifetime.

Oh, she'd made love before, if she could actually apply the label to that. Couplings would be a more adequate description. A handful of couplings that had turned out to be far less than memorable events. The experiences had been so forgettable that she would have been hard-pressed to recall the faces of any of the men who had shared, however briefly, a bed with her. At that time, to her, sex had become much ado about nothing.

But this, she knew, would be something she would always remember—vividly—even when she blew out a hundred candles on her birthday cake. Time would never dim the memory of this.

Olivia felt him withdraw, felt the mattress—rather than the earth—move as Rick fell back beside her. She waited for him to get up, to gather together his clothes and get dressed, behaving, more or less, as if nothing had happened.

Or, if not that, then she expected him to roll over and go to sleep, exhausted by the pinnacles they had both just climbed.

What she *didn't* expect him to do was what he did.

She didn't expect him to slip his arm around her and pull her close to him. Nor did she expect him to press a kiss to her temple as he released a sigh that sounded as if its source went down deeper than even his soul. After having her entire world rocked, she did not expect tenderness on top of that.

Yet that was exactly what she got.

"You are one incredible lady," he murmured against her temple. The words made her even warmer than his breath did as it danced along her skin all the way down to her neck.

"Me?"

In her estimation, she'd done nothing to merit his words. He was an incredible lover. A man who'd played her body as if it was a rare, finely tuned, precious violin. Yes, she'd responded to him but the comparison between the two of them couldn't be measured by any kind of instrument known to man.

Olivia turned in to him, expecting to see a smile of amusement on his lips.

He was smiling all right, but she could see that he was also serious. How was that possible? He was the one who'd made the earth not only move, but explode. It was all his doing, not hers. He had to know that.

"You," he confirmed. As he spoke, he toyed with a

strand of her hair, winding and unwinding it around his finger. Anticipation began to move through her. "I guess it's true what they say."

"What who says?"

"They," he repeated with a smile. "The all-important 'they.'"

"And what is it that they say?" she asked, still not following him but content to remain like this, lying here with him, feeling the heat of his body as it reached out to hers. This was the perfect moment. If she were to die now, this minute, she would die utterly content.

"That still waters run deep."

She thought of the past half hour, steeped in mounting frenzy. There'd been perpetual motion involved. "I wasn't aware that I was so *still*."

"Well, not strictly speaking," he admitted, a widening smile curving the corners of his mouth and going straight to her heart. "But talking to you someone might get the impression that you took yourself too seriously to let go like that." He tucked her against his side and before she could say anything about his evaluation, he added, "You took my breath away."

Any protest she might have had to offer died instantly. Another reaction rose in its place. Affection swirled through her and, while she knew it had no future and that she couldn't allow herself to get too caught up in this feeling, for the moment, for right here, right now, she gave herself permission to savor it. To revel in it. And to pretend, just for an instant, that it would last.

Olivia cupped her palm along his cheek, feeling things that had never had a place in her life before. "The feeling, Sheriff Santiago," she said, enunciating his title and name slowly, seductively, "is more than mutual." She teasingly brushed his lips with her own. "What's that expression?" It was a rhetorical question, she was well aware of the expression she was about to use. "Ridden hard and put away wet? That's just how I feel."

He did his best to look serious. "Is that a complaint?"

She laughed softly. "That is so far from a complaint, Sheriff, that it's not even remotely in the same time zone."

Humor glinted in his eyes. "So you wouldn't mind, if say, you and I went out for another ride?"

"You want to do it again?" she asked, staring at him, stunned. She would have thought that after a performance like that, he was done for the night.

Obviously she knew nothing about this man.

He grinned at her and she realized that she really liked his grin. "Nothing much else to do," he answered philosophically. "It's raining outside and the TV's down."

Another delighted laugh broke through. "You do know how to sweet-talk a girl, Sheriff."

"No, not a girl," he contradicted, lightly kissing the side of her neck. "A woman. Because you, lady, are *all* woman."

There went her heart again, she thought, pounding wildly and wickedly. "You really do know how to turn a phrase," she breathed as the fireworks inside of her began all over again.

It was the last thing she said to him for quite some time.

Chapter Fourteen

"I am very sorry to hear about your sister, Olivia, but you have a responsibility to the firm that cannot be suspended at will," the cold, scratchy tenor voice on the other end of the line informed her. "I am sure that you've considered the fact that your sister may never wake up from her coma. One way or the other, there will be staggering bills to pay. Your erstwhile dedication to her won't pay for a single IV. However, your position here at the firm will. Surely you can see that you have a moral obligation to return to us immediately."

Olivia sat on the bed in what had temporarily become her room, listening to the senior-senior partner, Harris Norvil, lecturing her. Mentally, she caught herself throwing up defenses and doing her best to block out the gray-haired man's words.

It was Friday morning, two days after she and Rick had sought shelter from the storm and discovered it in each other's arms. It'd been a full week since she'd arrived in Forever and she now realized that she would need to stay longer.

Wanting to give the firm a heads-up sooner than later, she'd called to request an extension for her leave of absence. That way, they could find someone to handle her cases. Initially, she expected to speak to the head administrative assistant, but the moment she identified herself to the woman, she was asked to please hold. The next voice she heard was the cold, sharp voice of Harris Norvil. He wielded guilt like a finely honed saber, slicing the air with every word he spoke.

This was not going to be easy. "I'm afraid I can't return immediately, Mr. Norvil."

She could almost see the man pulling back his bony shoulders beneath his hand-tailored suit, a dour expression on his face. His gray eyes narrowing into slits.

"Can't or won't?"

"Can't," she replied, trying very hard to maintain a respectful tone and not allow her temper to break through.

The man lived and breathed the firm, she understood that, but the firm did not define who and what she was any longer. She'd had a rude awakening this past week and realized what was really important. Burning the midnight oil at Norvil and Tyler was not it. She had a life outside the briefs and the long, drawn-out court procedures.

Even before this had come up, she had begun feeling disillusioned with the whole process. It occurred to her that victory in the courtroom wasn't about justice; it was about who was the most clever at blocking motions, trumping testimonies and manipulating the facts to their own best advantage. That left a bad taste in her mouth.

"My car broke down when I arrived in Forever," she

explained, "and the mechanic had to send out for parts. I'm told they're arriving today, possibly tomorrow."

She could tell by the way he breathed heavily that Norvil did not find the excuse satisfactory. "Take a plane."

"I'm afraid that there is no airport in the vicinity."

She heard Norvil mutter an oath. He made no effort to keep it inaudible. "Rent a car and drive back."

"There are no car rentals around here, either."

Norvil lost his temper. "Where the hell are you, Dogpatch?"

Ordinarily, the senior partner losing his temper would have made her retrace her steps and tread lightly, but she felt oddly combative, and also protective of the town that she herself had looked down upon only a few days earlier. What a difference a couple of days made.

"Not every town is as urban as Dallas, but Forever has its charm."

The people here were good people. They went out of their way to help one another out. And they'd been good to her. She and Tina had lived in the high-rise apartment for three years now and she still didn't even know her neighbors' names, much less feel comfortable enough to trust that neighbor with Bobby for a few hours. Yet she had absolutely no qualms about leaving the infant with Miss Joan or Lupe.

"All right," Norvil snapped, "we'll send a car for you."

He could send a coach made out of a pumpkin, drawn by four horses that had once been mice and she wasn't leaving, not without Tina.

"I'm sorry, sir," Olivia said firmly, "but I have to

respectfully decline your generous offer. I have to stay here until my sister can be transferred to another hospital."

There was silence on the other end of the line and she braced herself for an eruption. Norvil's were known to be legendary once they got underway. But when he finally spoke again, Norvil's voice was colder than ever, and exceedingly precise.

"All right, Ms. Blayne, one more week. But that's it. If you choose to remain there longer than that, we will be forced to terminate you and send your things to your apartment. Do I make myself clear?"

He was threatening her. And, for the sake of having a career to go back to at the end of this whole thing, she would let him get away with it. Worse, she would act grateful. God, but she hated this.

"Yes, sir, perfectly clear. That's very generous of you, Mr. Norvil. Thank you."

But she was talking to a dead line. Norvil had hung up. Muttering a curse, Olivia snapped her cell phone shut.

"Problem?"

She looked up to see Rick standing in the doorway. How much had he heard, she wondered. She hadn't thought to close the door. Things had gotten a great deal more relaxed between them since their return from the motel room. The magical night they'd spent together had stretched beyond its parameters, spilling out into the subsequent evenings that followed. She'd never known that being stranded could be so wonderful.

She blew out a long breath. "Not unless you call groveling a problem." She rose from the bed. "I just asked the senior partner at my firm for an extension on my emergency leave of absence. He made it sound as if I was asking for his last pint of blood."

Olivia forced a smile to her lips, refusing to fixate on the fact that she had, more than likely, torpedoed her chances of getting a raise this year. Norvil not only demanded team players—which was his right—but that those players live and breathe the firm to the exclusion of everything else—which *wasn't* his right.

Her eyes met Rick's. "Which isn't possible. Everyone knows the man runs on pure motor oil."

He came closer to her and touched her shoulder. She was hard-pressed to remember ever feeling anything more intimate, at least with her clothes on.

"You okay?" he asked.

A defiant smile rose to her lips as she tossed her head. "I am terrific."

He grinned in response. "You'll get no argument from me. So, are you ready to go?" he asked, crossing over to where Bobby lay in the playpen.

Rather than waiting for Olivia to make the first move, he picked up the baby and then grabbed hold of the diaper bag that was literally stuffed with everything that the infant would need for the day.

Rick appeared so comfortable doing that, she thought, feeling a familiar warmth stir within her. When had this happened? When had she started longing for what she'd always turned her back on? A husband, a child. A family of her own.

Tina had always been enough family for her. At times, maybe even too much family. And now, suddenly, she was thinking picket fences and all that went with them. What was going on with her?

Had to be something in the water. Or maybe with the town. When she'd arrived, the various citizens of Forever had been busy decorating for Christmas. Now, she thought, it was like wandering onto the set of *It's A Wonderful Life,* except that this was real.

Turning around with Bobby in his arms, Rick paused. "What are you thinking?"

The corners of her mouth curved just a little. "That maybe I'm the one who's in a coma and that this is all a dream."

"You certainly didn't act like someone in a coma last night," Rick pointed out with a grin.

Last night had been another magical night, except that there were no rats-on-steroids to drive her into his arms. It had taken just a look, the promise of a kiss, and she was there. Knowing full well their relationship was finite, she allowed herself to let down her defenses and *really* enjoy herself.

She wasn't quite sure how to respond to what he'd just said. When it came to legal matters, she had everything at her fingertips and there was no hesitation in her comebacks. But a lover's compliment put her in uncharted territory. She had no idea what to say or do, other than to savor it.

Before she could even attempt to form any sort of a response, her phone rang. Olivia didn't bother suppressing a sigh.

"Probably Norvil, calling to rescind the extension," she guessed. Pressing the talk button on the cell, she said, "Blayne."

"Miss Blayne? It's Dr. Baker."

The instant she heard the physician's voice, her hand tightened on the small cell, almost snapping it in half. Was he calling to tell her that Tina had slipped away in the night?

Tension rendered her whole body utterly rigid. She barely had enough oxygen in her lungs to be able to speak. "Yes, Doctor?"

Rick had been about to step out of the room to give her privacy, but he saw her grow pale and knew that his place was here, to help any way he could. When he heard Olivia say "doctor" he became alert, nearly as tense as she was.

"She's awake," Baker said without any preamble.

Olivia went numb.

Had she imagined what he'd just said? At this point, it was too wonderful to contemplate. Her breath was all but gone as she asked, "What?"

"Your sister's awake," the jovial voice on the other end declared. "I thought you might want to know in case you were planning to skip coming today."

"Not a chance," Olivia cried happily, tears filling her eyes. "Thank you. Thank you for calling. Thank you for being there for her," she added. She bit her lower lip to keep from babbling.

She'd gone to the hospital every day and every day, the doctor had made a point of coming in to give her an update of the hours since she'd been there last. He told her of any progress that had taken place, or any changes—both good and bad—that had been noted in the nurses' files.

"Just doing my job," he told her without any fanfare.

"I'll be by to look in on her later," he promised just before he hung up.

"Good news?" Rick surmised as she closed her cell phone. She gave him her answer by throwing her arms around him and the baby. Bobby squealed. "I think you're crowding him." Rick laughed. "So, what did the doctor say?"

"That Tina's awake. That she's finally awake." Olivia's voice cracked. She steepled her fingers before her lips, afraid of bursting into sobs. "She's going to be all right, Rick. Tina's really going to be all right."

He looked at her solemnly and merely nodded. And then a smile peeked through as he said, "Told you so."

"Go ahead and gloat." She laughed, blinking back tears. "I'm too happy to care. Besides, you earned the right. You told me not to give up—and you were right."

"I'm the sheriff," he reminded her. "I'm supposed to be right. It's in the town's bylaws." He glanced at the baby in his arms. "Do you want to take the baby with you to the hospital instead of dropping him of with Miss Joan?" he asked. She looked at him quizzically. "It might do your sister some good to see her son looking so well, especially if you decide to tell her about her boyfriend."

She should have thought of that, Olivia upbraided herself. Rick shouldn't have to be the voice of reason.

Her head was swimming, and it was hard for her to grab on to a coherent thought. She smiled at him, feeling incredibly close to this man she knew so little about.

"I'm glad you're here," she told him.

He told himself not to take the remark to heart. She

was just reacting to the situation and didn't mean what she said. Soon, she'd be leaving and it wasn't a good idea to allow himself to become too attached.

"Just doing my job."

That was the second time she'd heard that in the past five minutes. No one in these small towns thought they were doing anything out of the ordinary, going out of their ways for someone else. Collectively, these people were just the best people she'd ever encountered.

"C'mon," Rick told her, pressing a kiss to her forehead, "we'd better hit the road. If she's up to it, you and your sister have a lot of catching up to do. But you have to tell me one thing," he said as he ushered her out of the room, one arm cradling her nephew, the other pressed to the small of her back.

"Sure," she agreed freely, an act that took her completely by surprise and that she found oddly liberating, "if I can."

"If you're so happy—and you should be—why are you crying? Because you shouldn't be," he said. He had never been able to understand why women cried if they weren't upset or devastatingly unhappy.

Olivia couldn't explain the logistics, she just knew she was happy enough to burst, not to mention relieved. For some reason, this brought moisture to her eyes. She shrugged helplessly as she felt another wave of tears forming.

"Just happiness spilling out, I guess," she told him.

He shook his head as the three of them left the house. He didn't bother locking the door behind him. Her explanation hadn't really shed any light on the situation. "If you say so."

THOUGH NO TRAFFIC impeded the way, getting to the hospital seemed to take twice as long this time. Toward the end, Olivia grappled with the very real urge to jump out of the vehicle and run the rest of the way. The same feeling she'd had the first day Rick had driven her here.

She leaped out of the car before he'd barely pulled into a parking space. It was Rick who grounded her, who acted like the voice of reason. By example, he forced her to calm down and behave rationally, or at least with some semblance of rationality.

They entered the hospital together, although Olivia led the way by some several steps. When they reached the ICU, Rick hung back.

"Why don't I stay out here with Bobby and you go in first?" Rick suggested. "Spend a little time with her and see how well she's doing and what you think she might feel up to?"

Olivia nodded. Again, he was the calm in the middle of the storm. She should be the one thinking logically instead of acting so scattered.

Now that she stood outside her sister's room, she was almost afraid to enter. Afraid that Tina had slipped back into her coma, or that she'd sustained brain damage during the accident and was no longer the Tina she knew. She hadn't thought of that until just now and the prospect of it put fear into her heart.

Taking a deep breath, she slowly opened the door and walked into Tina's room.

Tina's eyes were closed. Olivia pressed her lips together, fearing the worst, that there had been a window of opportunity to catch her sister awake and she'd missed it. She hadn't gotten here fast enough.

She'd known someone whose cousin had come out of his coma for a full half hour before slipping back and dying the same day. She couldn't bear that. She just couldn't.

Starting to pray, she tiptoed over to her sister's bed and took hold of Tina's hand. "Please wake up, Tina," she begged in a fervent whisper. "Please wake up."

"Just five more minutes, Livy," Tina murmured. Her eyes were still shut.

Olivia suppressed a cry, tried to tamp down a sudden surge of joy. Tina always used to beg for more time each morning when she tried to get her up for school.

And then Tina opened her eyes, a very weak smile on her lips. It took her a second filled with disbelief to realize what was happening. Tina was playing a joke on her. It meant that Tina's mental faculties were working. No brain damage.

Thank you, God. I owe you. Big time.

"No, you get out of bed right now, Christina," Olivia said, trying to remember exactly what she used to say every morning as she bullied her sister out of bed. "School's not going to come to you, you have to go to it." And then she gave up the ruse, unable to continue. She blinked back tears. "Welcome back, kid. You gave me quite a scare."

Tina smiled weakly at her. "You came for me, Livy. I knew you would. I knew you would," she repeated, her voice growing reedy. And then her eyes filled with tears. "I'm sorry about the car."

Olivia shook her head. "Cars can be replaced, Tina."

She touched her sister's cheek. It felt cooler than she was happy about. "You can't. And you're still here," she added, giving her hand a small squeeze. "Everything's going to be all right," she promised.

Events began to come back to Tina. Memories unfurled like flags in the wind. Her last waking hours flashed through her mind.

Her eyes widened in horror.

"Bobby." Her fingers dug into her sister's wrist in alarm. "Oh God, Livy, I had to leave him on this cop's doorstep. Don said he wanted us all to die together. He was talking crazy, but I managed to convince him to let me leave the baby behind. I didn't have much time. And now I can't remember where—"

"Tina, I have him. I have him," Olivia cried, breaking into her sister's sob. "Bobby's safe."

"Thank you." Tina closed her eyes, relieved. "Thank you," she repeated. Tears seeped through her lashes onto her cheeks and then slid down until they reached all the way down her neck. "You always could manage things so much better than me."

"That'll change," Olivia promised her. "When you're better."

Tina opened her eyes again. "I only wish," she murmured softly.

"Look at me, Tina," Olivia ordered. "You *are* going to get better."

"But nothing's going to change," Tina cried sadly. "Don'll never let me go."

"Don's not a threat to you any longer," Olivia told her.

Tina shook her head, refusing to be comforted.

"You don't know him like I do, Livy. Don won't stop until he—"

"Tina, sweetheart." She took her sister's hand between hers. "He can't hurt you anymore. He can't hurt either one of you anymore," Olivia told her. "Tina, Don's dead."

Chapter Fifteen

For a moment, it was so quiet in Tina's room that all Olivia could hear were the machines as they monitored her sister's vital signs. Maybe she shouldn't have said anything yet. Tina seemed blindsided by the news. She was about to call for a nurse when Tina finally spoke.

"He's dead?" the younger woman asked in a small, still voice that was devoid of any emotion, any indication of what, if anything, she was feeling.

Olivia braced herself. For what, she didn't know. "Yes."

Tina's eyes held hers. Tina's were filled with disbelief and confusion. "You're sure?"

"Yes." Olivia thought she perceived an inkling of relief in her sister's voice. "Morgue, toe-tag, autopsy sure." What she would have wanted to add was "good riddance," but Tina had been in love with the monster, at least at one point, so she did her best to sound neutral. Most of all, she wanted to be supportive of her sister. "I'm sorry, Tina, but he is gone. The doctor told me that Don died immediately when the car struck the utility pole."

Tina's blue eyes shimmered as they filled with tears.

"That was what he wanted." She raised her chin ever so slightly, an unconscious sign of triumph that she had managed to survive. "Except that he wanted the baby and me to die with him."

How dare he? Olivia's hands clenched into fists. She struggled not to let her temper flare and rail at the man who was no longer there. "Yeah, well, I'm very, very glad it didn't happen that way." She heard the door opening and knew without turning around who had come in. Rick was bringing the baby in for Tina.

The man was good, she thought. He'd even had the timing for his entrance right.

"And so is someone else," she told Tina.

Turning, Olivia held out her arms and Rick passed Bobby to her. Though most doctors would argue against it, she was certain that Bobby recognized his mother. A contented sound escaped the small, rosebudlike mouth.

"Oh Bobby, Bobby, you're all right," Tina sobbed. She pressed the control attached to her bed until she was almost in a sitting position.

Olivia moved around so that Tina was able to see her infant son more easily.

"I think you're probably too weak to hold him, Tina, but I can hold him against you," Olivia offered, extending her arms so that Bobby could nuzzle against his mother.

Tina closed her eyes for a moment as she breathed in the very sweet, powdery smell that all babies had in common. When she opened her eyes, she looked at Olivia with gratitude. "This is all I need to get well, just to see my baby. I'm going to do better, Livy. I swear I'm going to do better."

Olivia smiled. "I have no doubts," she answered Tina with feeling.

For the first time since he'd entered, Tina became aware of the other person in the room.

"This is Sheriff Enrique Santiago, the man whose doorstep you left Bobby on," Olivia explained.

"Are you here to arrest me?" Tina asked hesitantly.

"No, ma'am, I'm here to see you reunited with your son," he told her. "Leaving him was clearly an act of desperation. You did it to save him. It's what mothers do," he assured her gently.

Not his mother, of course, he couldn't help thinking, but at least she'd had the presence of mind to leave his sister and him with her mother-in-law rather than skipping out on them entirely, leaving them in an empty apartment to fend for themselves.

OLIVIA AND BOBBY, with Rick keeping to the background, remained with Tina as long as they could. When she began showing signs of growing tired, they left, promising to return the next day.

Before leaving, Olivia stopped at the central desk and had her sister's attending physician paged.

Baker saw her standing in the hallway with the sheriff as he came around the corner from the emergency room. "I take it you saw her," the physician said. The smile on the man's somewhat craggy face was a combination of satisfaction and warmth.

She hadn't thought he had it in him to actually help Tina, but she was wrong. Olivia was more than willing—and happy—to give the surgeon his due. "I can't tell you how relieved I am to see my sister finally open her eyes again."

Baker laughed, nodding. His features softened. "You're not the only one. I've been at this doctoring gig a long time, but I still get a rush with each patient's recovery," he confessed.

His honesty surprised her. The doctors she knew were excellent, but for the most part, removed. There always seemed to be an invisible barrier between doctor and patient. Maybe it wasn't so bad in these small towns after all. "When do you think that she'll be up to being transferred?"

The surgeon thought for a moment before answering. "Tina needs to stay here a few more days," Baker told her. "Then, if everything continues on this path, she can go home."

He didn't actually mean home, did he? "To the hospital." It was half a question on her part.

Baker's smile widened as his glance took them both in. "Not unless she lives in one," he told her.

Olivia stared at him, afraid to believe what she thought he was saying. "You mean she can go home-home?" She heard Rick suppress a laugh behind her but she didn't turn around. She waited for the doctor's answer.

"Yes. Home-home," he said, echoing her phrase. "Tina'll need follow-up care, of course. For that she can see her own physician or, if you like," he continued, taking a prescription pad out of his pocket, "I can refer you to someone." He began writing the man's name and phone number. "Dr. Mike Delaney, he practices out in your area." Finished writing, he tore off the four-by-six sheet and handed it to her. "We interned together at Johns Hopkins in Baltimore. He's excellent."

Johns Hopkins was one of the best hospitals in the country, she thought. They didn't turn out mediocre doctors. The physicians who graduated from there were top-notch. And yet, Baker was here. It didn't make any sense to her. Very slowly, she folded the paper with one hand and slipped it into her purse.

"If you don't mind my asking, Dr. Baker—if you were good enough to attend Johns Hopkins, what are you doing here?"

The look on his face told her that this wasn't the first time he'd been asked the question. But there was no irritation in his voice as he said, "Because small towns need good doctors, too. Besides, Pine Ridge is my hometown. It feels good to give back a little something." His tone told her the subject was officially closed. "Now, your sister's doing fine. She has a remarkable constitution so, despite my being guardedly optimistic, I can honestly tell you that she's coming along like gangbusters."

She wanted to believe that, but she had always been the cautious type. It was better to be braced than devastated. "But she was in that coma for so long."

"Sometimes, the body knows best. Being in a coma allowed her body to focus exclusively on healing her wounds. And it obviously worked," he pronounced, pleased. Baker fished a card out of his other pocket and handed that to her as well. "If you think of any other questions, call me."

She looked down at the card in her hand, focusing on the phone number printed in black against the stark white background. "Is that the number of your service?"

"No," Baker told her, "that's the number to my cell. I find the personal touch works better in Pine Ridge. And it works better for me, too," he added.

She thanked him again with feeling, thinking how lucky Tina was that this man decided to "give something back" to the town where he'd been born. And then she, Rick and the baby left the hospital to go home.

She thought how good that phrase sounded, and then pushed back the thought and the feeling that the phrase generated before she started to get carried away. She knew the feeling had nowhere to go.

"THANK YOU FOR STAYING—at the hospital," she clarified when Rick glanced in her direction. For most of the trip home, she'd been quiet, pensive. He did his part and had left her alone. The radio droned on inaudibly in the background. "I was afraid you might leave, as usual." It just seemed right, having him there with her when she spoke to Tina.

"Special occasion." He then added in a neutral tone, "Seemed like the right thing to do."

He was constantly downplaying his actions. Didn't he know how unique he was? How good? "You've been really wonderful about all this. I don't know where to begin to thank you."

"You just did," he told her. Being on the receiving end of gratitude embarrassed him. He rolled her words over in his head a second time. "Actually, that sounded pretty final. You're not thinking of leaving just yet, are you?"

She shook her head. "I can't without Tina. I *was* going to have her transferred to a hospital in Dallas, but she really does seem to be getting excellent care here and the last thing I want to do is risk upsetting her progress. That means I'll stay in Forever until Dr. Baker releases Tina. I guess you're still stuck with me." It suddenly occurred to her that although she found the nights wonderful, Rick might feel he hadn't signed on for this length of time. Her eyes shifted to him. "Unless—"

He could see where this was going. Olivia was a beautiful, sharp woman, but not nearly as confident as she wanted the world to believe. Beneath the expensive suits and the aristocratic, classy lines was a small, somewhat insecure young girl who had never had the chance to lean on anyone for support. He found himself wanting to be the one whose shoulder she sought out.

"I wouldn't exactly call it 'stuck,' Livy," he told her.

She desperately wanted to ask him what he would call it, but was afraid of pushing her luck. This little gem he'd just dropped would have to be enough.

"Oh," she said.

"Besides," he continued, "I was thinking of putting you to work tonight."

"Oh?" This time, the single word was far more alert and cautious.

He nodded as he watched his high beams cut through the darkness on the road. "I've got a box of Christmas decorations that I've been meaning to put up. My sister's planning on coming home Christmas Day. She claims that the house looks happier when it's decorated for Christmas. So, if you don't mind joining me..."

Last year, she'd been too busy to do Christmas, and Tina was out of the house more than she was in, so there didn't seem to be a point. She hadn't even put up a tree—not even the small artificial kind. The upshot was that she felt as if Christmas had bypassed her.

Which meant she was clearly overdue.

The corners of her mouth curved deeply. "I don't mind," she assured him.

"Good."

The sight of his grin warmed her the rest of the way back to Forever.

INSTEAD OF GOING straight to his house, Rick surprised her by pulling up at the diner first.

Olivia eyed him quizzically.

"I thought since Miss Joan has been taking care of Bobby, she deserves an update about Bobby's mother."

She should have thought of that, Olivia berated herself. "Sure," she agreed cheerfully.

Rick stepped back, allowing her to enter first.

It was only when she was inside the diner that Olivia realized he had let her go in first on purpose rather than just being polite.

Miss Joan, Lupe, Rick's deputies, Mick the mechanic and several people she had come to know in town were inside the diner and they all shouted "Surprise!" the minute she walked in.

Dumbfounded, Olivia looked from the face of one person to the next, people who had been virtual strangers to her less than two weeks ago.

"What is this?" she asked Miss Joan.

Miss Joan came around the counter to stand beside her. As if she'd been doing it since he was born, she took Bobby into her arms.

"It's your party, honey. We're celebrating your good news—your sister coming out of her coma," the older woman explained in case the theme of the celebration still eluded her.

Olivia found herself without words again. Not a good thing for a trial lawyer, but what she couldn't find in words she more than made up for in feelings. Everything inside of her felt warmed as she basked in the thoughtfulness of these people who had seen fit to cross her path.

She enjoyed herself a great deal.

"HOW DID THEY FIND OUT?" Olivia asked Rick as, hours later, she stood up on tiptoe on the stepladder he'd provided to hang yet another ornament on the tree in his living room.

The tree was fragrant and the scent of pine was everywhere, nudging memories of Christmases gone by from the depths of her mind. She couldn't stop smiling.

"I called to tell them," Rick answered matter-of-factly as he attached a particularly delicate looking angel to a high branch.

But he'd been with her at the hospital the entire time, she thought. "When?"

Rick attached another ornament. "When I was in the hall with Bobby, giving you a few minutes alone with Tina."

Olivia climbed down to retrieve more ornaments. "You are sneaky, Sheriff."

"I prefer the word *clever* myself," he said with a grin.

Noting where she stood, Rick stopped what he was doing, caught her eye and pointed up toward the ceiling.

When she looked, Olivia saw that he had somehow managed to put up a mistletoe without her realizing it. The sheriff of Forever was just chock-full of surprises, she thought warmly.

"More of your cleverness?" she asked as he came closer.

"Absolutely," Rick said, enfolding her into his arms. "One of my better moments, actually."

She could already taste his lips on hers. "You'll get no argument from me."

His grin grew wider. "I really wasn't counting on one," Rick said just before he brought his mouth down on hers.

Olivia sighed with contentment, even as the passion began to build almost instantly, made that much more fierce because she knew her supply of moments like this was limited.

Tina was conscious, meaning she was getting better, and they would be on their way soon, back to Dallas. Back to the ninety-mile-an-hour life that she'd led.

And things would go back to normal for Rick as well. Without her.

Olivia wondered if, in a year's time, he would even remember her name or who she was.

The thought brought an ache into her heart. It wasn't supposed to be there. She'd told herself that she'd accepted these terms the first time she'd made love with

Rick. She'd known that this didn't have the earmarks of "forever" about it. She lived in Dallas and he lived in "Dogpatch," or at least a reasonable facsimile thereof. *And never the twain shall meet.*

Except that it had and he, as the saying went, had rocked her world. Rocked it each and every time they made love. She would never be the same.

"What do you say we finish working on the tree tomorrow?" Rick suggested. The wicked twinkle in his eye utterly fascinated her. Everything about the man fascinated her. She was hopeless. But she might as well enjoy what she had while she had it. Before it faded away.

She was more than willing to go along with his suggestion and nodded. "I always did like the minimalist look," she told him. She did her best to appear serious as she asked, "What do you have in mind?"

Rick surprised her by scooping her into his arms. "Guess."

Olivia laughed, lacing her arms around his neck. Glorying in the feel of his arms around her.

"You'd better do it fast," she coaxed. "Bobby's been asleep for a couple of hours already. He's due to wake up soon."

"Fast it is," Rick said agreeably, brushing his lips against hers just to tease her. "And then, if we have any more time, how do you feel about slow?"

He was kissing the side of her neck in between words, sending her body temperature soaring along with her pulse. Clouding her mind.

"Slow?"

"Uh-huh. Bone-melting, body-achingly slow," he elaborated.

His breath was hot along her skin and her core quickened. It was becoming a familiar response to him, to his very touch. What she was feeling was as close to yearning as she figured she had ever come.

Or ever would.

Her sigh came out ragged as anticipation raced rampantly all through her.

"Slow sounds wonderful. Maybe you should do that first," she managed to get out, each word emerging in slow motion, in direct contrast to the way her heart pounded.

"I am nothing if not a servant of the people," he told her dutifully, the words dancing along her breath-warmed flesh. "Your wish is my command."

"I'll remember that," she breathed with effort. "And I intend to hold you to it."

His eyes were already making love to her face, promising her things that had her whole body tingling with anticipation and excitement.

"See that you do," he deadpanned.

They'd reached his bedroom. Shifting, Rick closed the door with his elbow and then set her down on the comforter as gently as a snowflake.

Olivia held out her arms to him. "Shut up and kiss me."

"More good commands," Rick acknowledged with an approving nod of his head. He slid in next to her to obey this order first.

The kiss was passionate and only built from there.
Bobby did his part by sleeping for another full hour.
The hour didn't go to waste.

Chapter Sixteen

After much waiting for delinquent parts that seemed to take their own sweet time arriving from a dealer close to a hundred miles away, Mick announced with a bit of pleased fanfare that her freshly reupholstered—thanks to Miss Joan—car was finally ready to go.

The same could be said of Tina. Dr. Baker had released her sister from the hospital the night before, saying, oddly enough with the same sort of pleasure that Mick had displayed over the repaired vehicle, that Tina had made wonderful progress and that a full recovery was absolutely in her future.

Everything, it seemed to Olivia, was ready to go. Except for her.

At odds with her usual logical self, Olivia wanted to stay in Forever a little while longer. Stay, even though it wasn't practical or really possible. Her life, her work, her apartment, they were all back in Dallas. Harris Norvil had called her and said, because of the season, all was forgiven if she would return. He was giving her a last chance and she would be a fool not to snap it up.

There was nothing here in Forever for her. Nothing

except for a sheriff with hypnotic eyes and a mouth that drove her absolutely wild.

But that same mouth was not uttering words she needed to hear now. Packed and seemingly ready to depart, she was stalling, thanking Rick for his hospitality and for being so supportive during this whole ordeal. She was giving him every opportunity to say something, to "talk" her into staying even a week longer.

But Rick wasn't saying anything of the kind. He'd been silent throughout her entire little speech, as if he couldn't wait for her to be finished so he could get on with his day. Get on with his life.

And it was killing her.

Say something, damn it, she pleaded silently. *Tell me you want me to stay. Miss Joan told me you need a lawyer in Forever, but you never said anything about that, about my filling that slot. Or filling a place in your life. You didn't even say anything about my coming back for Christmas. Was everything just in my head?*

They stood there, almost like two strangers, with her making inept, awkward small talk. Two strangers instead of two lovers who had come to life in each other's arms, born again in each other's kisses.

Maybe it hadn't meant to him what it did to her. Olivia tried to shut out the ache and be philosophical about the way life turned out.

With a final, precise movement, she snapped the locks shut and put the suitcase on the floor beside the bed. She couldn't stall any longer.

"Listen," she said with forced brightness, "if you're ever in Dallas, just look me up. You'll have a place to stay."

"I'll keep that in mind," he replied stiffly.

He'd decided to turn down the interview for the position on the police force, but now he was having second thoughts about his second thoughts. Making up his mind one way or another required calm, quiet reflection, which he wasn't up to right now. His mind felt as if it was the center of a class-five hurricane, the antithesis of calm and quiet.

There was nothing left to do but walk her out. Picking up Olivia's suitcase, he carried it to the car for her. His gut was so utterly tied up in a knot, he felt like throwing up.

Rick turned from the car to see Olivia come out with Bobby in her arms and her sister walking slowly beside her.

He crossed to Tina and took her arm, threading it through his in order to give her the support she needed. Tina smiled her gratitude. In the few short days she'd spent here, she had come to like this tall, dark, handsome and somewhat stoic sheriff a great deal.

"Thank you for everything," Tina said as he opened the passenger door for her. She sank down on the seat, weary from the short trip she'd just taken. "And thank you for being so understanding about Bobby."

She knew without being told specifics that some other law enforcement officer might have turned the baby over to child services. That was still better by far than what Don had had in mind for the boy, but getting Bobby back would have meant going through hell.

"Just doing my job," Rick murmured, then realized how often he'd heard himself saying that these last couple of weeks or so.

He glanced over the roof of the vehicle. Olivia had just finished securing the baby in his infant seat and was turning toward the front of the car. Their eyes met and held. He felt his insides twisting again.

Damn it, stay woman. I can't ask you to give up everything for me. I don't have the right. But if you just said you wanted to stay, or at least that you didn't want to leave just yet, then I could tell you what I'm feeling. That I want you here with me.

But he remained silent.

Olivia saw the expression in his eyes, one she couldn't quite fathom. "Do you want to say something?" she asked, mentally crossing her fingers.

He wasn't conscious of the careless shrug that he gave, but she was.

"Just that I hope you have a safe trip." He held the door open for her and she got in, sitting behind the steering wheel. "You've got my number in case you run into trouble between here and Dallas."

She slid the seat belt tongue into the slot. "And what, you'll come riding to the rescue?"

He laughed shortly. There was no humor in the sound. "More like driving to the rescue and hey, it's the Texas way."

She nodded. This was pure torture. "We'll be fine." *If I don't break down and cry.* She looked at Tina, who was already strapped in. "Let's get you home, Tina."

Her sister breathed a sigh of relief. A look of tranquility seemed to come over her features. "Sounds good to me."

Olivia forced herself to smile as she started up the vehicle. "Yes, me, too."

Those were the last words he heard the woman who had his heart packed up in her suitcase say as he stepped back to let her leave.

He watched her drive away until the car was nothing more than a speck against the horizon, then remained there a little longer.

"How long will you go on being a jackass?"

The question came from Miss Joan as she poured a particularly inky cup of coffee for him. Rick had come in on his evening break, as he had been doing almost every evening ever since he'd become sheriff of this town. But, unlike all those other times, there was a heaviness to his step, a preoccupation about the expression on his face. Just as there had been for the past five days. Ever since that girl and her sister had left.

About to take a sip of the piping hot brew, he gazed up at the older woman. "What?"

Penciled-in dark brown eyebrows furrowed as she regarded Rick. She'd known him, man and boy, and prided herself on being able to read him better than he read himself. "You heard me. How much longer are you going to go on being a jackass?"

His took a sip, then another, before placing the cup back down on the counter. "Anything in particular you referring to?"

"Don't play games with me, boy," she warned sternly. "You know you want to go up there and see her. Be with her. Why don't you take that job offer that's been twisting in the wind and get on with your life?"

He'd only mentioned the possibility of going to Dallas for an interview. He hadn't said anything about the job actually being offered to him. "Anything you don't know, Miss Joan?"

"If that ever happens, you'll be the first to know," she promised, her expression the last word in drop-dead serious. Folding her hands together, she leaned over the counter and closer to him. "You know you're miserable without her. Anyone looking at you can see that. That friend of yours, Sam-something, he can get you on the force. You can go on being a law enforcement officer and still get the girl." She straightened up again, picking up her ever-present white cotton cloth and began polishing the counter. "If that's not the American dream, I don't know what is."

He didn't want to talk about it, not seriously. Not yet. He took another sip. "If I left, where would I get coffee like this?"

The cup was empty. She didn't refill it as was her habit. "I'll send you an urnful every Monday. Now quit talking and start packing."

He felt himself really vacillating. "I thought you liked having me around."

"I do. Only thing I like better is seeing you happy, not moping around all day with a hangdog expression on your face. Now, go." She punctuated her order by waving him on.

He circled the empty cup with his hands, staring down into it. "I'm thinking on it," was all he was willing to say at the moment.

"Think faster," she ordered as she went to tend to the customer who had just entered.

"IT's HIS, ISN'T IT?" Tina asked abruptly.

The question had come out of the blue, in the middle

of an inane conversation about the actual order of the articles cited in "The Twelve Days of Christmas."

Olivia stopped pretending that she had the slightest interest in decorating the tree she'd finally bought. Putting down her ornament, she turned to look at her sister. A nervousness undulated through her.

"Is what whose?"

Kindness and understanding flared in Tina's eyes. She was a far cry from the young woman who had stormed out of the apartment a short month ago. "The baby."

"You mean Bobby?" Olivia asked innocently, turning away. "You said that—"

Tina moved so that she was in front of her sister again. "You know, for a clever lawyer, you throw up a very poor smoke screen." She shook her head, but there was no judgment in her eyes. "No, not Bobby. I heard you throwing up this morning. And the morning before that. And the morning before that," she enumerated. Just a shade taller than her sister, she put her hand comfortingly on Olivia's shoulder. "I've been through this, Livy. Except that you, luckily, have a much nicer guy as the baby's father."

Where had this sudden urge to cry come from? She felt it scratching at her throat, trying to burst free. It took her a second to get it under control.

"I don't *have* anything," Olivia corrected her sister. "In all likelihood, I'll never see the man again." And just saying that hurt. Hurt like hell.

Tina had a simple solution. "You would if you went back down there."

Olivia stared at her, dumbfounded. "Just pop up? Tina, I can't go and—"

"No, not pop up," Tina contradicted. "I'm talking about going back there to live."

This time, Olivia laughed. The situation was far from funny, but Tina's simplistic take on it was. "Oh, even better. And just what would my excuse be?" she asked, then answered her own question. "You want me to walk up to Rick and say, 'Excuse me, Sheriff, but I believe I have something of yours? Some of your genes accidentally mingled with mine and it appears that I'm having your baby'?" She forced herself to pick up another ornament. "That, my dear, is a conversation stopper, not a conversation starter."

Tina took the ornament out of her hand and put it down. She bracketed Olivia's shoulders with her hands and looked into her eyes. "He deserves to know, Livy."

Olivia shook her head and shrugged out of Tina's hold. "Trust me, he'll be happier not knowing."

Tina picked up on the lead-in Olivia had given her. "Speaking of happy, you haven't been happy since we came back."

Olivia shrugged as she circled the tree, looking for the right place to hang the ornament she'd retrieved for a second time. "I've had a lot of work to catch up on. Nobody took up the slack while I was gone."

Tina saw through the flimsy excuse. "It's not the work and you know it." She glanced over her shoulder toward the room where Bobby was sleeping. "Why don't we just pack up and go back?"

That stopped Olivia in her tracks. It never occurred

to her that Tina would ever want to see that region of the state again.

"We? You mean you and Bobby, too? You actually want to move to Forever?"

Just a short while ago, the Tina she knew would have made some kind of snide remark about not being caught dead in a place where they rolled up the sidewalks after ten o'clock at night. This was quite a change—if she actually meant it.

But there was no indication that her sister was joking or pulling her leg. Tina looked—and sounded—sincere.

"It seems like a really nice, safe place to raise a kid. There're just bad memories for me here, Livy," she confessed. "I could start fresh there." Tina's eyes met hers. "Do it for Bobby and me if not for you."

"Like I don't see through that." Even so, she would have been willing to give it a try if not for one thing. "If Rick had given me the slightest indication that he wanted me to stay, maybe I could go back. But he didn't. He's probably forgotten all about me by now."

Tina stared at her incredulously. "In a week?"

"You'd be surprised how quickly men can develop amnesia—" The doorbell rang just then and she sighed. She was doing a lot of that lately. Sighing and throwing up and feeling as if her hormones were in the middle of a fierce tennis match. "That'll be the pizza I ordered. Could you do me a favor and get the door?"

"Sure." Tina left the room. A minute later, Olivia heard her sister opening the door. And then Tina called out, "It's not the pizza delivery guy, Liv."

The closer it got to Christmas, the more the local kids tried to hawk cards and wrapping paper and cookies even ants weren't interested in. She'd already bought more than her share. "Then tell whoever it is we don't want whatever they're selling."

"Don't you want to hear me out, first?"

The glass ornament slipped from her fingers, hitting the rug and rolling toward the base of the tree. Olivia turned from the eight-foot fir, her heart already pounding madly even as she told herself she was just imagining his voice.

But it wasn't her imagination.

Her mouth went dry.

He was standing in her living room, a black Stetson on his head, a tanned sheepskin jacket and worn jeans on his body and even more worn boots on his feet. All that was missing was the star.

"Rick."

He took off his hat and held it in his hands. If she didn't know better, she would have said he looked nervous. "Hi."

She blinked once. He was still there. "What are you doing here?"

"Feeling damn awkward," he admitted freely. "But it seemed like a good idea at the time."

Her brain felt as if it had gone into a deep freeze. "What did?"

Rick took a deep breath. "Coming here to tell you that I'm going to take a job with the Dallas police force."

Tina came to life. "I think I hear Bobby waking up," she announced. "I'll just go and look in on him." She paused to grin at the father of her sister's baby. "So great seeing you again, Rick," she told him, then gave him a quick kiss on the cheek before all but flying out of the room.

Rick ran the brim of his hat through his fingers. "She looks good," he commented.

"She is." They'd gone to see the doctor that Dr. Baker had recommended and he'd had nothing but encouraging words to say about Tina's obvious progress. "Getting stronger every day. But she can't act worth a damn." Olivia turned her attention back to him. Her heart pounded harder. He couldn't be saying what she thought she heard him saying. "So, you're really moving here?"

He nodded. "Seems like the thing to do. The commute would be a bear otherwise."

He had to be kidding. Didn't he? *Oh, please let him be kidding.* "Oh. That's too bad."

He thought she'd be happy that he was coming to Dallas. Had he misread the signs? "Why?" he asked cautiously.

She watched Rick's face carefully as she said, "Because Tina and I were just talking about moving to Forever."

Suddenly he was feeling a whole lot better. "You were? Why?"

She gave him Tina's reason, not her own. "Seems like a good place to raise a child. While we were there, there was definitely a feeling that everyone was looking out for Bobby. That wouldn't happen in Dallas. People don't take an interest in one another the way they do in Forever."

"It's a great place," he agreed enthusiastically. But he

needed to be absolutely sure before he let his happiness loose. "You're really serious?"

Was it her imagination, or were the lights on the tree suddenly glowing brighter? "I'm really serious."

His sigh of relief was huge. "Then I don't have to take that job on the Dallas PD and move here."

She needed more. She needed to have him spell things out. "Why would you *have to?*"

He looked at her as if she should know the answer to that. "To be near you."

She heard him, but she was reluctant to allow herself to believe what he was saying. Because she wanted it too much. "You'd give up everything to be near me?"

"Don't you get it, Livy? You *are* everything," he told her in a quiet, firm voice. Stepping forward, he opened his jacket and enfolded her in his arms. Next to his heart. "Are you prepared to make an honest man of me?"

She felt warm and safe and sheltered. Olivia lifted her head to look up at him. "Isn't it usually the other way around?"

"Times have changed," he informed her. "This is called equality." The smile on his lips faded as he watched her in earnest. "I know this is short notice, but it feels as if I've been waiting for you for a long, long time. I love you, Olivia." And then he set her world on its ear by asking, "Will you marry me?"

She felt like laughing and crying, all at the same time. She wanted to shout yes, but not before everything was out on the table.

Olivia pressed her lips together, then said, "You have to know something first."

He braced himself. Whatever it was, it didn't matter.

He'd handle it. As long as she was his in the end. "There's someone else?"

"In a way." She took a breath, but it didn't help. Taking a thousand breaths wouldn't make saying this any easier. "I'm pregnant." She saw him grow very still. Oh God, she'd lost him before she ever had him. "I don't know how, we did all the right things, but there you have it. I'm pregnant and the baby is yours."

"How long have you known?" he asked her quietly.

She was right, she'd lost him. Who wanted to have an instant family when he got married? "A week."

"Why didn't you call me?" His voice grew in volume. She still couldn't tell if he was angry about the baby—or excited. But she knew which side she was rooting for.

At first, she'd been tempted to call, but her more practical side had prevailed. "Because I know the kind of man you are and I didn't want you to feel you *had* to marry me."

His features softened, and she knew everything was going to be all right. "Now there you're wrong. I do have to marry you—because the thought of someone else holding either you or our baby would kill me. Now you have to say yes," he told her. "You'd be saving my life."

Olivia found herself back to the laughing/crying reaction again. She felt wonderful. "You are a crazy person, you know that?"

"You're stalling."

"Yes," she declared. "Yes, I love you. Yes, I'll marry you." She threaded her arms around his neck. Everything inside of her felt like singing. "Every day of the week, if you want."

"Just one day will be fine," he assured her. "Oh, wait." Pausing, he dug into the pocket of his sheepskin jacket. "Miss Joan gave me this mistletoe twig for luck, in case I needed help to get you to kiss me." He held it up over her head.

"You don't need a mistletoe for luck—or to get me to kiss you. But I'd better do it now before I decide this is all a dream, because I've been dying inside ever since I watched you disappear in my rearview mirror."

Tossing the mistletoe aside, he closed the sides of his jacket around her again, absorbing the heat of her body into his own. He couldn't remember the last time he'd felt this happy. Except with her. "Looks like we're going to have a merry Christmas after all."

Olivia turned her face up to his. "My thoughts, exactly."

They were the last thoughts she had for a very long while. Thinking would have only gotten in the way of what happened next.

* * * * *

Family Christmas
in Riverbend

SHIRLEY JUMP

New York Times bestselling author **Shirley Jump** didn't have the will-power to diet, nor the talent to master under-eye concealer, so she bowed out of a career in television and opted instead for a career where she could be paid to eat at her desk—writing. At first, seeking revenge on her children for their grocery store tantrums, she sold embarrassing essays about them to anthologies. However, it wasn't enough to feed her growing addiction to writing funny. So she turned to the world of romance novels, where messes are (usually) cleaned up before The End. In the worlds Shirley gets to create and control, the children listen to their parents, the husbands always remember holidays, and the housework is magically done by elves. Though she's thrilled to see her books in stores around the world, Shirley mostly writes because it gives her an excuse to avoid cleaning the toilets and helps feed her shoe habit. To learn more, visit her website at www. shirleyjump.com

To my husband and my children—
who have made every Christmas a magical,
wonderful time of year. There is no gift more
precious to me than hugging and kissing all
of you on Christmas morning.

CHAPTER ONE

Peace. Quiet. Tranquility.

That was what Olivia Perkins had been picturing
when she'd returned to Riverbend, Indiana, at the beginning of December. For the past year, Livia had thought
of Riverbend often, missing the calm she had found in
the little Indiana town in a way she'd never missed anything before.

A native New Yorker, Livia had always considered
herself a city girl. Until she'd spent three amazing, wonderful weeks in Riverbend last New Year's Eve, helping
her boss Jenna plan a birthday party. And now, she'd
gone and done it.

Moved here.

She'd bought a little house on a quiet side street,
loaded all her possessions into the back of a U-Haul, secured Piper in her car seat, then driven out here and settled in—just in time for her first Christmas in the sleepy
little town. She'd bought a tree from the Methodist
Church's lot—after a long, chatty conversation with
Earl Klein, who took a personal interest in every tree
and customer. He'd helped her tie it to her car and waved
off the bills she tried to hand him as a tip. As soon as
Livia got home, she'd set the tree up in her front room,

before she'd finished unpacking the stack of boxes in the kitchen.

Now Livia stood in that very kitchen and watched across the street as the neighbors draped strings of multicolored lights over a trio of thick, squat shrubs. It was the perfect complement to the herd of lighted reindeer on the right side of their lawn and the blinking wreath adorning their front door. Nearly every house on this street had the same Christmas touch, a neighborhood medley of red and green.

Livia sighed. It was all so…perfect. Like images on a holiday postcard. She wished she'd moved here earlier. In time to see the trick-or-treaters dashing up and down driveways, or the straw bales stacked on lawns for Thanksgiving.

She'd definitely lingered too long in New York. Understandable, she supposed. Change wasn't something she'd been very good at. At least not until a bright fall day in September that turned Livia's life upside down. In a good way.

Livia smiled at the thought of her three-month-old daughter, asleep just down the hall in the nursery. Amazing how one little baby could transform a grown woman's life. The moment she'd held her newborn daughter in her arms, Livia realized there was no other place on earth she wanted to raise her child but in Riverbend. The town had the perfect blend of hokey charm and Midwestern values that would wrap around Piper like a thick blanket.

She could just imagine Piper riding a bicycle down the town's quiet side streets while the neighbors waved and shouted a how-ya-doin'. She could see herself taking Piper downtown on Saturday afternoons for an ice cream cone where Mr. Duval would undoubtedly over-

indulge his youngest customer. Livia was already anticipating the delight in Piper's face the first time she saw
the rainbow of Christmas lights at the annual Riverbend
Winterfest and heard Santa's hearty ho-ho-ho.

Yes, Riverbend was perfect for raising a child. For
beginning a family, even if it was a family of just two.

Livia exited the kitchen and headed down to the
nursery, her hips swaying in time to the beat of the
Christmas music spilling from the stereo's speakers,
adding a Norman Rockwell air to the house. Piper slept
soundly, her tiny chest rising and falling with each whispered breath. God, she was a beautiful baby. A wave of
gratitude and love washed over Livia.

Piper had changed Livia's life in a hundred ways—
a hundred wonderful ways. Never for a second did she
regret the choice to raise her child alone. She'd do it better, she vowed, better than her own father had, and certainly better than her absent mother. Livia would make
sure Piper never knew that painful hole of losing a parent. But even as Livia made that silent promise, a part
of her whispered doubt.

Was she really saving Piper pain? Would Piper miss
what she had never had or known?

Livia tiptoed out of the nursery and tugged the door
shut. At the top of the stairs, she paused and thought of
the man who had unknowingly blessed her with Piper.

Edward Graham.

The owner of a nationwide chain of event venues, including the now closed Riverbend Banquet Hall, Edward
had swept her off her feet when she'd been here last year
and whisked her into one of those heady, unforgettable
romances. When she'd finally come up for air, she'd realized the one thing their whirlwind relationship had been

missing—substance. Edward was all about the charm, less about the long term.

She should have known something that started so fast would end up in flames. Edward had been a handsome but mysterious and private man who had let her into his bed but never fully into his heart. Like a fool, she'd hoped for more and stayed in Riverbend that winter for another week, waiting for him, before she finally realized he'd meant it when he'd said he was done with her, with their relationship, with the town. That he was never going to be marriage material, or anything even close to that. She'd returned to New York and buried herself in her work, running the New York branch of Jenna Pearson's party planning company.

Until she saw a tiny plus sign in the window of the pregnancy test.

That day, she'd thought of calling Edward, then stopped herself. Livia had heard through the grapevine that Edward had come back to town only long enough to sell his house, pack up his car and leave Riverbend for good. Without a word to her or to anyone else.

What had she expected, after the way they'd ended things? Still, it had hurt.

Not a little. A lot.

Now here she was again, in the town that had changed her in so many ways. Livia walked through the house, straightening this, arranging that.

Everything was perfect, exactly the way she liked it. The house was clean and neat, the decorations hung just so. The little house practically gleamed, as shiny as the gold star atop the tree that stood patiently in the corner, waiting for Piper's first Christmas. A half-dozen gifts for Piper sat under the branches, but Livia didn't need or want anything. She had Piper. And—

The front door flew open. "I hate this place!" A slam punctuated the sentence. The door shuddered in its hinges.

And Melody.

Livia shot a glance at the baby monitor on the counter, but there was nothing more than the whisper of air coming across the airwaves. Her heavy sleeper daughter hadn't stirred. Phew. "Why do you do that? You could have woken up the baby."

"Sorry." Melody dumped her coat and bag on the floor, then toed off her boots and kicked them aside. "I had a *really* bad day. You know how worked up I get when things go wrong."

"Yes I do." Too well. Livia retrieved Melody's things from the floor, giving her sister a hint-hint wave, which Melody ignored. Livia lined the shoes up by the door, put Melody's bag on the counter, and hung her coat up in the closet before returning to the kitchen.

Melody plopped into one of the kitchen chairs with a dramatic sigh. "I don't know why you thought living in this godforsaken town was a good idea. If I'd known this place didn't even have a Starbucks, for Pete's sake, I never would have come to visit."

So much for peace, quiet and tranquility. None of the three were words that she associated with her little sister. Who had, for some insane reason, decided to follow Livia to Riverbend. An afternoon visit had turned into an overnight stay, and was now verging on a permanent relocation.

"If you hate it so much, why do you stay?" Livia asked.

Melody crossed her arms over her chest and pouted. "Because I'm not going back to Boston until Carl gets a clue."

Carl, Melody's fiancé, who it turned out, had been engaged to, and pledging his eternal love to, a woman named Jackie at the same time. That hadn't gone over well with Melody, who had thrown a suitcase in her car and driven straight to Livia's new house. Livia had been tempted to give her sister a lecture about her tendency to choose every Mr. Wrong on the planet, but Melody had been crying so hard, Livia didn't have the heart. Instead, she made up the spare bed and ordered a large double-cheese pizza.

She'd figured Melody would cry for a couple days, then do what she always did—go back to the city, to her friends, her busy life and to yet another man. Instead, she'd stayed. And stayed. And stayed.

And complained nearly every single minute.

"Maybe you should look for a job," Livia said. "I'm sure it'll help take your mind off things. There's probably plenty of people in need of an interior decorator in this area."

Melody huffed. "*Home stager,* not interior decorator. They're two entirely different things."

Livia bit her lip. "Either way, I'm sure you could—"

"My car broke down right in the center of town," Melody interrupted. "I swear, this place hates me. Good thing that Earl guy was there. He towed it to his shop and gave me a ride home. I bet it's broken forever. It was making this whining noise and—"

"I'm sorry to interrupt, Melody, but I need to run an errand." Truth was, Livia had no interest in hearing the latest drama in Melody's life. There'd been the eyeliner meltdown first thing this morning, the stuck waffle in the toaster at breakfast and the too-small sweater in the dryer. And that was all before ten.

Livia grabbed her coat, flung her scarf around her

neck, then swiped her car keys off the table. "Can you stay? Piper should nap for another hour. If she gets up, just call me. You don't have to do anything."

"That's because you don't trust me."

"I do."

Melody arched a brow.

"Okay, maybe not entirely. But Piper's just a baby and you're…"

"The irresponsible little sister." Melody sighed. "I have grown up, you know."

"I really have to get to the store before dinner. Can we talk about this later?"

"Where are you going?" Melody's face lifted in hope. "Are you going somewhere fun? Can I come?"

"Just the grocery store. For, uh, milk and stuff." And whatever number of purchases could give Livia a few minutes of peace. Shopping alone was about the only way she'd get some. She loved her sister but Melody had a way of making every little thing into a BIG DEAL, complete with capital letters, wild gesticulating and over the top shouting. "You know how you hate grocery shopping. Besides, you promised you'd help out more and staying here while Piper sleeps is helping. Because you are living here for free, remember?"

Melody detoured for the sofa. She reached for the remote and flicked on the TV. "Okay, fine. But get me some chocolate milk, will you? And cookies. Oh, and chips, and some of those pizza bite things. You don't have anything good to eat around here."

"Because that stuff isn't good for you. If you'd just—"

Melody put up a hand to cut off Livia's argument. "Spare me the no-sugar life lecture. Geesh, Livia, you need to lighten up a little. Look at this place. You could eat off the floor. All five servings of vegetables and your whole grains, of course." She swiveled around to face her sister. A bright cascade of light from the television danced across her features. "A little fun won't kill you, you know."

"I gotta go. I'm not debating what I put in the cupboards or how often the house needs vacuumed. Again." Livia turned and headed out the door.

Winter had yet to breathe its snowy kiss over Riverbend. The air held a promise of snow, but over the last few days, there'd been nothing but one quick icy rainstorm. The cold world around her looked gray and bleak, not quite the postcard image of the holidays she'd had last year when she'd been here.

Livia drove the few blocks from her house to the main street of Riverbend. Melody's words ran through her mind. Yes, Livia liked things clean. And with a baby, it was doubly important to keep the environment organized, clean and healthy. Why couldn't Melody understand that?

Either way, Livia refused to let it get to her. Instead, she let the Christmas spirit filling Riverbend wash over her. Even without snow, it was a holiday oasis. What the town called "downtown" didn't even compare to a New York City block, but Livia loved it all the same. Small charming stores, all hung with Christmas wreaths and bright red bows, and friendly residents who had remembered her from last year and greeted her at every turn. Despite the gloomy weather, the town had Christmas cheer in abundance.

She parked in the side lot of the corner grocery store and headed inside. The electric-eye door whooshed shut behind her.

"Nice to see you again, Miss Perkins!" Cal, the store manager, sent her a quick wave.

"Thanks, Cal. How's business?"

"Busy as heck, thank the Lord. Seems everyone and their uncle is here in town for the holidays." Cal swung his wide frame out from behind the customer service counter. "How are things for you?"

"Just fine, just fine."

"Glad to hear it." A customer stepped up to the counter, so Cal sent her another wave and went back to work.

Livia grabbed a cart and started down the first aisle. She greeted Betsy Williams and Earl Klein, two lifelong Riverbend residents who'd been instant friends when she moved here. Most of the town was like that—friendly and warm.

No wonder Jenna had chosen to settle here after she'd married Stockton Grisham, her childhood sweetheart and owner of the elegant Rustica restaurant. Once the holidays were over, Livia would go to work for Jenna, part-time at first. Once she'd moved to Riverbend, Jenna had switched her event planning business focus from birthdays and weddings to charitable events, and had found fulfillment and happiness that Livia could hear in her voice. That was the kind of life Livia wanted, the kind of example she wanted to set for her daughter.

She wandered the aisles of the Sav-A-Lot. Livia hadn't really needed a thing at the store—except for an escape from Melody, and a moment of peace, a bit of time to herself, something she hadn't had in months. Christmas carols played on the sound system, and before long, Livia found herself singing along. Her spirits lifted, and the stress of Melody's stay abated. She loved her sister, she really did, but living with her—that was a whole other ball of wax.

She'd forgotten how difficult her little sister could be. Their mother had left when Melody was only six and

Livia ten. Melody had been far more affected by that than Livia, and had never really taken to Livia stepping into the mother hen role. There were days when Livia wished she'd been able to just be a kid, but their father had been working nonstop, and someone had to be in charge. Maybe it had been a mistake, but Livia had done the best she could.

Livia paused by a display of sparkling wine, her hips swaying in time to "Jingle Bell Rock."

"If I remember right, you were a Reisling girl."

The deep voice came from over her right shoulder, but she didn't need to turn to see who had spoken.

Edward.

Livia froze and willed herself to be cold as ice, but a shiver of heat ran through her all the same. Her heart raced, and the parts of her that refused to listen to common sense rang with awareness. *Edward.*

She swallowed hard, and wished the memories of her heart could overpower the memories of her body. Images flashed through her mind unbidden—his hands running over her body, his lips drifting down her neck, his voice, hot and low, whispering in her ear—but she pushed them away, cemented them behind the wall she'd put in place nearly a year ago.

She was done with him. D-O-N-E.

Finally, Livia turned. "Edward. I didn't realize you were in town."

"Just got in this morning. And the fridge is empty, so…" he held up a half-filled grocery basket, "here I am."

He was back? For how long? Didn't he wonder why she was here in town?

She told herself she didn't care, nor need to know, the answer to any of those questions. That it didn't affect her at all to see his piercing blue eyes. That she didn't want to reach up and push back the errant lock of dark brown hair that skimmed across his brows. That her gaze didn't drift to his mouth and wonder if he'd still taste as good now as he had then.

Edward.

She turned away, grabbed the first bottle of wine she saw and stood it in her cart. Even though she didn't need it, and probably wouldn't drink it. It was merely a prop, a means of escape. "Well, I'll let you get back to your shopping." She started to take a step.

Then he spoke again, and her body betrayed her once more. *"Livia."*

When he said her name like that, the memories rushed back in a wave, tumbling and tossing in her mind, breaking past her mental barriers. The steamy nights she'd spent in his arms, the playful mornings she'd spent in his bed, and then—

The heart-wrenching end.

The realization that their relationship had been something deep and meaningful to her—and not to him. That she'd been nothing more than a holiday—

Fling.

In the hundreds of moments since she'd wanted to pick up the phone and share the news about the baby. But every time, she had stopped. Before her fingers could dial, she remembered those last moments, the ones that had shattered all those silly schoolgirl emotions that Edward had awakened in her.

Damn, damn, damn. Why did he have to come back? At Christmas, of all times? She shook her head, willing him to go away. "I'm sorry, but I've got to—"

"Don't go," he said at the same time. He reached for her, but his hand fell short, and a whisper of cool air danced over her fingers. "Stay. Just for a second. Let's catch up, over some coffee or something."

"I don't think that's a good idea."

He offered her the lopsided grin that had haunted her nights for months after she'd returned to New York. "For old times? 'Auld Lang Syne' and all that?"

"That's for New Year's, Edward. It's Christmas. Ask me again in a few days."

"And will your answer change then?"

She shook her head, and something akin to a knife sliced through her heart. She thought of Piper, asleep in her crib back in the little house on Elm Street, completely unaware that her father wanted nothing to do with her. She thought of telling Edward about Piper, but stopped herself. She already knew his reaction. He didn't want their baby then, and he wouldn't now.

"No, it won't," she said. "We're done, and that's not going to change."

This time, Livia did walk away and headed down another aisle, before her common sense could be overruled again. And she fell for the only man who had ever truly broken her heart.

The log split with a sharp crack, the two halves landing on the ground with twin thuds. With the back of his hand, Edward swiped the beading sweat off his brow, then reached for another log. He swung the heavy axe up and over his head, then forward, watching the arrowed blade slice into the maple.

The pile of chopped wood beside him grew by another two chunks and the air held the sweet, earthy scent of fresh-cut logs, but the frustration in his chest had yet to subside. He laid the axe on its head, then dropped onto an overturned stump and took a breath.

Livia.

He'd heard she'd left Riverbend shortly before he had. He'd never expected that she'd return, much less settle down in the town.

Hell, he hadn't expected *he* would return. And he wouldn't have, if it had been his choice. Particularly not during the holidays. He'd been perfectly content to stay in his Chicago office, managing the remaining properties in his portfolio while he waited for a buyer for the company, and retreating to his apartment at the end of the day for a glass of bourbon and mindless television. Then the hospital had called, saying his father had had a heart attack, and Edward had gotten on the first plane back to Indiana. During his father's hospital stay, Edward had flitted back and forth between Riverbend and Chicago, and when Ray was finally ready to come home, Edward had put his company in the hands of his vice president and moved into his father's house. Truth be told, he hadn't been doing much of the day-to-day work before he handed it over. All that had done was make it official that Edward was no longer helming Graham Venues. Now here he was, chopping wood to stoke a fire that would keep his father warm.

"You're a stubborn man."

Edward turned and shot his father a grin. "Who do I think I learned it from?"

Raymond Graham scowled. "I told you I could chop my own wood. I'm not dead, you know."

True, but the heartiness had dimmed in Ray's features. He'd lost twenty pounds—something his already lean frame couldn't afford—and he seemed to have gained twenty years in his face. "Dad, you just had a massive heart attack—"

"One that would have killed a lesser man."

"Exactly my point. And that means you shouldn't be chopping wood or, hell, even standing out here in the cold." If anything could have pulled Edward out of his self-created prison, his father's illness was it. He'd stay long enough to get Ray back on his feet, to make sure his father was fully healed, then head somewhere else. Maybe somewhere warm.

Didn't matter as long as it was far from Riverbend and the mistakes that haunted him at every corner. Once upon a time, he'd thought he could be happy here.

He'd been wrong.

He wasn't the kind of man who settled down, had a couple kids and painted the porch on the weekends. He didn't know much about himself, but he knew that.

"Damn doctors," Ray said. "Always putting rules on me."

Edward looked at his father askance.

"All right, all right. I'll go back inside and bundle up under the blankets like a big baby. I'll even take a nap if it'll keep you from harping on me. I swear, you're worse than the nurses."

Edward grinned. "Call it payback, Dad, for all the lectures I got as a kid."

Ray waved off the words. "You ask me, you deserved them. You were always off in your own world. As distracted as a bee on the first day of spring. Biggest daydreamer I ever met."

Edward scoffed. "And look where it got me. I should have listened to you and gone to work at the factory."

His father let out a long breath that frosted in the cold air. "You did the best you could."

"It wasn't enough." Edward jerked off the stump, grabbed a pile of wood and started toward the house. But his mind wasn't on the woodpile or even what had

happened in this town last winter. It was on another winter, long in the past. In his bank account, he had millions, but it didn't matter. No amount of money bought
peace. Or forgiveness. "It wasn't nearly enough."

"That girl didn't get hurt because of you. It was an
accident. You keep blaming yourself for things you can't
control, son."

The words sliced through Edward, as cleanly as
the axe had slid through the wood. He froze, the cold,
hard logs clutched to his chest. He could see Miranda
Willett's face, her bright eager eyes the first day she
came to work. He'd hired her, but hadn't known the
nineteen-year-old very well. In their short interview,
she'd talked about working at the hall to save money
for college. Apparently she'd gotten early acceptance to
one that offered the perfect graphic design degree program she wanted, but even with scholarships, the school
was out of the financial reach of her parents. He'd half
heard her, thinking she was nice and earnest and good
enough for the server position he was filling. A few
minutes later, Edward had retreated to his office, buried himself in paperwork. The hall manager handled the
employees, and the day-to-day. Edward had been telling himself for months that he should spend more time
on the floor, getting to know the people who worked
for him. And now, when it came to a nineteen-year-old
server named Miranda, it was too late. She'd been so
young—too young to get hurt like that. If only—

He'd tread the path of If Only a thousand times and
it never erased the past. Or the horrific fire that had destroyed Miranda's life.

Or the mistakes Edward had made long before
Miranda Willett was even born. Mistakes that should
have taught him he was better off alone. Mistakes that

reminded him every day why he had no call planning a future with a woman like Livia. No matter how much he craved it.

"I should have never come back here," Edward said, the words icing in the cold air. "I can't change anything."

Then he headed into the house and stoked the fire, warming his father's house but not his own heart. That had gone cold last January when the place he had built his dreams upon went up in smoke. Taking an innocent person's future with it.

CHAPTER TWO

When Livia got home from the store, she spent a long time standing in the nursery she'd created in the tiny third bedroom of the house, really more of a glorified closet than a room, marveling at the miracle of her daughter.

Edward's daughter.

The beautiful child they'd created together—a child he'd made it very, very clear, he'd never want.

"He's the one missing out," Livia whispered to her daughter. Piper's tiny chest rose and fell beneath the pink fleece sleeper, her delicate hand curled into a tight ball. A dusting of blond hair whispered up and down with the slight breeze from the ceiling fan above, the one noise that seemed to lull Piper to sleep.

"Oh, Piper, if only he knew what a gift you are." She ran a finger down the silky softness of Piper's cheek.

Piper stirred, and opened her eyes. Big blue orbs took in the room, as if it were the first time she'd seen the space. Her gaze drifted over the cartoon zoo that decorated her bedding, then up the crib rails, until finally, locking on her mother's familiar face. Her three-month-old features lit with joy and she started to squirm, her hands and arms reaching. Livia reached down and curled her daughter into a tight embrace. She inhaled the soft strawberry scent of her skin, then pressed a kiss to Piper's cheek. Her heart swelled to bursting with love and gratitude for this place, for her life, and most of all, for her perfect minifamily of two. "Hey there, beetle."

Piper opened her mouth, and let out a half scream, half cry. Moment of peace over. Livia laughed. "Okay, okay, let's get right to the food."

She carried Piper back to the kitchen, then heated a bottle and slipped it into Piper's mouth. The baby sucked greedily, her cheeks hollowing with each slurp.

Livia looked down at her daughter and though Piper had light hair, she had her father's features, too. His eyes, the slight dimple in his left cheek, and most of all, his smile. For the hundredth time, she wondered if she should just show up on his doorstep with Piper.

I never want children, Livia. Never. I don't need that kind of albatross around my neck.

His last words to her, thrown at her in their final argument, had rung in Livia's ears for months. Every time she thought about telling him about Piper, she heard those words again. And kept her sweet daughter to herself. Rather than see Piper hurt by her father's rejection. Livia knew too well how a parent's indifference could hurt.

Once Piper was fed, Livia sat her in a bouncy seat while she put the groceries away, then set to work making some chicken and rice soup. She could have opened a can, or even served last night's leftover spaghetti and sauce, but instead she took the time to poach fresh chicken, throwing onions, garlic and spices into the water, then dice up carrots and celery.

Seeing Edward again had turned her inside out. She refused to think about him, to wonder how he was. To wonder if he had changed. Instead, she stayed busy in the kitchen. That was far better than daydreaming about a man who didn't want the same life she did. Cooking relaxed her, brought her back to ground. And so she cooked.

A half hour later, the kitchen smelled like heaven and steam from the simmering pot glazed the nearby windows. Livia mixed up a quick biscuit dough and plopped the doughy circles into the oven.

Melody came to stand in the kitchen, resting her head against the doorjamb. She eyed the pot with a dreamy, soft expression, then drew in a long inhale. An air of vulnerability, of openness, hung on Melody's delicate features. "Chicken and rice soup? Didn't Mom used to make that all the time?"

Livia nodded. "I'm surprised you remember."

"Yeah, me, too." Then the moment of vulnerability was gone before it even started. Melody stepped into the kitchen and gave Piper a quick kiss on the head. "Hey there, you smelly monkey."

"She hates being called that, you know."

"Then how come she just smiled at me?" Melody bent down to Piper and beeped her button nose. "'Cause you're a monkey, that's why."

Livia laughed. "You're a terrible aunt."

"Too bad, because I'm the only aunt she's got." Melody came to stand beside the stove. She picked up a spoon, dipped it into the soup and slurped up a taste. "Mmm. It tastes just like Mom's."

"It's from her recipe."

"Really?" Either the steam or the memory made Melody's eyes glisten, and Livia felt an echoing ache in her own heart for the mother they'd barely known before she'd walked out on her husband and children.

"Where'd you find it? I thought Dad got rid of everything."

Their father had done a massive purge of the house in the weeks after his wife left. It was as if he thought tossing boxes out the door would assuage his grief over the betrayal. It hadn't done anything but leave the house bare and lifeless, and made it seem as if their mother was a mere whisper of a memory, not a vibrant woman who had left them as quickly as a summer rainstorm.

It had been especially hard on Melody, who had fewer memories and mementos than Livia. What none of them had was answers, and it seemed all Livia had done for the past seventeen years was to try and cover up that gap in information and relationship.

Their father had bought a pair of big puffy chairs and a huge, ugly kitchen table to fill the space, but it wasn't the same. Maybe she could talk her father into visiting for Christmas. It would be good for all of them to get together. Still, a part of Livia doubted it would happen. Even when she'd lived in the same city as her father, he'd always been too busy for more than a quick hello. Either way, that was a mountain to climb another day.

"Before I moved, I stopped by Dad's house and while I was there, I went up to the attic," Livia said to Melody. "I guess I never really thought about whether there might be stuff up there, especially all these years later."

"Was there much?" Melody fiddled with the spoon, as if she could care less about the answer.

They rarely talked about their mother. Livia wondered sometimes if it was because Melody didn't like to be reminded of all the memories she'd lost. "There wasn't a whole lot," Livia said. "Mostly boxes filled with old Christmas decorations and our baby clothes. But in one of them, I found her cookbooks and her recipes."

Melody took another sip of soup. "I'm glad you did."

The moment of détente extended between them, and for a moment, Livia had hope that she and her sister could finally have the kind of bond other sisters had. As the protective oldest, Livia had never felt they were like other siblings. She'd been too worried about making sure Melody ate three meals and did well in school to do anything else, such as form a connection over checkers. Melody, with her loud music and dramatic moods, was the total opposite to Livia's quieter self. Piper had been a bridge for the two, but not enough.

Melody tossed the spoon. It landed with a clatter in the sink. "So, who's this Edward guy?"

Livia hadn't thought a few simple words could so radically change the mood in a room, but those words did it. She went from nostalgic warm fuzzies to frosty detachment in a second. "No one."

"That's not what I heard." Melody sing-songed the words. "Word about town is that you two used to date. I can't believe you broke up with him, sis. He is *yummy*."

"How do you know what he looks like?"

"He's in the paper today." Melody waved a copy of the *Riverbend News* at Livia. "Front page and everything."

"It's a small town. A dead deer on the road gets front page treatment." But still Livia took the paper from Melody and dropped into a kitchen chair to read the article.

Edward's smiling face stared back at her. It was an old photo, the one he'd used for publicity for the banquet hall. She knew the current look—a little messier, a soft layer of stubble across his jaw, and thicker, longer hair. But the eyes—the eyes were the same. A vibrant blue, so deep it seemed like she could drown in those eyes.

She jerked her attention away from his face and over to a small but conspicuous headline: Local Millionaire Back In Town?

The article was mainly speculation. Some gossip had noticed Edward's return and wondered if he'd come back to rebuild the banquet hall or just for a family holiday visit.

The building may not be smoldering any longer, but whispers about the tragic accident at Riverbend Banquet Hall last year are still in the air. Has Edward Graham returned to try again? Does he think Riverbend has forgotten what happened there? Forgotten how Miranda Willett suffered in the days since? The suddenly silent Graham didn't return repeated calls for comment.

Livia's heart panged. Edward didn't deserve that kind of vicious speculation. That fire hadn't been his fault. Yes, it had had a terrible consequence. She remembered reading the articles about Miranda's brush with death and her difficult months of recovery. The fire department had cleared Edward of all responsibility, noting he hadn't even been on the premises when the fire occurred.

She remembered that day clearly. She and Edward had gotten together for lunch, with a promise to see each other on Saturday. He'd gone back to the hall to get some work done before knocking off early to get some rest after a particularly hectic week.

The sirens had awakened Livia. The next morning, she'd seen what the fire trucks had been rushing to save. What she hadn't seen was Edward. They'd talked only once in the days after the fire—one long, heated argument that told her everything she thought about Edward was a lie. And that it was over between them.

She'd been living a dream, and that day had brought her screeching back into reality. Edward hadn't wanted her comfort, her advice, or anything else from her. He'd shoved her away, and that had been it.

Nevertheless, the Edward Graham she knew was never irresponsible. Never blasé about his business or the safety of his employees. It seemed no one else believed that, though. For a second, she thought of calling the reporter and telling her she had it all wrong.

Instead, Livia put the paper down.

Edward could—and probably would—fight his own battles. Except, he hadn't this time, which wasn't like the Edward she knew and remembered. Since his return, he'd apparently kept a very low profile. What happened to the ambitious business owner she used to know?

"I don't care what he's up to," Livia said to Melody and to herself. She crossed to the stove to check the soup. The rice was done, so she reached for the shredded, cooked chicken and began dropping it into the broth.

"*Sure* you don't." Melody grinned, then sobered. "Wait…if I do the math…is he…is Piper…?"

Livia sighed. "He's Piper's father."

"Wow. And he doesn't know?" Livia shook her head. Melody let out a low whistle. "Well, that explains a few things."

"Explains what?"

"Like why you were talking to him today at the supermarket."

Livia paused in adding the chicken. "How do you know that?"

"Livia, this town is smaller than a postage stamp.

Someone burps and there's a phone tree to alert the neighbors."

Livia shook her head. Melody had that right. "Betsy called you?"

"Nope. Earl. He stopped by to drop off my car. It's all fixed now. A broken fan belt, he said. Man, am I relieved. If it had been something bigger, I don't know how I would have afforded to pay the bill. That car is just a pain in the…"

Livia wasn't listening. Darn that Earl. He was one of the nicest people in Riverbend, but he had a tendency to play matchmaker. She should have known, after seeing him and Betsy—his lady friend, as he called her—in the market, that they'd say something. And of course, they had. Darn small towns.

Melody rattled on about her car. Livia ladled some soup into bowls, then placed them on the table and grabbed the biscuits from the oven. She sat down across from Livia and slathered butter all over until the biscuit glistened. Livia waved off the butter and tore off a piece of biscuit to dip into the soup. Piper sat between them, watching their meal. But Livia's mind wasn't on her dinner—it was on the article about Edward. Had he returned for good?

And if so, what was she going to do when he found out about Piper? In a town this small, it was inevitable.

"So, are you going to tell him?" Melody asked, as if she had read Livia's mind.

"I don't know." Livia sighed. "I just don't know."

"Don't you think he has a right to know?"

"Yes, but…"

"But what?"

Livia paused for a long moment. "But I don't want him hurting Piper, like…"

"Like Mom hurt us." Melody finished the sentence, the decades-old betrayal fresh in her eyes.

Livia nodded. "Yes."

"Okay." Melody took a sip of soup, then reached for the salt and added a bit of the spice to her bowl. "So, when are we getting a wreath?"

"Wreath?" Sometimes Livia couldn't follow Melody's non sequiters. It was as if her sister went through life only half listening. "We don't need a wreath."

"Mom used to say they're good luck. She always had a wreath." Melody shrugged. "If I had money, I'd get one for the house but you know, I gotta watch my funds."

"I know. You've told me that several times. And what exactly are you saving for?" Livia heard the bite in her tone, but it was too late to take the question back.

Melody scowled. "I don't know yet. Are you getting a wreath? I mean, we have to, don't we? We always did before. You know…Mom always did."

"I—" Livia cut off the sentence when she saw her sister's face. The hope in it, the dependence on her older sister to ensure the continuity that had been disrupted when their mother left. Livia had done all those same things—including buying a wreath every year. "Okay. As soon as we're done with dinner."

A smile curved across Melody's face, one of those peaceful smiles that rarely made an appearance. "Let's go together," she said. "And on the way, you can tell me all about this Edward. And how on earth you are resisting him a second time."

CHAPTER THREE

EDWARD had been standing in the cold for over an hour. One would think a decision like this would be easy to make. His father had pressed fifty dollars into his hand at dinner and told Edward to not come home until he had a little Christmas spirit strapped into the bed of Ray's pickup truck. Edward figured he'd be back home in ten minutes. Fifteen, tops.

"You see one you like?"

Edward turned toward Earl Klein, who had been patiently—or impatiently, depending on your perspective—waiting on him to make a decision. Edward had known Earl for most of his life and couldn't remember a Christmas when Earl didn't work the Methodist Church tree lot. "Not yet."

"Lord, have mercy and send me patience." Earl rolled his eyes. Not one to keep his opinions to himself, that Earl.

Why his father had sent him on this fool's errand, Edward didn't know. In all the years he'd known Ray, his father had never given two seconds of thought to whether they had a Christmas tree or not. Heck, Ray had hardly been home for the holidays, much less participated in them.

Edward's mother had been the one to hang the stockings, toss the tinsel onto the branches and play Bing Crosby. Ever since she'd died five years ago, Ray had skipped Christmas, as if it were just another date on the calendar. No tree, no stockings and sure as heck no Bing.

Then this year, Ray got a bug in his ear and sent Edward out into the cold to buy a tree. Never mind it was only a few days to Christmas and the entire exercise would be a waste, considering a snow pea probably had more Christmas spirit than Edward and Ray put together. They were working men, not sentimental men.

"What are you waiting on? Christmas?" Earl said, with nary a blink at his goofy joke. "Pick a tree already."

Edward waved at the stand of trees. He didn't know a Scotch pine from a Douglas fir. "Pick one for me."

Earl let out a long sigh. "It doesn't work that way, my boy. A Christmas tree is something personal. You gotta pick the one that speaks to you."

"Speaks to me?" He'd known Earl a long time, and though the man had his quirks, he'd never thought he was crazy. And a tree speaking to him—or to anyone for that matter—was crazy. "What's it going to say? Ho, ho, ho?"

"It's gotta say Christmas to you."

"They're Christmas trees, Earl. They all say Christmas."

"Yeah, but which one says it best? Which one is most like you?"

"Uh…that one." Edward waved at the nearest tree. A bluish-green one that tapered up from a fat base. For the hundredth time, he wondered what his father had been thinking. Still, if a tree made his father happy after the last few weeks of hell he'd been through, Edward was willing to put up with the cold and the tree conversations, such as they were. Didn't mean he had to get all merry and ho-ho-ho himself.

"Well, if you ask me—" Earl cut off the sentence, and a grin whisked across his face. "Oh, look, no need to ask me after all. Not when you have a better second opinion right here." He turned, and the gap between Earl and the trees opened up to reveal—

Livia.

Edward had to suck in an icy breath. He'd seen her just this afternoon and should have been prepared to run into her again, especially after Earl had let it drop that Livia was living in town now, but the sight of her tall, lithe body struck him hard in the gut.

She looked great, as if their time apart had agreed with her. She was slightly heavier than he remembered her, but the few extra pounds lent a softness to her features, rounded out her curves, in a way that made her seem more approachable.

Happier.

Damn. That was it. Livia looked happier without him than she had with him. Because of someone new? He told himself he didn't care, but damn it all, he did.

"Don't just stand there gawking at her," Earl said, giving Edward a little nudge. "Talk to the lady."

"Hi, Earl. I'm just here to get a wreath," Livia said to Earl, as if Edward wasn't even there. "Do you have any left?"

"I have a few," Earl said. "But right now, we need a woman's opinion." He stepped back and gestured toward the trees. "Which tree is more Edward?"

"I'm, uh, I'm really not qualified to make that decision. I'm sure whichever tree you choose will be fine." Livia started to turn away, and Edward knew he should let her go. What was it about her that kept drawing him in and making him dream about the impossible?

He'd done that once already today, but the thought of watching her get further and further away from him sent a pain through his heart. What was he doing? He knew what Livia wanted, and it wasn't what a man like him could give. All those words that came with a relationship—permanence, commitment, stability—weren't in his vocabulary.

"Yeah but you know me," he said, working a grin to his face that felt about as real as the fake snow decorating the cashier's register. All he knew was that he couldn't let her leave. Not yet. Not without seeing just a whisper of the Livia he remembered. God, he was torturing himself. "I could use a second opinion. My decor taste runs between hunting lodge and ice fishing shack."

That brought a smile. "I remember."

"So if you have a second, maybe you could help me."

I've missed your smile. Missed your laugh. Missed... everything.

Of course, he'd never say that. He couldn't. She deserved more than he had ever been able to offer.

She looked torn between staying and going. Then she seemed to reach some type of internal compromise and closed some of the distance between them. Damn, she had beautiful eyes. As rich and vibrant as the trees behind her.

"First, it helps to know where the tree is going," she said, giving a little wave as Earl walked off to deal with another customer while they chose Edward's tree.

"In the living room at my father's house."

"Right between his recliner and his gun rack?"

Edward laughed. "You know it."

Livia put a finger to her bottom lip. It was a gesture

he knew well, the one that said she was thinking. His mind darted to thoughts of kissing that lip. Tasting it.

"The Eastern White Pine is too wide," she said, drawing him back to his real reason for being here. "And I think this white spruce is too tall. Maybe try this Douglas fir."

"Sounds like you're talking about the three bears. This one is too big, this one is too tall, this one is *just right*." He drew out the last two words with a storytelling singsong voice. "I'll take your advice, Goldilocks."

This time, she did laugh. "Well, if you ask me, that one is perfect." Livia started to turn away. "Good luck with the tree."

"Wait." He reached for her, his gloved hand connecting with the thick wool of her knee-length coat. No skin contact, but the sheer act of touching her sent a searing heat through Edward.

What was he doing? He had no call to get involved with her again. He was leaving town as soon as Ray was back on his feet. And from what he had heard, Livia had put down roots in Riverbend. She intended to stay, and he wanted nothing more than to go.

Livia was the kind of woman who wanted it all— the white picket fence, the two kids, hell, even the dog. And he was the last man on earth who should be settling down, never mind doing the one thing Livia had always talked about doing—having kids.

The memory rose up, then hit him, as hard and fast as an uppercut. His little sister, one year younger, and a constant tagalong to everything Edward did. That day, his mother had called out, "Watch out for Katie," as he'd left, but Edward remembered only being annoyed and hurrying deep into the woods to meet his friends. And in the process, maybe lose his sister shadow.

Watch out for Katie.

In the end, he hadn't watched her. Had he?

Edward tried to shrug off the memories but they stayed, stubborn.

"Edward?" Livia's voice drew him back. "Do you need something else?"

He needed her smile. Just one more time. He wanted to be selfish just a little longer and take the balm that Livia's presence offered. Then he'd let her go again. For good. "One cup of coffee," he said. "To thank you for helping me."

"I really need to go. I'm supposed to pick out a wreath and—"

"I can do that, sis." A younger, darker haired version of Livia emerged from the maze of trees. In one arm, she held a plastic carrier with a baby inside—a little girl if the pink snowsuit was any indication. "You must be Edward. I'm Melody. Livia's little sister."

He shook with her. "Nice to meet you."

"We should go get that wreath," Livia said. Her face had paled, and her eyes were wide. She was leaning toward her sister and the baby, one hand out as if to drag them both away.

"I already got one." Melody raised her other arm and showed off a wide circle of evergreen, decorated with a giant red bow and white sprigs of faux berries. "Mission accomplished."

"Okay, then let's—"

"I'll go home and hang this," Melody interrupted, "and you go for coffee with Edward. You deserve a break, sis."

"What about…?" Livia let the question hang in the air. Enough that Edward knew she was discussing something private, something she didn't want Edward to be privy to. He sensed an undertow of something more to the entire conversation. What, he didn't know.

Melody waved a hand in dismissal. "I've got *that* under control. I can handle…it."

"I don't know." Livia looked to her sister, then to the parking lot. "I really shouldn't."

"One cup," Edward repeated, knowing he should let her leave. What was he going to do? Suddenly turn into Mr. Commitment? "I promise to have you home before bedtime."

A flush rose in her cheeks and he cursed silently. He shouldn't have mentioned bed.

Try as he might not to think about Livia and bed in the same sentence, his brain refused to disconnect the two. Because he knew what it was like to hold her long into the night, knew exactly where to touch her to bring that wide, sweet smile to her lips, knew the soft sounds of pleasure she made when he entered her, and knew most of all the warm comfort of her satiated body curved into his. In her arms, he'd found the one thing he'd never found anywhere else. Peace.

Damn. She was temptation embodied.

"Just one cup?" Livia asked.

"We can do some catching up," he said, though he wondered if that was any part of his real reason for asking to see her. "You can tell me about what you've been up to in the last year."

An innocuous conversation, the kind two old friends had. Yeah, that was what he wanted.

Liar.

The baby fussed, her pixie face working up from contentment to a full-out cry. Edward backed up a few steps—not that he thought Melody was going to hand him the kid or anything—but because the whole moment made him uncomfortable. Kids were something Edward had always steered clear of, and for good reason.

The baby's presence reminded him of his last argument with Livia. She'd wanted to know where their relationship was going, and he'd told her nowhere further than where it was. He'd perfected the art of the no-commitment relationship, and that was what he wanted with Livia. No marriage, no permanence, and definitely no kids.

Livia had asked him why, and he'd lied. He'd kept his most grievous sin to himself. He'd been selfish then, too, unwilling to see the trusting, loving light in her eyes dim.

Watch out for Katie.

No, no kids. Not for him. Ever.

Now her sister had a child, and—

The baby seemed to be leaning toward Livia. Before he could think about why, Livia took the child out of the carrier and the pink bundle settled happily into the crook of Livia's arms. And in that second, the truth slammed into him. The year apart. The baby. The last time they'd slept together—

The mirror image—*his* image—reflected back at him, as clear as a summer sky.

Could it be?

His pulse thundered in his head, as he faced the last thing he'd ever wanted. A child.

"I've, uh, been up to a lot. A lot I haven't told you about," Livia said, and her face softened when she gazed down at the baby. Before she even said the words, he knew. Knew what she was going to say, knew what that mirror image meant, and knew the truth. "I'd like you to meet your daughter, Edward."

* * *

The steaming mug of decaf sat between Livia's hands, erasing winter's chill. Beside her, Piper sat in her baby seat, gumming a rattle, oblivious to the tension in the small space. Edward sat across from her, holding a mug of his own. His car, parked in front of the diner, had a green missile-shaped tree now roped to the roof, but Edward didn't look at all as if he wanted to celebrate the holiday.

She could see the stress of the last year in the lines in his face, the shaggy ends of his hair, the wrinkles in his T-shirt. The Edward she had known had always been in control of everything from his appearance to his company. And now he looked…almost lost.

What had she expected, springing that kind of news on him? And what the heck had she been thinking, telling him about Piper when she'd vowed never to do that?

Yet when the moment had come, she'd realized that regardless of how they might have ended things or what he'd said at the end, she couldn't deny him the opportunity to love Piper. She wasn't that kind of woman, and never would be. It was only right that she tell him. After that, it was Edward's choice whether to be involved or not. Right now, she couldn't read him either way.

"I just want you to know, I don't expect you to do anything. Piper and I are doing just fine on our own." There, she'd said it. Gotten the worst part out of the way first.

Coffee churned in her stomach. She pushed the mug to the side. She aligned the silverware. Then the salt and pepper shakers.

"You named her Piper?"

Livia nodded.

He had to swallow hard before he could work any words to his throat. "Nice name."

"You told me a story once, about how you had a relative with that nickname—"

"She was always talking, like a baby bird," Edward said softly. "So we called her Piper."

"It was a sweet story and I always thought it was a cute name. So when Piper was born…" She shrugged and looked away, not wanting him to see that it was partly about her wanting to hold on to a piece of Edward, even when she knew he wasn't coming back.

Edward didn't say anything for a long moment. Then he steeled again and whatever emotion he'd been feeling disappeared. "When did you know?"

Only three other people sat in the diner. An elderly couple in a booth at the back, sharing a platter of French fries. A skinny man in his thirties read the *Riverbend News* while he waited on his order. The room was hushed, as if the entire town was trying to eavesdrop.

"I found out I was pregnant a few weeks after I moved back to New York." She remembered standing in her bathroom, staring at the positive home pregnancy test with a mix of joy and fear. Her first instinct had been to call Edward, but then she'd remembered his vehemence about not wanting children, and put the phone down again. And every day since, she had wrapped this tight cocoon around her and her child. Just the two of them, like a family in miniature. They were just fine without Edward.

But as she sat here, watching the news sink into Edward, she realized she'd been lying to herself all these months. A part of her always had wanted Edward to share in the miracle of Piper. Wanted to see him laugh over her expressions, delight in counting her fingers and toes, marvel at her peaceful, sleepy face.

A part of her had been waiting all this time for some

sunset reunion where they all went off and made a happy family. The sinking feeling in her gut as his features went stone cold told her that wasn't likely to happen.

"Are you sure it's mine?"

Anger washed over Livia in a sharp, fast wave. *It?* How could he call sweet Piper it? Then she took in a breath, and admitted to herself it was a legitimate question. She and Edward hadn't dated very long—just a few weeks—and any man would question an ex showing up a year later, baby in tow. "Yes, I'm sure."

"There wasn't another—"

"There's been nobody but you." The admission slipped out, her temper making her say more than she wanted to.

"Then that makes it mine."

"That 'it' is our child, Edward. She has a name and a personality."

"Forgive me if I'm having a little trouble dealing with this surprise," he said. "It's been almost a year, Livia. You could have said something. You knew how to get a hold of me."

How she wanted to just run out of the diner. But taking the time to gather up baby, diaper bag, car seat and purse didn't make for the fast, stormy exit she wanted. "Like I said, you don't have to 'deal with it' at all. Piper and I are just fine without you. So don't worry about making us another thing on your To Do list. You already made it clear that you weren't interested in the albatross of a child. We'll be fine without you around."

The last had stung. He recoiled, and for a second, she thought he was going to leave. Instead, he signaled to the waitress for a refill, then crossed his hands one over the other and leaned toward her. "Knowing you, I have no doubt that's true. I've never known a more resourceful, strong and creative woman."

The compliment took her by surprise. A warm flush flooded her face. Thank God they could be civil about this. In a few minutes, they'd say goodbye and Livia could go back to her quiet life in the little Riverbend house. Maybe send Edward a picture or two over the years. She told herself it didn't hurt at all. That he'd stayed true to his vow not to be a father, not to commit to her, and she shouldn't be upset at all. "Thank you." She moved to gather up her things. "I'll see you around town then."

"I'm not finished." He put up a finger. "But—"

Livia's throat tightened and she stopped moving. But? What kind of *but* could Edward possibly have? She'd told him he could forget about her and Piper. Go back to his life and leave them be. A part of her prayed he'd do just that. And another part prayed harder that he'd do the opposite. "But what?"

"I'm not the kind of man who will abandon my responsibilities."

"Responsibility? Is that how you see our baby?"

"It is a responsibility. Wouldn't you agree?"

"No, Edward, I wouldn't. She's a child. *Our* child. And she deserves to be loved."

"And provided for."

She let out a gust and jerked away from him. "I didn't tell you so you could give me money. I don't want your money. I told you because I thought you deserved to know. In case…" she looked away, bit her lip. "In case you wanted to be a real father."

The seconds ticked by. The tears Livia had tried so hard to hold back began to drop and puddle on the table. He shifted in his seat, seeming to grow more uncomfortable with the silence and her emotions. Beside Livia, Piper mmm-mmmed around her rattle.

Edward cleared his throat. "You know I can't do that."

"You made that perfectly clear before." Acid burned in her gut. Why had she agreed to coffee?

"And nothing has changed in that regard. However…" he steepled his fingers, "I am willing to help you in any other way you need. I am financially stable, and would provide handsomely for both of you."

"I don't want your—"

"Before you say no, think about the advantages." He ticked them off on his fingers, as if this were an accounting program. "The child will be well provided for. Nice home, best schools, everything. If you want to live here, fine. I'll buy you or build you whatever house you want and make sure everything is covered. You and the child will never have a worry."

The reality of his words slapped her hard. "You make it sound like another one of your business deals."

"Think of it as an arrangement. One that takes care of both of you for the rest of your lives."

"And you won't have to get emotionally involved. Be a husband or even a parent to *the child*. No changing diapers, no afternoon feedings, no late night cuddling. But oh, there will be a full bank account. Even if our lives are as empty as air. You can't just throw money at us and hope we'll go away. That isn't how it works, Edward." Now she did get up, thrusting her arms into her coat and grabbing all the paraphernalia around her, scooping up Piper's car seat last. "Piper and I don't want or need your money, Edward."

Then she and Piper walked out the door, the words she hadn't spoken ringing in her mind.

All I ever wanted was you.

CHAPTER FOUR

WELL. That hadn't gone well. Nor had it gone at all how he'd expected.

He'd hoped to handle that with more finesse. To make Livia see the smartest choice was to take his money. The child could have a good life, one where she didn't want for anything.

Anything? his mind whispered.

He ignored the doubts. He wouldn't make a good father, nor a good husband. Livia and the child were better off alone than in a home filled with disappointment.

Still, the sight of Livia walking away, clearly not intending to see him again, hurt. She was angry, and probably rightly so.

Then why had he made that offer? Probably driven by that desperate need he'd always had to make everything right. If Edward had to encapsulate himself in a few words, it would be "the man who wanted to make things right." He had always kept his little corner of the corporate world neat and tidy. Until the fire had shown him how little he had under his control.

Now Livia was springing this…this *baby* on him. He was reminded once again that a split second of acting without thinking could lead to a disaster. One he had tried to contain with money. Apparently, not very well, given the way Livia had stormed out of the diner.

He'd done exactly what she'd accused him of doing—trying to tidy up a loose end with a blank check. Livia didn't understand, though, that anything more, anything smacking of forming a "family" would only leave her angrier in the end. Best to stay detached, uninvolved, by offering only financial support.

He had no business getting involved with Livia again. A woman like that deserved a man who could give her everything—a beautiful home, financial security and, most of all, his heart. Edward could do two out of three. Unfortunately, it was the one he couldn't do that Livia wanted most.

He took a sip of his coffee but the brew had gone cold in the minutes he'd been sitting there. He pushed the coffee to the side and signaled for the check.

"You look like a man who needs a piece of pie."

Edward turned around. "Hey, Earl."

Earl dropped into the seat opposite Edward, without waiting for an invitation. He undid the flaps on his plaid hunter's cap, and laid it and a pair of brown leather gloves to the side. He sent a wave to the waitress, already on her way over with Edward's check in her hand. "Two pieces of whatever pie you have on special today, Annie."

"Caramel pecan okay with you?"

Earl grinned. "Aw, you know that's my favorite. But for God's sake, don't go telling Betsy that. She thinks I favor her blueberry." Annie chuckled and headed toward the kitchen.

"Thanks, Earl, but I don't want any pie. And honestly, I should get going to…" Edward's voice trailed off as he realized his agenda had been clear for a long, long time. "Well, to get some things done."

"You ain't had pie until you've had the caramel pecan here," Earl said. "And believe me, it'll cure most anything that ails you."

"I'm not sick."

Earl arched a brow but didn't say anything.

"Besides, I haven't got time for pie." Edward started to rise.

Earl laid a hand on his arm. "Everyone has time for pie. Sit down and visit with me. Entertain an old man."

Edward sat. He had nowhere else to go, except for bringing the tree home to his father. And right now, Edward wasn't exactly in a deck-the-halls mood.

"So, how's your dad doing?" Earl asked. "I was thinking of swinging by there tomorrow. See if he's up to letting me beat him at cards."

"He's okay," Edward said. "A little down. Some card playing would be good for him."

"Hell, you can't blame the man. A heart attack can bring anyone to his knees. And you know your dad." Earl smiled. "I've never known a busier man than Ray. Hell, he was rebuilding a trannie at the kitchen table the day he got home from the hospital."

Edward smiled. "I remember. He wasn't too happy when I locked up his tools. He told me I was trying to kill him when I told him I'd tie him to the couch if he didn't sit down and rest."

Earl chuckled. "So I take it he's not doing so well with following doctor's orders?"

"What do you think?"

That brought another laugh out of Earl. "I'd think something was wrong with Ray if he *didn't* give the doctor a hard time."

That was his father, through and through—determined to work even if it put his health in danger. Edward had barely seen his father when he'd been a child, and even now, they seemed to…dance around each other, rather than have a meaningful conversation. Edward was nothing if not his father's son—far more comfortable at his desk than in a relationship.

Annie brought the pie and left Edward's check on the table beside his plate. "Enjoy."

"Thanks, Annie." Earl shot her a grin, then dove in to the gooey piece. He swallowed, and his smile widened. "What'd I tell you? Best pie around."

Edward took a bite, then nodded his agreement. He'd eaten here many times over the years, but had never had dessert. For a second, the sweet taste reminded him of Livia, of the peachy softness of her skin. He could still remember how she'd tasted. Of cinnamon and vanilla, or so it had seemed to him, the kind of delicious combination that had him coming back for more and more.

Until he'd realized a union between them was never going to work. That she wanted things out of him that he couldn't give. He still couldn't, even as he'd seen in her eyes that a part of her had hoped for more.

If only she knew what she was asking of him.

He pushed the pie aside, and drained the rest of his coffee, even though it was a cold caffeine sludge that churned in his gut.

"It's great that Livia's back in town," Earl said. "Isn't it?"

Edward tried to act as if he wasn't affected at all by the mention of Livia's name. "Mm," he answered noncommittally. He figured it wasn't going to take much for people to fit together the baby and his past relationship with Livia. But the longer he could put off dealing with that, the better.

Right now, he didn't know how he wanted to handle it. A good man would step up and be a father, create a cozy family of three. Livia had made it clear, though, that she didn't want a semblance of family. She wanted the whole thing or nothing at all.

He couldn't give her that. But maybe they could come to some sort of a compromise that would take care of her and the child. If nothing else, he would make her see the reason of taking his money.

"She's a beautiful woman," Earl said. "Can't believe you let her go."

"It was a mutual decision." He'd broken her heart and she'd told him she never wanted to see him again. As mutual as it could get.

"Well, if you ask me, a woman like that doesn't come around every day. You find one, you should scoop her up, and make it legal soon as you can."

"Then why haven't you proposed to Betsy?" Edward asked. Best way to get the spotlight off yourself…shine it on someone else.

Earl scowled. "I'm an old man. Set in my ways. I don't want someone telling me when to go to bed and what to eat for supper."

"She turned you down, huh?"

"Twice." Earl let out a gust. "That woman is more stubborn than a mule in mud."

Edward chuckled. "Sounds like true love."

A goofy grin took over Earl's face and lit in the older man's eyes. He might complain about Betsy, but it was clear she had stolen his heart. Jealousy filled Edward that Earl had found such an elusive thing as happiness with another person.

"Might be true love. Just might be." Earl forked up another huge bite of pie, but paused before eating. "Anyway, I have to admit, I had an ulterior motive for treating you to some pie."

Edward put a few bills on top of his check, enough to cover the cost of the desserts and a generous tip. "Really?"

"Yup." He ate another bite, clearly not about to interrupt his dessert with talking. Edward waited. And not too patiently. Finally, Earl finished his piece of pie and pushed the plate aside. "I need a favor."

"Anything. You know that." Earl had been a good friend to Edward and his father over the years, acting almost like a second father. The kind of neighbor who shouted warnings when a teenage Edward drove too fast, and offered counsel when Edward had broken up with his first girlfriend. Who'd crowed as loud as a proud father when Edward's company had gone national. He'd always liked Earl and considered him part of the family.

"These joints ain't getting any younger, and with these cold winter days…" Earl shivered. "Anyway, I could use some help at the tree lot. Just for the next couple days. Christmas is just around the corner, and ain't nobody buying a tree after the big man comes down the chimney."

"True." Edward was about to decline, then realized he didn't have anything else to do besides care for his father. Ray was none too happy to be mollycoddled. It was only a matter of time before the two butted heads. Again. Edward's company was in the capable hands of his vice president while Edward was here, and waiting to sell the whole corporation to an interested investor.

What better way to while away those days than by helping a friend? "Sure, I can help out."

"Terrific. You know I love to work that lot myself, but I…well, I need my rest."

Concern filled Edward. Earl had seemed fine, but Edward knew too well how a hearty exterior could mask a bigger problem. "Everything okay?"

"Yep. I'm fine," Earl said. "Just doing too much is all. Betsy and the doc told me to take it easy." Earl glanced away, then gestured toward Edward's pie. "You gonna finish that?"

"All yours." Edward slid it across to Earl.

Earl waved toward Annie and gestured for a drink. "I better get something to wash this down. If Betsy tastes Annie's pies on me when I get home, there'll be hell to pay."

Edward laughed. He knew Betsy nearly as well as he did Earl. She was about as warm and fuzzy as a cactus, but apparently the grizzled auto mechanic had found something to love in the cantankerous B&B owner. Good for him.

When Annie dropped off a glass of water, Earl finished his pie and chugged back the liquid. Then he dropped a few more bills on top of Edward's and got to his feet. "I sure appreciate your help. It'll do you good, to get out in the fresh air. Do something with your day. Besides brooding like a mother hen about things you can't change." He clapped a hand on Edward's shoulder. "You'll be better for it. You'll see."

Then Earl was gone, leaving Edward wondering whether he'd just made a huge mistake or taken a huge step forward.

* * *

"You need to stay in bed all day." Livia crossed to the bathroom and rinsed off the thermometer, then put it on the nightstand beside her sister. "I'll warm up some of the leftover chicken and rice soup before I leave. Do you want a cold cloth for your head?"

Melody flopped back against the pillows. "Why can't you stay home? Who's going to take care of me?"

Livia bit her lip at the whine in Melody's voice. Melody could be so much more self-sufficient, if only she chose to be. Right now, though, Livia didn't have time for a lecture on independence. "I'll only be gone a couple hours. I laid out everything you could possibly need, so all you have to do is stay in bed and get better."

Melody pouted. "Call in sick. Stay here. Take care of me."

"I can't. I'm sorry." Livia left the room and heated up some leftover chicken and rice soup on the stove. As she was bringing it back to Melody's bedroom, she ran through her mental list. Diaper bag packed. Piper's carrier and snowsuit by the door, waiting for Livia to get Piper up from her nap and bundle her up. She laid the soup on the nightstand, beside the television remote, a hot pot of tea and a stack of magazines. "I'll be back before you know it. If you want something special for dinner, text me and I'll pick stuff up at the store."

Melody let out a long, dramatic sigh. "I suppose I'll take care of myself."

Livia wondered if all this was her fault. If she'd babied Melody too much in the years since their mother had left. Trying to step into a role that really shouldn't be filled by a sister. Melody was perfectly capable of taking care of herself, but still a twinge of guilt ran through Livia at the thought of leaving her alone when she was sick.

"Are you sure you know my cell number?" Livia asked. "Maybe I should write it down."

"Livia, you've had the same phone number for three years. Of course I know it."

"Okay." Livia bit her lip, thinking. "There are extra tissues under the bathroom sink and a stack of blankets in the closet—"

"If I get cold. I know, I know." Melody buried herself further in the covers. "I guess I can get up and get them myself."

Livia retrieved a pair of cotton blankets from the closet and draped them over Melody. "Don't forget to shut off the stove if you make more tea. Better yet, use the microwave."

"I know, I know. You are such a worrywart."

Livia arched a brow. "Don't I have good reason to worry?"

"Hey, that flood…thing," she waved her hand vaguely, "wasn't my fault. Entirely."

"Just turn off things when you're done with them, okay? And get well, sis." She gave Melody a quick hug, then headed into the nursery. Melody kept on grumbling, but Livia didn't stop. She'd promised Earl and she couldn't let him down.

As always, the sight of her sleeping baby curled around Livia's heart. She smiled, then reached into the crib. The second her hands met Piper's body, the baby woke up. She let out a little cry at first, which shifted to a gurgle when her blue eyes locked on Livia's. "Hey, beetle." Livia nestled a kiss in Piper's dusting of hair, then held her close.

"We've got work to do today," she said as she laid Piper on the changing table and put on a new diaper. The fresh, sweet scent of baby brushed at Livia's senses, and she paused long enough to give Piper a raspberry kiss on her belly. Piper gurgled and kicked her feet, her hands reaching for—and getting a good chunk of—Livia's hair. Laughing, Livia untangled her hair from Piper's steel grip, and finished dressing her daughter in a festive red and white jumper.

Once Piper was bundled in her snowsuit and strapped into the car seat, Livia headed out the door before Melody could convince her to stay. A few minutes later, she'd driven the short distance across Riverbend, pulling into a space at the back of the church. Such a small thing, to love that everything essential in this small town was located within a radius of minutes. It was a homey, warm and quiet community. She could barely remember the hustle and bustle of New York. And more, couldn't imagine ever returning. This was where she and Piper belonged, she knew it.

Except Riverbend came with Edward, at least for now. He hadn't bought another house, as far as she knew, and hadn't sold his business, either, as far as she knew, so surely he wasn't planning on staying. If he did—

What then?

It wasn't as if they were going to get married. Clearly, Edward was no more interested in a long-term relationship today than he had been last year. How could he have just thrown the money card on the table like that? It was so cold, so impersonal…

So indicative of the man he'd turned out to be. A man who wanted no depth in his life, only fluff.

She didn't want to marry him, anyway, because she knew it would be nothing more than a sham, constructed because they had a child. A mistake, that's what that would be.

Hadn't she already seen how a marriage built on a

shaky foundation could crumble? How unhappy two people could make each other, even if they had the best intentions? Leaving their children to flounder in the wake of bad decisions. The best thing she could do was stay away from Edward and concentrate on her daughter.

"We're going to have fun today," she whispered to Piper as she unlatched the car seat. "I'll do all the hard work, you just sit there and look cute. Which you do perfectly, if you ask your mama."

Piper blew a bubble and worked a smile onto her face. The white snowsuit made her look like a bundled marshmallow, but the jaunty red and white cap on her head added a burst of Christmas spirit. Livia knew she was probably biased, but she thought Piper was the cutest baby in the universe.

Every day with Piper was precious as gold, a true gift. She could think of nothing more she wanted.

Nothing? her mind whispered. *Are you sure you're not missing out on anything?*

Nothing, she told herself. Nothing at all.

Livia propped Piper on her hip, loving the way the baby's fist curled around Livia's collar. She swung the diaper bag over the opposite shoulder and headed into the tree lot. There was a decent selection, considering how few days were left until the holiday.

Several people milled about the aisles of trees. Then the group parted, and Livia's steps stuttered. Edward. Who looked as surprised to see her as she was to see him. "What are you doing here?"

"Working Earl's shift for him."

"But…that's why I'm here." Her mind circled back to the conversation with Earl the day before. Had she misunderstood him? Arrived on the wrong day? No, Earl had called and asked her to take his shift for the next few days. His exact words, "These joints ain't getting any younger, and with these cold winter days…Anyway, I could use some help at the tree lot." She'd said yes, of course. Earl was a good friend, and if he needed help, she'd be there.

Except if Edward was here. She couldn't work with him. Not now, not when her heart was still stinging from him throwing money at her and their baby, as if that would solve everything. "Well, it seems you have it all under control. I guess I'll come back tomorrow."

"I'm supposed to be working that shift, too." Then Edward shook his head and understanding dawned on his features. He chuckled. "Earl. Riverbend's own Dear Abby."

"What do you mean?"

Edward leaned in close to her so the other people wouldn't overhear. When he did, his breath tickled along her neck and she remembered.

Oh, she remembered it all.

Her pulse skipped, her breath stuttered. She could almost feel Edward's fingers dancing along her collarbone, dipping into the V of her shirt, slipping down her side, over her buttocks, awakening her senses inch by excruciating inch. She'd never known a man who took such time, such care, with something so simple as a caress.

"I think we're being set up." He drew back a little, and she told herself she was glad. "I do believe Earl's matchmaking."

"Oh, he wouldn't." She thought back again to the conversation she'd had on the phone. Earl had asked her about Edward twice and seemed overly interested in whether she'd seen Edward again. The pieces fell into place. She should have known better. If there was one thing Earl Klein believed in, it was that everyone should get their happy ending. "You're right. He is. Oh my goodness. And I fell for it, hook, line and sinker."

Edward nodded, and a slight grin curved on his face. "He's good at it. Very good."

Livia was suddenly aware—very aware—of how close Edward was. Of how her body reacted, even as she willed her hormones to play dead. Of how her heart still leaped at his grin, even as she remembered, too well, how he had broken her heart. She knew even more now how easily he could break her heart again.

Except, in this little snippet of time, she'd glimpsed the Edward she'd met last year, the one who had swept her off her feet. The one with a ready smile, a twinkle to his eye, a tease in his voice. Oh, how she'd missed that. Craved it.

She was immune to those charms, she told herself. Older, wiser. Not making that mistake twice.

She shifted Piper on to the opposite hip and blew her bangs off her forehead. "Well, you can leave if you want and I can handle Earl's shift. Surely there doesn't need to be two of us here."

"And you're going to do what? Put the kid on the ground while you tie a tree to someone's car roof?"

The kid. Not our baby. Not Piper.

Her chin jutted out. "I'll be fine."

He scowled. "Don't be stubborn, Livia. You can't do this alone. I'll stay."

She started to turn away, pressing Piper to her chest, as if their child could be a wall against hurt. But it only reminded her that Edward hadn't wanted the miracle they had made together. Why did she keep hoping? Keep believing in the impossible? "I should go, then."

He reached for her—the second time he'd touched her in as many days—and her heart skipped a beat. "Stay. You're a better salesperson than me. I'll do all the heavy lifting and grunting."

"Like a Neanderthal?" The words slipped out like a reflex.

A slight smile curved across his face. "Ah yes, Neanderthal. I do believe someone once called me that."

She couldn't help herself and laughed at the memory. Did he remember, too? Did he think about their time together? "You *were* being particularly manly that day. Moving all those boxes. And, uh, everything else."

"I remember."

The moment extended between them, heated and heavy. Oh, she remembered, too. She'd been at the banquet hall that day, helping Edward move boxes of files to a storage room. It had been hard, sweaty work, but they had laughed through most of the job, and as the day drew to a close and the last of the boxes were stacked, they had realized how alone they were in the dimly lit, overly warm storage space. Livia had peeled off her sweatshirt, and Edward had let out a slight groan, then taken her in his arms in a crushing, powerful kiss. Boxes had fallen to the floor, papers spilling in a wide circle, but they hadn't noticed. It had been a frenzied rush to have each other, to taste and touch as much as they could, as quickly as they could. Livia had had no idea fast, hot sex could be so amazing and fulfilling.

Now, Edward's gaze drifted down, over her face, then held on her lips. Was he thinking of that moment in the storage room? Was he picturing her arching beneath him, just as she was remembering the hard strength of his back beneath her hands? The blissful, amazing moment when he'd entered her, and brought her to new heights?

An ache built inside of Livia. She had missed him so much. She opened her mouth to say something, anything. Then Piper let out a cry and started to fuss in Livia's arms, and the moment was broken. Livia stepped back. Back to reality, not to things she shouldn't want. But her mind was a foggy mess. "I better get her, uh, something to, uh, play with. You know, a…a…"

"Rattle?"

"Exactly. That darn mommy brain." A nervous laugh, and then she spun away to search the diaper bag on the ground beside her for a toy, any toy, and any reason to avoid Edward's gaze.

"That's not like you," he said.

"What isn't?" She handed the rattle to Piper, who promptly stuck it in her mouth.

"To be so…discombobulated."

"Me?" She let out another little laugh. Why was he standing so close? And why was she still so easily affected by him? She knew better, darn it. "Lately, I never feel like I have anything together."

He smiled. "I find that hard to believe."

His eyes had darkened, his body had tensed, and she could read the message emanating from him as clear as a sunny day. She wasn't the only one remembering that moment in the storage room. She may have thought that history was dead and buried.

But she was wrong.

Piper had leaned over Livia's shoulder, working at that rattle, totally uninterested in the adults. But Livia was interested. Oh, yeah. Very interested.

She watched Edward's mouth. Remembered how his

lips felt on hers. What kind of magic he could work with nothing more than a touch.

And she wanted that again. Very much. She forgot everything else, especially all those very good reasons she'd had for staying away from him. All she wanted now was Edward. "Edward." His name escaped her in a whisper.

He closed the distance between them, until barely a breath of air stood in the space. "You look like you have everything under control right now." His voice was deep, husky and laden with a meaning she knew well.

She could step away. She could change the subject. She could do a hundred things to head off what was coming next.

She did none of them.

His hand came up to cup her jaw and Livia leaned into the touch. Oh, how she had missed him. His thumb drifted over her lips, and she parted them, wanting to taste him, to know him again.

"*Almost* everything under control," he said, his voice a dark growl. Then he leaned in and kissed her.

His mouth didn't just meet hers—it caressed hers. Lips drifting slowly over hers at first, tasting, relearning, exploring. Then his hand came up to cup the back of her head, and he leaned in closer. She yielded to him, opening her mouth, curving into his kiss, his touch.

It was sweet and hard all at the same time, the kind of kiss that made her body sing, her heartbeat dance. She wanted it to last forever, wanted it to end right now.

Before she fell for him again.

Livia pulled back and broke off the kiss. Her body ached in protest. "We…we can't do that," she said. "We're not…"

His gaze still lingered on her lips. "Not what?"

"Together anymore." The two words sounded harsh and cold. Livia stepped back again, and cradled Piper closer to her chest. This was what was important. This was what would last. This was what needed her attention, her full focus. Her child. Not the man who had broken her heart and who would only lead her down a dead end path. At the same time, an older woman came around the cluster of trees and walked up to Edward. Saved by the customer bell. Thank goodness.

"Young man, I could use some help. I really can't decide," the woman said. She was about five feet tall and had a head of white hair that poufed around her features. She clutched her purse to her chest like an arsenal, but had the look of a sweet grandma. "They're all so beautiful. Do you think you could give me a hand? I want a tree that will match my house. It's all done in Colonial style, you know. Which one do you think is best for that?"

"Uh…" Edward shot Livia a help-me glance. He had that deer-in-the-headlights look, and she bit back a laugh. "Livia here would know," he added. "She's practically an interior designer."

"Well, not practically. But I'd be glad to help." Regardless of everything, she couldn't let him flounder through this. And having something to do would keep her thoughts from returning to that kiss, and to what it might be or might not be. She shifted Piper on her hip—it was amazing how quickly such a tiny package could get heavy—then pointed to a short, squat balsam fir on their right. "This one would be great, ma'am, if you have the space. It reminds me of the kind of tree my mom liked. She had a Colonial style home, too."

"Oh, that looks perfect. I'll take it."

A few minutes later, the woman had paid for the

tree. Edward fed it through the netting machine, which wrapped the tree in a bright orange net, then loaded it onto the woman's car. He double-checked the fastenings, then leaned toward her window. "Are you going to need help with that when you get home, ma'am?"

"Oh, what a sweet man. No, I'll be fine. My grandson is coming over to help me set it up."

Livia watched from the sidelines. Edward had had nothing but kindness for the older woman, and patience as she searched her wallet for the correct amount of money, and then her calling him young man.

The Edward she had met a year ago had been charming, yes, but with a Dead End sign around his heart. But had she glimpsed another side of him today? Something more?

She told herself she only cared for Piper's sake. Her sole focus now was her baby, not a relationship. If that was so, then why had she kissed him back?

Didn't matter why. She wouldn't do it again. Period.

After their customer had left, Edward rejoined Livia. "Did your mom really have a Colonial style home?"

"I think," she said. "Sometimes it's hard to remember what it was like before my father got rid of all her stuff." A flood of emotions washed over her and Livia exhaled, willing them away. "It seems it was that way."

"Well, it was a nice touch."

"Thanks. It was the truth, at least the truth as I remember it."

"And did you have a tree like the one that lady bought?"

Livia's gaze went to the distance, to years so far in the past the memories held cobwebs. "I don't really remember," she lied. She remembered the holidays, nearly every single one. The ones before her mother left, when at least there was a semblance of a family get-together, and the empty ones after when her father gave up on celebrating and left his daughters in charge. "When I was a kid, Christmas…well, it was a stressful time."

"It is for lots of people."

"Yeah," Livia said. "But most of them don't leave town after New Year's."

His gaze sought hers. "Are we still talking about your mother? Or us?"

"We have customers," she said, and excused herself to help a young couple select a small, inexpensive tree. Edward let the subject drop and they worked together like that for a couple hours, with Livia shifting Piper from one side to the other as the baby's weight seemed to increase. Melody called twice, complaining that her soup had gone cold, then that there was nothing to watch on TV. Every time, Livia assured her sister she'd be home soon and until then, Melody could manage. Still, she was glad for the interruptions because it kept her from thinking about kissing Edward again. Or about a past that she couldn't change.

When the last customer had left, Edward headed over to Livia. "You should take a break. Sit in the office for a while with…the kid."

As soon as Edward called Piper, their child, "the kid," a reality check hit her square in the gut. He hadn't changed. He hadn't become a family man overnight and he probably never would. One kiss didn't change a thing. Neither did one tender conversation about Livia's fractured childhood. In the end, with Edward Graham, it all came down to practicalities and "responsibilities." To a relationship without messy entanglements.

She didn't want Piper and herself to be a "responsibility." Ever.

"Yeah, you're right. I could use a break." But she didn't mean from holding her daughter—rather from dealing with her daughter's father. And all the disappointments that sat heavy in her chest.

Livia headed inside, stripped off Piper's snowsuit, and plopped the baby in the car seat. Piper settled happily into the rocking base. She sat there, staring at Livia with big wide eyes.

Livia sighed. "What are we doing here, beetle?"

Piper gummed her fist.

"Being around him is torture." Livia plopped her chin into her hands. "What was Earl thinking?"

Piper kept drooling on her fingers, not offering an opinion on anything other than the yumminess of her own hand.

"Okay, well, we agreed to do this for Earl. So we'll tough it out." And, she figured, in the process, she might be able to make some contacts for future events. She made a mental note to bring business cards next time. Once the holiday was over, Jenna would be back from her honeymoon and Livia would join her at the events company, ready to start working on the preparations for the scheduled spring and summer events.

But still, a part of Livia hurt. The part that kept on hoping, like a stubborn sun on a rainy day, that Edward would take one look at his child and fall as madly in love as Livia had. That he would see and understand why it meant so much to Livia for her child to know *both* parents. Even though Livia told herself that her mother's leaving hadn't affected her, she knew deep down inside that it had. There were days when she felt a piece of herself missing, like an aching hole where a tooth used to be. She couldn't redo her own childhood, but she could make sure Piper didn't lack for love.

Her cell phone rang again. Livia knew without look-ing that it would be Melody. "What's up, Melody?"

"Where's the cold medicine?"

"In the bathroom cabinet. In the box labeled Cold and Flu."

A rustling of objects, a couple coughs from Melody. "Geez, Liv. You have them alphabetized."

"It makes it easier to find things."

"You have too much time on your hands." Melody sneezed, then let out a pity-me moan. "I think my fe-ver's worse. I'm dying here."

"You'll be fine. It's just a cold."

"I think it's worse than that, Livia. I might need to go to the hospital."

Melody had always been like this—every cut surely merited stitches, every sniffle spelled a trip to the doc-tor, every worry meant something bad was on its way. "I'll be home soon. My shift is almost up here. Do you want something special for dinner?"

"A new body." Melody coughed and sneezed on the other end.

Livia laughed. "I don't think they have those at the Sav-A-Lot. But I'll check."

"Okay." Melody sounded miserable. "Hurry home. *Please*. I'm so tired of taking care of myself. And I'm a terrible nurse. You're much better."

"I'll be home soon," Livia repeated." I promise."

Livia ended the call. At the same time, the door opened and Edward stepped inside, ushering in a cold breeze. Every time she looked at him, though, she felt heat curl in her gut. Darn it all.

Parts of her hadn't forgotten what it was like to be with him. Not one bit.

"Sorry," he said. "Just thought I'd get a cup of coffee while we had a break."

"Okay."

He crossed to the pot, poured a mug, then gestured toward a second one. "Want some?"

"Please." She tipped Piper's chair again, sending a happy smile across Piper's face. While the chair rocked, Livia stretched and worked out the kinks in her back. "For such a little creature, you sure can wear your mama out."

"One sugar and a little cream, right?" Edward asked.

She nodded, trying not to be touched that he remembered such a tiny detail. It didn't mean anything. Not a thing at all.

Edward brought the coffees and took the seat across from Livia. He held the mug between his palms, his gaze on the dark brew inside, and not on her or Piper, still happily gnawing away at her fist. "Can I ask you something?"

"Sure." She sipped her coffee. Edward had made it exactly the way she liked it. Still, in that first perfect sip, she had to wonder if it was because he cared or because he was a stickler for details. It had to be the latter.

"Why'd you come back?"

"To Riverbend?"

He nodded. "I thought you were a New York girl, through and through."

"I thought so, too. But then I fell in love with this town. And when I had Piper," Livia pushed at the chair's base again, and Piper gurgled as she rocked back and forth, "I realized there was no other place on earth where I wanted to raise my child."

"It is a good place for a family." He took a sip of coffee and a long silence extended between them. Tension hunched his shoulders, wrote lines across his face. She waited, sensing he wanted to say something. Maybe something she didn't want to hear.

"I'm sorry about yesterday," Edward said. "I shouldn't have offered you money like that. It was just…I didn't want you to worry about providing for the child. I'm sure being a single mother is hard."

It came down again to practicalities and sensible decisions for Edward. She shouldn't be surprised. He was all about tallying the numbers and weighing the pros and cons.

She glanced over at sweet, happy Piper, and felt a smile steal across her face. When it came to a child, Livia had learned, all those lists went out the window. "The joys far outweigh the work," she said softly. "Piper is a dream baby."

He cleared his throat. "Well, if you ever need anything, you know how to get hold of me."

He might as well have handed her a business card, considering all the emotion in his words. She let out a gust and got to her feet. A happy Santa clock chimed the hour on the wall with a few short notes from "Here Comes Santa Claus."

"How can you sit there, not three feet from your own daughter, and not fall madly in love with her? Talk about her like she's a goldfish in a bowl or a plant in a pot? She's a living, breathing human, Edward, who happens to share half your DNA."

"I know that." He scowled into his coffee. "And I'm prepared to take care of her and you, however you need."

"We don't want your money!" She shook her head. "Are you really that cold? What happened to the man I met last year?"

The man I just kissed. The man I thought still existed deep down inside. Even though I know better.

Santa tick-tocked on the wall, his booted feet swinging back and forth with each minute. Outside, the lights from the Winterfest blinked a bright pattern on the walls. But inside the room, the tension was anything but festive.

"You knew I wasn't interested in marriage or children when you met me, Livia." Edward said. "So don't stand there and act like it's a surprise."

"That was before…" she trailed a finger along Piper's satin cheek and her frustration ebbed, "before Piper was born."

"I can't just change overnight into some goo-goo, ga-ga guy." He pushed away from the table and crossed to the coffeepot, refilling his cup even though it was still half-full. "Don't ask more of me than I can give, Livia."

She heard the pain in his voice, saw it in the set of his shoulders. There was more going on here, something Edward was leaving unsaid. Was it just about the fire? Or more?

The Livia she had been before would have gone to him, offered comfort. But this Livia had one priority—Piper—and if Edward chose not to be involved, she wasn't going to force him. The last thing she wanted was to see her daughter brokenhearted.

Like Livia had been a year ago. Heck, five minutes ago. She steeled her resolve once again. Piper came first. Everything else, even Livia's own heart, was secondary.

"I don't expect anything out of you, Edward. And neither does your daughter." Then she gathered up the car seat and diaper bag and headed back out into the cold.

CHAPTER FIVE

"You look worse than I feel." Ray plopped into his re-cliner, and picked up the remote. "You watching this?"

Edward jerked his attention to his father. He had barely noticed Ray entering the room, and hardly heard what he said. Heck, he hadn't paid much attention to anything in the last hour. Edward had come home from the tree lot, checked his messages on his cell—and only because he wanted to silence the beeping voice mail in-dicator—then he'd headed into the living room and... well, done nothing. "Watching what?"

Ray shook his head, then clicked over to a military history channel. The sound of gunfire rat-a-tatted in the background. "What's wrong with you today?"

"Nothing. Just tired."

"From selling a few Christmas trees?"

"No." Though the few hours he'd spent at the church lot had been challenging in other ways, they hadn't been physically tough. He could still see the hurt in Livia's eyes, the hope that he would magically turn into the kind of man she wanted and needed. A part of him wondered if he could, then the realistic side of him remembered that he, of all people, had no business trying to be a tra-ditional family man, much less raise a child.

No matter how much he had enjoyed that kiss—and

damn, he had enjoyed it. A lot. But all he'd done by kissing Livia was open a door to a path he already knew
was a dead end.

Edward knew where his comfort zone was—at work.
It wasn't in a relationship where he had to open his heart
and lay bare his soul. Except in the past year, work had
ceased to be the salvation he knew. He felt as if he were
floundering, trying to find his footing again.

What he needed to focus on was things he could control. Like unloading the company that he no longer had
the heart to run. Then getting the hell out of Riverbend,
once and for all. Edward leaned forward on his knees.
"I have a buyer for the business."

"Well, good." Then the celebration faded from Ray's
features. "That's what you wanted, isn't it?"

"Yeah." Though now that it was a reality and there
was a contract sitting in the fax machine, Edward wasn't
as thrilled as he had expected to be. For nearly a year,
all he'd wanted was the weight of the business off his
shoulders. To be free of a responsibility that had become
a curse after the fire.

"You gonna take the offer? Or negotiate for more?"

"I think…" he paused, let out a breath, "I'm going to
think about it."

He told himself it was because he had so much on
his mind. That he was still reeling from the news that
he had a child.

A child.

With Livia.

Edward still couldn't quite wrap his head around that
concept. He looked at the baby, and looked at Livia, and
wondered how on earth that had all come to be. And what
he was going to do about it all from this day forward.

Kissing her wasn't the best thing to do. Hadn't

stopped him from doing it, though. Or wanting to do it all over again.

He swore under his breath. He was a mess. No, he'd *made* a mess. The problem was how to clean it up when Livia had made it clear she wanted all—or nothing.

Ray leaned back in his chair and eyed Edward with surprise. "Think about it? You, the son who has never hesitated on anything?"

"I thought I wanted to unload it, get away from the memories and responsibilities, but…"

"That company is as much a part of you as the nose on your face. I know that. Hell, half the town knows that. Except maybe you." Ray muted the television and shifted toward his son. His wise light blue eyes zeroed in on Edward. "What else is bothering you?"

Edward cast his father a curious glance. "Since when did we have touchy-feely conversations?"

"What, a man can't ask how his son is doing?"

"You can, it's just…you never did before."

"Yeah, well, it isn't my best skill." Ray shifted in his seat. "I'm better when there's a desk or something in front of me."

Edward chuckled. "Me, too."

Ray paused for a moment. His gaze dropped to his hands. "Listen, I may not have been around much when you were a kid, but I know you. I see myself in you. The good and the bad."

"Dad—"

"Don't try to sugarcoat it, Edward. I left your mother to raise you and your sister. I wish I hadn't, but you know what they say about wishes—"

"That and fifty cents will get you a cup of coffee." Edward recited his father's favorite saying without missing a beat.

Ray chuckled. "Yeah, and probably not even that in today's economy." He let out a breath, then met his son's gaze. "Anyway, I'm here now, and I'm paying attention. At least more than I did before. And that means I can tell when you got more on your mind than how the stock market did today."

Edward let out a long breath. The information was going to be public knowledge soon, if it wasn't already. He needed to at least tell his father. "Livia had a baby."

Ray arched a brow. "Yours?"

Edward nodded. At the same time, he realized he had no doubts that the baby was his. She looked a little like him, but more, everything he knew about Livia pointed to a responsible and honest woman. "She didn't tell me until a couple days ago."

"Why would she wait like that? I only met her a couple times but she never struck me as the kind that would keep that kind of thing from a man."

"Because…" Edward sighed, "when we were dating, I told her I never wanted to settle down, much less have children. Or anything to do with them."

"Well, that'll do it." Ray leaned his elbows on his knees. "But now the kid is here, so what are you going to do?"

"I don't know." He offered his father a weak grin. "Think about that, too."

Ray snorted. "If you ask me, you're going in the wrong direction. All this thinking is doing nothing for you. You should go see your baby, go to work, keep yourself occupied, instead of running from your responsibilities and sitting around here moping."

"I'm not moping and I'm sure as hell not running from anything. I'm here, taking care of you."

Ray snorted. "And how many days have you spent in the office since the fire?"

"I've been busy, Dad. You know that." Edward's gaze went to the pile of books stacked on the floor by Ray's chair. Not his father's face. Because even Edward could feel the lie underneath his words.

"Yeah, busy running, like I said. Moving out of town, heading to one city after another, then on that foolish trip to Europe, then back here." Ray waved his hands, as if encompassing the whole world in his gestures. "Hell, I don't think you have spent more than a handful of days at work. You used to be there day in and day out."

"My office here is gone, remember? I can't just up and go to Chicago every day, and still be here for you. And why are you complaining? You're the one who just told me you worked too much and lived too little."

Ray waved off that argument. "It's called finding balance, Edward. You can do both. You just gotta keep from having all your eggs in one henhouse. You ever heard of that marvel called the Internet? I hear you can accomplish amazing things with just an email."

Edward scowled. Leave it to his father to zero in on the solution—and the truth. "Pete's doing a good job in my shoes."

"As good as you could do?"

No, but Edward wasn't going to admit that. He'd always been a bit of a control freak about his company, and letting someone else be in charge had never been on his radar. Until everything he worked for went up in smoke, ruining someone else's life in the process. That day, he'd lost his footing, his surety about the way he ran his company, and hadn't wanted to sit behind that big cherry desk ever again. He made a good show at working for a while but really he'd been nothing more than a figurehead. He hadn't rebuilt the banquet hall. Hadn't done a damned thing. Just let it sit. "Doesn't matter. I'm selling."

"As you've said. And yet, you're still holding the reins." Ray got up, and crossed to his son, then laid a gentle hand on Edward's shoulder. "Before you sign anything, think long and hard. Learn from my mistakes. I buried my head in the sand for too many years and missed out on life. On your mother. On you." He gave Edward's shoulder a squeeze. "I regret that, more than I can tell you. Don't do the same thing."

"You were fine, Dad."

"No, I wasn't, and you know it. So quit doing things you're just going to regret later."

Ray headed into the kitchen, his steps slow but surer today than the day before. His father was on the mend.

While Edward was still in an emotional ICU.

Livia considered taking the coward's way out. Feigning an illness or a sudden, mysterious trip, anything other than going back to the tree lot and working with Edward. In the end, it was Piper who decided things.

The baby lay on a pink blanket trimmed with white bunnies in the middle of the living room floor, kicking her feet and waving her hands and just…being herself. Livia took one look at her and knew she couldn't deny Piper anything. Even access to her father.

Piper might be too young to be able to tell one male face from another, but Livia was convinced that Piper had an innate sense that this man was important to her. Yesterday, she had perked up whenever Edward spoke, her head swiveling in his direction, as if seeking the other half of her DNA.

So she bundled the baby up, filled the diaper bag

with bottles and diapers and toys, then headed upstairs to Melody's room. Her sister had spent all day yesterday in bed, and would probably do the same today. A rush of guilt ran through Livia, but she reminded herself Melody was an adult and a few hours on her own wouldn't hurt her. "I'm heading out now. Do you need anything else?"

Melody's eyes were red, her nose even redder, and she had a look of such sheer misery that Livia again considered staying home. "I'm still waiting on that head transplant," Melody said, the words coming out in a thick cold-influenced voice.

Livia laughed. "I'll see what I can do about that."

"Are you leaving the monkey here? It won't be easy holding her while you're selling trees and stuff."

"No. You're sick. You can't watch her, and I don't want her to catch your cold."

Melody pouted. "Truth is, you don't trust me."

"I…I do."

Melody barked out a laugh. "Right. You've never trusted me. The only time you've ever left Piper with me is when she's sleeping."

"Taking care of a baby can be tough. There's a lot to worry about."

"And what? I'm too young to worry? Too immature to handle a diaper change?"

"I never said that."

"You didn't have to."

The silence hung between them for a long time. Livia wanted to take it all back, but she knew her little sister was right. Livia didn't trust capricious Melody with Piper's care. Heck, she barely trusted anyone.

Melody tossed the remote to the other side of the bed.

"There's nothing on TV. I'm so bored." She drew the last word out in one long sound.

"Get something to read."

"Like a book?" Melody's nose crinkled. "I don't think so."

"You know, there are a lot of books out there you might actually enjoy. Not everything reads like an English assignment."

"I'd rather have company." Melody shifted onto one elbow and her eyes brightened with an idea. "I have an idea. Why don't you invite Edward to dinner?"

"For one, I am not dating Edward—"

"Why not? He's sexy as heck." Melody coughed, then dabbed at her nose with a tissue.

"For another," Livia went on, "you're sick and shouldn't be around anyone."

"I'll just lie on the sofa while you guys entertain me." To demonstrate, Melody flopped back against the pillows. "You won't even know I'm here."

"For a third," Livia continued, "if I invite anyone to dinner, it won't be Edward."

"Why not?"

Livia let out a gust and busied herself with folding the clothes that had fallen out of Melody's clean laundry pile and onto the floor. Her sister had never been especially neat, and when she was sick or tired, her room became a hazmat zone. Livia straightened and piled, organizing what she could. "Why don't I get you some books to read?"

"Are you trying to avoid the topic?"

"Of course not."

"Liar." Melody rolled onto her side and propped her head on her hand. "Why don't you want to talk about him?"

"Because there's nothing to talk about."

"There's Piper."

"He's…not interested in Piper." The words choked out of her throat. Finally stating the truth burned. No matter how much she hoped, she couldn't pull off a miracle.

"What? Really? Are you sure?"

Livia nodded. Her vision blurred, and she kept on refolding the same shirt because she couldn't see the stupid seams.

"Maybe there's more to it than you know," Melody said softly.

Livia jerked to her feet and dropped the rumpled shirt onto the laundry pile. "Really, Melody? Was there more involved with Mom, too? Because I seem to remember her just running out the door and never coming back. Like we were goldfish she didn't want anymore."

Tears swam in Melody's eyes and she shook her head. "I don't know."

Livia rushed to the side of the bed. "I'm sorry, Mel. I shouldn't have said that."

Melody refused to look at her. She just shook her head and thumbed through channels on the television. Regret coursed through Livia. All her life, she'd tried to shield Melody from the harsh truth about their mother. As if by not saying it, she could avoid hurting her sister.

"Listen, why don't I go get those books?" Livia said, forcing brightness into her voice.

"Fine." Melody shrugged. "Find me something that won't put me to sleep."

Livia came back with several suspense novels, a half dozen romance novels and a new pot of hot tea. "I'm sure you'll find something you like out of these. I'll be back at five."

Melody waved her off and sank back into the pillows

with a pout. Livia lingered a moment longer, then headed out the door. Livia wished she'd never stepped into the minefield of their mother's disappearance. When she got home, she'd smooth things over with Melody.

The air was crisp and cold, the kind of winter day that hinted at snow. Livia breathed in the clean, fresh air and offered up a silent wish for a little snowfall. She wanted Piper's first Christmas to be perfect—a regular winter wonderland of beauty. Hopefully Mother Nature would cooperate.

What about Edward?

Melody's words came back to her. *Maybe there's more to it than you know.*

What more could there be? He didn't want anything to do with being a father and the sooner she gave up hoping for the opposite, the better.

When she pulled into the church parking lot, she saw that Edward had beaten her there again today. The tree lot was empty, and the festive strings of white lights drooped a bit in the spaces that had held trees just a few days before. Across the street, the town Winterfest stood ready and waiting for tonight's festivities. A miniature village fronted the park, while Santa's Workshop—complete with a real reindeer in a pen beside the shed that housed Mr. and Mrs. Claus, played by CJ and Jessica Hamilton—sat in the back, waiting for the magic time when the sun set and the lights came on, and the Christmas world came alive. CJ, a former set designer, had turned the Winterfest into a destination for Riverbend and all the surrounding communities. She'd heard attendance this year was nearly double last year's. Maybe tonight Livia would take Piper over there. Piper wouldn't know who Santa was, of course, but she'd love the bright lights and Christmas music.

Right now, though, Piper wasn't loving anything. As soon as Livia stopped the car, Piper started crying from her seat in the back. Her face reddened. Her fists pumped, and she let out a wail that seemed to echo in the enclosed space.

"Hey, hey, what's the matter?" Livia got out of her side of the car and came around to unbuckle Piper, who was working herself up into a bigger fit. Livia sighed. It looked to be a grumpy baby day, not nearly as easy as yesterday. She tugged Piper out of the car seat, slung the diaper bag and seat's handle over one arm, then carried Piper in the other. Maybe a few minutes against her mother's side would soothe her.

And if not, maybe they'd get lucky and have few customers. With only a handful of days remaining until Christmas—and even fewer trees left to choose from—chances were good there wouldn't be too many people shopping today.

Piper fidgeted against Livia's hip as she carried her through the maze of trees. Her cries reduced in volume—barely. "It'll be okay, baby," Livia soothed, running a palm down Piper's snowsuit padded back. "Just a couple hours today. Then we'll go home, and I'll give you a nice warm bath before bedtime. Sound like a plan?"

Piper let out a wail. Clearly, waiting for the bath was not acceptable. She squirmed and fussed, her firsts pumping at the air. Livia dug in the diaper bag for a toy—which Piper rejected—then another one, but neither pacified the baby. She rubbed at her eyes and let out another wail.

A middle-aged couple rounded the corner at the edge of the lot, the wife curved into her husband's arms as they walked. They didn't say much, just looked at the trees bordering the sidewalk. Livia increased her pace to reach the center of the lot where Edward surely was, and undoubtedly in need of help. Piper kept on crying.

"Sorry I'm late," Livia said, the words escaping her in a hurried breath. Partly because she was flustered from dealing with Piper, and partly because every time she saw Edward, her pulse tripped. He stood there, tall and handsome, his knee-length black wool coat the perfect offset to his dark hair and deep blue eyes. Beneath the coat, he wore a white button-down shirt and a pair of well-worn jeans, a combination of sexy and business-man that nearly took her breath away.

Why did this man have such an effect on her? Every time she saw him, he reduced her willpower with merely a glance. She'd fallen for those blue eyes once before, blind to his faults. She wouldn't do it a second time. Kiss or no kiss.

"No problem," Edward said. "It's been slow. No customers yet."

It was an ordinary, regular conversation. Yet Livia sensed an undercurrent of words left unsaid, issues yet to be resolved.

Not to mention kisses that had opened a Pandora's Box she'd vowed to shut. Again. Everything inside her—the part that was so used to running from her problems and pretending they didn't exist—wanted to leave. But she didn't. Because the minute she had held Piper in her arms, she had decided to face everything in life from there on out head-on. And that included Edward Graham.

"There's a couple over there by the last few Scotch pines." She pointed and Edward's gaze followed. "Once we've helped them, maybe we could take a few minutes to—"

"You have to take those customers, Livia. I...I can't."

He seemed to have gone cold. He stood as rigid as a statue, his face unreadable.

"What? Why?"

"I just...can't."

Piper twisted and pushed at Livia, and seemed to be working up to another wail. Livia dug in the diaper bag for a pacifier, but Piper wanted none of that, either. She was reaching—

For Edward.

He hadn't noticed, but Livia had. For whatever reason, he didn't want to deal with the customers and she didn't want to trek over there with a fussy baby. A child having a crying fit didn't exactly encourage sales or lift holiday spirits.

Right now, Piper wanted, of all things, Edward. Well, who was she to deny her daughter?

"Okay, I will," Livia said. "On one condition."

"What?"

"You take Piper." As if hearing the offer, Piper leaned even further toward Edward, her arms out, her hands reaching. "She's not in the best of moods and I don't think a crying baby helps make the sale."

His eyes widened and he took an imperceptible step back. "Me? Take...her?"

She nodded. "You can go inside to the office, where it's warm. Just plop her in the car seat and rock her. I think she's tired. Chances are, she'll fall asleep before you can say boo."

Livia knew she could take the baby with her—it wouldn't be an ideal situation, by any means—but as she watched Piper leaning more and more away from her mother and more and more toward Edward's familiar voice, she knew she had to at least try to get Edward involved, for Piper's sake. The little kernel of hope that resided inside Livia held on to the thought that maybe, just maybe, he'd hold Piper and fall as madly in love with their daughter as Livia had.

Maybe.

"I don't know." Edward gave the baby a wary glance. Piper had at least stopped crying, as if she knew she was the subject of debate.

"Either that, or deal with the customers." She shot him a grin. "Your choice. I swear, Piper doesn't bite. Most of the time."

He took another look at the couple across the way. A shadow dropped over his features. "Okay."

She got the sense he was avoiding something, but what, she wasn't sure. She glanced again at the couple out in the lot. They didn't look familiar. Not that she knew everyone in town. Still, Livia couldn't understand why Edward was so upset.

Once again, he had shut her out rather than opening up. Just like last year. Damn, she needed to learn her lesson better.

Either way, someone needed to greet the customers before they got frustrated and left. "You want to take her?"

"Yeah."

A flicker of worry ran through Livia. Melody was right. Livia could count on one hand the number of times she'd let someone else hold her baby. Okay, so she was a bit of a control freak, but Piper was the most precious thing in Livia's life. Taking a chance was simply out of the question.

Then she remembered that this was Edward, the same man who had once touched her so gently, she cried. He would never do anyone harm, and she knew that as well as she knew herself.

And, more than that, he was Piper's father. Of all the people in the world, she was sure he would watch over her safety, regardless of everything else.

"Be careful with her," Livia said.

"Of course." Though he looked dubious, clearly someone who didn't know the first thing about babies.

"If she's still fussy, you can put her in the car seat. Just be sure to latch the strap so she won't fall out."

He glanced at the seat, then at the baby. "Can do. I'll be fine, Livia. Now can you just go deal with those… customers?"

"Sure, sure." What was bothering Edward? He seemed as anxious to leave as a vampire at sunrise. She wanted to ask, but didn't. If anything, his closed and guarded features reminded her that Edward Graham preferred to keep his emotions close to his chest rather than let her into his heart.

She handed over the diaper bag, then the seat, then Piper. As soon as he had the baby, he spun on his heel and headed into the trailer housing the office. He wasn't much of a holidays guy—she knew that—but this was more than just avoiding a little caroling.

He'd shut the door on her as effectively as he shut the door to the trailer. Disappointment curdled in her stomach but she pushed it away. She crossed to the couple, who were staring up the seven-foot length of a reedy pine. "Hi, I'm Livia. Can I help you find something?"

"Well, we're looking for a tree," the woman said, then paused to glance up at her husband. They were in their late forties, and seemed dwarfed by the thick black coats they wore. "I…I think."

"We've always bought a tree," her husband said, his voice quiet. "But this year…"

"We weren't sure." Tears shimmered in the woman's eyes. She looked up at her husband again, and bit her lip. "Miranda is the one who loves trees."

Miranda.

The name clicked in Livia's mind. And then she knew. Why Edward was avoiding this family. Why he'd disappeared inside. She glanced over at the trailer serving as a temporary office for the tree lot, and saw Edward, his back to the window, sitting at the table. Piper's car seat rocked back and forth before him. She couldn't tell if the baby was still crying, but she knew one thing for sure.

Edward was still hurting.

And here was Miranda Willett's family, a visual reminder of the pain the fire had caused. No wonder Edward hadn't had the courage to face them. And no wonder they looked so lost and hurt. Her heart softened, for him, for these people. Another part of her hurt because he had chosen again to leave Livia out of the picture, and let her figure it out herself. What would it take for this man to open up?

"I don't know, Rich," Miranda's mother said. "She told us specifically no tree this year."

Her husband sighed. "I know. But she needs something. I hate seeing her so sad."

The couple glanced at the trees, then at each other. Finally, Mrs. Willett nodded. "A tree it is, then."

"What kind of tree does she like?" Livia asked gently.

A soft, pained look settled on Miranda's mother's face. "She likes the scraggly little trees. The ones nobody else wants."

"When she was little, she was always bringing something or other home," her father said, echoing his wife's expression. "We drew the line at rodents, but let her keep most everything else."

Livia could hear the memories in their voices, the tender love they had for their daughter. She wanted to ask how Miranda was doing, but it was clear that regardless of her physical recovery, she was far from healed emotionally. Undoubtedly, this would be a hard Christmas for the entire Willett family. If picking the perfect tree for them could help ease some of that pain, Livia would stay in the cold for as long as it took. "She sounds like a wonderful girl."

"She is." Then the mother's voice caught and she buried her face in her husband's shoulder. He drew her close and held her for a long time. Finally, Mrs. Willett drew herself up and swiped the tears off her face. "I'm sorry. This has just been so hard on all of us."

"Please, don't apologize. I understand. Let's go find a tree that she would love," Livia said. Miranda's parents nodded, then followed her to the other side of the lot. There weren't many trees left to choose from—a few fat, picture-perfect ones and a couple that had broken branches. Livia circled past those, then stopped by one she had seen yesterday. A skinny tree, shy a few branches of being full, leaned against the church's brick exterior. It looked lonely and sad, like the proverbial Charlie Brown Christmas tree. "We have plenty of regular trees left, as I'm sure you saw, but this one…"

"Needs a little love." Miranda's mother turned to Livia. Tears glistened in her eyes, but they were partnered this time with a smile. Mrs. Willett danced her fingers along the tree's delicate branches. "It's perfect. Thank you."

Livia nodded. Her throat clogged. "I'll get it wrapped up for you."

Miranda's father hefted the tree onto his shoulder and carried it to the register, then fished in his pocket for some money. Livia waved the money off. "No charge."

"We can pay for it."

"Consider it a Christmas gift. Earl would have insisted, I'm sure." She may not have known Earl Klein very long, but she knew he took care of the people of Riverbend as if every one of them was a relative. And if anyone in this town needed taking care of, it was the Willett family.

Livia leaned over, picked up the tree, then tipped it to load it into the netting machine. The big blue metal machine, with its neon orange netting seemed like a relatively straightforward process.

For someone who had used the machine before.

She'd done sales yesterday, and Edward had done all the labor. She hadn't thought to pay attention to how the trees were actually packaged and then loaded onto the customer's cars. In truth, she had no idea how to use it. She wrestled with the machine for a few minutes, pushed this button, that one, pulled a lever that jerked a chunk of netting up into a rat's nest. Finally, she gave up. "Um…let me get someone to help with this…thing."

"I'd help but I spend all day behind a desk." Miranda's father shrugged and looked just as perplexed as Livia felt. "Machinery's not exactly my area of expertise."

"That's okay. I know just who to get." Assuming, that was, that he'd come out here to help.

Edward had to move on past that fire sometime. Maybe starting with something as simple as wrapping a tree could be the first step. She glanced at the Willetts. Would seeing Edward upset them? Or would it give everyone a chance for forgiveness? She thought of the stoic, yet broken man who'd returned to Riverbend, a man she once loved, and knew she had to take that chance. He may never open up to her, but he owed it to himself to move past this tragedy.

Livia took a deep breath and headed for the trailer. A burst of heat greeted her when she opened the door. "Edward, I—"

She stopped talking. Her words disappeared as she took in the vision before her.

Edward stood by the filing cabinets, Piper laying across his arms like a load of wood, while he swayed back and forth. He maintained a distance between his chest and Piper's tiny body, as if he didn't want to quite commit to holding her, but it was a start.

He was holding their daughter. Actually holding her.

Livia's heart flipped over in her chest, and she blinked, sure she was seeing things. But no, it was real. It was Edward.

And their daughter.

He turned when Livia entered. "Shhh. She's almost asleep," he whispered.

"You're…you're holding her. More or less." She stepped closer, forcing herself not to step in there and hold Piper herself because even she knew him just touching the baby was a huge step forward. "But you might want to hold her tighter, though."

"Sorry." He shifted his position but didn't bring the baby any closer. It was as if she were a time bomb and he was hoping like hell she wouldn't go off. "I got kind of desperate when she wouldn't stop crying." He gave Livia a grin, the lopsided smile that he used to have, the one that had made her fall in love with him. And a part of her, she knew, had started falling for him again.

Dared to hope that this one moment could turn into two, then three, then four, then forever. It was only one sliver of time, she reminded herself. It didn't mean anything.

But her heart refused to accept that. Refused to accept the lessons she had already learned. Edward Graham had no intentions of building a relationship of any depth.

Yet she saw how he had looked at Piper in that unguarded moment before he knew Livia was in the room. She had seen the tenderness on his face and dared to dream of more. Of having it all—Edward a part of the circle of her and Piper. Hope was a stubborn thing.

Could this be the part of Edward he had kept hidden from her last year? Fueled by guilt over the fire, or fear of a commitment, or something else? Or was it merely a moment, and nothing more?

"I hate to bother you," she said, "but I really need your help out there. I can't get that netting thing to work."

She stopped short of telling him the Willetts were still out there. If she did, she was afraid he'd say no without even giving the encounter a chance.

"Can do. Uh, but what about…?" He gestured with his chin toward the sleeping Piper.

"Don't disturb her until you absolutely have to. That's always worked well for me." Livia smiled, then noticed the slight grimace on Edward's features from the awkward extra weight. "Except, well, I bet that position is a bit uncomfortable. Here. I can take her from you if you want."

"Sure." He cleared his throat, then transferred the baby to Livia. "She was getting heavy anyway."

And as Edward handed his daughter back to Livia, he transformed again, his features wiped as cleanly as an eraser on a chalkboard. In one second, he went from the soft man with a tender spot in his heart for the sleeping baby in his arms to the distant man who had told her he had no business being a family man.

Then. Or ever.

CHAPTER SIX

EDWARD WATCHED THE baby curl into Livia's chest, like a puppy settling onto a bed. Tenderness filled Livia's face, warmed her eyes. The love between mother and daughter was clear, and for a moment, he felt an emptiness, as if his arms had been severed and he had lost a part of himself. He'd had a few minutes there—a window of time, really—where he'd considered...

Considered things a man like him had no business considering.

What had he been thinking? That he could just step into the father's role, merely because he shared some DNA? He couldn't give Livia or the child false hope like that. It wasn't fair to either of them. He wasn't a man who opened up, settled down. Even if for a minute, he'd thought—

Didn't matter. He'd do well from here on out to act less and think more.

Except, he wasn't really thinking about the hard stuff, was he? He was avoiding it today, as much as he'd avoided it a year ago. Doing what he did best—everything but delve into the recesses of his heart.

He cleared his throat. "What do you need help with?"

Livia cupped the back of her daughter's head with a gentle touch, as if she was shielding Piper from Edward's sudden indifference. He didn't know if she realized the change in her body language or not, but he couldn't blame her. He'd made his position clear.

"I don't know how to work the netting machine," Livia said. "I think I got the tree stuck inside it. Or the net. Something is, anyway."

"It's persnickety. I can fix that." This was the role where Edward felt most comfortable—solving problems, getting things running smoothly again. Dealing with relationships and children, not so much. He told himself it was better this way. Better for him, better for Livia, and most of all, better for the child. Still, a sense of loss hung in the air around him.

Before he took a step, Livia laid a hand on his shoulder. "Wait. You should know that it's the tree Miranda's parents bought. I wasn't going to tell you, but then I realized it would be wrong to have you walk out there and not know."

Just hearing the girl's name again drew him up short. He glanced out the window and saw the Willetts standing by the register, huddled together in the cold. Just like they had been that day.

Edward sucked in a sharp breath, but it didn't stop the mental images. The Willetts, huddled together, unaware of the dusting of snow and ash coating their hair, their shoulders. They stood outside the burning hell of the Riverbend Banquet Hall, staring at the charred skeleton that held their daughter's body hostage. The screaming had stopped, and that was the worst part. The silence that filled the spaces in between the firemen's shouts, the noise from the hoses and the crackle of the flames.

Three firemen dove into the building, while everyone held their breath and prayed for a miracle. After what seemed an interminable wait, they'd emerged, Miranda a limp doll in the arms of the first man. The Willetts had rushed forward, and the EMTs sprang into action. The Riverbend fire chief had cornered Edward, and by the time he'd finished answering the chief's questions, the Willetts were gone.

All that day and the next, he'd told himself he needed to go see them and Miranda, to apologize. But when he got inside the hospital in Indianapolis and saw the phalanx of friends and family waiting outside Miranda's room, it had been like a wall saying, "Stay out." Miranda had been a popular girl at Riverbend High, and the paper covered her injuries and recovery for days afterwards. Every story was a reminder to Edward of how he had failed. How his bad choices had resulted in years of suffering for the vivacious Miranda.

He'd left town after that. Leaving the words he wanted to say tucked inside him, where they'd done nothing but eat away at his conscience.

"Do you want to talk about it?" Livia asked. "I know this has to be hard."

"No, I don't want to talk about it. What is it with people thinking that if you talk something out, it'll get better? There's nothing I can say that can make what happened go away."

"I didn't mean—"

"What am I going to say to them, Livia? 'I'm sorry for ruining your daughter's life'?" He turned away from the window. "'For making every holiday for the rest of your lives a painful reminder of what happened'?"

Livia's hand trailed down his arm, until she was holding his hand. It was a comforting gesture, nothing more, but still, Edward could feel every ounce of that contact in each pump of his heart. She wanted him to open up, to push past his guilt. She didn't understand that if he let that wall come down, he'd fall apart.

"Tell them you're sorry," Livia said, her green eyes steady on his. "Start there."

"I'm sorry?" He shook his head and broke away from her. "That's not nearly enough."

"No. But it's a start. And you have to start somewhere." Her face held kindness, understanding, encouragement. Concern, care. A hundred things that other people showed and felt, that allowed other people to move forward, live full lives.

Everyone but him. He wasn't built that way, he wanted to say, but Livia's steady support kept on contradicting him. Even last year, she'd wanted him to *talk* about it. To work through his guilt with her by his side. It sounded all so simple, so ordinary. But he lacked the wiring to be that kind of open person.

No, he worked better on his own. Alone. Not in tandem.

Livia had crossed to the door, clearly intending to go out there with him. "You stay here," he said. "Keep the kid warm. I'll handle it."

He walked outside before she could argue. As much as he wanted her there, he knew two things—one, he was better facing this alone, and two, the more he got used to having Livia around, the more he'd start reconsidering a relationship. Not a mistake he could afford to make.

Edward buttoned his coat and headed for the netting machine. Livia's advice came back to him, but when he reached the Willetts and opened his mouth to speak, instead, he said, "Can I help you?"

It took a second for Richard Willett to recognize

Edward. When he did, steel filled his gaze. "What the hell are you doing here?"

"Working the lot. Livia said you needed help getting the tree bundled."

He'd had a hundred things he wanted to say to the Willett family, and none of them included the words *lot, tree* or *bundled.* But he couldn't seem to find a way to get around to the right words. They lodged in his gut instead. Again.

"We don't need your help." Richard started to tug on the tree, but it refused to budge. One of the branches had gotten jammed in the netting machine. Beside him, Alicia, Miranda's mother, watched the exchange.

"Let me get that," Edward said.

Richard let out a low curse and looked away. His wife put a calming hand on his chest, but it did little to temper the red in his cheeks or the hard set of his jaw.

Edward reinserted the tree, attached the clamp hook to the base, then turned on the machine. In one smooth, slow movement, it pulled the tree through the attached funnel, wrapping the bright orange net around the branches at the same time, sealing the entire tree in a neat, portable package. When it was done, Edward cut the end of the net, tied it off, and hoisted the tree onto his shoulder.

The Willetts hadn't said a word. The entire operation took only a few seconds, but to Edward, the heavy silence made it seem like ten hours. "Do you want me to carry this out to your car?"

Richard Willett reached over and took the tree from Edward. "I think you've done enough. Don't you?" Then he turned and headed for his car, with his wife hurrying to keep pace.

When their car peeled away and disappeared down

the street in a flash of red lights, Edward didn't think about the tree lot. About Livia. About anything other than leaving.

Damn. He thought he'd dealt with what happened. Given the sharp slice of guilt shredding his insides, he hadn't. At all.

He crossed the street, walking at a fast clip, trying to put as much distance between himself and his memories as he could. Unfortunately, he didn't think Riverbend—hell, the entire world—was big enough for that.

There were times when Livia wondered if Earl Klein possessed psychic abilities. Within five minutes of Edward stalking off the lot, Earl had pulled into the parking lot. Livia had been standing in the trailer, debating how she was going to run the lot literally single-handedly, with Piper in her arms, when Earl came striding into the tree lot's office, wearing a friendly smile and that silly plaid hunter's cap of his. "How's it going?" he asked.

"Slow today. Just one sale so far."

"It's the end of the season. Most folks have either bought their trees or are waiting till Christmas Eve." Earl looked around the trailer. "Where's your partner in crime?"

"He, uh…had to leave." Livia unstrapped Piper and held the sleeping baby against her.

"Well, that ain't right. I'm sure you and the pipsqueak here," at that, he tapped Piper's nose, "could sell all the trees just with a smile, but you need a man to do the heavy lifting."

"I can—"

"You may be a super woman, Miss Livia, but you

ain't Superwoman." He leaned in and nodded his own agreement. "Looks like I showed up just in time."

"I thought you were taking a few days off."

Earl waved off that suggestion. "You know what happens when a man has too much time on his hands?"

She shook her head.

"He watches too much TV. Every time I turn around, there's another bunch of overindulged teenagers raising a ruckus on a beach. Or a judge telling some fool what he already knows. That he's an idiot."

Livia laughed. "Everyone gets their fifteen minutes."

"Yeah, but no one said I had to watch it." Earl scowled. "Which is why I'd rather be out here with the trees."

"A little help would be nice," Livia admitted. She shifted Piper's weight against her chest. Asleep, the baby seemed to weigh a hundred percent more. She wasn't looking forward to carting Piper all over the tree lot during her nap, but she'd promised Earl she would help.

"You have a more important job to do besides sell a couple trees," Earl said. "You gotta go find Edward and talk some sense into him. I saw the Willetts leaving." He let out a heavy sigh. "Couldn't have been easy on Edward."

"It wasn't." She told Earl about what had happened with the Willetts, about giving them the tree, then getting it stuck in the machine and sending Edward out to help.

Earl nodded. "That was mighty nice of you, with the tree."

"I'll pay for it myself," she said. "I just didn't think it was right to charge them."

Earl dismissed that notion. "You did exactly what I

would have done." Then he sighed. "Poor Edward. That poor boy is suffering."

"Yeah." She thought of how Edward had looked when he'd walked away. Shoulders hunched, head down. She hadn't heard the entire exchange with the Willetts, but had watched it from the office and knew it hadn't gone well. Regardless, she wasn't about to go track Edward down. He'd made it clear a year ago, and again today, that he had no intentions of talking about his emotions. She'd just be pushing against a wall. "I should stay and help you. If you get busy—"

"My Betsy's coming to give me a hand. I called her just before I came in here, figuring you'd say that." Earl grinned. "Seems to me you've plum run out of excuses to stay."

"I—" She saw the determination in Earl's eyes and conceded defeat. She knew it wouldn't do any good, but she suspected Earl wouldn't believe her. "Okay, I'll go."

"Good." Earl picked up Livia's coat and held it out to her. "No better time than now."

"Piper really should finish her nap. I'll go later."

As if on cue, the trailer door opened again and Betsy stepped inside. She shot Piper a smile first, then seemed to realize Livia was there and gave her a smile, too. Clearly, Betsy's heart had already been stolen by the little bundle of pink and white.

"I'm here to help," Betsy said. "And I'd like to start helping with that little precious one right there."

"Oh, I don't know…" Livia knew Betsy well enough and had let her hold Piper a few times when she'd run into Betsy at church or the market. But leaving the baby here? Her protective mother instincts came roaring forward, even though she knew Betsy and Earl and knew they considered Piper an adopted grandchild. Seemed lately the entire world was out to prove Melody right and to put Livia to the test. "She can be a handful."

Betsy parked a fist on her ample hip. "She's no such thing. Why, that Piper is the most beautiful and perfect baby in the world."

Livia laughed. "Okay." Deep inside, she knew Earl and Betsy would care for Piper, guard her like two tigers with a newborn cub. She handed over Piper, feeling the familiar tug of sadness every time she let Piper out of her arms. "The diaper bag is over there, and if you want, she can sleep in her car seat."

"We'll be fine. Don't you worry." Betsy had already settled into the office chair and was leaning back, with Piper snuggled close. The baby, adept at sleeping most anywhere, curled up on Betsy without waking.

Livia brushed a gentle kiss across Piper's head. "Thank you."

"No, thank *you*," Betsy whispered. "Holding this little girl is like holding a slice of heaven."

Livia smiled, and turned to Earl. "You sure you don't need me to stay?"

He shook his head. "Edward needs you more. That man's hurting, and he needs a friend."

She sighed. "I know. But I don't think I'm the friend he needs." But she buttoned her coat and stepped out into the cold anyway. Because she knew no matter what had happened between herself and Edward, if he needed her, she would be there.

Even if doing so broke her heart.

It was a long time before Edward even noticed the cold. He'd walked far and fast, and when he reached the edge of Riverbend, he'd turned around and walked back. Eventually, he'd have to return to the lot and pick up his car. Winter nipped at the exposed areas around his coat, but he didn't feel the chill. His frustration and anger fueled a fire that couldn't be tamped by Mother Nature.

He didn't realize he'd detoured until his feet stopped moving and he saw where he had ended up. His breath lodged in his throat, and his chest constricted.

Was it ever going to get easier?

He wanted to walk—no, run—away, but his feet refused to move, as if a part of him demanded he look, demanded he see. Demanded he deal with it once and for all.

The fire.

There were still ruts in the ground from the heavy wheels of the fire trucks, forming a frozen moat around what had once been a twelve-thousand-square-foot building. A few timbers stood defiant, like charred stick figures refusing to be downed. Against the stark gray landscape, the remains of the Riverbend Banquet Hall seemed sad and lonely. Forgotten.

But Edward hadn't forgotten. Not when he'd left town, not when he'd gone to Europe, not when he'd put the business up for sale. He hadn't forgotten. At all.

"I can't believe any of it's still here."

He turned at the sound of Livia's voice. "What are you doing here? Where's the baby?"

"Earl and Betsy showed up after you left. They kidnapped Piper and shoved me out the door." She laughed, then sobered and met his gaze. "They insisted on babysitting so I could talk to you."

He scowled. "I don't need to talk. I need to be alone." The wind kicked up and nipped along the exposed parts of him, skating down his back. Surely the biting cold bothered Livia, too, but she didn't show it. Nor did she leave.

"Do you think maybe that's part of the problem?" She took a step closer. There was no escaping those wide green eyes and a gaze that he swore could see right through him. "All that being alone, and no talking?"

"What problem? I don't have a problem."

She pursed her lips and didn't say anything. It was the same argument they'd had last year. Always, Livia had pressed him to talk, to open up, and he had resisted. He preferred to retreat, to deal with things himself.

Except, what good had it done him over the past year to deny and ignore? It hadn't made anything better. In fact, he was pretty sure he felt worse now. Especially after letting a year pass without doing a damned thing or speaking up. He'd walled himself off and ended up alone. Miserable.

"Okay." He let out a sigh. "Maybe you have a point."

They didn't say anything for a long while. The guilt kept churning in his gut, didn't go anywhere. Livia stood beside him, staring at the same bleak scene. Her mere presence offered a comfort and peace. "What happened that night?"

A bird flew overhead, letting out an angry squawk at the intruders. A car drove past them, wheels crunching on the cold, ice-dusted road. Above them, clouds formed in puffy poodle-like bunches, floating in a pack across the sky. But before him, the world had stood still, caught in a tragic, year-old time warp.

Was he stuck there, too? Was that why he kept trying to shed everything that once used to matter so much to him? First, his relationship with Livia, then his home in Riverbend, then his business? If he talked about it, if he began to exorcise those demons, maybe he could move out of this cement-filled purgatory.

But still he couldn't speak.

"A year ago, you didn't want to talk about it," Livia said.

"I deal better on my own."

"Do you?"

Winter held the question tight in its frosty grip. Did he? Had he? Really?

He'd pushed her away once, and here he was, back in nearly the same place all over again. Circling, circling… and never moving forward.

"I had gone home around six that night," he said finally, the words seeming to come of their own volition, as if his voice was overriding every other part of him. "We had a wedding scheduled for the next afternoon, and I wanted a little time off before coming in to run that. I didn't always run stuff, you know?"

She nodded.

"But the bigger my company got, I found I liked taking over from time to time. It was like getting back to my roots. So when I was in Baltimore, I'd spend a night or two running the concert hall. Or work concessions at the stadium in Boston. It kept me grounded, kept me in touch with the company."

"I remember you telling me that."

"Riverbend was where I liked to be best, though. This was my first property. Every time I got out from behind my desk, it was like those early days all over again." Or it had been, at least, before…

"Miranda and a few other employees stayed late to handle a small party," Edward went on, the words scraping past his throat, but not stopping. "A celebration for a local band that had made its first CD. Nothing big, and I figured they could take care of it. And since I was overseeing the wedding on Saturday, I wanted to cut the night short." He closed his eyes, and it was like he was there again. Heading out the door, a hurried goodbye over his shoulder. The door closing, the banquet hall forgotten—

Until the call from the fire department at one that morning.

He didn't want to continue. He wanted to keep all of this...this pain and regret locked inside him, but what good had that done him? Facing it was harder, but in the end, would it be better?

Maybe.

He thought of his father, who had waited until his late fifties—and a massive heart attack—to start opening up. Did Edward really want to repeat that?

"I went home, went to bed early," he went on. All this time, he hadn't talked about it to anyone other than the firemen who'd interviewed him that night. And now it seemed like the words were practically tripping over his tongue in their rush to be out in the open. "It had been a hard week—I'd had to let go a manager at one of the Chicago facilities, and had spent half the day renegotiating the lease on the Indianapolis property. I was stressed, and tired, and just didn't want to deal with anything." His breath frosted in a cloud around his face, but he barely noticed the dipping temperatures or the graying sky. "I should have stayed."

"But you said it was a small party. Surely something the employees could handle, and normally did."

"Normally, yes, they could have. But it was an inexperienced staff, and I should have known better. The facilities manager was new, too, and I should have stayed, did a double check." He took a few steps forward, crossing over the border of frozen mud ridges and up to what had once been the front door. "Damn it. I should have known."

Livia was beside him, her hand on his shoulder, her presence almost a balm. "You can't predict the future. Not then. Not now."

He shook his head, unwilling and unable to release himself so easily. The regrets held tight to him, a band around his chest, a thick fist in his throat. But still he kept talking. "The band stayed late, long after the rental time, and the staff joined in on the party. They weren't supposed to, and they knew that, but a lot of them were friends with the band and I guess they figured…"

"If the cat's away, the mice will play."

He nodded. "Miranda was in the back, putting away the linens and stacking cardboard boxes to go out with the trash, when—" he shook his head, trying to erase the images, but they stayed, stubborn "—a frayed electrical cord caught fire. Apparently the band brought their own equipment and one of the cords wasn't in the best of shape. Normally, I would have checked that kind of thing if I was there. But I had gone home and the manager was inexperienced…" He let out a curse. "The fire spread quickly, igniting the cardboard, and…in seconds, the whole building was on fire. Everyone got out right away, everyone except…"

He couldn't say it, couldn't finish the sentence. He closed his eyes and he saw the slim nineteen-year-old, her eyes wide and frightened, seeing no escape from the encroaching fire. He had dreamed that image a thousand times in the year since the fire. Heard her terrorized scream in his ears, as if he'd been there.

"Richard ran for the building," Edward said, softer now. "He was screaming his daughter's name, determined to find her himself. The firemen pulled him back, but he kept lunging for the building. Then three firemen went in and God, it seemed like forever before they came back out. Smoke was coming off her body, Livia. Smoke." Edward shook his head, pinched at his eyes. "Damn it. Damn it all to hell."

Livia's arm went around his shoulder, her head against his chest. "It wasn't your fault."

He tried to pull away but Livia held firm. "I was the owner. Didn't matter how big the company was, or how much time I spent behind a desk. In the end, I was the one responsible. I should have made sure everything was okay. And now that girl can't go to college or do anything. Do you know she wanted to be a graphic designer?"

Livia shook her head.

"Something in the music industry. Album covers or something. I remember her telling me when she came in for the interview. How that would let her combine the two things she loved most—music and art. And now…" He closed his eyes and shook his head. *"I should have stayed."*

He'd said that to himself over and over since that night. If only he had stayed. If only he had double-checked the band equipment himself. If only he had kept the promises he'd made.

But he hadn't. And this time, Miranda Willett had paid the price. He couldn't even think about the pain and suffering she had endured every day since that night. If he did, he had a feeling he'd fall apart, and not be able to put himself together again. If he could trade places with her—for a day, for a month, for eternity—he would.

"You can't be anywhere twenty-four hours a day, Edward. No one can be."

He shrugged off her touch and crossed to the streaked cement foundation. In a few steps, he stood in the center of the hall, or what had once been the center. A year ago, the Riverbend Banquet Hall had been booked nearly every day. It had been one of several shining stars in his business constellation. He'd thought he had the world by the tail, when really he hadn't had anything at all.

He bent down and curled his fist around a charred piece of wood. It crumbled in his grasp, turning to ash with one touch. He cursed again. The regrets crowded around him, squeezing at his chest. "She suffered that day and every day since," he said, his words a harsh rasp, "and that's all my fault."

"It was an accident. Surely you know that." Livia came around to face him, forcing his gaze to focus on her face, instead of the burned shell of the building. Her deep green eyes bored into his. "Oh, Edward, Why don't you believe that?"

"I…" His gaze darted back to the devastation before him. A minute more, and Miranda would have died. That bright, vibrant girl, permanently hurt because he had gone home early. That was what he hadn't been able to say last year, and even now, he still couldn't. "I can't."

"If you don't, you can't move forward. And you need to move forward, Edward. Not just for you, but for our daughter, too." She reached for him, and he saw the hope in her eyes, the belief in him.

She didn't know everything, though. Didn't know how he had let people down, over and over again. This wasn't one mistake. It was many.

Watch out for Katie.

Watch out for Miranda.

In the end, he hadn't watched out for anyone. Except himself.

He jerked to his feet. Better to do this now than to let Livia keep building that hope that someday, he'd turn into the husband, the father she wanted. He knew better than to try to be a part of a family. To be responsible for anyone's child, even his own. He was no good at this, no good at all.

"I'll support the baby financially," he said. "But don't expect more out of me than that."

She reached for him again. "What happened to the man who held Piper and danced with her to get her to sleep?"

"I was just trying to get her to sleep."

"Liar."

She was there, confronting him, over and over. She refused to see that he could be anything other than what he was. He exhaled, and wished he had never come back to town. This was a hell of a lot harder than he'd expected it to be.

Because he knew how painful it had been to excise Livia from his life once before. He wasn't sure he could do it again, especially now that Piper had been added to the mix.

God, it hurt. He steeled himself and tucked the feelings away in the back of his mind. Best to do it now, fast, before he reconsidered. She deserved a man who could be open with her, who could let her into his heart. He had tried—and stopped short of giving her all.

"Stop asking more from me than I can give, Livia," he said, and didn't meet her gaze. Because if he did, he might not be able to finish the sentence. She didn't need a broken man, one who had let down everyone around him. She deserved more. "Money, fine. House, fine. Education, fine."

"This is about more than the fire, Edward." She came

around to face him, those beautiful, inquisitive green eyes. "What aren't you telling me?"

"Nothing." He tried to move away, but she stuck with him. "Why is it so important to you to create some fairy tale out of our lives? To keep pushing me to be something I'm not?"

She recoiled, and he wanted to take the words back. "You think raising our child together is a fairy tale?"

"I think you're looking for something that you didn't have."

Her jaw dropped. Her eyes widened.

And he hated himself.

"You don't mean that," she said, the words a pained, choked whisper.

He was on a train he couldn't stop, the words barreling down a suicidal track. All he wanted was to be away from this place, away from this subject, and most of all, away from everything he wanted and couldn't have. He wanted to retreat to his desk, to the quiet solitude of work. Not deal with the tsunami of emotions whirling inside him. So he lashed out, knowing it was wrong, knowing she and Piper might end up despising him. But if he didn't, Livia would go on hoping.

"Your mother ran off and your father pretty much checked out," Edward said. "You had to raise your sister, and you vowed early on that you would never do that to your own children—"

"I know I said that but I didn't mean—"

"So that's what you're trying to do now, isn't it? Trying to create that perfect family for your child by forcing me into some mold of the perfect father. All so that she doesn't have to know what it's like to go along with just one parent and a well-meaning sister?"

Tears swam in her eyes, and Edward wanted to undo

the damage, but the words were there, and there was nothing he could do to take them back. If he wavered at all, Livia would keep on hoping and dreaming for the both of them. Maybe if she hated him, she'd give up this idea that he could be some Utopian husband and father.

"This isn't the same thing, Edward. Not at all."

"Maybe not. But either way, I—" he drew in a breath and surveyed the decaying remains of his dreams "—I can't be the man you want me to be. I'm sorry."

CHAPTER SEVEN

LIVIA CRIED UNTIL her tears were as dried as her heart. She'd walked away, leaving Edward standing amid the ruins of the banquet hall, and then retrieved Piper, hurrying out of the tree lot before Earl and Betsy could ask her any questions. They'd seen the upset on her face, but let her go without too much prodding. Thank God.

Piper had gone to bed early, and Livia had told Melody she had a headache and was going to bed early, too. Livia's bedroom door had barely finished latching behind her when the tears started.

Why had she thought Edward had changed? Just because of something she'd glimpsed inside a trailer?

He hadn't changed at all. He was still the closed-off man she met last year. The one she had fallen for so hard that she didn't realize until it was too late that he hadn't fallen for her, too.

Deep in her heart she'd always thought he'd change his mind, that what he'd said last year was some kind of knee-jerk reaction to their discussion about marriage and to the shock of the fire. But she'd been wrong. So very, very wrong.

Livia poured more tears into her pillow, but it didn't ease the ache in her heart. She clutched it to her chest, and tugged the blanket up until it covered most of her face. But even here, buried in the dark, silent comfort of her bed, she couldn't find peace.

A soft knock sounded on her door. "Livia?"

Livia feigned sleep. No way was she going to get up to make Melody more tea or help her find the remote or entertain her because there was nothing good on TV.

"I know you're awake. Can I come in?"

Livia sighed. "Can't it wait until morning? I'm… tired."

Melody either didn't care or didn't hear what Livia had to say. She came in the room, and dropped onto the edge of Livia's bed. "Liv—"

"Please, Melody, just let me be. I'll get whatever you need tomorrow." She buried her head deeper into the pillow and prayed her sister would take the hint.

"Liv." Melody paused. "Livia, look at me."

When it became clear that Melody wasn't about to leave, Livia rolled over and looked up at her little sister. In the dark, Melody's eyes seemed wider and lighter. "What?"

"What's the matter?" Melody asked.

She must have heard her crying. "Nothing."

Melody smiled. "Liar. I know that look anywhere. Someone broke your heart. Someone named Edward, I bet."

Livia draped her arm over her eyes. Damn, they hurt. "I just want to go to sleep."

"That's the worst thing you can do. You should talk about it. Sleeping just delays the problem."

Despite everything, a slight smile worked its way to Livia's face. "Where have I heard that before?"

"You said it to me. A hundred times at least. Remember the seventh grade dance? When Ryan

Spartan stood me up? And all I wanted to do was stay in bed and cry and sleep?"

"I made you get up and get dressed."

"And go to the dance and show that Ryan what he missed out." Melody grinned. "Did I ever tell you he spent the entire night in the corner, while his date flirted with another guy? He kept glancing over at me, and I knew he was regretting what he'd done."

"Really?"

Melody nodded. "Going by myself showed me that I could be okay, no matter what. And not to mention, taught Ryan a lesson or two. Which is why I'm telling you to do the same thing."

"Get dressed and go to the dance?"

Melody shook her head. "Get dressed and go to the Winterfest. You've been dying to go, and it's only open for two more nights."

"I don't want to go to that. I'm not in a Christmas mood."

"Because," Melody reached forward, took Livia's hands and hauled her into a sitting position, "you're lying in this bed, wallowing in self-pity."

"I'm not."

Melody glanced at her askance. "I've done it enough to recognize it in you. Now get up, get dressed and show that Edward Graham that he's the biggest idiot to walk the earth."

"I can't go out. Piper—"

"Will be fine with me here. I'm feeling better." Melody smoothed a hand across the comforter. "Besides, I've been thinking. Being sick gives you a lot of time to do that, you know."

Livia nodded.

"And I realized I let you do a lot for me. And you let

it happen." Melody wagged a finger at her. "I…well, it's just easier that way."

Livia sighed. Her sister was right. Melody needed something, and Livia provided it, slipping into the old role of surrogate mother as easily as slipping on a pair of socks. "I guess we got into a routine—"

"And never got out of it." Melody kept on tracing the floral pattern on the comforter. "Do you know why I came here? Instead of going to Dad's?"

Livia shook her head.

"Because I count on you, Livia. Because you're the one who's always going to…" Melody's gaze returned to her sister's. "Well, always tell me the truth. Whether I like it or not."

"I don't do it to hurt you, Melody." She reached for her little sister's hand. "I worry about you, that's all."

Melody gave Livia's fingers a squeeze. "I know. And that's why you have to stop. Worrying about me, that is."

Livia shook her head. "Mel, I can't—"

"You have to. It's time you lived your own life. And stopped being my mom."

"I don't mind."

"I know that. But I do." Melody cocked her head and gave Livia her familiar mischievous smile. "And if you don't let me stand on my own two feet, I'll never learn how to do it."

Livia grinned. "How did you get so wise?"

"Listening to you, sis." Melody reached forward and drew Livia into a hug. "Just listening to you."

The Winterfest was in full swing by the time Livia arrived. She hadn't wanted to go, but Melody had insisted, even going so far as to toss a pair of jeans and a sweater onto the bed and refusing to leave the room until Livia got dressed. Livia had finally acquiesced. Melody was right. Staying in bed and wallowing in self-pity wasn't going to help anything. Piper was already tucked in for the night so Livia left her home with Melody.

Livia wandered the town park, marveling at Santa's village—complete with a real reindeer—and the gingerbread family set up outside a small gingerbread village. She got a pretzel from the vendor stand and a cup of hot chocolate made by the local Girl Scout troop. In the center of the park, she could see a group decorating the gazebo in preparation for tomorrow night's big dance.

Suddenly, it was too much. She didn't want to go to the Winterfest alone. Ever since she'd arrived in Riverbend, she'd dreamed of coming here with Piper. Seeing the delight on her daughter's face as she took in the sights and sounds and got her first picture with Santa.

And yes, a part of her, buried deep inside, had pictured Edward in that little tableau, too. A crazy, impossible wish. One sentimental wish she had hung on to for a long time, because a part of her heart had never let go. He'd never loved her the way she loved him, and yet…

She turned away and headed out of the park. She hit the sidewalk and waited for a car to pass so that she could cross. She was going home. Despite Melody's advice, Livia didn't think going out by herself was working out.

She sensed him before she saw him. The spicy notes of his cologne danced on the breeze, teased at her senses. Edward was here. Behind her. But she stood her ground and didn't pivot toward him.

"I think this is yours."

She glanced over her shoulder. Edward was holding out one of Piper's toys. The small stuffed animal looked so incongruous in his big hand. Behind them, the sights and sounds of the Winterfest continued, bright and merry. "Where did you get that?"

He thumbed toward the tree lot across the street. "She must have dropped it when she was in the office. I found it there when I went back to get my car. I came by the house to drop it off, and your sister said you were here."

And he had tracked her down to bring it to her? Why? It was something that could have waited. Was he just trying to make her miserable? Trying to confuse the issue? Every time she thought it was over, he showed up again. What did Edward Graham want?

"Oh. Okay, thanks." She took the small stuffed giraffe and tucked it into her coat pocket. "Have a nice night." She stepped off the curb and crossed toward the small well lit diner on the corner of Main. Inside, she could see Earl and Betsy sitting at one of the window booths.

Edward walked right beside her. "Not going to the Winterfest?"

"I'm not in a holiday mood right now."

"Me neither. I've never been much for Christmas."

She whirled around to face him. "Then what are you doing?"

"Just out, trying to enjoy the evening. Feels like snow, don't you think?"

"No, I meant, what are you doing with me? What do you want?" She shook her head and stopped walking. She could feel the tears rising up again. She blinked, willing them away. "Just stop, Edward. I'm not a yo-yo that you can jerk back and forth." She turned away again. And waited for him to leave.

He didn't. "I'm not trying to jerk you back and forth. I…" He let out a long breath. "I can't let it end like this."

"End? When did we begin?"

"A year ago. Or have you forgotten? And now we have a child."

Still, "a child," not our child or our baby. "I'm not having this conversation." She started to move away, but Edward grabbed her arm.

"I was out of line earlier today, Livia. I'm sorry." He dropped her arm, and moved back, as if he finally realized she didn't want him to touch her. "I shouldn't have said half of what I said."

"Then why did you say it?" Now the tears choked in her throat.

He looked past her, at something far in the distance, something, she suspected, didn't even exist in this time, in this place. "It's a long story."

She wanted to tell him too bad, it was too late, but that stubborn cloud of hope in her chest refused to give up on Edward Graham so easily. She had glimpsed something in him, something real and true, as if he had pulled back a curtain. All this time, she'd thought Edward was a cold man, incapable of love, then she'd seen him this week, being kind to an elderly woman, dancing with Piper in the trailer and opening his heart at the ruins of the banquet hall. Was there more? "So tell me."

"Not here. I…" He let out a breath. "I just want to forget all that tonight." He put out his hand and nodded toward the diner. "Grab some coffee? Some pie?"

What was she thinking? Go with him? After she had just spent the better part of the evening crying over him? She was out here to forget him, not take the same wrong turn again. No matter what unguarded moments she might have seen, in the end, it came back to the same answer.

Edward wasn't a settle-down kind of guy and she wasn't dumb enough to let him break her heart a second time. No. There'd be no pie. And no more silly hope.

"I don't think that's a good idea." She tugged her hand out of his. Then Livia hurried away, before her common sense was overridden by heartbreak.

Edward should have gone home. He fully intended to do that, after that insane attempt to make up to Livia. Did he really think a piece of caramel pecan would be enough to heal the wounds he'd made?

He had thought he'd done the right thing when they'd been standing outside the remains of the banquet hall. He'd broken it off, severing that tie once and for all, and telling himself it was the best thing for all of them. He'd done it once before, he could do it again. Even if it hurt ten times more the second time.

Then he'd found Piper's toy on the floor of the tree lot office, and his mind had rocketed back to holding his daughter, to the soft comfort of her strawberry-scented skin, and he'd realized something.

No matter how hard he tried to push Livia away, how hard he tried to avoid being a father, that little pipsqueak had already grown in his heart. He missed her, damn it, and missed her mother most of all.

But he'd messed everything up. Every time he tried to make it better, easier, really, it got worse. For a man who had successfully built a mega business from the ground up, he was having a lot of trouble with something so simple as relating to one woman. What was it about him that made it almost impossible to open his heart?

She'd asked him what he wanted. It was a question he still couldn't answer. All he did know was that he didn't want to let go of Livia, not yet. For her sake, he should stop. Walk away—and keep walking. Simply by holding on, he hurt her.

But as he headed toward his car, his steps made a detour and he found himself in the parking lot of the Methodist church. A handful of trees remained, lit by the string of lights that surrounded the tree lot. The sales office had shut down an hour or so earlier. A small hand-lettered sign—complete with a greasy thumbprint that undoubtedly belonged to Earl—was propped up in the trailer's window. TOMORROW IS CHRISTMAS EVE! GET YOUR TREE IN TIME FOR SANTA'S VISIT! OPEN AT NINE A.M.

The lot was quiet, peaceful, with just the soft under-tow of the music from the Winterfest playing in the air. It was as if the world had stopped on Christmas Day in this little corner of Riverbend.

Edward rounded the corner and found Livia standing beside a lone, skinny pine tree. She reached out and slid a hand down one of the branches. A few needles dropped into her palm, then drifted to the ground.

He hesitated. The golden light of the streetlamp framed her and cast a soft glow over her delicate features. She had an ethereal quality to her, as if at any moment she could disappear. He wanted to reach out and hold her. But he didn't. "Livia?"

She turned and jerked a bit in surprise. "Edward. What are you doing here?"

He shrugged and moved closer. "I didn't want to go home. My dad is probably asleep in front of the TV, while some war movie blasts his eardrums. And I wasn't in the mood to be my only company."

A bittersweet smile stole across her face. "Me either."

He took another step closer to her. In the darkened, intimate confines of the tree lot, he was a hundred times more aware of her. Of how close she was, how alone they were. How far apart they'd drifted in the last year. Even as he knew he shouldn't, he wanted to close that gap, to have a taste of that happiness just one more time. "Are you thinking of buying a tree?"

She shook her head. "I already have one. And a wreath, thanks to my sister. Got the house all Christmas-ed up."

There was a melancholy note in her voice. He took another step, and now he could catch the fragrant notes of her perfume, watch the twinkling lights dance across her features. "I bet it looks beautiful."

She nodded. Then turned back to the scraggly pine and caught another handful of needles. "So much work, just for one day."

"Most people would think it's worth the effort. Don't you?"

"Some days, yes. Some days…" She took a breath. "You asked me a couple days ago about my mother and Christmas."

"I'm sorry. I shouldn't have. I know it's a difficult subject." Livia hadn't told him much about her childhood, just that her mother had walked out on her children while they were young and never come back. When her father didn't step into the parental role, Livia stepped up and raised her younger sister.

He hadn't shared much, if anything, about his own childhood, and yet curiosity to know more about her burned in his chest.

"And then tonight," she went on, "when you said what you did—"

"I'm sorry. I didn't mean any of it." Regret weighed inside him.

"No, you were right, Edward. I keep telling myself that you're wrong, but you're not. I am trying to force you into this little perfect family because ever since that baby was born, all I've ever wanted is to give Piper what I never had."

"Livia—"

She put up a hand. "Let me…let me tell you about Christmas at my house. And then maybe you'll understand a little more."

"Okay."

The pine needles coursed across her palm, and Livia watched for a moment as they tumbled end over end. "When I was a little girl, Christmas was always my dad's thing. It was like he was trying so hard to make it perfect, to make her happy. But my mom would complain about the mess, complain about the extra chores of decorating. So my dad would be the one to get the tree out of the attic. We had a plastic one. Less mess, you know? Anyway, Melody and I would help him set it up, and though we fought over putting on the star, we each had our favorite ornaments to hang. There weren't very many. My mom thought they were a waste of money, but the ones we did have, the three of us would hang." She tipped her palm and the needles spilled onto the pavement. "That was all we ever had. A tree. No stockings or cookie jar Santas. Just the tree. But when you're little, it's enough."

"Nothing else?" He'd grown up in this town, where Christmas was practically considered a sport. Decorations had been—and still were—a friendly neighborhood competition.

She shook her head. "It was a battle just to get that

tree, believe me. I always wondered about that. About why my mother didn't like Christmas."

He'd never known a mother who didn't celebrate holidays with an all-out effort. His own mother had been the driving force behind Christmas when he'd been little. But then after Katie died—

He cut that thought off right in its tracks.

"Why do you think she felt that way?" he asked.

Livia thought for a long moment, her face turned to the moonlit sky. Clouds drifted across the full moon, causing it to drop a gauzy light over the town, a glow over her features. "I think it just reminded her of the box she was in. All those holiday family gatherings and family activities, and most of all, family expectations. I think she always felt trapped by being a mother."

"And that's why you think she left?" he asked the question with a gentle touch, almost afraid to push her down the dark corridor she hated, but sensing she needed to talk about this. Livia clutched those pine needles like they might escape, the same tight way she held on to her emotions. Pot calling the kettle black, he thought, because he did the same thing. "Is that why, Liv?"

Livia nodded. Tears glistened in her eyes and her face crumpled, as if the last brick in her emotional wall had been removed. "Was it really too much to ask?" she asked, her voice small and shredded. "To have a cookie jar Santa?"

His heart broke for her. For the years without stockings and cookie jar Santas and most of all, without a mother. For Livia Perkins, the holiday wasn't about decorations or a Christmas ham. It was about the absence of a mother who loved and cherished her family. About growing up in charge of everything. Poor Livia, trying so hard all her life to fill shoes she didn't fit.

He drew her to him and cradled her head against his chest. She hesitated only a second, then curved into him, and he pressed a kiss to her forehead. "No, Livia, it's not too much. Not at all."

She turned toward him, her face still filled with doubt. He pressed another kiss to her forehead, then a second further down, along her nose. Then she tipped up higher, and his lips came down a third time and met hers.

Kissing Livia was like coming home. Connection arced inside him, the kind of connection that came with someone who knew you better than you knew yourself. She tasted of everything that had ever been sweet and good in his life.

She let out a soft mew, and any noble intentions he might have had disappeared with that sound. He crushed Livia's body against his, hands roaming down her back, wanting as much of her as he could have. Her breasts pressed against his chest, and his body reacted, an erection rising hard and fast, pulse throbbing in his head, demanding more.

But he reined in his desire. Now was not the time, nor the place. And he already knew where caving to his desires got him—in bed with Livia and considering the kind of future he knew he couldn't have. She deserved a man who gave her his whole heart.

So he drew back, but didn't let her go. Not quite yet. "I'm sorry. I…" He let out a gust. "You know what, I'm not sorry. I'm glad I kissed you."

"You're…glad?"

"I've been wanting to kiss you again ever since the other day." Damn, why did he keep complicating this? "I've thought about almost nothing else. I have missed kissing you, Livia."

She tried to hold back a smile, but it burst on her face like a sunrise. "I've missed kissing you, too."

"Then we should do more of that." He danced another kiss along her lips. He wanted to hold onto this moment. To capture the happiness he felt, bottle it up and save it for those dark lonely days ahead. "A lot more."

Her smile held, then fell, a little at a time. "Why?"

"What do you mean, why? Because it feels good." He leaned in to kiss her again, but she put up a hand and stopped him.

"But where's it going to go? To a relationship? To marriage?"

The cold hard reality of their situation thrust itself between them. The happiness he'd been trying so hard to grasp flitted into the ether.

"I'm not made for that, Livia."

"Why not? Because it's hard to open up? To build a relationship? You think it's easy for me? I don't want to spin my wheels and end up in the same place as we did a year ago. I want more now."

"More?"

"A *real* marriage, Edward. The kind where we're both madly in love with each other, and we're building a happy family. You of all people should understand why that's important to me after what I just told you. I don't want your money, I don't want Piper and me to be your 'responsibility.' I want you to be here, to be with us—" on the last word, her voice broke "—because you love us and can't imagine life without me and our daughter."

He released her and stepped away. She didn't understand what she was asking of him, and why he couldn't give it to her. It wasn't a matter of not wanting that dream—it was a matter of not being the kind of man to fulfill it. Hell, he'd never learned how to be that kind of man. Why did Livia keep thinking he could magically change? "Why does it have to be all or nothing with you, Livia?"

"Because I deserve it all, Edward. And so does Piper." She moved forward, put a soft hand on his shoulder. "And so do you."

CHAPTER EIGHT

"Snow today, that's the word." Ray settled into the kitchen chair opposite his son with a mug of coffee and a handful of cookies. Sugar Santa cookies, with sprinklings of red sugar. Probably came from Samantha MacGregor's bakery, and most likely delivered by Sam herself, who'd already sent over a basket of carrot and bran muffins. "About darn time. It's not Christmas without a little snow."

"Since when did you get the Christmas spirit? You got the tree, the cookies. Heck, I half expect you to start wearing reindeer antlers."

"No antlers. I ain't going that far." Ray chuckled, then shrugged. "I dunno. I guess it's only been the last couple weeks or so. Nothing like a little heart attack wake-up call. I realized I've been missing out all these years. On you, on Christmas trees, you name it. Working too hard and taking care too little. Your mother always did all that stuff and when she was gone—" Ray sighed.

Edward nodded. "I know. It wasn't the same." And it had been a hard road to build a relationship with his father that extended beyond small talk. Living together had forced them to talk, though, which was probably a good thing.

"Caroline, God rest her soul, was the heart of this

family." Ray glanced out the window, his eyes misting. "There are days when I miss her so much, it's hard to breathe."

Edward saw the deep love in his father's eyes, still strong after all these years, and envied the emotion. "What's it like? To love someone that much that they're...almost a part of your soul?"

A smile stole across his father's face. "It's like becoming more of who you are. It's like the other person brings out the best in you and makes you want to be even better. I tell ya, I was never half as good a person as Caroline. But I tried." Ray crossed his hands on the table. "I sure wish I'd learned that lesson sooner, while she was still here and we could have had something... more. I always thought if I worked hard and provided well, I'd show her how much I cared. I guess I didn't realize until the end that all she ever wanted was for me to be here."

Edward nodded. His mother had sat at this very kitchen table on hundreds of nights waiting for Ray to come home from work. After Katie had died, it was as if his mother needed Ray to be around even more, to hold together the three parts remaining in her family. "She loved you, Dad."

"I know. And I didn't know what a hell of a gift that was until it was gone." His gaze returned to his son's.

"You never told me."

"I'm not much for talking. Never was, and after Katie died—" Pain creased Ray's features. "I just thought it'd be easier not to talk at all."

Edward nodded. "Me, too."

The two men exchanged a glance. They'd become each other's emotional twins in many ways. "Not the smartest thing I could have done. Your mother needed me you needed me, and I was…"

"Not there."

"Yeah. Sorry."

"It's okay, Dad."

Ray let out a cough, clearly still a little uncomfortable with the hard talk. "Anyway, when you find love, you hold on tight. You do whatever it takes to make it work. Because believe me, that kind of love doesn't come along every day."

Edward twirled his coffee cup in his hands. "I don't know if I'm wired that way."

"You are. You just don't like to flip that emotional switch. I know, I'm the same way. It was hard for me to become a man who talked about what he thought, how he felt. I had to learn, because I didn't want to miss one more day, not when I came so close to…" He shuddered. "Anyway, that didn't happen. Sometimes, son, you gotta open your heart to see what's on the other side."

"Kinda like having open-heart surgery?"

Ray laughed. "Yeah, kinda."

They sat quiet for a while, two men sharing memories of a woman they had both loved dearly. Edward digested his father's advice. Maybe his father was right—or maybe he was just thinking his son could be more than he really was. Then again, Ray had changed, albeit very late in life. Was there still time for Edward to learn a new way of connecting?

He rose, refilled his coffee, and leaned back against the counter. He'd enjoyed these quiet days with his father. After all this was over, Edward vowed to spend more time here in this bright kitchen in Riverbend.

Ray got to his feet, then leaned against the counter beside his son. "Now when am I going to meet this grandchild of mine?"

"Meet her?"

"You didn't think I'd let her first Christmas go by without at least a howdy-do? I even got her a gift."

"You bought Piper a gift?" His father was full of surprises today. "How? When?"

"Soon as you told me about her. I can use the internet as easily as anyone else, and wouldn't you know, they'll ship your items lickety-split." Ray snapped his fingers. "Amazing, that Internet."

Edward leaned back and studied the man he used to think he knew as well as himself. "You surprise me, Dad."

"Good. I meant to. I wasn't the best father for you, but I can change that with this little baby. And so can you."

"I just found out about her a few days ago. I haven't even had time to be a father."

Ray waved that off. "I don't care if you found out three days or three years ago. It's never too late to be a good father. At least that's my new motto."

"I don't know, Dad." Edward turned to the sink. He started the water and added soap to wash the few dishes from breakfast. True, Ray had changed a lot since his heart attack, but it was a whole lot different to build a relationship with another adult than to care for a baby. A baby who would grow to depend on Edward to be there, forever and ever. Once he stepped into that quagmire, he knew getting out wouldn't be that easy.

"You know what the right thing is to do. Problem is, you're just too damned scared to do it."

"I'm not scared." Edward rinsed a glass, then set it in the strainer to dry.

"Okay, then prove it." Ray laid a hand on Edward's shoulder, a firm grip that said he was serious about the invitation. "Dinner is at five. I expect to see my new granddaughter and her mother here at the kitchen table."

Christmas Eve.

Livia sat in a rocking chair by the window in Piper's nursery, her daughter on her lap, while Piper sucked down her second bottle of the day. The rest of the morning stretched ahead of Livia, more or less empty of responsibilities.

There was the house to clean, of course. And Piper to feed, dress and bathe. But no shift at the tree lot, no plans for the evening except possibly taking Piper to the Winterfest. All the presents had been bought and wrapped and stowed under the tree. A ham sat in the refrigerator, waiting for Christmas dinner. Tonight, she planned on ordering pizza—Melody's favorite meal, and a concession Livia had made for the holiday.

She'd called her father first thing this morning and when he said he wouldn't make it to Riverbend for Christmas, she promised to fly out there with Piper after the holiday was over. He'd seemed reluctant to have the company, saying he had work to do, but she'd insisted. If she could convince Melody to go along too, maybe they'd have a true family holiday. One way or another, she was going to build this family and keep it together. For Piper's sake, if nothing else.

Piper looked up at her mother as she drank, her blue eyes wide and seeming to ask questions Livia had no answers to. Like what she was going to do about Edward.

Edward.

Livia's fingers went to her lips, tracing where he had kissed her. The man knew how to kiss, that was for sure.

It was keeping a relationship together that he had trouble with. The problem was, a large part of her still cared about him and still hoped for the impossible. It was as if she'd had a taste of something delicious and couldn't accept that the recipe was a temporary one.

"Oh, baby," she whispered to Piper, "half of me hopes he moves to Costa Rica. The other half hopes he stays right here." Piper didn't have an opinion on anything other than her bottle.

Down the hall, she heard the soft chime of the doorbell. "Melody?" Livia called down. "Can you get that? I'm feeding Piper."

"Okay," Melody answered. The door opened, then there was the sound of Melody greeting someone. Probably Earl, who had said he was going to stop by today with a thank-you gift for working the tree lot. She'd told him he didn't need to thank her, but he'd insisted.

"Piper's almost done," Livia called to her sister. "Tell Earl I'll be there in a few minutes."

Footsteps sounded in the hall. A second later, the nursery door nudged open and Edward, not Melody, not Earl, stepped into the nursery. "Your sister said you were in here."

Every time she saw Edward, it was like seeing him again for the first time. She forced herself to maintain a neutral face, to not betray her hurt and disappointment that he hadn't changed, that he still wanted a relationship with about as much depth as a puddle.

This was the future, she told herself. Edward stopping by from time to time, to see their child. It wouldn't be the traditional family environment she'd dreamed of, but it would be enough. It would have to be.

"Sorry. It's feeding time at the zoo." Livia smiled,

then gave Piper's head a gentle rub. "I'm almost done if you want to wait—"

"I'm fine. I can talk to you here." He leaned against the doorjamb.

Livia adjusted her arm under Piper's head, then repositioned the bottle. "So what did you come by for?"

"My father is inviting you to Christmas Eve dinner at his house."

"Your father? The man who never cooked." She raised a dubious brow. She'd met Raymond Graham a few times and had instantly liked the cantankerous softie. He'd made it clear one time that cooking was something he didn't believe in doing, "not when there's a perfectly good pizza shop in town that delivers," as he'd said.

"I didn't say it would be good. I just said he invited you, your sister, and…" Edward let out a breath, "his granddaughter."

It wasn't the words *my daughter* or even Piper's name, but it was a step forward from *the child*. Maybe someday down the road they'd progress to Edward having an actual relationship with his daughter. That would be enough, Livia reminded herself.

Even if she didn't believe it, even if it hurt to think of seeing him all the time and not being with him. How on earth was she going to sit across a dinner table from him tonight?

She'd find a way. Piper came first, and everything else, including Livia's broken heart, came second. "Sure, that sounds great. Can I bring anything?"

"I…don't know. I'll ask him. I'm kind of new at this company-for-dinner thing myself."

"I remember." The words escaped her in a quiet rush. When she and Edward had been dating last year, his kitchen had been as bare as an empty box. They usually either ate at restaurants or brought home extras from the banquet hall. The one time he'd invited her for dinner at his house, he'd forgotten to shop for the meal and ended up calling down to Rustica and ordering a delivered meal. "You are great at ordering takeout, though."

He chuckled. "We all have our skills in life."

"We do indeed." She glanced down at Piper. "What's your skill going to be, baby girl? President? Nuclear physicist? Pianist?" Piper, of course, didn't answer, but Livia didn't care. She just marveled at her child, and the peaceful look on her face as she finished her meal. "This is my favorite time of day, when I feed her. It's just a few minutes of the two of us being quiet. It makes me slow down, focus on nothing but Piper. It may sound silly, but it really helps me focus on what's important."

Edward watched them for a long moment, then he came a little further into the room. He seemed hesitant, unsure if he was even invited. "Do you think…maybe I can do it?"

It took a second before Livia realized Edward was asking to feed Piper. She tried not to get her hopes up, but they rose all the same. She stood, keeping Piper's bottle still in her mouth, and vacated the rocking chair. "Sure. Have a seat and I'll put her in your arms."

His big frame seemed to dwarf the delicate white chair, but he settled into it without complaint. "Now what?"

"Put out your arms." When he did, she leaned forward, and gently placed Piper in his arms. At first, Edward sat stiff, Piper again lying like a log on his forearms. Livia couldn't help but laugh. "Relax. She doesn't bite." Livia eased the baby back against Edward's chest, settling Piper into the nook of his arms, then she reached for Edward's right hand, and placed it on top of the bottle. "Just keep that right there, and you'll have a happy little girl."

He shifted but didn't bring Piper a whole lot closer to him, as if he was afraid to get too near the baby. "Doesn't she need to burp or…breathe or something?"

Livia chuckled. "Burping is at the end, and she breathes while she drinks. Watch."

Edward leaned down and watched as Piper paused in drinking. Her nostrils flared with an inhale, then she started drinking again after the exhale. She repeated the action over and over, as the formula level dropped more and more inside the bottle. As the bottle drained, Edward seemed to relax and shifted Piper a tiny bit closer. "Wow. She's got it down to a science."

"Yup. A genius already."

Edward's gaze swept over Livia's features, and a smile curved across his face. "I love the way you look at her."

"The way I look at Piper?"

"You just…love her so much. And it shows."

Livia trailed a finger along Piper's cheek. "She's easy to love. I loved her before she was born, but love her more every day I spend with her."

"But don't you worry that you'll—" he looked down at the baby and then his demeanor tightened again "—let her down?"

"Of course I do. I worry about that every day. But all I can do is my best." Livia shrugged.

Piper had finished the bottle and Edward took it out of her mouth and set it on the end table. The baby lay in his arms, blinking up at him, as if wondering who the new chef was. "What if your best isn't good enough?"

"I don't think about that, Edward. I worry about what

I feed her. I worry about keeping her dry and warm. I worry about keeping the house clean and as germ-free as possible. But I don't worry about things that could be dozens of years away. Filling my head with what-ifs only distracts me from the most important thing."

"And what's that?"

She knelt down beside him and the baby. "Loving her. That's the easiest thing to do. And the most important. Don't you agree?"

He didn't answer. As if on cue, Piper started to squirm. Edward held the baby toward Livia. "I think she needs to be burped or something."

"You can do it, if you want. It's not all that hard."

Doubt filled his eyes, and he looked about ready to bolt from the room. Feeding had been easy, because Piper had just lain there and done all the work. But burping was a more involved, hands-on job, and Edward looked about as comfortable with that idea as a bull walking across thin ice. "I...I don't want to screw it up."

Livia's first instinct was to take Piper and make this easier on Edward. To take control of the situation, something Melody accused her of all the time. But in the long run, that hadn't gotten the results Livia wanted, had it? She'd allowed Edward to have the distance he wanted, rather than letting him just...deal. Like she had from the day she'd found out she was pregnant. If she had called him that day and told him about the baby on the way, would he be as awkward around her as he was? Would he have had more time to warm to the idea, maybe even look forward to the baby's arrival? Or would he have remained the same closed-emotions man she'd met last year?

She propped a fist on her hip. "Are you telling me the man who has successfully built a banquet hall into a national venues company is afraid to burp a fourteen-pound baby?"

"This is different. She's living, breathing...I could hurt her."

She nearly laughed at the worry in big, strong Edward's face. She'd never seen a man look more uncomfortable and unsure of himself. Edward, too, of all people, who had impressed her from the start with his command of his company and of a room. He'd been confident, charming, sure of everything.

Apparently sure of everything but babies.

"I'm right here, Edward. You can do it." She pressed his hands upward, guiding Piper into place against his shoulder. She felt him stiffen when the baby made contact. "It's okay. You won't hurt her. Now, rub her back in a circle, then pat."

He did as Livia instructed, but with a feather touch. "Like this?"

"A little harder. You gotta work that air out of her. Don't worry. You won't break her."

He patted more firmly and in seconds, was rewarded with a very loud, very long belch. "Holy cow. She did that?"

"Yep. Takes after her daddy that way." She tossed him a teasing grin.

"Hey." But then Edward's face softened, and he turned to peek at Piper. "You got quite a set of lungs on you, kid."

Piper reached up a chubby little fist, and grabbed Edward's nose. She tugged at him, holding tight with tiny fingers to the prominent feature. Piper's eyes widened, and she stared at Edward, not moving, not making a sound, as if she were memorizing him.

For a moment, Edward's gaze locked on Piper's too.

The two of them, so similar in features, looking like mirror images of each other. Then Piper let out a squeal, and a little joyous bounce. Livia knew that look—Piper was happy.

Edward shifted his nose out of her grasp. "Uh…I think she's done eating. You want to take her?"

Livia nodded, trying not to be disappointed that Edward had abdicated so quickly. She took the baby, then got to her feet. "Thanks."

"Yeah, no problem." He got out of the chair and gestured toward it. "All yours again."

"I'd love to sit down, but it's time to get dressed and start our day." She crossed to the changing table, laid Piper down, and reached for a new diaper. Under Livia's watchful hand, Piper kicked and gurgled, reaching toward the mobile hanging over her head.

Edward lingered by the door, as if he didn't want to leave yet. "You did a nice job decorating for Christmas. Wait till you see my father's tree. It's pretty pitiful. But in our defense, it was decorated by two guys."

Livia laughed. She finished putting on Piper's diaper and helped the baby wriggle out of her pajamas. "I don't care. And Piper won't notice at all."

Edward still hung just inside the room, and Livia got the sense that he was working up to saying something. She busied herself with dressing Piper in a clean onesie, then a bright red sweat suit with a fuzzy Santa head on the front. It wasn't until Livia was sliding thick white socks onto Piper's feet that Edward finally spoke.

"When I was a kid, Christmas was a big family thing," he said, his gaze on Piper, but Livia sensed he wasn't really seeing anything. "My mom loved Christmas, and she made sure every single holiday was a production. Or at least, she used to."

Piper was all dressed, so Livia picked her up and held her to her chest. She wondered why Edward was still here. Why he kept saying one thing and doing another. It was as if everything inside him was a conflict. As much as her head told her to run away, that he was only going to shut her out again, and she should end the torture of seeing him, her heart told her to give him one more chance. Because the man she'd glimpsed a couple times this week was in there, somewhere. "I bet that was nice."

He nodded. "I was in charge of hanging the ornaments and my sister was in charge of the tinsel. They still had tinsel in those days. Godawful mess it made, but my mother loved it. She said it gave the tree sparkle."

"I didn't know you had a sister."

He swallowed hard and looked toward the wall. "I don't talk about her much."

And then Livia knew. The pieces began to come together. "Is she…the Piper you mentioned?"

He nodded and his eyes glistened with unshed tears. "She was a talker from the day she born. My mom would say, 'Katie-girl, you're always piping up about something or other.' And that's how she got the nickname."

"I had no idea. I'm sorry. I—"

"No, it's perfect. I'm honored, actually, that you would do that." His gaze lit on his sister's namesake for a moment. "It means more to me than you can know."

"I'm glad, then. And if our little girl's vocal abilities are any indication, I think she's going to grow into that name quite well."

A smile flitted across his face. "I agree."

"So why did you never tell me you had a sister?"

Edward didn't answer the question. Not directly, anyway. He ran a hand down the string of the mobile hanging over the changing table, capturing the little zebra at the end and letting it bounce against his palm. "When she was six, Katie was starting to doubt Santa. I think one of the kids at school said something to her and she came home, all upset. Anyway, that year, she wanted proof that Santa existed. She wrote him a long letter, mailed it herself, and wouldn't tell any of us what she wrote in there or what she asked for."

"I bet lots of kids have done the same thing." Livia swayed a little with Piper, hoping to keep the baby happy long enough for Edward to finish his story. She knew, in that intuitive sense of someone who has been close to another person, that telling it was important. To him, and maybe to closing a long-open wound. "What happened at Christmas if no one saw the letter?"

"Well, she let it slip to me one day what she really wanted. A red bicycle. Bright red with a white seat." He chuckled softly at the memory but Livia could hear the raw edge in that laugh. "That was what she had her heart set on, and she told me if she got it, then she'd know Santa was real." He crossed to the window, looking out at the bleak, gray landscape. The promised snow had yet to start falling and the entire town seemed caught in a dreary bubble of anticipation. "I told my mom, and of course, she went right out and bought a bicycle. Katie was overjoyed on Christmas morning, and the first thing she did when she saw that bike was hug me. It was like our special secret, that Santa was real."

"Edward, that's so sweet."

"We were typical siblings. Rarely got along. Didn't hug much, if ever. So that one hug was a big deal. I just didn't know how big at the time. God, I wish I had." He paused, took in a long breath. "I really wish I had known."

"Known what?"

He leaned a palm on the cold glass, spreading his fingers against the bleak view. "That it was the last hug I'd ever receive from her. I guess I never realized how much I loved my little sister until—"

The room in the air stilled. Livia caught her breath.

"—until she wasn't there anymore," he finished. His voice cracked.

"Not…not there anymore?"

He nodded, and it seemed like his shoulders dropped under an invisible weight. "Katie, oh, she was my shadow. Everywhere I went, she had to go, too. Drove me out my mind. I was a boy, I had boy things to do. And the worst thing you can have is your little sister tagging along."

Livia glanced at Piper and wondered if there would ever be a sibling to tag along with her. Someone to fight over toys with, someone to hug when a thunderstorm crashed overhead, someone to spill secrets to and share cookies with. As much as Melody sometimes drove her crazy, Livia was glad to have her sister.

"It was Christmas break," Edward went on, his voice softer now, lost in a day decades past, "and I was going to play in the woods behind our house with my friends. We had it in our heads to build a snow fort." He pivoted toward her. "Crazy things kids do when they're bored, you know?"

She nodded. Didn't speak.

He turned back to the window, seeing, she was sure, another wintry day. A day off from school, filled with the kind of empty agenda children enjoyed every day. The world bright and limitless. Edward, totally unaware of the shadows lurking around the corner.

"Katie wanted to tag along," he said. "I complained,

tried to talk Katie into staying home, but she really wanted to be with the 'big boys,' as she used to call us. The last thing my mother said before we left was…" His voice trailed off, then he took in a deep breath, and tried again. "The last thing she said was, *'Watch out for Katie.'*" Those last four words seemed to rip from his throat. He shuddered out a long breath and grabbed at the windowsill with both hands, pressing his forehead to the cold glass. "Watch out for Katie. And I couldn't even do that." The words were a sob, not a sentence.

Livia crossed to Edward and laid a gentle hand on his shoulder. He tensed, then relaxed, but didn't turn toward her. She almost didn't want to press this, to ask anything more, because this was clearly a hurt that reached deep inside his soul, but she also knew that letting this fester even one more day was no good for Edward. "Tell me what happened."

Long moments passed. Cars went by on the street outside, the microwave let out a series of beeps, and Piper squirmed a little in Livia's arms. When Edward spoke again, his voice was hushed and hoarse.

"She…she fell, right over the edge and into a ravine. It was snowy and icy, and we were hurrying through the woods, and she was struggling to keep up because it was hilly and slippery, but all I wanted to do was lose her, because I didn't want her tagging along. And then she fell, and all I heard was her calling for me—*Edward, Edward*—and I thought she just wanted me to wait up, and I didn't want to do that, because I was annoyed she was even there." The words spilled from him in a rush. "So I kept going. And going. And by the time I realized she wasn't behind me anymore—" He cut off the sentence, and his eyes welled. "It…it was too late. I couldn't do anything. I tried, but I couldn't get her out of there. I couldn't save her." Now he turned to face Livia, his face crumpled with regret. "I tried, Livia, I tried so hard."

"Oh, Edward, you were only seven. What could you do?" She could imagine the scene. The boys, tromping through the woods, laughing, joking, and then the realization that one person was missing. Returning through the woods, calling Katie's name, and then…seeing her crumpled at the bottom of a ravine.

All the pieces finally fell into place. Edward's considerable guilt over an accidental fire, and another hurt girl. His refusal to have children, to get close to them. To even consider being a parent. "All these years, you carried this guilt with you for something that was an accident," she said. "Edward, you were a child yourself. Nobody could expect you to see this coming, to prevent it, or to save her."

He shook his head again, stronger this time. "That's no excuse."

"I'm not saying it's an excuse. It's a reality. You were a little boy. Annoyed with his little sister. Every boy in the world has felt that way at least a hundred times."

Edward spun around and in his eyes, she saw the intolerable weight of his regrets. *"I didn't stop,"* he said, the words slow and sharp, like lashes against his back. "I could have saved her, Livia. Don't you understand that? It was my fault. Mine. And my mother was never the same after that day. She died because she never found happiness again after Katie died. I did that, Livia. *I* did that."

"Oh, Edward." Her heart broke for him, and she wished he could see himself the way she saw him. A man who tried his best, day after day, and still couldn't escape the weight of his past. "You've always been the strong one. Maybe too strong. You take the world on your shoulders when it has plenty of other people to help carry the load." She reached up and cupped his cheek and waited until his eyes connected with hers. "You made a simple, understandable choice. More than twenty years ago. Surely you don't blame—"

"Yes, I can keep blaming myself, Livia. Don't you see? I'm no good watching over other people. Katie, Miranda…" His voice trailed off and his face shattered when he took in their child, now asleep on Livia's shoulders. "Piper."

"There are no guarantees in this life, Edward. All you do is the best you can."

"But what if my best isn't good enough? What if she gets hurt, too?" He shook his head, and looked away, as if merely the sight of Piper's innocent, cherubic face undid him.

"You'll never know unless you try." She shifted closer to him, turning until he could see Piper's sleepy face.

But he moved away, putting distance between himself and his child, and most of all, between himself and Livia. "I'm sorry. I can't take that chance."

She watched him standing in the shadows of the nursery, a broken man who had kept all this pain to himself for so long. He had a chance now to have everything and he was throwing it away. Closing the door between them. Again.

She reached down and took his hand. She gripped his palm firmly, trying to tell him with her touch how much she believed in Edward Graham. "Come with me."

"Where are we going?"

"To make amends." She smiled up at him. "And maybe then, you'll realize that doing the best you can is the only thing you can do."

CHAPTER NINE

EDWARD had gone along with Livia's mysterious plan for the first hour, mainly because she wouldn't answer any questions and wouldn't tell him what they were doing at a superstore about five miles outside of Riverbend. He'd pushed the cart while she loaded it, wondering about the purchases. They didn't buy much, mostly a laptop computer. For Piper? He didn't understand it, and Livia wasn't talking.

It wasn't that he couldn't afford it—Edward's company had done very, very well and money was not a problem for him—it was that he wasn't used to being in the passenger's seat. He wondered if perhaps Livia was keeping him in the dark on purpose, to get him to loosen the reins a little on his life.

Truth be told, he felt drained, empty, after telling Livia about Katie. Her unwavering support of him filled him, and for the first time since his little sister died, Edward began to feel the bonds of that self-created prison begin to ease. He had opened his heart, let Livia peek inside…and it had all been okay. Maybe he could change.

And in the end, maybe find…

Peace.

And boy, did he need that.

"Who is all this for?" he asked after they had loaded their purchases into the back of her car, then settled Piper inside and got in themselves.

"You'll see." She put her car in gear and pulled out of the store parking lot. The sky above was still gray, not so much as a single flake of the predicted snow. Didn't look like the storm was ever going to make an appearance.

"Livia, I'd really like to know what the plan is."

She laughed. "This drives you crazy, doesn't it?"

"What?"

"Not being in control. The boss had to hand over control to someone else for a change."

"I've already done that," he said. "My vice president is in charge of my company right now."

She snorted. "Uh-huh. And how in charge is he?"

"What do you mean?"

"I mean, did you step back, hands-off entirely, or is he following your directions to the T? Doing everything the Edward Graham way?" She eyed him before returning her attention to the road.

"Well, it's important that there's a cohesiveness to the leadership and—"

"Just as I thought." She turned to him and grinned. "We are two of a kind, Edward. Two control freaks who can't let other people be in charge."

"I let you drive today." He pointed to the steering wheel. He didn't add that there hadn't been much choice in that arena, considering Livia had a car seat and he didn't.

She chuckled. "And how many times did you try to give me directions? Even though you didn't even know where we were going."

He smiled. He'd been caught—nailed to a board with

precision by Livia. Sometimes he wondered if anyone knew him as well as this woman. She'd been right about everything—about his inability to give up control, about his vice president following precisely in Edward's footsteps. Hell, he hadn't even been able to sign the documents to sell the company yet. All this talk of moving forward and getting out from under the yoke of CEO, and he hadn't really taken one step in that direction. Maybe that was part of it, too—the tighter he held the reins, the less risk he had to take. Was he doing the same thing with his heart? With Livia? "I was trying to guess what you were up to."

"And were you right?"

He laughed, and thought of where they'd ended up. He'd expected a restaurant. Maybe a trip to a baby store to load up Piper with enough clothes for the next seven years. "Not even close."

"Good." A self-satisfied smile curved across her face.

"You look like a cat that caught a mouse."

She laughed, and he realized how much he had missed her laugh. She had a melodic, sweet voice, and when Livia laughed, it was like putting notes to that music. "Not quite."

"So are you going to at least tell me why we are doing this mystery thing we're doing?"

"For you to get past the panic stage."

"The what?"

She turned right, heading back into Riverbend. "Before I had Piper, I'd wake up all the time in the middle of the night, worried to death about everything. From whether I could provide for her to whether I'd remember to change her diaper. I was a wreck by the time I had her, so sure I'd screw up something. But you know what a baby teaches you pretty quickly?"

He shook his head.

"The minute that baby arrives, it's sink or swim. And really, even when you sink—" she paused at a stop sign and glanced at Piper in the rearview mirror "—like the time I cut her finger when I was trying to trim her nails, then bumped her head on the shelf hurrying to get her finger under some cold water, sometimes you learn that you can handle it. That in the end, it'll all work out fine. That worrying about the what-ifs did nothing but waste time."

He sobered. The light mood of the morning had disappeared. "Sometimes those what-ifs come true."

"And sometimes the results weren't nearly as disastrous as you suspected." She took a right, then stopped the car in front of a small two-story Cape-style house.

His blood froze. He saw now why Livia had driven. If he'd been behind the wheel, he never would have turned down this street, much less stopped at this house. What was Livia thinking? This wasn't going to make anything better. "Why are we here?"

"Because it's time, Edward." She laid a hand over his. "It's time."

She was right. But that didn't mean he liked the fact. He wanted nothing more than to stay in this car and not go inside that house. But where had avoidance gotten him in the last year? Nowhere good, that was for sure. Instead of moving on, he'd been wallowing in regrets. And in doing so, in thinking he was best at working through this on his own, he'd once lost the best woman he'd ever met, driving her and his child away.

If he didn't do this, he knew—knew as well as he knew his own name—that his past would keep on being the biggest obstacle to his future. A future that he was beginning to hope would always include Livia.

"Okay." He reached for the door handle and got out of Livia's car.

She got out too, then retrieved Piper from her car seat in the back. She slung the diaper bag over one shoulder, then stepped onto the sidewalk beside Edward. Her smaller hand slipped into his. He squeezed her fingers. "If I forget to tell you later...thank you."

Livia turned a smile on him. "You're welcome."

He nodded, then took a step forward. And another. A crisp winter wind blew against him, but he kept going forward.

Until he reached Miranda Willett's front step. And finally faced what he'd done his best to avoid for nearly a year.

The door opened before they pushed the bell. "What the hell are you doing here?" Richard Willett's face held a stone-cold anger.

"I came by to deliver a long overdue apology," Edward said. "Very long overdue."

The anger ebbed a little in Richard's face. He stood in the doorway, hesitating. Finally, he let out a long breath, like releasing air from a balloon, and stepped back to allow Edward and Livia entry. "Come in, then."

They stepped inside a bright, warm home. The walls were covered in soft shades of blue and white. White Christmas lights swagged the archway between the living room and dining room, then cascaded down the staircase. And in the corner stood the scraggly pine tree from the tree lot. Livia was surprised to see it covered in ornaments, so many she was sure the tree would topple from the weight.

Alicia Willett had been sitting in a chair by the window, a newspaper on her lap. She rose, then crossed to

Edward and Livia. She followed Livia's gaze. "The tree looks beautiful, doesn't it?"

"Yes. It does. A big improvement over how it looked in the lot, too."

"Miranda tends to go a little crazy at Christmas. She puts Mrs. Claus to shame. And even though she insisted she didn't want a tree—didn't want a Christmas at all, in fact—as soon as we got it set up, she had her dad get the ornaments out of the attic and insisted we hang them up together. Every last one." A tender look filled Alicia's eyes. She stood by the tree and fingered a hand-made gingerbread man. "Miranda's been making ornaments for as long as I can remember. When we look at this tree, it's like seeing her grow up all over again."

Edward cleared his throat. "Can I speak to her?"

The Willetts looked at each other, their faces filled with the protective caution of parents. It was a look Livia knew well. If she could have created a giant bubble to cushion Piper for the rest of her life, she would have.

Finally, Miranda's mother nodded. "Okay. I think that will be all right."

Richard tensed. "I don't want to upset her."

"Richard, we have to let her go sometime. She's a big girl. As she reminds us all the time. She can handle this."

"Follow me." Richard headed up the staircase, with Edward on his heels, and Livia bringing up the rear. From her perch on Livia's hip, Piper looked around, wide-eyed at the new surroundings.

Richard stopped halfway up and turned to face them. "Do you have any idea what my daughter's been through?" He didn't wait for an answer. "Six surgeries. Four skin grafts. And down the road, more surgeries as the scar tissues contract. She wears a pressure suit on half her body for twenty-three hours a day. And the pain—" Richard cursed and shook his head. "It's been a nightmare. The medical bills are astronomical, I'm sure. But someone paid—" He cut off his sentence and stared at Edward, pieces clicking together. "You?"

"It was the least I could do."

Richard considered Edward for a long time. A hundred emotions washed over his face, as he realized the man he'd been blaming all these months had been the one footing hundreds of thousands in medical bills. "Well, thank you. We'll pay you back—"

Edward put up a hand. "I don't want your money. I'll pay for her care for as long as she needs it. Whatever she needs."

"Thank you." Richard's voice was gruff. He turned and continued up the stairs. They stopped at the top of the stairs, then Richard knocked on the first door on the right. "Miranda, you have company."

There was a muffled okay from the other side, then Richard turned the knob and opened the door. He stepped inside the room first, then turned to allow Edward and Livia to enter.

The first thing Livia noticed was the album covers. Some faded, some dog-eared, some as pristine as the day they were printed. It has been years since she'd seen actual LPs, but Miranda was apparently a fan of rock music and the artistic LP covers created years ago. Instead of wallpaper, she had all the classics lining her walls—the Rolling Stones, The Beatles, Led Zeppelin. An ancient computer sat on a small desk by her bedside, along with a stack of books on graphic design and music magazines. Classic rock played loud on the stereo on the bookcase, shivering the Christmas lights hung from corner to corner of the ceiling.

Miranda sat in the center of a double bed, propped up by a half-dozen fluffy white pillows. A thick white comforter covered part of her legs, but not enough to block the view of the pressure suit compressing the bottom half of her body. Long tubular bandages covered her arms. Her hair was cut in a short, boyish style, but Livia could still see the bald patches where her scalp had burned. Her face had been mostly spared, thank God, except for a few patches marked by unnaturally white blotches.

No wonder Edward hadn't wanted to come. For a second, Livia considered leaving, but they were here now, and it was, as she'd said, far past time Edward dealt with his demons.

Richard thumbed down the volume on the stereo. "I'll let you all talk." Then he left the room, giving his daughter one last concerned glance.

"Hey, Mr. Graham." Miranda smiled, and it seemed to transform her face from scarred to beautiful. "What are you doing here?"

"I wanted to see how you were doing. And to apologize to your family and to you." Edward took two steps closer to the bed. "I should have come sooner, long before this. And said I was sorry a long time ago."

"For what?" Miranda looked genuinely perplexed. "I mean, me and the other servers are the ones that had that party afterwards. Your instructions were very clear and I…well, I didn't listen. If I had, I wouldn't have been in the building that night."

Livia had expected anger from Miranda. After all, the girl had suffered, and she was more than entitled to her share of fury. Instead, she saw a girl who hadn't let the fire beat down her sunny personality. Or let anyone else shoulder the blame for her decisions.

"I should have stayed," Edward said. "It was my hall, and I always make sure everything is right before I leave, but that night…" He threw up his hands. "I have no excuse. I'm sorry this happened to you, Miranda. Deeply sorry."

Her eyes watered. She nodded. "Thank you. And I'm sorry your hall burned down. We never intended for anything to happen."

He crossed to the bed and dropped into the chair across from Miranda. He laid a hand over Miranda's, the same way Livia had done to his earlier. She glanced at his hand and smiled, as if his touch brought her a feeling of acceptance, of forgiveness. "I know, Miranda. I don't blame you at all."

"I thought…" Miranda's lower lip trembled. "I thought you were mad at me for the fire. Like, that's your whole business. And if we hadn't had that party, it wouldn't be gone now."

"I was never mad at you. I stayed away because…" He heaved a sigh. "It was easier than facing what had happened to you. I blame myself entirely."

"Oh, Mr. Graham, don't. I'm going to be okay. I've had to wait before I could start college—" at that a wistfulness filled her eyes, and her gaze swept the album covers on her walls "—but I'll get there soon enough. Maybe not Pratt. I mean, that one's out of my price range, but somewhere."

Edward looked at Livia. Understanding dawned in his eyes. "Well, maybe I can help a bit with that. I have to get something out of the car. I'll be right back."

He hurried out of the room. Piper started to fuss, clearly done with being carried around. Livia shifted the baby's weight to the other hip.

"What's her name?" Miranda asked.

"Piper." Livia saw the interest in the girl's eyes and moved a little closer. "Do you want to meet her?"

Miranda nodded, then hesitated. "But don't you think all this—" she waved a hand over her body "—will scare her?"

"Not at all. Piper might beep your nose—that's her new thing—but she won't be bothered one bit." Livia sat on the edge of the bed, then balanced Piper on her knee. Piper turned toward the new person and made a gaa noise.

Miranda leaned forward, and slid a finger into Piper's fist. "Hey, there, Piper."

Piper gurgled and squeezed Miranda's hand. She kicked her feet and pumped her little fists. Miranda laughed. Wonder filled her face. "I think she likes me."

"What's not to like?" Livia said softly, her voice catching on the last words. "Look at you, Miranda. You're a strong, smart and upbeat girl, despite everything you've been through. A lesser person wouldn't have your attitude, your smile. I can only hope Piper grows up with those same qualities."

Miranda's eyes misted, and she dropped her gaze to the baby. For a long while, she didn't say anything, and neither did Livia. They let Piper do the talking.

Edward came back in the room, holding the bag from the store. He took in the scene on the bed and gave Livia a grateful smile. Then he plopped the bag beside Miranda and returned to his place in the chair. "I think we have just what you need here, so you don't have to put your dreams on hold one more day. Merry Christmas, Miranda."

Edward reached into the bag and pulled out the laptop they had bought earlier. He had questioned Livia about the need for so much memory and a good graphics card, but now she saw that he understood. He added two graphic design software programs to the pile. "Livia and I picked this out earlier today. And we're pretty sure this set up should be just what you need to practice your design work."

For a long second, Miranda didn't say anything. She just stared at the gift, clearly stunned. Then her eyes watered and she hugged the laptop to her chest, the software boxes spilling onto her lap. "Oh my God, this is so awesome. More than I could ever dream of having. Thank you. Thank you so much."

Edward shrugged. "It's nothing. Truly."

Miranda lowered the laptop and cocked her head to study Edward. "But why would you do this for me? I didn't work for you very long, and I burned down your hall and—"

"You didn't destroy anything, Miranda. In fact, this Christmas, I think you helped me make a lot of things very, very right. And if anyone knows the importance of pursuing your dreams, it's me. I started with that banquet hall when I was fresh out of college and it grew into a national business, bigger than I could have imagined. You have a talent. And you need to pursue it."

Miranda sighed. "That's a dream, Mr. Graham. It's way too expensive to go to Pratt and besides, I have to stay here and have surgeries and stuff." She let out another long breath. "Someday, maybe."

"I'm sure you can start online with them."

"Maybe."

He leaned back and feigned thinking. "You know, I'm starting a scholarship fund. It was a scholarship that helped pay for me to go to business college, and without it, I doubt I'd be where I am today. But mine would be more for kids who had suffered…setbacks and needed a little help to get to college."

"That sounds like a great idea."

"And I want you to be the first recipient."

It took a moment for the words to sink in. "Really?" Her eyes widened and a tentative smile appeared on her face.

"Yeah."

"Because of—" she glanced down at the pressure suit and the scars "—what the fire did to me?"

"No. Because of what the fire has taught me." He reached out and laid a gentle hand on her arm. "I can't change the past, but I can change the future. For me, for you, and for other students down the road."

"I'm really going to be able to do this? Really?"

Edward laughed, and for the first time since she'd returned to Riverbend, Livia saw real joy in his features. "Really, really."

"Oh my gosh. Oh my gosh. Oh my gosh!" Miranda's fingers danced along her lips. Then the realization that this was real, and was going to happen, burst on her face like a sunrise. "Dad! Mom! Come here!"

A thunder of footsteps sounded on the stairs. The door burst the rest of the way open and the Willetts hurried in, breathless. Richard cast a sharp glance at Edward. "What'd you do?"

Edward waved toward Miranda. "Let her tell you."

"What is it? Are you okay, honey?" Alicia asked. "Are you in pain?"

"No, I'm fantastic. And I'm going to college. Starting today." She beamed at Edward. "Mr. Graham is giving me a scholarship. I want to check out and see if Pratt is offering online classes, so I can take those until I'm ready for real classes." Then she held up the computer.

"And he bought me this laptop, and all the software I need to design."

"Really?" Her mother stared at Edward, then Miranda.

Miranda laughed. "That's what I said. And he said really, really."

A flush filled Edward's face. "I'm just trying to help us all have a new start here."

Richard shook his head, then put out his hand to shake Edward's. "Seems I've judged you wrong."

"No, you haven't."

"You've done a good thing. More than anyone could ask." Richard swallowed hard then faced Edward. "Thank you."

"No, thank you. You've raised a wonderful and gracious girl. And I hope when she completes that degree, she comes to work for my company."

"You mean it?" Miranda asked.

"Of course. Not as part of the wait staff, but in the offices, helping the marketing department. Unless some record label grabs you first for their marketing arm. We do a lot of concerts at our other venues, Miranda. And I bet you'd be great working in that department."

"I'd love that." She flipped open the laptop and powered it on. "I'm going to get started right now. From this day forward," Miranda said, "my life is changing and I am pursuing my dreams."

"Me too," Edward said softly, as he and Livia and Piper left the room, and the happy, crying Willett family. "Me too."

CHAPTER TEN

"You're gonna wear a hole in that carpet," Ray said from his post by the Christmas tree, where he was hanging a few more ornaments unearthed from the attic that morning. "You're as nervous as a cat in a rocking chair factory."

Edward laughed and stopped his constant motion in front of the window. "Sorry, Dad. I hate waiting."

"Especially when you're waiting on a pretty woman." Ray put the empty box to the side. "A woman who's got your heart?"

Edward stared out the window. The gray day had seemed to brighten, and he could almost smell the coming snow in the air. Or maybe it was just his attitude that had changed. For the first time in forever, he was looking forward to Christmas nearly as much as he had when he'd been a little boy. "I think so."

After the afternoon they'd spent visiting Miranda, Livia had dropped Edward off at his father's house and promised to return for dinner. They hadn't talked much on the ride home—it was close to Piper's nap time and she hadn't been happy about being in the car instead of in her crib at home. So any conversation they tried to have had been interrupted by one very loudly complaining baby. Edward had tried to soothe Piper, since he was in the passenger's seat and more free to reach back there, but she was overtired and having none of it. That little taste of Livia's life made him sympathize with the work she obviously put in raising their child. It wasn't all smiles and beep-beeps on the nose. Yet, even as he'd tried—and failed—to coax a smile to his daughter's face, he'd realized he was doing something far more important.

Being a parent.

It was a new feeling, one he was still trying on, like a new pair of shoes.

When he got home, Edward had gone outside and hit the wood pile again. He'd needed clear, cold air in his lungs and some time to himself. To think. His father had let him chop for an hour, as if sensing his son needed to be alone.

With every swoop of the axe, the world became a little clearer to Edward. It was as if he'd made the first steps today at the Willett house—no, he'd made those first steps when Livia had taken his hand in the nursery and told him it was time to make amends. All afternoon, he'd thought she meant with the Willetts.

The wood stacked up beside him, the scent of freshly slivered logs filling the air. And the healing process began.

Because Edward realized the one he needed to make amends with wasn't Miranda. Or her parents.

But himself.

He had begun, ever so slowly, to open his heart. To his father, to Livia, to Piper, to other people. And it wasn't nearly as difficult as he'd expected.

Now he couldn't wait to see Livia and tell her. Still, he paced, worried that it was too late. That he had damaged their relationship beyond repair.

"Glad to hear you're moving forward. It's about time." Ray flicked off the television and turned on the stereo. Classical versions of Christmas music filled the house. "There. That should set the mood."

Edward chuckled and shook his head. "Since when did you become Cupid?"

"Since I realized what a good thing a great wife can be." Ray's eyes brimmed with emotion, but he shrugged it off with a gruff gust. "You better realize that, too, my boy. You're not getting any younger."

"Nothing's stopping you from dating again yourself, you know."

Ray patted his chest. "Once this ticker's ready to rock, I'll be taking some twirls on the dance floor again."

"Good for you."

"I'm glad you did what you did today for the Willett girl," Ray said. "Just talking to her and the family was a big step. One in the right direction."

"Yeah." Edward let out a long breath. It hadn't been easy, and had been a moment he'd resisted for a year, but the look on Miranda's face had made it all worthwhile. "I agree."

"So…you still going to sell the company?"

Edward thought about it for a moment. He had an offer on the table for his company—a generous one and one that could let him sit around and count his money for years. He'd already achieved his financial goals—to become a millionaire before he was thirty—but found once he had the money in his account, that there was no better or greater challenge than the next one. It wasn't about the money. It was about seeing if he could grow the company to new levels every year. Expand beyond banquet halls and into concert venues, then to theaters and outdoor amphitheaters. To go nationwide, then maybe someday, global. In the end, though, it was that very challenge that had been part of what cost him his relationship with Livia.

Could he still do that, but manage to be here and be involved? He thought of Livia, then Piper. That alone was enough motivation to find a way to have it all. "I'm going to keep the company, but I'm going to do things differently from here on out."

"How?"

"I'm going to make time. So that in the end—" he glanced out the window and watched as Livia pulled into the driveway, with their daughter tucked safely in the back seat, making his heart leap and his pulse race "—I don't have a single regret."

Ray clapped his son on the shoulder. "I'm proud of you, son." His voice was hoarse, and he let out a little cough, covering for the emotion, then he turned away and settled into his recliner.

The doorbell rang and Edward crossed to answer it. He pulled open the door to see Livia and Piper, their cheeks rosy from the cold. Behind them was Melody, holding a foil-covered dish. Edward's heart sang, and he had to force himself not to crush Livia in a hug.

"Merry Christmas," Edward said, the words feeling a little foreign on his tongue. Geez, had it been that long since he'd felt festive? "Well, Christmas Eve."

She smiled one of the hundred different smiles of hers that he loved. "Merry Christmas to you, too."

"We brought mac and cheese," Melody said, holding up the dish. The sharp scent of cheddar cheese wafted up to greet him. "Livia disagrees, but in my opinion, carbs go with everything. And mac and cheese…well, that's the bomb."

"It's whole wheat pasta," Livia added. "Only slightly unhealthy."

Edward chuckled. Leave it to Livia to health up an artery-clogging dish. "Thank you. I know my dad's going to be in heaven." He slid the diaper bag off Livia's arm and put it on his own. "Come on in."

"I'm going to go put this in the oven to warm up," Melody said. "Three-fifty, right?"

Livia nodded, and Melody headed off to the kitchen. Livia waved a greeting at Edward's father. "Nice to see you again, Mr. Graham."

"Oh, you know it's always Ray to you, Miss Livia." He gestured toward his son, and didn't move out of his recliner. Maybe his father was feeling bad today, which sent a rush of concern through Edward. "Hey, Edward, go get my grandbaby for me, and bring her to me. Let Livia have a minute to herself without her arms all full."

Edward reached out, and Piper leaned toward him, her face animated and happy. She settled into his arms without complaint and laid her head on his shoulder. Her weight felt comfortable against him, almost…perfect. His fingers brushed against the soft dewy skin of her legs where her jumper had ridden up, and he inhaled the strawberry sweet scent of her skin. She was…perfect. Absolutely freaking perfect.

A curious feeling of peace and joy stole over Edward and settled in the deepest recesses of his heart. So this was what it felt like.

Damn.

And he'd almost missed it. Almost given it all up. Almost.

"I think she recognizes her father," Livia said softly. She rested her hand on Piper's back and smiled at the scene before her.

"I think you're right." He reached up and hesitated only a second before placing a palm against the downy hair on the back of Piper's head. She curved into the touch and cooed. In that instant, he felt a swell of something that he was pretty sure was love.

She was his daughter. And she knew it.

He leaned in and met Piper's face with his own. She stared at him, blinking. Then her lips widened, and he could swear a smile curved across her face. "Hey there."

Piper gurgled and bounced in his arms. She reached out and grabbed his nose. Livia stood to the side, watching them. She looked ready to grab the baby at any time, but Edward had this under control. And he wanted to prove that to Livia. Prove he was ready—and willing—to step into his role as Piper's father.

He reached out and pressed a finger to Piper's nose. "Beep."

She laughed, and bounced some more. Squeezed his nose so hard, he was surprised she didn't break it.

So he did it again. "Beep!"

She squealed and bounced again and again. Her eyes were wide—his eyes, the same blue—and her face was lit with joy. An echoing feeling exploded inside him. So this was what it was like. Amazing.

So he did it again. "Beep!"

They played the game over and over again, and each time, Piper got more and more excited. Finally, Edward stopped—to protect his own nose, which was beginning to hurt. He crossed to his father and settled Piper in Ray's lap. "Careful. The kid's got quite the grip."

When he looked at Piper, Ray's entire demeanor melted like ice cream under the sun. "Hey, kiddo."

She stared at him, unblinking. Then Piper turned to look at Edward, and her face broke into a smile.

Ray glanced up at Edward. He grinned. "Seems she knows who her daddy is."

"She does indeed." Edward ruffled Piper's hair. Then he realized that his father wasn't feeling bad at all—he'd merely been concocting a way to get his son to handle Piper. "You're a smart man, Dad."

Ray chuckled. "You gotta be to raise a son like you." Then Ray reached out and trailed a finger along Piper's cheek. "Ah, kiddo…you look just like another Piper I know."

Edward's heart nearly broke for his father. He could hear the pain in Ray's voice, but it was mixed with wonder and happiness, too. As if this little fifteen pounds of baby had finally healed a wound that had been open far too long. Edward could feel it in the room, and when his gaze connected with Livia's he saw that she did, too. He bent down beside his father, and let Piper's fingers curl around his thumb. "She does, doesn't she?"

They both could see it—the features that so resembled Katie's. It was as if God had given the Graham family a second chance to make it right. To open their circle this time, rather than closing it off like before. Edward watched Ray marvel over his granddaughter and decided that nothing was going to keep him from being a part of Piper's life.

A beeping sounded in the kitchen and Melody came rushing into the room. "Uh, something's going off. I hope I didn't burn the casserole."

"It's probably the ham. I can get it." Ray started to rise.

"Don't worry about it, Ray. I can take care of it," Livia said and followed Melody into the kitchen.

"Go." Ray shooed at Edward. "Finish dinner for me,

if you don't mind. I'm going to spend some time with my granddaughter."

"Don't let her wear you out. You're supposed to be resting."

"I will, I promise." Ray sighed, then smiled. "I guess I'll follow my doctor's orders a little closer. I want to be around to teach this sweet little girl how to reel in a bass."

Edward smiled and gave his father's shoulder a squeeze. "I'm glad to hear that, Dad. Really glad."

Ray's hand covered Edward's. "Me, too." The two men's eyes met and then they each looked away. They were still Grahams, after all, and a mushy moment wasn't part of the family DNA.

Livia couldn't stay busy enough in the kitchen. She removed the ham from the oven, then turned off the timer, and set to work carving it. She knew she should let the meat rest, but she didn't want to go back in the living room and face Edward. Not yet.

What did he want? Every time he turned around, he told her he didn't want to be a father, didn't want to be anything more than a financial donor in Piper's life, that he was the same man he had been before, closed off emotionally. And then just now, he played with her, engaged with her—

And got her hopes up.

"Damn!" Livia put down the knife.

Melody arched a brow. "What did that ham ever do to you? That thing's a mess. Here, let me do it."

"You? Carve a ham?" Livia let out a snort. "Right."

"I'm not totally incompetent in the kitchen," Melody said, then she grinned. "I just act that way so you'll wait on me."

Livia swatted her sister, then stepped away from the carving board. Melody had a point—Livia did cater to her sister. Perhaps if she stepped away more often, Melody wouldn't be so dependent. She made a vow to let Melody stand on her own two feet from here on out. "I don't know what's wrong with me."

"You're all discombobulated by a man. I know. I've been there myself." Melody sliced the ham into perfectly even pieces, and used the knife to lay them in a concentric pattern on the platter. Exactly the way Livia had done it a hundred times. Apparently Melody had been paying attention.

"I am not," Livia hissed. She turned toward the cabinet and started reaching for plates so Melody wouldn't see the lie in her eyes. She was discombobulated by Edward, but she was in no mood to talk about it. All she could hope was for dinner to go quickly. Thank goodness Melody had been feeling better and well enough to come along, and hopefully run a little interference.

Ever since they'd left the Willett house, Livia had been torn—between wanting to believe in the Edward she had seen today and being afraid that it wouldn't last. That just when she began to depend on him, to be there, to be a part of her life, he'd shut down and close her out.

"Mmm-hmm," Melody said, clearly not believing her sister at all. Then her voice brightened. "Oh, hi, Edward. Come to help?"

Livia stilled, her hand on the pile of dinner plates. Just hearing his name made her heart trip. Maybe she should have never settled in Riverbend if it was always going to remind her of that man. Best choice for Piper or not, running into him all the time—or hearing people talk about him—was going to be painful.

"Let me get those." His voice was dark and low over her shoulder, and she wanted to melt into his chest.

She didn't.

"Sure." She spun away and nearly winged her hip when she yanked open the silverware drawer. The forks and knives shuddered with a metal clatter.

"I'm going to go put this on the table," Melody said and then disappeared with the platter of ham, leaving Edward and Livia alone.

"I should get the table set," Livia said, grabbing a bunch of silverware and turning away from the drawer. At the same time, Edward turned toward her. The tines of the forks and blades of the butter knives came within inches of his stomach.

He smiled. "You're a dangerous woman."

"Sorry. I'll—" She ducked to the right, but he put a hand on her arm.

"Why are you avoiding me?"

"I'm not. I'm…busy."

He took the silverware out of her hands and laid it on the counter. "Now you're not."

"We have to get the table set for dinner. The ham will get cold—"

"Ham tastes just as good cold as it does warm. It can wait. I want to talk to you." He tipped a finger under her chin and turned her face until she was looking at him. "Why are you avoiding me?"

She wanted to leave the room, but Edward blocked her way. He wanted an answer, and she owed him at least that. Maybe then he would drop it and see that they weren't made for each other. That what she wanted and what he was willing to give were totally different things.

"I…I saw what you did for Miranda," she said. "You

did even more than I thought you would. In that moment, you were an Edward I never saw before."

"And why is that a bad thing?"

"Because…" She couldn't say it. Couldn't look at him. She turned away, unable to voice the words that had tumbled inside her all afternoon.

Because I fell in love with you again when I saw that.

"Because." A lame answer, but the only one she was going to give him.

Edward studied her for a long second, then he turned to call over his shoulder. "Dad, Livia and I are going to take a walk. You and Melody should eat. You don't have to wait on us."

"If that ham's ready, I'm not waiting on anything," his father shouted back from the living room.

"Take care of the baby, will you?"

Ray chuckled. "You know I will. In fact, I'm going to spoil her mercilessly and shower her with noisy toys."

Edward chuckled, then tugged two winter coats off the hook by the back door and held one out to Livia. "Come on. I want to talk to you."

"Edward—"

"Just hear me out. If you don't like what I have to say, you can always come back for ham and macaroni." He held the coat and waited for her to take it.

She shrugged one arm into the jacket, then hesitated. "Piper—"

"Will be fine. Your sister is here and so is my dad. Who happens to have a little childcare experience of his own." Edward slid Livia's other arm into the coat. "I turned out reasonably well, so I'm sure Piper will do just fine."

She'd run out of excuses. So she buttoned her coat, waited for him to do the same, and then they headed out into the cold together. The temperature had dropped a few degrees while they were inside, and Livia closed the neck of the coat against the slight wind. They walked down the driveway and turned right onto the sidewalk. Some of the holiday lights were coming on, as dusk deepened its hues from pale pink to dark purple.

"First, I want to thank you." Edward's words frosted in the cold. "For the shopping trip and for getting me to see Miranda and her family today. How did you know that's what I needed?"

She sidestepped a crack in the sidewalk. "I know you pretty well."

"That you do. Better than I know myself." He slid a glance her way. "You're quite the mind reader. I had no idea how much I needed to do that—not just for Miranda, but for myself—until after we left."

"You're welcome," Livia said. Now Miranda and Edward could move forward. There was that, at least, to take comfort in. "She seemed really happy with the laptop."

"All thanks to you." He chuckled. "I didn't know what you were thinking when you had me buy it. But I trusted you. Good thing."

She shrugged. "I just tried to think like you today at the store. I knew if you got past the fear of seeing her, that you'd want to do something for her. And you had mentioned her wanting to go to college for graphic design, so that seemed like the perfect gift."

He chuckled. "You thought like me? How'd that work out?"

"Well for a while there, I was tempted to watch a football game and have a few beers."

He laughed. "Glad you didn't."

"It is Christmas Eve, after all. I'll save that for the

Super Bowl." She flashed him a grin, then sobered. "I thought the scholarship was a very generous idea."

"What good is money if I can't give to other people? I've made more than enough, and I don't need much to live on. All this time, that money has pretty much sat in the bank, not doing a damned bit of good. Though I have tried to take care of my dad. He lives in the same house we've always lived in, still stokes his woodstove with wood he chops himself, even though I've offered to build him a brand-new house, pay his heating bills for the rest of his life, whatever he wants. He does it because he says there's history in that house. Roots. The things he believes in and holds dear. And no amount of money can give him that."

Livia smiled. She hadn't realized that Edward's cantankerous father had such sentimental tendencies. "Who knew an old softie lurked under Ray's gruff exterior?"

"He just does that to keep up appearances." Edward paused while they turned the corner onto Maple Street. "He's not the only one."

"You're not like your father."

"I'm more like my father than I ever realized." He shoved his hands into the pockets of his coat. "My father worked a million hours a week when I was a kid. He was never home, and it got worse after Katie died. He never talked, never told me how he was feeling. We had almost no relationship. He was doing exactly what I've always done—running away from the pain instead of dealing with it."

"He suffered a terrible loss. It's to be expected, I'm sure." If she ever lost Piper, she had no idea how she'd ever go on again. A loss like that was too big to comprehend, to even begin to wrap her mind around. She could only imagine how hard it had been for the Grahams.

"Yes, but he did all that at the cost of the child he already had. I never saw my father. I didn't get to know him until after my mother died. And even then, our relationship was strained at best, until he had his heart attack. We're still learning how to build a relationship together. I did the same thing with you after the fire. I kept telling myself it would be better if I worked through how I felt alone. That's how I always operated—feelings tucked inside, as if that helped anything. It didn't. All I did was drive a wedge between us." Edward stopped walking and faced Livia. "I don't want that to happen with me and Piper."

"It won't. I'll be sure you see her as much as you want to."

"I want to see her every day."

Livia nodded. He was going to be a part of their daughter's life. It was what she had hoped for, all this time. Then why did she hesitate? "Okay. I'm sure we can work something out."

"No, you're not understanding me, Livia. I want to put Piper to bed and I want to wake up in the morning and see her. I want to watch her smear oatmeal on her face and hear her laugh when I blow bubbles into the air. I want to teach her to ride a bike and warn her about teenage boys, and see her go off to school in the morning." Edward reached for Livia's hands and held them in his own. His deep blue gazed locked on hers. "I want us to be a family, Livia. A real family." He took a deep breath, then smiled. "I want to marry you."

Marry Edward.

It was what she'd wanted him to say—what she'd prayed to hear from the day she found out she was pregnant. She had what she'd told him she wanted now, but as the words sank in and the cold air settled around her, she hesitated again. A choking fear rose in her chest. She pulled her hands out of his and stepped back. "I...I can't do that, Edward. We didn't date very long and just because we have a baby is no reason to get married and..." her voice trailed off. The rush of excuses exhausted.

"And you're terrified to settle down." He closed the distance between them, and his deep blue gaze met hers. Knowing, understanding and seeing past her walls. "For all your talk, Olivia Perkins, deep down inside you're afraid to make a permanent connection."

"I am not."

"Oh yeah? Prove it to me." He tipped her chin to meet his. "Marry me."

Her heart raced so fast, she was sure it would beat right out of her chest. She caught a deep breath, held it. This was what she wanted. Why didn't she just say yes? "I need some time to think about this."

He let out a gust. "You know, all this time I thought it was just me who had the problem opening up, making a commitment. But I'm getting the feeling that either you don't really want me or you don't want to be tied down."

"I..." She exhaled, then faced the truth. It had been there, all this time, heck, all her life, and she'd never had to say it aloud. Until now. "I don't want to be let down."

His gaze softened. "Like your mother did to you and Melody."

She nodded and cursed the tears that rose in her eyes. She thought of the future Edward was proposing and felt nothing but fear. So many things could go wrong. They could start with the best of intentions, and end up apart. The one hurt the most by that would be Piper. Her protective instincts warned her to step away, to head off the damage before it started. "What's to stop you from leaving next week or next month or next year? Raising a child is hard, Edward. It's demanding. Babies are crying and dirty and needy—all the time. And you're going to have days when you are going to want to run away and let someone else do the tough work."

"I'm sure we'll both have those days. But we can get through it together. Give us a chance, Livia."

She turned away and fingered a swag of white lights draped across a short picket fence bordering the sidewalk. The sun had dropped behind the horizon and all around her, Christmas lights began to come on, blinking their little bits of magic. "After my mother left," she said, "I vowed that when I grew up, my kids would have a perfect Christmas. Trees and stockings and wreaths and everything they needed. And I tried this year, I really did. I wanted Piper to have everything I never had. And—" her voice broke "—I still failed."

"You didn't fail at all. You're a wonderful mother. That's the only gift she needs."

"No, that's not true. I didn't get her the one gift she really wants."

"What's that?"

She shook her head and pulled away. He hadn't said the words and she wasn't going to force them out of him. Love, she wanted to scream, that was what she was looking for. He had opened up so much already, but he had yet to open his heart all the way to her. Without that, she couldn't take a chance. "I can't do this, Edward."

"You mean you can't take a risk."

"What if it doesn't work out? What will happen to Piper then?" She glanced out at the neighborhood, all looking so peaceful and perfect.

"Aren't you the one who lectured me about not worrying about the things you can't control?"

"But don't you see? I can control this. I can head this off before it disintegrates. Before Piper is left—" Livia cut off her sentence. And now the tears came anyway, strong and determined. "To raise herself."

"Oh, Livia," he said, softly, reaching for her, "that wouldn't happen."

She stepped away from him, putting as much distance between them as she could on the small sidewalk. She turned her face up to the dark, clear sky. "I wish it would snow. Then Piper's first Christmas would be perfect."

"It still can be." He took her hand, ran his fingers along hers. "Believe in miracles, Livia. They can and do happen."

She shook her head. How many times had she tried to believe in the miracle of her mother's return? Of things that never happened, never came to pass? No, it was far better that she protect Piper now, rather than leave her daughter in the same situation later in life. "I believe in what I can see, Edward. And I don't see a future for us. I thought I did, but I was wrong."

Then she headed back to his father's house to collect her child and to leave before she put stock in something that could never be.

CHAPTER ELEVEN

EDWARD stood by the Christmas tree in his father's front room, watching the multicolored lights blink on and off. The scent of ham and macaroni and cheese still lingered in the air, but the holiday spirit had left when Livia did. His father was in the kitchen, cursing over a crossword puzzle.

How had that gone so wrong? He'd been sure, when he asked her to marry him that she'd say yes. He wanted the same thing she did—a family. He loved her, he wanted to be with her and Piper...what could be holding her back?

The doorbell rang, dragging Edward out of his thoughts. "Earl," he said when he answered the door. "What brings you by on Christmas Eve?"

Earl doffed his plaid hunting cap and gave Edward a hearty hello. "I wanted to thank you for working the tree lot."

"No problem. It was my pleasure."

Earl handed him two slim pieces of paper. "It ain't much, in the way of thank-yous, but I figured you'd get some enjoyment out of these. My Betsy and I are going, so we're hoping to see you all there, too."

"Two tickets to the New Year's Eve party at Rustica?"

Edward started to hand them back, then reconsidered. He gave Earl a grin. "You do know you are the most obvious matchmaker in Riverbend, don't you?"

Earl chuckled. "All I'm trying to do is build up Riverbend's population. It's my civic duty."

"I don't think Cupid ever thought of that angle."

Earl tapped his head. "Some of us are smarter than your average guy in diapers."

Edward laughed. "Well, that population is definitely increasing by one. I'm moving back. And rebuilding the hall. In fact, I'm moving my corporate headquarters here, too, so I'll be around a lot more."

"That's really good to hear." Earl clapped Edward on the shoulder. "So…is there any hope you'll be living in a house built for three?"

"I don't know about that." He sighed and crossed his arms over his chest. "I asked her to marry me. She turned me down."

"Hell, I've asked Betsy three times." Earl grinned. "She's a stubborn woman, my Betsy."

"What are you going to do?"

He shrugged. "Keep asking. A man can't give up on the woman he loves. I know Betsy. She'll come around." He planted his cap on his head and redid the flaps. "She's a worrywart, and I think she just wants to know that I love her more than anything under the sun, and that I'll always be around, before she puts my ring on her finger."

"Earl, you're a fixture in this place. I can't imagine you going anywhere."

"That's what I keep telling Betsy. That she's stuck with me till the end of time." Earl turned and took a step off the porch, then turned back. "Looks like snow."

"That's what they keep saying. But it hasn't happened yet."

"Just keep believing," Earl said. "You never know what Santa will bring you on Christmas mornin'."

Melody had been following Livia around for the better part of an hour. She'd stuck close to her when she put Piper down for a nap. Hovered while Livia started a load of laundry and folded another one. And always with the same goal—to try to get Livia to talk about Edward. Which Livia had thus far avoided doing, ever since they left Ray's house. But Melody was not easily deterred.

"I brought home some leftovers for you," Melody said. "It's not good to go around on an empty stomach."

Livia threw the last few pieces of dirty laundry into the machine and added some detergent. "Hey, that's my advice."

"Yup. I listen more than you think, too."

"Well…good." Livia pushed start on the washer, then leaned against the machine. "I'm sorry. Thank you for helping at Ray's and for packing up some leftovers for me. I appreciate it."

"Enough to tell me what happened on that walk?"

"I really don't want to talk about that." She tried to leave the laundry room, but Melody blocked her exit.

"I know you think I'm bad at relationships."

"I never said that."

"You didn't have to. It's practically public knowledge." Melody let out a little self-deprecating laugh. "But at least I know why I run instead of stay. Carl's screw-up notwithstanding, most of the time, it's me leaving, even when things are great. Like you just did."

"I don't—"

"You do. You ran from Riverbend when things didn't work out between you and Edward. And once he was gone, you ran right back here. Because it was safe to—he'd already left. No danger of running into him again."

"Or so I thought."

"And you know why you do that?"

Livia propped a fist on her hip. "Hey, when did you become the analyst of my love life?"

"Since forever. You're my big sister, Liv. I watched everything you did." A tender smile stole across Melody's face, a rare moment of vulnerability in a sister who didn't like to let others peek inside her soul. "And I tried to live up to the example you set."

"You did?" Livia had never realized that about Melody. She'd been so busy worrying about making sure Melody was brought up right, that she never lacked for love or attention, that she hadn't thought about an example.

"Of course I did," Melody said. "I loved you and envied you and copied you all my life. You're my big sister."

Sister. Not surrogate mother, but sister. The kind of sister you played checkers with and joked with, and shared memories with. *Sister.*

"You really think of me as your sister?" Livia asked. A smile curved across her face, and she felt her shoulders ease, as if the burden she had put on herself when she'd stepped into the maternal role all those years ago had finally eased.

Melody nodded. "Yup, sisters. Complete with all the fights over boys and hair products, and sweater sharing." There was a tease in her voice, but no mistaking the love there, too.

Livia drew Melody into a warm, tight hug. She held her little sister for a long time, while tears dampened each of their shoulders. "I love you, Mel."

"I love you too, Livia." Then Melody drew back and cupped Livia's face. Melody's green eyes were serious, and determined. "This time, I'm going to tell *you* what to do. Because I think you've been worrying too much about everyone else—me, Piper, heck, the people in this town—than you have about finding your own happiness."

"I don't…" Then Livia considered her sister's words. How many years had she done exactly that? Shelving her own life, to take care of those around her. It had become second nature, and even now, when she knew in her heart that she loved Edward, she kept pushing him away. "Maybe I do."

Melody nodded, and a knowing look lit her eyes. "So, take the smelly monkey to the Winterfest. Let her see Santa. And then go track down that hunk of a guy who's madly in love with you and tell him you want to marry him."

"How do you know he's madly in love with me?"

"It's written all over his face, sis. He was so starry-eyed, he was practically tripping over his feet today." Melody let out a long sigh. "I would give my right arm to have a man look at me like that."

"You will someday."

Melody waved that off. "We'll worry about someday later. Right now, you have an amazing man to go find. So go." She took Livia's arm and practically dragged her out of the laundry room. "You can even borrow my sweater if you want."

Just before she left, Livia turned to her sister and gave

her one more hug. "You're the smartest and best sister anyone could ask for."

"That's 'cause I learned from the best," Melody said with a smile.

The Winterfest party was in full swing by the time Edward arrived. He had a few hours until the clock turned past midnight, and Christmas Eve gave way to Christmas Day. Some time yet to pull off a miracle.

At first, he didn't see Livia anywhere. Had her sister been wrong when he'd stopped by the house, looking for Livia? Had Livia opted out of the Winterfest after all?

Then he saw her, Piper perched on one hip, standing before the gingerbread family display. Piper was reaching for the brightly lit people, clearly fascinated. Edward hung back for a moment, just watching his daughter take in the world. Everything was a discovery for her—new people, new situations, new experiences. And if everything worked out, he'd be right there, catching every single second.

Livia turned just then—did she sense him behind her?—and a smile curved across her heart-shaped face. It was yet another of the dozens of smiles of hers that he loved. Then the smile disappeared, and as he closed the distance between them, he started praying for a miracle again.

"What are you doing here?" she said.

"Looking for you. And my daughter." He took a step forward, and as he did, Piper noticed him and leaned toward him. He grinned like a fool, ridiculously happy every time his child recognized him. Such a simple thing, and yet so huge to him. "It's Christmas. We should spend it together."

"You want to go to the Winterfest. With us."

It wasn't even a question. It was more disbelief framed in a sentence. "Why is that so hard to believe?"

"Because you're not a holiday guy."

"Hey, don't judge me by that tree. My dad and I aren't exactly decorators." He took another step forward, noting Piper still leaning in his direction. Then the joke faded from his voice, and he caught Livia's gaze with his own. "You're right. Up until this year, I wasn't much of a holiday guy. I guess after Katie died, Christmas was never the same. I never really felt like celebrating again."

"I know what you mean. We tried, after my mother left, but it was like there was always a hole." She sighed and fiddled with Piper's snowsuit.

"Exactly. I thought I was just fine like that, fine being by myself, but I was wrong." He waited until her gaze met his. "When you left the house tonight, that's what I felt. Like there was a hole where my family should be. I don't want to feel that way anymore, Livia."

"Edward…I can't." She spun away, and Piper let out a squeal of protest. She leaned her little body over Livia's shoulder, making her intentions clear. Piper wanted her daddy, but her mother was speeding off in the opposite direction.

Then the answer came to him, so fast and furious, it was like a slap upside the head. Livia wanted proof. Tangible proof that he was serious. That he loved her and their daughter, and he wasn't going to run from any of that. That was the one thing he had never given her before. She'd fallen for him last year, and he'd kept all his emotional cards close to his chest. Time to let them show.

He stepped around Livia, stopping her departure, and put his hands out. Piper bounced and reached again. "Can I hold her?"

Livia hesitated only a fraction of an instant. Then she read the body language of her daughter, and the clear interest of her daughter's father, and handed Piper to him. The baby settled against Edward's chest and began to coo. Wonder filled Livia's features. "Look at her. She's so...happy."

"Good." He nuzzled a kiss along Piper's forehead. The action felt so natural, so right, he couldn't believe he hadn't done it before. He vowed to do all of this a lot more often. "Now, what say we get your mommy to come with us for a little while?"

Livia shook her head. "I should probably be getting her to bed. It's getting late."

"Piper, tell your mommy that she's never going to believe I can be a great dad and a great husband if she doesn't give me a chance to prove it to her." He nuzzled Piper again, and she let out a stream of baby babble.

"Edward—"

"Don't forget to tell Mommy that Christmas is no time for arguing." Edward took Piper's hand and helped the baby wag a cautioning finger at Livia. "See? She agrees."

Livia opened her mouth again, as if she might do that very thing, then shut it again. She rolled her eyes, but a grin played at the corners of her lips. "You win. Or rather, Piper does. Where are we going?"

"To tell Santa what we want for Christmas. If you don't tell him, he can't bring it." Edward beeped Piper's nose, which made the baby squeal with delight. "Isn't that right, Piper?"

"Okay, but just for a little while. It is, after all, almost bedtime." Livia walked alongside Edward as they crossed the park, waving to people they knew, and headed for the small red house marked Santa's Village.

C.J. Hamilton sat in the big chair on the porch of the little house, decked out as the big guy himself, looking pretty realistic in his thick white beard and bushy eyebrows, too. Clearly, he'd brought a lot of Hollywood tricks with him when he'd moved to Riverbend. Beside him stood his wife, Jessica, in a matching red dress and black boots, a perfect Mrs. Claus. In a pen to the right of Santa's house was a live reindeer—an annual fixture at the Winterfest and a kid favorite. Tonight, though, the line of children was down to just one, probably because most of them wanted to get home early in case Santa dropped down their chimney first. When the last child left, C.J. reached for Piper.

"Ho, ho, ho. Who do we have here?" C.J. did a perfect imitation of Kris Kringle, complete with a shake of his temporary pillow-formed jelly belly.

"Piper Graham," Edward said, leaning forward to place his daughter on C.J.'s lap.

C.J. glanced up at Edward with a blink of surprise. "Seems Santa has already blessed your house this year."

"He has." Edward felt a goofy grin spread across his face. Proud as hell to show off his beautiful daughter. Why had he ever thought he didn't want this? Right now, he wanted to shout it from the rooftops, tell it to the world, that this incredible child was his. "He has indeed."

"Congratulations," Jessica said, drawing Livia into a quick hug. "She's beautiful."

"Thank you." Livia watched her daughter, sitting on Santa's lap and delighting at the new face. And Edward watched them both, completely smitten with the girls in his life.

"Well, well, little girl, what do you want for Christmas?" C.J. leaned in toward Piper, as if she might whisper in his ear. Instead she grabbed his beard and gave it a tug. "Ah, she says she wants a beard of her own."

Edward and Livia laughed. "If she ends up with a beard," Livia said. "I'm going to have a long talk with my obstetrician."

"I'm thinking…teddy bear," C.J. said, gently untangling his beard from Piper's grasp. "What do you say, Piper?"

She babbled and bounced. Apparently in complete agreement. C.J. laughed, gave Piper a little tap on the nose, then handed her back to Edward. He and Livia said goodbye to C.J. and Jessica and started across the park again. All around them, people were soaking up the last few hours of the Winterfest—playing at the carnival games, sipping at hot chocolate, nibbling at pretzels.

"I can take her if she's getting too heavy," Livia said.

"She's just fine. Isn't that right?" Edward glanced over at Piper, and she gave him a toothless grin. "I think we're about all done at the Winterfest. But before you run back home, Livia, I want to show you something."

"What?"

"You'll have to trust me just a little longer to find out." With Piper balanced on one hip, he took Livia's hand, and together they headed out of the park and across the street. He glanced up at the sky and hoped Mother Nature would cooperate with his plan. If not, he'd improvise.

"The tree lot?" Livia paused when they stopped at their destination, her brows knitted in confusion. "Isn't it closed now?"

"Yup. But there was one tree left. One lonely little tree, with no one to love it." He tugged her around the corner, to a small stubby tree, too short for most people's tastes, and too tall for a tabletop. He'd plopped it into a metal tree stand earlier tonight, and done his best to take it from scraggly to Christmasy.

"Did you do this?" She crossed to the tree and fingered the strings of lights decorating the tree, the scattering of red and gold ornaments dangling from the branches. It wasn't much, but it was the best he could do in such a short period of time and with his own admittedly limited decorating skills. From her seat in his arms, Piper stared at the tree, fascinated by the lights. "Why?"

"Because I thought our first tree should be just ours. And, this tree lot was where we started again—"

"I remember. The wreath. And the cup of coffee. And that kiss." Her smile widened, and he hoped it was because she enjoyed the memories. Because he did—especially the kiss.

"I thought it would be special to return here," he said, "with you and my daughter. To start our first Christmas together, right here."

Her gaze roamed over the tree again. "It's...perfect. I love it, Edward. Thank you."

He came up behind her, and his breath whispered along her neck, lifting the delicate tendrils of her dark hair. How he wanted to kiss her, hold her. "Santa forgot to ask you what you want for Christmas, Livia."

"Nothing. I have everything I need." She gave her daughter's hand a little squeeze, then met his gaze. "Really, I do."

"Oh, I don't know about that." He bent down, Piper balanced on his hip, and withdrew a package from beneath the tree. "Let's give this to Mommy, okay?" Piper gurgled and bounced in agreement. He gave her a kiss on the temple and she reached for his nose, keeping up the constant stream of baby babble. "Piper says, 'Open it.'"

Livia took the package from him and gave him a curious look. "What's this?"

"Open it and see."

She undid the wrapping paper. It fluttered to the ground in a big red and green square. He watched her, waiting, his breath caught in his throat, for the moment when it all clicked. Then, there it was, a sharp inhale of breath, and the smile that he had grown to love lit up her face, her eyes, everything. "A cookie jar Santa?"

He nodded.

Tears welled in her eyes, and she clutched the box to her chest. A porcelain Santa face, jolly, merry, ready for holidays to come, decorated the front. "Edward...I...oh, my, it's exactly right. Just the kind I always imagined. That one silly little thing I missed at Christmas."

"It's not silly, not at all. I want every Christmas from here on out to be perfect, for both of us. No more ghosts from the past, Livia. We can start fresh, this year, this moment. The three of us." He tipped his head toward the box. "And the cookie jar Santa."

"I...I don't know what to say."

She'd already said it all, with the look on her face. He'd hoped, when he bought the silly kitschy thing and wrapped it earlier this evening, that she would see the gift the way he did—as a new beginning, where nothing was missing. And then, as if Mother Nature agreed, something white whispered past Livia's cheek, then another, and another.

"Oh my. It's snowing." Livia turned her face to the sky, to meet the first snowflakes. They tumbled fast and thick, coating the branches of the tree with white. "Just in time for Piper's first Christmas."

He smiled. "I told you to believe in miracles."

"You did." She caught a sprinkling of snow in her palm, blew it off, then caught another handful. "That's a hard thing for a control freak to do."

"I know. You're preaching to the choir, Livia." Then he nodded toward the gift, his heart caught in his throat. "There's more. Look inside."

"What? Cookies too?" She opened the box, and pried off the lid of the cookie jar. A gasp escaped her, and she paused before reaching inside to pull out the small velvet box.

Before Livia could say anything, Edward took the box from her and got down on one knee, balancing Piper on the other leg. He held the ring box out to Livia, cupped in both his large palm and Piper's little one. The baby looked down at the soft box, probably wondering if she could eat it.

"I know getting married is a huge leap of faith for you. Faith in me, in us. But hear me out."

She bit her lip and nodded.

"From this day forward, I want us to be a family," he said. "We'll live here, in a little house on a quiet side

street, and teach Piper to walk and ride a bike and dig
for bugs." Livia smiled at the last, and he took that as
a good sign, and kept talking. "I promise to make you
happy, to make you smile, because I sure as hell love
your smiles, Livia. Every single one of them. But most
of all, I promise to be there and to talk to you, and let
you in my heart, my soul. Today, tomorrow and all the
days after that." Tears glimmered anew in her eyes, and
she bit her lip in that way he loved. He thumbed open
the box's lid. "Because I love you, Livia, and I love our
daughter, and I want you to marry me, and make us a
family."

Piper let out a soft coo, as if she was marveling at
the ring, too. Edward pressed his head to Piper's and inhaled her sweet, incredible baby scent. While he waited
for the answer to the most important question he'd ever
asked.

"I...I love you too," Livia said, but still she didn't take
the ring. "I always have. I'm just so afraid, Edward."

He rose, put the box in her palm and covered her hand
with his own. "Then stand next to me, Livia. I'll hold
on to you." He held her gaze, steady and sure. "I'm not
going anywhere. Ever."

The tears brimmed on her eyelashes, then slid down
in one slow trickle. He could see her struggle with letting go, with trusting. She took in a deep breath, then
met his gaze, the cookie jar Santa still clutched to her
chest. Her green eyes locked on his and after what
seemed an interminable moment, she nodded, and a
smile burst on her face. "Yes, Edward, yes, I'll marry
you."

His heart exploded with joy. He drew Livia into a
tight embrace, creating the warm, perfect circle of him,

Livia and Piper. He'd been all over the world, to every major destination there was, and yet he couldn't imagine another place he would rather be than right here in this little town standing by this sad little tree with the woman and daughter he loved.

She drew back and looked up at him with a smile. Between them, Piper babbled softly. "You never told me what you want for Christmas, Edward."

"I already have it all," Edward said softly, then kissed his wife-to-be as the snow dusted them with a winter kiss. "And I'm never letting it go. Merry Christmas, Livia."

"Merry Christmas, Edward." Then she curved into his arms, and completed his life.

* * * * *

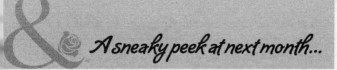

A sneaky peek at next month...

Cherish™

ROMANCE TO MELT THE HEART EVERY TIME

My wish list for next month's titles...

In stores from 18th November 2011:

☐ Firefighter Under the Mistletoe – Melissa McClone

& A Marine for Christmas – Beth Andrews

☐ Unwrapping the Playboy – Marie Ferrarella

& The Playboy's Gift – Teresa Carpenter

☐ Christmas in Cold Creek – RaeAnne Thayne

In stores from 2nd December 2011:

☐ Expecting the Boss's Baby – Christine Rimmer

& Twins Under His Tree – Karen Rose Smith

☐ Snowbound with Her Hero – Rebecca Winters

Available at WHSmith, Tesco, Asda, Eason, Amazon and Apple

Just can't wait?

Visit us Online

You can buy our books online a month before they hit the shops! **www.millsandboon.co.uk**

Special Offers

Every month we put together collections and longer reads written by your favourite authors.

Here are some of next month's highlights— and don't miss our fabulous discount online!

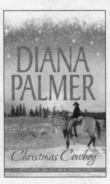

On sale 18th November On sale 18th November On sale 18th November

Have Your Say

You've just finished your book.
So what did you think?

We'd love to hear your thoughts on our
'Have your say' online panel
www.millsandboon.co.uk/haveyoursay

- 🌹 Easy to use
- 🌹 Short questionnaire
- 🌹 Chance to win Mills & Boon® goodies